The Most Important
CATCH

By Jaclyn M. Hawkes

Spirit Dance Books

The Most Important
CATCH

By Jaclyn M. Hawkes

ACKNOWLEDGMENTS

To those who made this book come together, Anissa, Karlene, Tristi, and Thomas, a sincere thank you. And thank you as well to the beautiful redheaded girl on the motorcycle who took her helmet off to give us directions one sunny afternoon in Hoytsville.

The Most Important Catch
By Jaclyn M. Hawkes
Copyright © March 2012 Jaclyn M. Hawkes
All rights reserved.
Published and distributed by Spirit Dance Books.LLC

Spiritdancebooks.com 1-855-648-5559

Cover design by Thomas Gasu

Printed in USA

First Printing March 2012

Library of Congress cataloguing in publication data

ISBN: 978-0-9851648-0-5

Dedication

This book is dedicated to my husband, who has long been my best friend. He encourages me to never quit trying and picks me up and dusts me off when I sometimes crash and burn. I would be lost without him.

It is also dedicated to my sons, who play an awesome game of football, but are still gentle men off the field. I'm honored to be their mom.

Chapter One

North Carolina

As their meeting with the coaches ended, Robby Robideaux stood up and moved toward his friend Jason to touch base about what time they were going to be leaving for the airport in the morning. He absently accepted a courier envelope a waiter held out to him, slipped a finger under the seal, and opened it as he turned back to his conversation. "Seven forty-five? That should be long enough to make it through security if we only have carry-ons. I'll pick you up." He glanced down at the papers he'd pulled from the envelope, swallowed a gasp, and hurriedly shoved them back inside. *Holy Toledo!*

He looked up, hoping no one else had seen the suggestive photos of a woman with far too few clothes on that he'd pulled from the seemingly innocuous express envelope. Geez, these things usually came in heavily perfumed pink letters or in elegantly wrapped packages and he knew not to open them; but this one had taken him by surprise. He'd expected business correspondence this time.

Jason looked at him sympathetically, and Robby rolled his eyes and shook his head as he bent to retrieve the piece of paper he'd dropped in his hurry to hide the pictures. What were these women thinking? Didn't they listen to the news at all? Just this week there were two reports of women who had been assaulted by professional athletes. Not that he was that kind of a guy, but these women didn't know that. They didn't know him from Jack the Ripper! Were there no nice girls left in the whole wide world?

He checked to make sure that the plain paper he had dropped didn't feel like a photo before he turned it over. It was a note and he would have just shoved it back in as well, except that it only said five words which jumped off the page at him. "Meet me on the balcony."

The hair on the back of his neck stood on end as he resisted the urge to even turn his head to glance at the balcony overlooking the main dining room where he was standing. Even the fact that he was a 240 pound All-Pro football player didn't stop his dread at the thought of another stalker. He hated this! How had she even known he was going to be meeting here? And, what courier service had delivered this to him?

Stepping to his left where he was far enough underneath the balcony to keep anyone above him from seeing him, he set the note carefully on a table beside him, knowing it would be dusted for fingerprints, and pulled out his phone. This meeting had been only head coaches, their staff, and a handful of the most senior players. He glanced at his phone as he went to call security. He never let anyone near his phone, but he still wondered if someone had managed to plant something in it again to track him and listen in on calls. It seemed absolutely paranoid, but it had happened to him twice before.

His suspicions were confirmed when he'd no sooner asked for security than there was a disturbance on the balcony above him, and then glass shattering and the sound of a women's heels rushing out the back. He ran a hand through his hair with a sigh, hoping this was just a one-time fluke. The last thing he needed right now was another psycho female.

Jason looked down at the note sitting on the white linen and then looked all around the restaurant as well. As quarterback for the Carolina Panthers, Jason had had more than his own share of unsolicited, and decidedly unwanted, female attention forced on him. He knew exactly what Robby was dealing with here.

At least Robby didn't have a sweet wife and daughter like Jason did. Jason had to worry about keeping them safe now, too. A year ago, Jason had gotten love letters and nude photos, and his wife had gotten a blood-covered death threat.

Robby sighed inwardly, wondering if the level of his success meant that he would never have any sense of peace or normalcy in his life forever. He loved what he did and where he was professionally, but there were things that came with this fame and money that sucked the life right out of him.

Illinois

As the heavy metal doors shut with a clang behind her, Kelly Campbell squinted in the brightness of the late afternoon sun. She turned to glance at the austere tan building she had just left. It was only a psychiatric hospital, and she was a nurse, not a patient, but sometimes that building felt more like a prison. She took a deep breath and tried to rid her nose of the nasty institutional smell of commercial disinfectant, but even the thickness of the air here in Chicago wasn't enough to kill that odor.

She rolled her shoulders and headed for her car, wondering if this was really all there was. She'd spent years getting her RN and finding what she thought would be a fulfilling career, but just two months of this job was beginning to make her question if she'd made a mistake.

At first it hadn't been too bad. She knew that helping these mentally ill patients was a worthy work, and when one of the seemingly sharp, young doctors had started asking her out, it had been a rush. But it was a short lived one. Dr. Peter Holmes was handsome and for a short while she'd thought he was completely charming, but now she was beginning to wonder. There was something strange going on here at this facility, and it involved him. She just hadn't figured out what it was yet.

Altium Pinnacle Institute was supposed to be state-of-the-art and heavily involved in studies to license the latest promising drugs; but there were times that she wondered if all of that wasn't a glossed-over excuse for using people who were hopelessly troubled to experiment on without repercussion. And after what she'd found out today, she was sure that one of those patients had died day before yesterday.

She'd been there when he'd begun to struggle to breathe, and when he'd flat-lined, she'd called for help as she began CPR. Peter and another doctor had come into the room and had, in fact, sent her away to do something else. Then, later, he told her that the patient had been fine and had been sent to another nearby hospital to be cared for. Today she had come across the patient's file on Peter's desk when she had been waiting to meet him for lunch. What she had read in that file made her wonder more than ever.

All reference to any medical incident had been sanitized out of the record, if it had ever even been recorded. And the file stated that he was still here in treatment, but Kelly knew that he had been taken somewhere that afternoon and was no longer in the building. After finding his file this afternoon, she had looked. He wasn't here anywhere. She'd even checked with the other hospital, but they had no record of him.

She probably wouldn't have even realized there was a problem if Peter hadn't acted so strangely when she asked after the patient. Then, when Peter had walked into his office to find her reading the file, he had recommended that she keep herself out of other people's business. He did it in such a thinly veiled, threatening way that mental red flags had popped up all over the place.

Actually, thinking about it, there had been red flags for a while now for her. When Peter had first asked her out, she had accepted, even though he wasn't a member of the Church. Her own mother had been introduced to the church by a man she'd dated.

Kelly had always been taught to be willing to take people at face value, whether they were members or not, but Peter didn't necessarily return the respect she gave him with respect for her religion. So far, he'd always found a way to belittle her beliefs, anytime she brought them up. Now that she thought about it, any attraction she had had for him had suddenly been lost in the questions she had about his ethics and character.

Lately, Kelly had even been wondering if he had a racket going there in the hospital, selling prescription pain pills. Twice she had come upon him and one of the staff exchanging something, and Peter had walked away pocketing a wad that looked like bills. The second time, Kelly had even seen the white tablets in the plastic bag the other nurse stuffed into her scrubs.

At the time it had seemed too preposterous to even consider, but after the file today, she wondered if she had been ridiculously naïve.

As Kelly pulled out of the staff parking lot, she looked back up at the dreary building one more time. Maybe she was wrong about all of these crazy questions. A successful and well respected physician wouldn't jeopardize his entire future with these kinds of stunts, would he? Wouldn't the risks far outweigh the pay offs? Maybe she was just being too imaginative. But then again, there was a phenomenal amount of money in pharmaceuticals, both the ones that were being tested in the trials, and the addictive ones that people were willing to sell their souls for.

As Kelly thought back on what she had learned that day, she shook her head. This wasn't her imagination. There were things going on here at this facility that were dark and ugly. It wasn't just what she had seen or heard or read. Kelly could actually feel the darkness in the very air around her sometimes when she was there.

She finally realized what the mental red flags were. They were promptings Kelly was receiving. Once she thought about it, she was sure. The Spirit had been witnessing to her that something definitely wasn't right. Now, she just had to figure out what the Spirit was prompting her to do.

She was so troubled about it all that later that night, she couldn't seem to fall off to sleep. She called her Uncle Roy to talk to him about it, even though it was nearly eleven at night. She didn't want to bother her mother. Her mother had done more than her share of dealing with Kelly's troubles over the years of raising her alone after Kelly's father had walked out when Kelly was two. And her friends would think she was nuts to question such a great job and seemingly wonderful boyfriend. But she needed more wisdom than she had on this one. Her Uncle Roy had always been the deep well she had gone to when she needed counsel.

She woke him up. She could hear that in his voice, but he was his ever-patient and concerned self anyway. She explained what was going on at work and what concerned her, and then told him she thought she was being prompted to do something, she just wasn't sure what.

When she finally paused and waited for him to say something, she heard him yawn before he said, "Kelly, you know as well as I do how to recognize the Spirit by now. Don't you hesitate for a moment to act on it, when you feel you should. As for what you need to be doing, that depends a lot on just what really is going on.

"My first inclination is to tell you to quit your job and just get out of there, but if you really believe that they are somehow harming relatively helpless people with the drug trials, then you should try to find a way to stop them. And dealing addictive prescription drugs is just as bad as any street dealer out there. In fact, it's worse because a physician has taken an oath to be a healer. He's a trusted medical professional, and is being horribly unethical.

"That being said, the amount of money that we're talking about here could put you in more danger than the patients, or any addict. If they were to find out that you were going to blow the whistle, you might be the next body that disappears with a sanitized record. Whatever you decide, be very, very careful."

She had wondered if she could be in danger if she said something, but having her uncle voice her fears out loud was a wake-up call. She still wasn't sure how to proceed and asked him, "What do you think I should do about it all?"

He sighed tiredly. "I don't know sweetheart. Keep listening to the Spirit and it will guide you. I'd guess you need to have a concrete idea about what is going on before you can go to the authorities, anyway. See what you think as you go back to work. Just keep your eyes and ears open, and be careful. If you see anything questionable, document it thoroughly. When you do know for sure that something is going on, we'll discreetly go to the police. Then you should probably quit and go somewhere else.

"In the meantime, you don't have to go out with Dr. Holmes. You're a precious daughter of God. Don't settle for less than the best man this world has to offer."

He always said stuff like that to her and she never tired of hearing it. Counsel like that had gotten her through her toughest teenage years. "Thank you, Uncle Roy. Thanks for telling me that, and for letting me wake you up and bugging you with my issues. I think I can go to sleep now. I love you."

"I love you too. Get some sleep and keep me in the loop. G'night." She smiled as she hung up and turned out her bedside light.

Robby Robideaux stood behind the realtor and looked around while he waited for her to unlock the heavy wooden door of the farmhouse. Everything from the house to the pasture fence looked weathered, but that was actually part of the charm to him. Under the peeling varnish and warped trim boards, this whole farmstead was masterfully built. Whoever had done the original log work had been a craftsman. Everything was still straight and square even though this house was more than a hundred and twenty years old.

As unusual as the old house was, it had all the qualifications he had laid out for the realtor. First and foremost was seclusion. He wanted peace and tranquility and security. It had acreage and was well built, but would still keep its almost frontier charm once it was refurbished the way he was hoping. Even though the buildings were of hand hewn logs, an earlier remodel had been done to add indoor plumbing and electricity.

And, it was within forty minutes of Charlotte, which was another stipulation. As a wide receiver for the Carolina Panthers, he wanted to be able to actually spend time wherever he ended up buying, so it needed to be close to the stadium and the airport. It was also close to both a river and a lake and had a stream right in the yard.

Jason came up the walk behind him, carrying his one-year-old daughter Shania on his shoulders, tickling her as he walked. He was looking around too. "It couldn't be more opposite than your condo. That's for sure. And no one who ever saw it would think it belonged to an NFL superstar. I'm sure you'll find the seclusion that you've decided you need lately."

The realtor opened the door and went on to the far side of

the house, opening doors and windows as she went. Jason and Robby went inside, as Jason added, "I think this is just a stage that you're going through, and as soon as you find the right woman, all the publicity hype won't be such a big deal. If you were at peace and married, half the women in the modern world would finally quit hounding you. The press would find another eligible bachelor with looks and money to torture."

Robby shook his head and laughed. "Whatever you say, Jase. As you stand there carrying your daughter. You've just gotten so comfortable that you've forgotten that some of the rest of us would like to find a decent woman and have a family. It may be a stage, but right now I'm feeling incredibly burnt-out with it all. I can hardly face coming and going from my place lately. Moving to the end of the earth is sounding better and better." He ran a hand through his hair and added almost tiredly, "I wish summer camp was this week; maybe getting back into the season is all I need. That, and a break from money hungry women."

"How do you know it's the money?" Jason's grin glowed white against his skin of the deepest brown. "I think it's your charm that makes them stampede. Rutledge makes more than you and he doesn't have your trouble. It's that pretty French look you have to you. That, and the fact that you don't fool around. You're like the ultimate challenge for nasty girls."

Robby slapped him on the back as he went past, ignoring the ribbing. "Hey, look at this great wood floor! This is cool! I like it beat up, just like it is." This was exactly what he had in mind when he decided that he was going to buy a neat, old farmhouse. "What do you think? Should I buy it?"

Swinging Shania down off his shoulders, Jason shrugged. "I think you're nuts, but buy it if you want, Rocker. It is cool. It reminds me of a pioneer museum, but it's not like it's going to break you. Go for it."

Robby continued walking through the house, then went out and looked into a couple of the out buildings. Listening to the birds in the trees around him, and the sound of the creek that ran along the edge of the yard, he made his decision. The whole place was steeped in a wonderful peace. It was just what he wanted.

It was going to be a huge project though. He looked back at the house. He'd have to begin looking for a contractor to start fixing it up. There was a ton of maintenance to be done before it would be livable.

The week had gone relatively well, considering. After talking to her uncle, Kelly had had every intention of going in to work the next day and telling Peter that she wasn't really interested in seeing him again, but early that morning she changed her mind. Sometimes he almost didn't seem to notice she was with him when he was talking to some of the staff. First thing, as she'd walked in and said hello, he'd been discussing something about how miraculously quickly this trial was going. He and the other doctor he'd been talking to had laughed. It gave her the impression that the joke was the speed of the trials.

Was that what was going on? Were they shortcutting the legal trial length in order to get the drugs approved more quickly? She consciously decided to keep stringing Peter along until she could find out what their secret was that made them laugh so suspiciously. He put an arm around her shoulder and walked her down the hall to his office, without so much as a second glance at her afterward.

As she stood in front of his office door, she wondered if he thought she was too simple minded to question his behavior at times. She knew there had been people in her life who assumed she was stupid, because she was pretty.

It had happened a lot, actually. Even one of her professors had insinuated that nursing school might be too rigorous for someone who "looked like her". It was frustrating, but had also come in handy a time or two. Maybe this was one of those times.

Peter opened the door. Still without looking at her, he walked inside.

Closing the door behind them, he finally turned to look at her as he stepped toward her with a half smile. He pulled her into a loose hug. "Kelly. We haven't seen enough of each other lately. We should remedy that. Can you have dinner with me tonight?"

He went to hug her more tightly and she pushed against his chest. "I have to get to work, Peter. Dinner would be great. I get off at six tonight. Then, I'll run home and change."

Taking the hand that held him away, he kissed it. "Are you finally going to let me come in?" He went to kiss it again with a look that made her decidedly uncomfortable.

Gently, but insistently, she pulled the hand out of his grip and pushed him away again with a smile to buffer the push and her answer, as she said, "I have to go to work, Peter. I'll see you tonight."

Still dating him when she knew deep down she was no longer the slightest bit interested, made her feel guilty. Especially when she knew she was never going to be more intimate with him physically; something he was probably expecting. But she decided she owed it to these mentally ill people whom she had come to truly care so much about to find out if there was a problem here for sure.

Later that afternoon, she was bent down in a storage room, digging for some dressings that were placed in the wrong cubicles, when someone came into the room from the far end.

She was just about to look up, when she recognized Peter's almost slick voice and the voice of the other doctor, Crowther, who seemed to be in on whatever questionable issue Peter was involved in. Instinctively, she stayed below the counter level and began to pray for safety as her heart began to pound.

The two were talking as if they were discussing the latest television sitcom, but, in fact, they were speaking openly about what drug trial files needed to be gone over that day to change the records. The only time their voices even had a hint of intensity was when they spoke briefly about the death of the patient the week before.

Peter tried to be matter-of-fact, "Okay, so we learned the hard way what not to prescribe together, and how much is too much, but it's gonna be okay. He'd never had so much as a phone call from family. We're still perfect and this one will be under wraps within the next couple of months. In the meantime, we'll just say he was considered recovered and released. We have no idea where he went after leaving here."

He paused and then admonished almost gruffly, "Stay cool, Crowther. Just remember how much you're getting paid for this and it all falls back into perspective. Retirement at thirty-five is a beautiful thing."

Kelly closed her eyes and grimaced, absolutely sick to her stomach. How had she ever been able to stand this guy? For just a second, she thought she was toasted when she heard footsteps in her direction, but then the two turned and went back out the door they came in. She breathed a deep sigh of relief. For a minute or two, she stayed quietly in the storage room trying to analyze her feelings. What was she supposed to be doing here?

Uncle Roy said to keep following the Spirit. What was the Spirit trying to tell her? It was so hard to figure out sometimes. She prayed silently for understanding, then stood and walked back out to finish what she was working on.

Even though she had decided to keep seeing Peter for the time being, she couldn't stand the thought of facing him tonight. By mid afternoon, she was almost grateful for a pounding headache that kicked in so she could beg off on their dinner date and just go home. Peter appeared empathetic and honestly disappointed when he said, "You work afternoons for the next three days and I won't be able to do anything with you. Can I have a rain check for Friday then?"

She searched his eyes for a second. She should say yes. She still didn't feel like she had enough to get the police involved. "Dinner on Friday. It's a date. Thanks for understanding tonight." She went home and nursed the worst headache she'd ever had in her life. She'd had tension headaches before, but nothing like this.

On Thursday she busted Peter in a clandestine meeting again with one of the women who she suspected was hooked on pain pills. This time, when she saw the two of them sneak into the linen supply area with a pointed look, she did some sneaking of her own. She ducked in behind the huge hamper that held the soiled sheets, held her breath, and then sighed inwardly when her suspicions were confirmed. Not only was Peter selling narcotics, he was totally gouging this poor, desperate woman as well from the sound of things. She waited for them to leave the area before she stood up to leave herself.

Boy, Kelly Shaye Campbell, you picked a doozy of a guy this time. How had she not realized this man was a total snake in all these weeks?

On Friday morning, when another patient collapsed with the exact symptoms as the last time, and the same scenario took place afterward, she knew, without a doubt, that there was a problem--a big problem. It had only been nine days since the first death, at least the first death that she was aware of, and she recognized that both of these individuals just happened to be people who had no family that ever checked on them, visited, or even called.

That afternoon, when Peter was out of the building, she pulled the dead woman's file and began to study it. She was completely focused on it when she heard his voice. "What are you up to, Kelly?" She jumped and looked up and into his eyes. They were definitely not happy eyes. She felt her stomach knot in fear, even as she tried to act like nothing was going on.

"I'm just checking Julia's treatment records, trying to see if we made any mistakes that would make her sick like that." *Sick, yeah, like dead you mean.* "Maybe we gave her the wrong medication or something. Do you think that could have been it? I've heard of that happening on those crazy shows on TV. One time, I heard they accidentally gave a woman the wrong meds. It was for men, and she got male pattern baldness. It was awful!"

Kelly sounded like a complete idiot to herself, but she hoped Peter was buying in on the ditzy stuff. The hard glint in his eye didn't soften a bit. He took the file from her hands and placed it firmly under his arm. "You should be more careful what you nose into, Kelly. You could really open a can of worms that you wouldn't like. This facility could be sued or something." His eyes narrowed, icily. "Or something even worse." Finally, she saw the snake try to sheath its fangs when he blinked, and then asked, far too smoothly, "Are we still on for dinner?"

With that one innocent sounding question, her heart almost stopped. After what she had just seen in his eyes, she knew that if she ever went to dinner with him, she'd never make it home. Ever.

Trying desperately to act calm, she answered, "We are. Seven o'clock? I'll be ready."

He gave her a half smile. "Good." He looked her up and down. "I'll be looking forward to it."

When he turned and walked away, Kelly had to actually concentrate to breathe. She knew she was in more trouble than she'd ever imagined in her life.

She glanced at her watch. Three-twenty-five. She got off at five tonight. She had three hours and thirty-five minutes to disappear before two deadly doctors and the pharmaceutical companies behind them tried to silence her forever. She had no problem interpreting the red flag prompting this time. It was screaming RUN like a flashing beacon!

Her first thought was to head right out the door this second, just as fast as she could go, but she knew that would tip Peter off instantly that she was going to run. For the rest of her shift, she tried to work as usual and to act perfectly normal when Peter stuck his head in three different times to look for her. He must have seen the panic in her eyes when she'd looked up as he caught her reading the files.

As she worked, she tried to formulate a plan. The police first! No matter what happened to her, this had to be stopped. She'd go straight from work to the police and tell them everything she knew. Hopefully, that would be the end of the deaths from these drugs. Then, she either had to convince the police to protect her, or run just as far and as fast as she could without Peter and whoever else was in on this mess finding her.

She couldn't do it. She had no doubt that these guys had enough drug company money behind them to chase her to the end of the earth, and it didn't take a great deal of imagination to know what would happen to her when they found her. She'd have to make the police understand how serious this was. There was no way she could just hide.

Even as she was telling herself that, she was still getting the distinct feeling that she needed to run anyway. As she worked, she wrestled with herself mentally. Running was crazy! How could she pull it off? They'd find her car and trace her credit cards, phone calls, and the whole nine yards. She'd seen enough movies to understand that she didn't even know all the ways they could track her down.

Still, she felt like that was what she was supposed to do, and she tried to figure out how she could get away with it. It would have been slightly possible if she had a month to figure it all out. There wasn't a chance that she could pull it off in less than two hours.

She was still having a tumultuous mental tug of war as she walked into the police station at exactly six minutes after five that night. She tried to calm her nerves and explain at the same time, but it wasn't going all that well. She'd been referred to a Lt. Hartvigson; the man in charge of drug fraud, prescription drug dealing and abuse, and had been talking about ninety miles an hour for more than twenty minutes, when she looked up into the man's cool, gray eyes and realized that he hadn't taken one note. Not one.

He was watching her intently, and almost smiling a little, and she thought, *this guy either doesn't believe a word I'm saying, doesn't care, or he's in on it as well.* From the disinterested way he was watching her, she almost believed it was the latter.

She glanced at her watch and her heart sank. She now had an hour and thirty-two minutes to completely disappear. She looked up at the cool investigator and said, "I'm sorry. I forgot I have a dinner date tonight. I'll have to come back tomorrow." She gave him one last glance, stood up and walked out. How could she do this? She couldn't do this! She had to.

On the way to the car, she stopped at a pay phone and called her cousin. "Rye." She didn't even give him a greeting. "Ryley, I'm in trouble. Big trouble. Can you come get me at Riverside Park like immediately? I mean immediately! Bring a set of empty saddle bags. Please."

He hesitated for no more than a second, "Sure, Kel. I'll

be there in five."

"Oh, thank you, Ryley. Hurry!" As an afterthought, she added, "And pray, Ryley. Pray for me like my life depends on it!"

At the park she took the pocket knife out of her purse and hardly even hesitated as she sliced the inside of her forearm. The only way this was going to work was if she could convince them that she hadn't run away, but had somehow been killed or kidnapped. She let her blood drip onto the seat of the car, down the side of the door, and onto the floor, as she waited for Ryley.

After a minute or two, she carefully wrapped the cut tightly with a bandage out of the emergency kit in her car, then tossed her purse and let it spill into the blood. She'd have to leave it all to make it look real.

It didn't matter anyway. Once she was gone she couldn't use any of the cards or phone or they'd be able to find her. She always tried to keep two, one hundred dollar bills hidden in her wallet in case of an emergency. She stuffed them into her pocket with the bloody pocket knife, grateful that her mother had always encouraged her to keep cash, and wishing she'd kept more. This was definitely an emergency.

When Ryley showed up, she jumped across to the back of his motorcycle, still carefully holding the bandage, so no blood got near him. He looked at her, and she could tell he wanted to know what was going on, but he must have been able to tell that it was a dire emergency because all he asked was, "Where to?"

"My apartment. Hurry! But don't get a ticket. Wait... Give me your helmet. We can't be seen." He helped her wind her long, red-brown hair into a loose knot and pulled the helmet over the top of it, and they hit the road.

At her apartment, she used a hidden key to get in, and in less than two minutes she'd taken three changes of clothes that she almost never wore and was back behind him on the bike. On the way out of the parking lot, she saw Peter's car coming in the other entrance. Instinctively, she leaned into Ryley and ducked her face. She'd missed Peter by maybe forty-five seconds.

She had Ryley take her back to his motorcycle shop. At a stop light on the way, she tried to tell him what had happened.

When she asked if he could let her take one of his older bikes and some leathers, he was concerned. "Kelly, you hate motorcycles. Ever since you wrecked so bad when you were seventeen. What are you thinking?"

"I'm thinking I need to disappear in the most unlikely manner, or someone else is going to make me disappear, Ryley. Hopefully, when they find my car and the blood and my purse, and when it seems like nothing was taken from my apartment, they'll think I'm in that river or long dead. No one will think I'd leave on a motorcycle, and with luck, no one will realize that one of your old bikes is missing."

At the shop, she hurriedly pulled leathers on over her scrubs, transferred the saddle bags, stuffed her hair up into a tinted helmet again, and hugged him goodbye. "Take care of my mom. Somehow, I'll get word to you, when I can."

He handed her a wad of bills, a heavy gold man's wrist band, and a motorcycle title. "Here's almost fourteen hundred bucks, Kel. That's all I have here. If you run out of money, sell the gold and the bike."

She looked up at him and tears filled her eyes as she hugged him. "Thank you, Rye. Someday, I'll repay you."

He grinned, almost sadly. "See that you do, Kel. Take care. Good luck and be safe."

She tried not to let a tear escape as she nodded and clicked down the tinted helmet shield. "Bye, Rye. Love you." She gunned the bike out of the shop's back door.

She had almost made it to the interstate when the significance of the bills and gold Ryley had given her hit. She had little money and no way to get more. That had entered her chaotic thoughts when she'd first realized she couldn't take her cards, but then had slipped her mind in the mix of things.

How would she live? How could she survive? She couldn't even get another job using her own name and social security number. She was going to have to be so careful with her finances. She struggled not to let worries about money compound the fear she was already fighting as she roared away.

She had been riding on I-90 a full five minutes before she truly felt like she could breathe. Then, it was still another fifteen or twenty minutes before her legs quit quivering. She hadn't driven a motorcycle in more than six years, since her terrible accident when she was seventeen, but that thought hardly crossed her mind right now. All the other things like the need to run for her life and shock and adrenaline were far too strong for mere nerves to affect her. Her world had tied itself in a knot so fast she hadn't even had a chance to realize it fully. She raised a hand to glance at the watch on her wrist. It still wasn't even seven o'clock yet. She wondered how long it would be before someone told her mother they had found her bloody car.

Chapter 2

She was somewhere in northern Ohio, and had been on the road for more than five hours, when it started to rain. She felt the first cold drops hit her hands and glanced up at the night sky, wondering what was going on. She couldn't see a thing after looking at the light from the headlight, but the moisture and electricity in the air felt like a storm. She looked all around, wondering how far she was from the nearest hotel or motel. She hoped it wasn't far. Motorcycles, leathers, and rain didn't exactly mesh well.

When she finally did find a place, she was soaked to the skin and her hands were so cold she could hardly let go of the bike as she wearily climbed off. What she had found was a small motel with rooms all in a row on the ground level. It felt perfect to her, and she pulled the waterlogged saddle bags off, hauled them inside, then triple locked the door behind her. Once it was locked, she went to lean against it, but her helmet clunked solidly. With a sigh, she straightened up and took the helmet off. Walking into the bathroom, she set it and the bags right into the sink, so they wouldn't make a mess dripping.

She had to literally peel the wet leathers off. The black dye had stained right through her scrubs, and her skin looked like a young child's drawing of a leopard. She hung the leathers on the closet rod on hangers and put the laundry bag under them to catch the inky drips. Then looked around to see what this far-from-luxury hotel had to offer in the way of toiletries. She didn't even have a toothbrush with her.

She found a tiny bottle of shampoo, a packet of hand lotion, and the makings for coffee. It could have been worse. At least she could wash her hair.

As cold and tired as she was, even the tiny shower and its wimpy stream of water felt like nirvana. She wished she hadn't let herself bleed quite so much before leaving her car. She felt completely chilled and light headed from it. The leopard spots didn't wash all the way off, and she was glad that at least her face wasn't spotted. She dug through the saddlebags and realized that she hadn't brought anything that even remotely resembled pajamas. Settling for clean undies and a T-shirt, she wished, unsuccessfully, for a Book of Mormon to be tucked in next to the Gideon Bible on the bedside table. It didn't really matter. She was far too tired to read, but it would have been comforting.

She prayed and lay down, hoping her fatigue would make her brain slow down and let her exhausted body rest. Without pajamas, the room was cold and she got back up to try to figure out how to work the third world heater. Feeling lonelier and more whiney by the minute, she finally had to remind herself that she had nothing to complain about. The pioneer women would have given about anything to have a warm, dry, comfortable bed with clean, crisp sheets to stop and fall into at the end of a long day of walking. She could have been sleeping on the prairie in a number of wet petticoats tonight.

At length, she finally did fall into a dream-laden sleep, full of disjointed images of patients and Peter and the blood in her car, beside the swirling black water of a river. When she woke up five hours later, drenched in sweat, she was only marginally less tired than when she had gone to sleep. She pulled herself up in the bed and realized the room was sweltering from the funny little heater. Getting up, she turned it off and peeked out of the drapes to see if the rain had stopped.

It was no longer raining, but the sky was leaden and the clouds were low and bleak. That was just about the way she was feeling this morning. She had no idea what her plan was and instinctively knelt beside the bed. God had gotten her safely this far. She knew He could do anything, and she was going to need His help all the way on this one.

When she had finished praying, she lingered for a moment or two there on her knees. She hadn't realized just how much fear was gripping her until the sweet peace brought on by her prayer began to seep into her heart. She had to calm down and get a plan and trust more, or she was going to be a basket case. Okay, so she was in a mess, but this was ridiculous.

On the bedside table, she found a small pad and a pen.

She climbed back into the bed to brainstorm a plan. She struggled at first, and then decided that she needed to take stock and figure out exactly where she was to start with. She sat and looked at the notepad for several minutes, then gave up planning as moot. Before she could plan, she needed to calm down and try to listen for what God would have her do right now.

Setting the notepad aside for the time being, she called the motel office and told them she'd be staying another night, requested not to have maid service and asked about the nearest food and store. She at least needed a toothbrush and some things for her hair. Turning on the TV for some background noise, while she was dressing she was unpleasantly surprised to realize that even two states away, she was now a news story. She hoped Ryley had been able to talk to her mom before someone told her she'd gone missing.

It was only a short segment on the noon news, but it came at just the right time for her to take into consideration that people could recognize her, even here in Ohio. That was another issue she'd have to worry about. Getting safely away would be pointless, if someone here reported seeing her.

She looked at the shiny, striking, brownish red hair that hung clear down her back objectively. Her hair was a huge part of her own personal self image, but that wouldn't matter a bit if she was dead. She'd have to cut it all off and dye it. Just the thought broke her heart, but there was nothing for it. For now, she'd hide it under the helmet and then tie the t-shirt around it like a scarf, until she could buy something to hide it with, and get it cut and colored.

At least her leathers were mostly dry this morning. She slipped them back on, put the helmet on before stepping out and went in search of food. It had been since yesterday's lunch that she'd eaten anything, and she was so hungry she was shaky. At the first fast food drive-through she came to, she bought enough food to last her at least through the day, so she wouldn't have to go out any more than absolutely necessary.

With food in her bags, she stopped, got gas and bought a tooth brush and Band-Aids at the gas station convenience store without ever taking the tinted helmet off. Then, she rode back to her room. She ate and did her best to pull the cut on her arm neatly closed with the Band-Aids, put a Do Not Disturb sign on her outer door knob, and went back to bed. While she lay there before going back to sleep, she tried to plan what she was going to do next, but not a whole lot came to mind.

She didn't know where she was going, or what she was going to do when she got there. And to top it all off, she knew that Peter and those involved in his scheming were still doing whatever it was that had recently killed two pathetically troubled people. She also knew, without a doubt, that the policeman she had met with the night before wasn't going to do a thing to follow up on what she had told him.

Finally, before she drifted off, she decided to take it all to God and trust him with it. He was all-knowing. He would take her where she needed to be if she could just listen close enough to understand His promptings. Somehow, this was all going to work out all right.

Peter Holmes slammed his desk drawer in complete disgust. He'd planned to do plenty to Kelly Campbell when he got his hands on her last night, but he'd never even gotten the chance. And the cops were breathing down his neck anyway! They were investigating him as a possible suspect! The last thing he needed was real police snooping around here.

Nothing had gone right from the second he had found Kelly reading that dead woman's file the afternoon before. And now, on top of everything else, he had this rogue police officer demanding a cut of the money from his narcotic sales! How had he even known that Peter was selling? It had to have been one of the staffers who bought from him. Someone must have gotten busted, but the guy was coming for money, instead of prosecuting.

At least it was the cop who was already willing to look the other way about some things; although, he had smugly intimated that he knew that Peter had, in fact, killed her. But he was willing to overlook that in the investigation if Peter was fully cooperative. Which was simply crooked cop speak for if he got paid off enough, and it galled Peter to have to try to keep his name clear of Kelly's disappearance. What a mess!

He should have realized sooner that Kelly wasn't just an incredibly beautiful woman. If he'd known how smart she was under that porcelain doll face and figure, he'd have been more careful about keeping his sketchy practices hidden from her. And he should have known that she wouldn't let something questionable go, as churchy as he'd found her to be. She'd always had to be honorable to the Nth degree, even if it was just in accepting exact change from the cashier. At first it had been a cute quirk, but yesterday it had threatened to blow the lid off of his whole life.

He had a sweet set up here. Take money from the patients and insurance companies. Take money from the addicts. And take a lot of money from the drug companies or getting their incredibly lucrative new medicines licensed with the FDA. Short-cutting the trials from time to time had just been the icing on the cake. They were sometimes even twice as lucrative, if the trial records were cooked a bit to cut costs.

Some of these mentally ill patients were perfect for this because they were struggling too hard to get through the day to worry about checking into the details. And, if deadly mistakes were made, often times they were so far removed from any support network that not a soul in the world was even aware that their useless lives were accidentally snuffed out. In a way, he was helping them. It had to be merciful to cut short a miserable existence, didn't it?

He leaned back and put his feet up on his desk for a moment, but his receptionist walked in and handed him a message that he needed to talk to the cops investigating Kelly's disappearance again. He swore as he read it. He'd actually been the one to bring Kelly's disappearance to light last night, when he'd been trying to figure out where she'd gotten to, but that hadn't stopped the police from including him in the list of possible suspects.

He swore viciously at her again. It'd just serve her right if she really had been kidnapped or killed or whatever at that park last night. Hopefully, someone had done his dirty work for him, although what he'd had in mind before getting rid of her would have been a great little distraction for him. He'd wanted to get close to her physically from the very first day he'd seen her walking down the hall of the hospital with that shining fall of glorious hair and fascinating green eyes. She had certainly been attractive, that was for sure.

Still, he wasn't convinced that Kelly had truly been a victim here. It was just too much of a coincidence. She'd known he was going to have to get rid of her the second she had looked up at him when he'd spoken to her as she read the file yesterday. He'd seen that realization in her eyes. But even as smart as she was, could she have pulled off literally dropping off the face of the earth in a matter of just a few minutes last night?

If she had run, she had no car or ID or purse or clothes or anything. At least that's what the police were saying. And they had found blood in her car. A lot of it. What was up with that? Could she have even staged that?

Of course she could, but would she have? He didn't know what to think yet. As soon as the heat from the authorities was off of him as a suspect, he intended to find out. He'd find her if she ever surfaced, no matter where she was. He had too much at stake here to risk losing it on a sexy nurse with hair like an auburn headed vixen. He hoped she was dead and that her disappearance was just a coincidence. But it was suspect.

Sharon Campbell felt like she was going to shatter. Kelly had been missing for more than twenty-four hours now, and there wasn't a single encouraging clue to ease the unbelievable ache and horror that made Sharon feel like cold, brittle glass to the core of her heart. She had never in her wildest nightmares dreamed of a day as painful as this last one had been.

Finally, this afternoon, she had asked her personal physician to prescribe something that would let her rest and find some peace. So far, every time she tried to close her eyes to let her exhausted body sleep, the ensuing blackness swam with images of all the terrible things that could have happened to her beautiful, sweet daughter.

Her brother, Roy, had been beside her every second of the time, as had a myriad of policemen and press and even volunteers who had started looking for Kelly as soon as her bloody car had been discovered. There had even been a whole group of wonderful people who had immediately begun to distribute flyers with Kelly's photo on them to every conceivable place in the Chicago-land area. Everyone had been so wonderful to try to help but that hadn't been able to fix the horrible void in her chest at what had happened to her only child last night.

She took the doctor's prescribed tranquilizer, then sadly retired to her room and tried to go to bed. Why would someone hurt her gentle, kind, smart daughter? As she finally felt the strong medicine begin to settle her mind down, there was a knock at her door. Roy and his son, Ryley, came into her bedroom and shut the door behind them. As far as she knew, the only people left here in her house were they and Roy's wife and small daughters, so she wondered why the closed door.

Roy took her hand and Ryley sat on the other side of the bed and said, "Aunt Sharon, there's something I need to tell you. Please forgive me for not telling you sooner. Under the circumstances, I felt like I couldn't. I hope you'll agree with me, once you hear it all."

When Kelly woke up again, she was hungry and ate another of the sandwiches she'd bought earlier, pondering while she chewed. Part of her head was telling her that if she just stayed inside her room, no one would be able to see her and therefore find her, but another part of her brain was telling her that she needed to get as far from home as fast as she could go. She sat on the bed, eating and dozing, until the running part won, and she decided to get up and get on the road.

It was nearly eight o'clock in the evening and although it was late April, it would be full dark before she got out of town. Here again, she was torn. At night it would be harder to recognize her, and there would be less people around when she stopped for gas or food, but driving across the country on a motorcycle by herself was scary enough, without doing it in the middle of the blackest of nights.

She finally decided to leave now anyway, feeling like it was urgent that she get away. But that belly-deep fear was back when she rolled onto the interstate, feeling entirely alone in the world except for a myriad of scary monsters that lurked just beyond the headlight of the bike beneath her.

A couple of times it spattered rain on her again, and toward morning it actually began to snow. She pulled the motorcycle into the porte-cochere of a hotel somewhere in Pennsylvania in disgust. It was nearly May for crying out loud! What was up with it snowing? At least this hotel was big enough to have an on-site restaurant and she'd be able to order in room service. She took off her helmet and tied her head up with her bright t-shirt, hoping that she'd someday be able to comb the tangles out of hair that hadn't seen conditioner or a hairbrush in two days.

When she didn't have a major credit card number to leave at the front desk, she had to put an extra hundred dollars down as a refundable deposit, but it was a much nicer hotel than the first one. She was pleasantly reassured when she found a full basket of little bottles of lotions and shampoos on the bathroom counter. Not only that, but she could set a real thermostat and pull room-darkening blinds before falling with a sigh into the crisp sheets. She'd made it through again and prayed an incredibly grateful, even if an incredibly tired prayer.

The next day, she wore a towel on her head to go down to the gift shop to buy a hair brush. It was a little unorthodox, but it beat the heck out of someone seeing her hair and recognizing her. Maybe someone would think she'd been swimming in the hotel pool or something.

With a heavy heart, she bought several things, including a pair of scissors, and went back up to the room. She needed to cut her hair off today, and it killed her. She'd never had short hair in her life.

After she finally got all the tangles out, she decided to order in breakfast before lopping it all off. It actually ended up being a chef salad because breakfast wasn't served after eleven a.m., but whether she had breakfast food for breakfast or not, was the least of her worries. Even after eating, she hesitated as she stood at the mirror with her scissors. She could just keep the helmet on for one more day, and she didn't have the hair color yet, anyway. It was rationalization, but she went with it. Cutting her hair felt like the last straw after having to leave her home and family for who knew how long.

After another nap, she was back out on the bike. As she pulled out of the hotel parking lot, another single snowflake hit her helmet shield, and she made an executive decision to turn south at the next interstate junction she came to. Snow in May. What was going on here? She stopped at the first truck stop she came to and bought a pair of leather gloves. As an added benefit, they covered her bright pink nail polish

The leather gloves came in handy that evening. She had pulled off the highway to get food and gas, and although she never took her helmet off, she still found herself the object of attention from a couple of car loads of what looked like high school boys on a road trip, and she was glad her bright nail polish was covered. At first, they were just throwing out comments and random expletives, but once back on the highway, they began to pull up and around her, swerving back and forth, being idiots.

For the first time this trip, fear about driving a motorcycle gripped her, as she remembered how she'd laid a bike down when she'd been cut off on a highway as a seventeen year old.

She had spent weeks in the hospital recovering from it afterward, and still had scars on her ankles to show for it. Pure adrenaline kicked in when she gunned the bike and decided to get away from these punks. Life was far too precious to mess around with a bunch of teenagers who didn't understand the risks they were taking.

She sped off through traffic in the early evening, slanting sun, and became even more concerned when the two cars tried to keep up with her. They were weaving in and out just like she was. It was foolish for a motorcyclist, but it was total insanity for a larger vehicle.

She was twenty minutes into this stupidity when she sighted a group of about twelve bikers up ahead on Harleys and breathed a sigh of relief. The bikers could at times be intimidating, but right now they looked like a gang of guardian angels. She pulled up and attached herself to the rear of the group. When the cars came up and continued to goof around, the bikers clued in fast. Suddenly, the whole group of them pulled back to surround the teens' cars.

The two carloads of teen boys exited at the next off ramp, and Kelly felt the knot in the pit of her stomach begin to loosen. She'd never traveled like this by herself and still struggled with a heavy burden of fear, in spite of her constant prayer. She was a long way from home, and no one in the world knew where she was or if she was okay. That scared her more than she dared to admit. She was so grateful that the fact she was female was hidden under layers of black leather and a tinted helmet. Half an hour later, she waved thank you to the bikers as she took the freeway exit.

That night, she pulled off to find a room as it got dark. She'd already been so nervous and driving all night alone again with the threat of rain still was too much. She approached a small, unimpressive motel and waited until she was standing in the office before she took her helmet off.

The scruffy, middle-aged man behind the desk looked her up and down with all but a leer as her hair fell out and cascaded down her back. The look in his eyes set off the red flags again, and she decided to simply ask for directions back instead of getting a room after all.

She had the helmet back on again, and was sitting on the bike, when she saw the man get into a truck and pull out behind her. She was glad she'd filled up with gas before looking for a room. When he signaled to get onto the interstate behind her, she got on the throttle and decided to just get gone now. She had no idea if this guy was following her, or if he just had somewhere to go right at this particular time, but she wasn't waiting around to find out.

After all out speeding for more than fifteen miles, she got off the interstate and looked again for a room, this time in a bigger, nicer hotel, and she left her helmet on even at the front desk. She pulled her saddle bags and took them clear inside the room and had the door locked, chained, and bolted, before she took the helmet off this time. The security of that dead bolt was a welcome thing.

There was a *Book of Mormon* in her room that night, and it brought an emotion that was almost overwhelming when she picked it up to read. It was a tangible reminder that God was out there, watching over her. She'd let that thought slip some times today. It had definitely been a spirit of fear she'd been traveling with instead of a spirit of power, and she needed to never let that happen again. She called down to the front desk and asked if there was any way she could buy the Book of Mormon. She went to sleep that night feeling a peace she hadn't felt in what seemed like a year, but had actually only been a few days.

The next morning, as she went to gas up, she found that the gas gauge was sticking and had to tap on it with her gloved hand to get it to work. She'd have to remember to watch herself so she didn't get stranded.

That day was the best one yet as far as travel and stress. The clouds finally cleared up and, in fact, it was almost too warm in the afternoon sun. She never took her helmet off at all and had no trouble with anyone that she met, so she wasn't worrying quite so much about being recognized. Surely a missing woman in the Chicago area wouldn't be a story clear down here in Virginia.

Still, to be safe, she left her helmet on again as she checked into a hotel near Roanoke. It never hurt to be safe and it made the rationalization that she could keep her hair unchanged more plausible. She really didn't want to cut her hair off, or even change the color. Somehow, she felt like she would lose the last of herself if she did.

Before leaving town the next morning, she found the public library and went in and pulled up a couple of the Chicago papers to see what was going on back home. She cried when she saw the pictures of her mother in tears wondering what had happened to her. Ryley must not have told her mother what she'd done, right at first. Her mother could have never faked the deep sadness that was etched onto her face in the photos. As she thought about it, maybe that was the reason Ryley had held back. It was brutal to do to her mom, but it would keep her safer if Peter and the others truly believed she was dead.

She crossed the state line into North Carolina just before

noon that morning, and looked all around her in interest. She didn't think she had ever been in a more naturally pretty place. The lush spring greens and the beautiful hills, valleys, and streams were like a tourism guide in real life. What a truly lovely place.

The gas gauge quit completely that morning. Kelly must have been thinking about her mother because she felt the bike chug that afternoon and switched over to her reserve tank without realizing she was even close to running out of gas. She was out in the country and prayed again, for about the thousandth time since this nightmare had begun, for God to watch over her.

When she began to wonder if she was going to reach civilization before she reached a gas station, she pulled off the interstate. She wasn't sure what would be better, being stranded on the surface roads or the interstate, but the smaller roads seemed less intimidating.

No town had come into sight when her motorcycle chugged into silence and coasted to a stop beneath her, and she opted for prayer again over swearing. How had she been foolish enough to let this happen? She could have sworn she had plenty of gas yet.

Prayer helped. It always did, and she was strangely at peace when she climbed off the bike and began to push it down a quiet country highway in the late afternoon. If she hadn't been too warm in her black leather, she would have probably really enjoyed the tranquil stillness, broken only by the occasional birdsong.

Chapter 3

Robby finally made it off the plane, and picked up his Land Rover from the long term parking. With a stretch, he pointed its hood toward the airport exit toll booths. It had been a tiring five days of fundraising for his foundation for less-fortunate children. He'd been successful and raised a lot of money, but he was more than ready for some down time and freedom from the spot light.

He sighed when he neared his condominium complex and recognized two of the cars parked out in front of the visitor's entrance. He was really not in the mood to dodge the advances of these two all but predatory women. What? Did they have nothing better to do than wait around all day, watching to see if he was pulling into his building's parking garage?

He wished he could just come out and be ornery enough to tell them all off for good. Then, maybe he could get them to leave him the heck alone. He hated that kind of thing though. And it would never have worked anyway. If these two left him alone, he'd just have to deal with several more in their places. It wasn't that he was being egotistical. He was smart enough to know that it really had nothing to do with him, or even his talents, or looks. He was just famous and had a lot of money. He'd worked hard to get to where he was, but sometimes it wasn't all fun and football.

He circled the block, then on an impulse, decided to go out to his new farm house. There wasn't much there yet to make it a home, but the moment the thought popped into his head, he felt it was a good idea. He hoped that meant he would, indeed, find the peace and security there he was hoping for.

The realtor had given him the final closing documents and the keys the afternoon he left, and he'd been dying to get out there ever since it had officially become his. He wished he'd had time to hire someone to start fixing it up. It would have been great to be able to just go out there right now and not have it be empty and run down.

He made a mental note to begin tomorrow trying to find someone to start both maintenance and caretaking. He wanted to be able to begin using it as soon as possible. For the next two and a half months before training camp officially started, it would be great to be able to go out there.

Halfway between two small towns, and smack dab in the middle of nowhere, he came upon a kid in black leather, pushing a motorcycle. He looked around, wondering where the boy had come from. There was just nothing out here, and he didn't look like a local farm boy on his way to his fields in black leather and a helmet. Robby stopped beside the motorcycle and rolled down his window, hoping he wouldn't be recognized in his ball cap and sunglasses. "Engine trouble, or are you just out of gas?"

The tinted helmet shook. "Just out of gas." Wow, this guy had a young voice.

With the familiar wish to be able to help those around him because he was so blessed himself, he wondered if he dared to offer a ride. The situation seemed relatively safe. He doubted the youth would be pushing the bike if he was just looking for someone to mug. "Can I give you a lift in to the station? I could bring you back."

The helmet shook again. "Thanks, but no. I'll be fine."

He pushed the bike past Robby's vehicle, and Robby had to let it roll backwards to ask again. "C'mon, dude. It's like eight more miles to the nearest station. Are you sure?"

The kid hardly even turned his head to say, "I'm sure. Thanks for the offer."

Sighing, he pulled out. Whatever. At least he'd tried. Stubborn hard head. That bike was going to weigh ten thousand pounds by the time that not very huge kid got it pushed into Tolke. On an impulse, he turned around. He went back to the station, bought and filled a gas can, and took it back to the wary youth. There was no reason not to. It's not like he couldn't afford the time or the money.

The kid had pushed the bike more than a quarter of a mile in the time it took to get the gas can and return. Robby had to hand it to him. He was spunky to turn down a ride rather than deal with a stranger. He stopped, lifted the gas can out, and then drove on to his little farm. Doing his good turn for the day helped to improve his mood immensely over what it had been when he'd driven past his condo. He got out at his new home of sorts with a sense that life was really good when you thought about it.

Kelly had been praying pretty much nonstop since she'd realized she was out of gas. Her Heavenly Father had rewarded her prayers with an uncanny sense of peace, given this situation. As she trudged along, out of breath from pushing the heavy bike, she looked around her and thought to herself, *I'll have to quit running sometime. Maybe this is God's way of telling me this is the place.* It was certainly beautiful and peaceful enough. She'd never lived out in the country before.

She tensed when a Land Rover came her direction, and tensed even more when it slowed and the window came down. Walking the bike had her feeling extremely vulnerable right now.

The face she saw when the window finished descending made her lose her train of thought for just a second or two. She had never seen a more gorgeous man in her life. He'd looked at the bike for a moment before addressing her, and she was able to remember how to speak, but only just barely. Man! They didn't make men like that in Illinois!

He asked about what was up with her bike and then offered her a ride to get gas. She was finally able to focus on what he was saying instead of what she was seeing. The fear made itself known again when he offered her a ride, and she breathed a sigh of relief when he drove off, even though she also breathed a sigh of regret. It was too bad she couldn't take a picture of that face and keep it forever. He had been flat out beautiful.

He'd turned and gone the other way, and Kelly didn't think much about it, until she'd pushed the bike what felt like ten more miles and he showed up again. This time he just set a gas can out onto the road, got back in, and went on his way. Kelly could have kissed him, even if he hadn't been drop-dead attractive. The bike had gotten heavier and heavier by the minute. She dumped the gas in, then wondered if she should leave the gas can here in case he came back by this way or take it with her into the nearest station and leave it there.

Being that the guy drove a nice car, she opted for taking it to the station. It was probably needed there more anyway. Maybe she could describe him, and the locals could get it back to him for her. She thought about describing him as she drove the ten minutes or so to the town. How could you ever try to describe a man like that to someone without totally embarrassing yourself? She grinned to herself and it felt good. She could just see the local North Carolinians watching her try to describe such a man. They'd laugh out loud. She knew she would. He'd been the ultimate in her twenty-three years.

When she finally made it to the station, she stretched her back as she let the tank fill. She was tired to the bone. She'd used muscles in the last five days she hadn't been aware that she even owned before, and the constant travel and stress wore her out.

She asked the station clerk to recommend someone who might be able to repair the gas gauge for her. There was no way she was doing this again --unless she could bargain for the adorable gasoline deliveryman. Just seeing him had definitely been worth the hassle of the whole thing.

The clerk sent her to a shop several blocks away on the main drag of the town. She glanced at her watch, wondering if the place would still be open. She tried to figure out what time it was here locally, or even what day it was and came up with honest blanks on both accounts. She was a mess. She was lucky she even remembered her name after this week. Of course, that didn't really matter any more. She couldn't use her real name right now anyway.

The shop was open, but they couldn't fix the gauge until the day after next because they had to order in the part. Kelly made the arrangements and asked about a hotel, then went off down the street in search of a room and some rest. The hotel they recommended wasn't big and wouldn't have room service, but there was a Pancake House across the parking lot. She got off her bike and stood beside it, wondering what to do. She'd be staying in this town for a couple of days, and wondered if keeping the helmet on all the time would be more conspicuous than just taking it off.

Maybe now was the time to finally cut her hair. She loved it, but it was becoming more hassle than it was worth. And no hair, no matter how stunning, would be worth being found over. There was a grocery store across the street from the hotel, and she decided with resignation to get the hair dye and chop it all off after all. It didn't really matter.

With a tired sigh, she reached up and took the helmet off. With another stretch, she walked into the hotel office.

Robby was on his way back through the town of Tolke when he noticed the leather clad biker in the parking lot in front of the hotel. He was glad to see that the young man had made it in okay. Robby stopped at the light right in front of the biker, and glanced back over just as the kid reached up and took off his helmet. Instantly, about two feet of auburn hair cascaded down her back.

He was floored to realize that the stubborn kid who had refused the ride had, in fact, been a girl. She turned to reach into the saddle bags of the bike, and he was even more floored to see her face. She wasn't just a girl; she was exquisite!

He was so busy staring, that he almost missed the fact the light changed. He pulled forward, glancing in his rearview mirror as he went. Holy Toledo, she was pretty! He could understand even better why she had turned him down, but that had never happened before in his life. It was so refreshing, he had to laugh.

Jason would hassle him for days about his reaction if he told him. He glanced in his mirror one more time. As she went inside the hotel, the last rays of the sun caught her hair and turned it into a deep red-brown flame. Holy Toledo! He hadn't seen hair like that since his mission to Ireland, where he'd found that he definitely had a thing for red.

He drove home almost in a daze and was clear into his

parking garage and getting out of the Rover before he thought about the women he had been trying to avoid earlier. Even being buzzed by the front door didn't bring him out of his reverie. He answered the intercom and when the voice of a woman named Jenna, who he had zero interest in, asked him if she could come up and visit, he didn't hesitate. "Jenn, I just got home, and I'm tired. I'm sorry, but not tonight." He let go of the button, and didn't even feel guilty. He was too busy thinking about the surprise that hair had been tumbling out of that helmet. Man, that had been hair!

He unpacked, looked through a handful of mail, and checked his answering machine. For once, deleting call after call after call didn't discourage him. He couldn't believe he was honestly intrigued, but it was actually kind of fun. He puttered around his house and decided he was going to Tolke early in the morning for a leisurely breakfast at the Pancake House.

Trying for rational thought this morning was a tad nebulous. Every few minutes he found himself in pause mode, thinking about that deep red-brown flame hair and china doll face. He tried to plan for actual accomplishment on his trip to Tolke, and to think of things that needed done out at the house after breakfast, but his brain was completely off. He was enroute before he had any kind of logical plan. He laughed at himself again. Jason would torture him if he saw what a zone he was in.

The drive itself helped him to focus, and by the time he was seated in the dining room of the little restaurant, he was beginning to have a game plan for the day. After looking around to make sure she wasn't already seated, he took out a pen and began making a list on a napkin. He'd been going to just hire everything done at the house, but since he was already almost there this morning, he might as well plan to get started. Cleaning first. He was in the process of making a shopping list of supplies when she walked into the room.

The waitress who was seating her placed her at the table that was almost touching his and he had to wonder if this was just a coincidence. He hoped not. She glanced up at him, but didn't say anything as she began to read the menu. The waitress stopped at his table to get his order, and he remembered he hadn't even looked at the menu yet, so he asked, "Do you have a house special breakfast?"

"Yes, we do. Ham, eggs, grits, toast and fruit. This morning, I believe it's cantaloupe."

"Bring me that then, please. And orange juice."

"Coming right up."

He tried to go back to his shopping list and ignore the fact that his brain was short circuiting, but it was a rout. He was almost relieved when his breakfast did come out in just a few minutes. He caught her looking at him, and a moment later, when the waitress came back, she ordered the same thing. When the waitress was gone again, he asked the girl with the hair, "Did you ever get your gas gauge fixed?"

She looked at him in surprise, with an expression that, if he didn't know better, he'd describe as anxious. "How did you know I needed my gas gauge fixed?"

He shrugged. "You ran out of gas yesterday. Isn't it just logical that that doesn't happen unless you're a mindless wonder or the gauge is broken? Can they get it working?"

She gave a miniscule head shake. "Tomorrow. They have to order the parts from somewhere. Thank you for the gas, by the way. I'd probably still be pushing."

"You're welcome." After another bite or two he asked, "Are you from around here?"

There was a hesitant pause before she admitted, "No."

"Where are you headed?"

She glanced around quickly and he could have sworn he saw fear in those green eyes. "South."

He looked up at her answer. "Just south?"

There was an almost inaudible sigh. "Just south." Her breakfast came and they ate in silence for a few minutes, while he thought about her answer.

Finally, he asked, "What are you going to do when you go south?"

She must have been trying for flippant, but what he got was sad, when she said, "I'm going to ride until I feel like stopping and then look for a job for awhile." He nodded and went back to eating. There it was, then. Tomorrow she was leaving for she didn't even know where. For some reason that depressed him.

He finished eating and left a generous tip. On standing, he said, "Good luck going just south." He paid his bill and went to leave, but looked back at her table one more time before going out the door. Their eyes met for just an instant. He'd been right. For some reason, just going south made her sad and fearful. He climbed into the Rover, more intrigued than ever. The eyes were as striking as the hair.

The whole time he was cleaning the bathroom at the farm house, he was thoughtful. Too thoughtful, apparently. While he was scrubbing above the tub, he inadvertently cleaned six tiles right off the wall. He gave a half-hearted smile. He'd known it was going to be a project. At least the water and electricity were on and the propane tank had been filled. It would come along.

He left at dark, wishing he at least had a bed so he could stay out here if he wanted.

The next morning, he was awake before it was even light and was thinking again. For some reason, he wanted to go back to Tolke and have breakfast once more. He thought about that and shook his head. Now there was a less than brilliant idea. It would waste his time and frustrate the tar out of him. The first thing that had entered his mind upon waking this morning, was to go back to the Pancake House and offer her the job of being a caretaker at his new farmhouse. It was nuts and he knew it, but it kept lingering in his head. There was something about that girl.

Obviously, there *was* something about that girl. Most of the women he knew he tried to avoid, but he didn't know one thing about this girl and was seriously thinking about offering to have her work right in one of his houses. That was crazy when he didn't know anything about her. He worked around his house for awhile, but when the thought was persistent, and kept popping into his head, he began to wonder if God wasn't calling and Robby was trying to ignore Him by saying it wasn't logical.

He thought back to the look he had seen in her eyes as he stepped out the door of the Pancake House yesterday. He'd seen fear and sadness there. Maybe it was God, trying to get him to help someone who needed it. Who knew? He went in and got dressed to go to Tolke. He'd try to listen for inspiration as he drove. Worst case scenario, he'd have a pretty drive and come home.

During the twenty-five minute drive, he went back over everything that had happened since he'd come around a gentle curve and seen the leather clad kid pushing the motorcycle up ahead. He remembered that she'd never once hesitated to turn down his offer of the ride, and the reason he'd simply set the gas out of his vehicle was that he was worried it would be refused as well. His thoughts were comforting. There was certainly nothing in their short time together that would lead him to believe she was after either him or his money, or that she was dishonest or dangerous. In fact, just the opposite had been true. She had tried to completely avoid him. His gut feeling was she was the one in danger.

He got to the restaurant and pulled in, glad to note that the black motorcycle was still parked in front of the hotel next door. He pulled his ball cap on and the dark sunglasses he'd become accustomed to wearing almost like a shield against being recognized and went inside. This time he was seated near the back of the restaurant. He had to wonder to himself one more time about the coincidence thing when she was seated right next to him again ten minutes later.

They had actually eaten most of their meal when unexpectedly, she asked him, "So are you from around here?"

He shook his head and smiled. "No, but I've been here for six years. Well, not here, but over in Charlotte."

He could feel her hesitation before she asked, "What do you do in Charlotte?"

What to tell her? She obviously had no idea that he was a pro football player, and he so didn't want any more money grubbers after him because of it. "I work for a big corporation there." That was true, just not terribly concise. "I'm in acquisition." He'd never really put it that way, but wasn't that what a wide receiver did? Try to acquire passes? She clearly wasn't a huge football fan or she'd have already recognized him. "What is it that you do?"

He could almost see her trying to come up with an answer for that. At length she said, "A little of whatever." He didn't think for a minute that her definition of what she did was any closer to being exact than his was. Perhaps she had a good reason for skirting things like he did.

He was still trying to figure out what to think about her, and finally decided that he truly felt like he'd been prompted to come here this morning. He would have to trust his gut on this one. Still, he hesitated to tell her it was his own house he was offering. "Are you going to try to find any certain job in particular, or are you open to a little of whatever?"

Her gaze looked off to the window for a second while she considered that. At length, she said, "I don't know. I guess I'll take what I can get when it comes right down to it."

She looked back at him and he said, "I know of someone who's looking for a caretaker for an old house he just bought. It hasn't been fixed up yet, but I think he plans to eventually. However, it's near here. Would you ever consider staying around here? It's pretty secluded. It might be lonely, but it would include a place to stay."

Her eyes met his and almost seemed to question what he was asking. After considering it for a minute, she answered, "Yeah, I would consider staying here if I felt like I could trust the man. When will he need someone?"

Robby had to think about that and finally grinned and said, "I guess it would depend on how tough you are. It's a house, and it has water and lights and heat and everything, but he's just barely bought it. It hasn't even been furnished yet. You could probably come anytime, but it needs work to be nice." She seemed to be thinking, and he offered, "I have the keys with me today. It's about a ten minute drive from here, if you want to see it."

She started nodding her head, albeit hesitantly, "I'd like that. My bike will be ready to go by nine-thirty or so. I could go anytime after that."

He almost started to say that she could ride with him now, but then he remembered she had refused that the first day, and he didn't want to spook her again for no reason. It was only wise for a young woman not to get into a car with a stranger, and he respected that. In the meantime, he could do some more shopping. There were a thousand things to be bought before his house would really be livable.

They arranged to meet back at nine-thirty, and he left with her still sitting at the table looking thoughtful.

That morning Kelly's day had started with her appreciating that the hotel here in Tolke, North Carolina had been her most comfortable stay so far, but still, she knew she needed to be moving on to somewhere. She had no idea where that somewhere was, and she had decided not to keep worrying about it, knowing she couldn't even leave until the gas gauge was working properly. She woke up at sunrise, and then lay there for a minute, trying to think things through logically. She wished she could call her mother and her Uncle Roy. It was awful to feel so alone.

She reached for her Book of Mormon. For some reason, reading about Moroni helped that feeling. It was almost as if just reading about his loneliness made her remember that she was never truly alone. God was always there with her if she'd just reach out for Him.

After reading she got up, showered, and got ready to go eat. As she dried her hair, she looked over at the scissors and box of hair dye sitting on the counter. She should just get it over with. She'd been putting it off for days, but it needed done. She picked up the scissors and felt so terrible about it that she put them right back down. Maybe after eating she'd try again. She went outside and walked to the restaurant across the parking lot.

The new gas gauge should be up and running in just an hour or two. Then she'd have to decide where she was headed next. She looked around, wondering if she could be inspired about what would be the best plan just by looking in a certain direction, but no, it wasn't as simple as that.

She had to go about this logically. She needed to hide where she could be safe, and she needed to find a way to earn a living. She had money now, but it wouldn't last long, and she had absolutely no idea how long she'd have to stay running like this. At least until she could find a way to stop Peter and the others from hurting anyone else, and being a threat to her.

Just a safe place and a job didn't sound like that tall of an order, but from where she was right now, and with no legal ID, she had no idea what to do or where to go. She said another prayer in her heart as she walked. It was down to just her and God now, and she was putting all of her faith in Him and not trusting to her own understanding. When she remembered to do it, the peace that it brought was unbelievably comforting.

On her way across the parking lot she saw the white Land Rover. It made her perk up. Maybe he was here having breakfast again. She wished she had the guts to talk to him if he was. There had been something about him that was so comforting. Maybe it was just that he had brought her the gas she had needed, but at any rate he had left the most unusual impression on her. Men didn't typically have that deep of an effect on her.

Of course men didn't typically look like that either, but it was more than just the fact that he was beautiful.

Inside the restaurant, she saw him instantly, and it was almost weird when the waitress seated her right next to him again. He glanced at her and then went back to quietly eating, and she wondered what she could say to open up a conversation with him. At length she asked him the same question he had first asked her yesterday morning about whether he was from around here.

It was uncanny the way the conversation turned almost immediately to a way she could possibly have that safe place to hide and a way to make money. She felt like she wanted to look skyward and say, "Thank you". There was still the question about not having ID, but when she knew so surely that God's hand was in all of this, she didn't doubt for a second that that could be handled, too.

Chapter 4

By nine-thirty, Robby had bought more cleaning supplies, some paper plates, cups and utensils, and a handful of easy foods for when he worked there. He was trying to think of things he'd need, but his brain had begun short circuiting again the way it had before when he'd first seen her, and his thoughts weren't terribly cohesive. He loaded his purchases to his car with a self conscious grin. *Yup, Jason would definitely be having a good time with this one.*

He pulled back into the parking lot between the hotel and Pancake House, and just a few minutes later she pulled in behind him, completely hidden by her leathers and helmet. To see her now, you'd never know this biker dude was, in fact, an exquisitely beautiful young woman. He headed out onto the highway without saying anything to her, and on the short drive tried to listen for that anxious feeling that would be warning him if this was a wrong move. Over the years he'd made enough of them that he certainly knew what that feeling was like, but even listening as well as he could with no brain at the moment, he was ridiculously at peace and drove on. He felt good about this. It would remain to be seen what the auburn haired beauty on the bike behind him would think about it all.

Kelly followed the Land Rover out of the town and right back to the place she'd first seen this guy when she was pushing the motorcycle. On looking back, she was grateful all over again for his gift of the gas. She'd probably still be pushing if he hadn't gone and brought it to her.

It had been a pure-hearted good deed for him to do it, and it made her feel more comfortable about following him out to a house that he'd come right out and said would be lonely and secluded.

This morning, she'd been worried about finding a safe place to hide where she wouldn't be recognized and a way to support herself. Now, just an hour or two later, she may have found a way that was ideal. A caretaker job that included a place to stay and seclusion, filled the bill like a charm. What it was like still remained to be seen, but so far she wasn't having any of those pesky red flag issues that had begun to be far too familiar lately.

Stopping at a locked gate in the middle of pretty much nowhere, the man in the Rover got out, opened the gate, and then continued on up the gravel road behind it. From the gate, she could see nothing but fields, woods, and a winding stream, but just a few minutes up the road an old farmstead appeared around a bend. She pulled up behind him and climbed off the bike, looking all around at the neat, old, weathered buildings with an incredibly overgrown yard threatening to take control around them. She wished her Uncle Roy could have seen this. He'd have been in heaven. It was like the ultimate This Old House project.

She pulled off the helmet and set it on the seat and zipped off her leather jacket to leave it there as well. Without even waiting for him, she walked up on the porch and, instead of going to the front door, she walked over to the weathered log wall and leaned in to study the squared off logs. Hearing him step up onto the porch behind her she said, "Wow. These are hand hewn logs. Look, you can actually see the axe marks on these."

She backed up to tip her head up and look at the whole house again. "Look at this place. Can you imagine the work that went in to building this?" She went to the corner and looked at the notch where the logs fit together.

She shook her head and turned back to her host. "This is incredible. And look at it. It's weathered, but there's no rot and it's all still straight and square and tight. How did your friend ever find this? It's awesome!"

He laughed at her. "What, are you some kind of old log home buff? How do you know what a hand hewn log looks like?"

Looking somewhat sheepish, she admitted, "Uh, well.

This Old House has been my favorite TV program forever. My uncle and I love it. He's a builder. The rest of the family think we're nuts, but I love that stuff." He was looking at her a little skeptically, and she hesitated. "I know. It's not terribly feminine. My mother hated it. I used to make a point of painting my fingernails as I watched just to make her think I was still girly. She still wasn't very happy about it."

He shook his head and grinned. "My mother wanted an MD, so she wasn't all that thrilled with me either. I know how you feel." He unlocked the door and went inside. "It needs a ton of work and he's just getting started with it, but it has some great potential."

Inside, she leaned down and stroked the dusty wood floor. It had to have been the original floor and was distressed and scuffed and marvelous. It was heart pine with the tightest grooves and a natural mellow patina that could only come from years and years and years. She stood up and glanced up at him to see him watching her and it made her a little embarrassed. He probably thought she was crazy.

Turning away, she went past him into the kitchen and kept looking around. The kitchen was a project. The walls and floors were cool, but the old cabinets were garbage and needed to be ripped out and replaced.

Behind her he said, "The house itself is great, but there are some issues. These cabinets are one of them. The plan is to refurbish the place without losing the frontier charm, if possible. The kitchen is hard because he wants to keep the old feel but still have it be a working kitchen with nice appliances. It's going to take a lot, but should be really cool when it's done."

"What does he want, as far as a caretaker? Do you know?"

He shook his head. "Not exactly. I think what he wants is someone to make sure things are secure here when he's out of town and that when he comes to visit it's clean and the heat is on and there are fresh milk and eggs in the refrigerator. Does that make sense?"

"Yes, I think it makes sense. If you had a second home that's what you would want, isn't it? Where would I stay here?

You mentioned that it would include a place to stay."

He paused and looked all around. "You know, I don't know. For the time being you'd have to keep staying at the hotel there in Tolke until he can get a contractor to come out and make it livable, but I'm sure he'd pay for it. I don't know if you'd stay right in the house or build another little place for the caretaker's quarters. I don't think he has everything all worked out yet. He just got the keys for it last week."

She continued walking as they talked and peeked into several of the doors that stood open. It was a great old house and she'd love to stay here. The only question was whether the seclusion that would keep her from being found would scare her or be too lonely. She'd never lived out of the city in her life. At any rate, she felt like it was the answer to her prayers. She turned back to him. "What is this guy like? When can I meet him?"

He stood looking like he wasn't sure how to answer that question and finally said, "He's a good man. You'd definitely be safe here with him. I'd trust my mother and sisters with him. In fact, he's actually a bit of a recluse as far as women are concerned. I'm not sure when he could meet you. For the time being you'd have to simply work through me. But he's honest and easy to get along with and generous."

She nodded, studying him and trying to decide whether she could trust his judgment of his friend, and then looked around one more time. "Okay, so when do I start?"

"You don't even want to know what he'd pay?"

"I did forget to ask that, didn't I? What does he pay?"

He chuckled. "I have no idea. What do caretakers make?"

She shook her head and laughed. "I haven't a clue. Find out and get me a list of exactly what this guy wants, and in the meantime, I'll get started on his project. Will he care if I dig in without checking with him first?"

"I'm sure he won't care." He dug into a pocket and took out a pair of keys. "This one is the gate and this one is the house. Come out to my car and let me get some information." He looked up. "I'm Robby, by the way. Robby Robideaux." He extended a hand. "Sorry. I almost forgot that I didn't introduce myself."

With just a split second of hesitation, she said, "And I'm Kelly Shane."

At the car he found a piece of paper, ripped it in two, and handed her half. "Okay, for now just give me your name and phone number. I'll talk to someone and find out what all information I have to get from you and whatever legal forms I need filled out. I don't usually do this, so I have no idea what I need." He wrote a number on the other paper and handed it to her. "Here's my home phone number. You'll probably just get my machine, but leave a message if there's a problem. I'll get back to you."

She waited for his pen as she said, "I didn't bring my phone with. I'm sorry. So there's no number. I'll call you with the number from the hotel. Is there a phone here? A land line?"

He looked up. "I don't know. I've never even thought about that. We'll have to go see. Did you see a phone in there? If not, we can arrange to have one installed soon."

"I can't remember seeing one." She handed him the paper with just her first and middle name on it. "I'll go back in and look."

He handed her a couple bags of groceries. "Would you mind helping me carry these in and I'll come look with you?" They loaded the bags in and set them on a dusty countertop. "Just set them there for now and I'll wipe out at least one of these cupboards before I go to hold them. As you're working, make a list of what needs to be bought and we'll eventually get this place furnished."

After making another short tour, she turned back to him. "No phone, but there are some old jacks. I'm not sure if the lines are still good, but there has been a phone hooked up here at some time."

"I'll call about having a line installed. If they have to tear the whole road up to bring in lines, it may be better just to use cell phones exclusively."

They went back out to the Rover and brought another load of bags in. On the way she paused and looked at the other buildings. Nodding, she asked, "What are they?"

He shook his head. "I don't even know for sure. That nearest one is a garage, and the one across the lawn the realtor thought was an old fashioned summer kitchen. There's a stable and a granary and I believe the smaller building used to be a smokehouse. I have no idea which is which. In all honesty, I've never explored them. I believe the fence encloses a small pasture. It's about the only thing that has been used around here in years. I'm not sure why the last owner hasn't used it."

She set the bags on the counter and, seeing that one held a bag of dishcloths and detergent, she ripped the package open and began to wipe out the inside of a couple of the cabinets and then dry them with another cloth. While she did that, he'd been sorting the bags and when the cupboards were dry, they stood side by side and loaded food into one and dishes and utensils into the other and then took the cleaning supplies to the laundry room next door and did the same thing with them.

When he went to throw the grocery bags away, he stopped and seemed to realize that he hadn't even gotten a garbage can yet, and instead stuffed all the bags inside one and tossed it under the sink. "I'll try to remember to bring a garbage can out with me next time. And if they can get the phone lines in soon, I'll call you and get your list and bring it out, too."

On the way back toward the front door, she looked all around. "This really will be a big project, but it will probably be a lot of fun too. I don't know that I've ever tried to start up housekeeping from scratch before. I think all my college apartments were at least partially furnished. This will be an adventure! Do you think he'll care if I explore the outbuildings?"

"No. I'd think he'd expect you to. Come on, I'll look through some of them with you."

"Oh, good. I'm not typically afraid of small creatures, but it will still be good to have someone with me in case of any surprises. I'd guess that in all this wild yard and long unused buildings, there will be a few."

She hadn't taken but about two more steps when the grass in front of her did indeed move, and he said, "There would be one of your small creatures now. For the most part I think they should be relatively harmless, but there are some snakes here that can be extremely poisonous so watch your step. I'll also see about getting someone out here to try to tame this yard a little."

She tripped over a trailing vine on a small slope. "This yard may be more of a project than the house. North Carolina must be incredibly fertile to have everything grow this out of control. I wonder how the early settlers were able to keep it cleared to farm and garden."

"I'll bet they had to work at it."

As they reached one of the buildings, she nodded. "I'm sure they did. This must be the garage with these big doors." They pulled one of the doors ajar and stepped into the dim interior. He went and pulled a cobwebby string that hung from the light fixture in the center of the ceiling, and she laughed. "That thing needs to be in a museum."

"What? The old garage light museum?" She laughed again at his stupid pun and it made him laugh in return.

"There's an old garage light museum? I don't believe I'm familiar with that particular one."

"There's a museum for everything somewhere isn't there? Check out this oil can. It's right off of the *Wizard of Oz*."

"Hey, maybe they could display it in the garage light museum. Okay, maybe not. But, maybe some people oil their garage lights."

"Yeah, I think it was the Lord of the Flame who started Chicago on fire that night. That's about what would happen if you oiled that light. Check out these old jars full of nails. The glass is all but blue."

She picked up one of the jars and held it to the light. "Why is it blue? They're all blue. Did they use to make glass blue or something?"

"I don't think they made it blue. Somehow when it ages it goes blue. The antique buffs love it. Supposedly the bluer it is the more valuable."

"Well, then some of these old jars full of stuff are worth something. Look at this one. It has all kinds of flaws in the glass." She held it up to the light as well. "Hey, this one is green. Does that mean anything?"

He laughed. "The blue tidbit was as good as it gets from

me. Old bottles in a garage are not my specialty. I guess this one is going to take some work before it will fit a car inside. Let's go to the next building and then I have to get going. I've got meetings this afternoon.

The next one was the stable and it was far cleaner than the garage. There wasn't much left inside other than some dusty harness that hung on a wall and old straw and droppings in the stalls. There were some built in grain bins and feeders and one of the gates had a broken hinge and hung crooked. She pointed at it. "That's the first truly broken thing that I've seen here. Whoever built this place must have been a gifted craftsman, and then someone has maintained it over the years. The whole place is incredible."

They headed back toward his car. "I'm glad you think so. Maybe that will help when the caretaking gets boring or lonely." He went to get into his car. "Be sure and lock up when you leave, and lock the gate behind you. I'll see about getting a phone as soon as possible. Take care."

He shut the door and drove away as Kelly watched his car go down the gravel lane in amazement. The most handsome man she had ever met had hired her on the spot when she needed it desperately and then worked beside her and visited like they'd been friends forever. Being with him this morning had been the most comfortable thing in the world. She could hardly believe it.

He had taken a chance on hiring her. She knew it and determined right then to make sure he didn't regret it. She would earn her wage, whatever it was, and then some. That way maybe when he or his friend figured out that she didn't have any ID or social security card right now, it wouldn't make them boot her out on her ear.

She headed back into the house and started right into cleaning with determination. She had no vacuum or broom, so she had to just make do with wiping off counters and cupboards and washing sinks, tubs and windows.

By the time the sun began to set in the west over the ridgeline, she had made a sizeable dent in the grime. The house looked much brighter now that the light could come in the windows unfiltered. She'd worked hard and was tired, but happy, and looked forward to coming back out here tomorrow to hit it for another day. It was going to be a fun project.

There was nothing to write with yet, so she made as good a mental list as possible, locked the door securely behind her, and went out and climbed on her bike to head back to the hotel for the night. Before she lay down to sleep that night, she thanked her Father in Heaven for making sure Robby Robideaux was driving down that country road in North Carolina those couple of days ago. He had definitely been the answer to her prayers several times, so far.

The restaurant felt a little lonely the next morning without him, but she was looking forward to getting back out to the farm house enough, that it wasn't a big deal. After eating, she stopped at the grocery store and bought a small broom and dust pan and then laughed at herself as she tried to figure out how to strap it onto her bike to get it out there. It was a good thing there weren't many people out and about right then, because she certainly wasn't very inconspicuous, biking along with her broom in tow.

Once there, she swept the house out thoroughly and then went outside to finish exploring the other outbuildings. She'd been wondering about where she would stay out here with a male boss who stayed in the house. Staying in a house with someone she didn't even know was a bit frightening to her, and even if she got to know him, it didn't really seem appropriate somehow. She was thinking about that as she explored the other few buildings.

There were several pleasant surprises for her. One was that in what she assumed was the granary she found several pieces of old furniture. They were dusty, but upon wiping them with her hand they were still beautiful and seemed sturdy enough. There was an antique bedroom set of dark wood that consisted of a sleigh bed, dresser, and night stand. There were no mattresses, but the rest of it would clean up nicely and fit the style of the old house perfectly.

There was also a much more rustic bed that appeared to be made out of heavy plain boards that almost looked liked weathered barn wood. It was obviously old and hand made, but still seemed to be structurally as solid as the rest of the farmstead.

She could just see the bed with a white cotton bedspread and pillows on it. There was also a small, plain kitchen table that resembled the bed, which was perfect for this house.

Behind the furniture were some ancient, striped ticking feather mattresses, but judging from the rustling sounds she heard when she approached, they were definitely not going to be usable, which was just as well. Going retro with a mattress didn't sound like such a great idea. Decent sleep was important enough to warrant the latest luxury.

Next, she peeked inside the smoke house. She'd never seen anything even remotely like it and was fascinated by the blackened interior full of hooks and racks that still smelled like a bacon factory. She couldn't even begin to imagine raising enough food to feed a real family without going to the grocery store every few days. How had those people survived?

There was an outhouse tucked under a huge old bush that she had no interest in peeking into, and a chicken house that was empty, except for nesting boxes and roosts. Finally, the last building on her circuit was what Robby had called the summer kitchen. She wasn't sure what a summer kitchen was, but on opening the Dutch door she was very pleasantly surprised.

It was large, probably twenty by twenty, with big windows that made it appear bright and cheerful, and when she discovered a farmhouse sink in the corner with a few cupboards and a short counter, she had a sudden thought that maybe this was where she would end up living. It was big enough to add a small bathroom near the sink, and she could absolutely envision the more rustic of the beds with the white bedspread and matching airy white curtains blowing in the breeze from the big windows.

The small, rustic table would fit perfectly nearby. She could even picture a bouquet of wildflowers in a mason jar in the center of it and more flowers growing on the wide shelves that had been built outside the windows. It would be perfect to live in. She made a mental note to ask Robby if that would be okay the next time she spoke to him.

On the way back into the house, she tripped over the same pesky trailing vine and determined that it had to go just as soon as she found something to cut it with. She'd brought a notepad and pen from the hotel this time, and, after beginning a list with the word pruners, she wandered from room to room trying to envision what each needed eventually and trying to prioritize what she needed to get started on first.

There were so many things on her list that she needed, but after her struggle with just the broom on the motorcycle this morning, she was at Robby's mercy to pick up anything much larger than hand tools. That was actually somewhat disappointing to her. After finding the beds and discovering the summer kitchen, she wanted to start on fixing up these rooms the way she could so clearly envision them. She was sure that Robby had only wanted her to clean and help furnish and organize things here, and that he intended to hire a contractor to do the remodeling part of the project. But, some of the things were going to be pretty small scale, and she didn't think he would mind if she pitched in.

In her list making, she decided that the main bathroom needed to be the first priority for a number of reasons. First off, no matter who was doing the renovation, they would need a working restroom, and when she'd been cleaning in there, she'd knocked more tiles off a wall that was already missing several. Because the actual walls were of log, protecting them from the moisture of a bathroom was vital to keep them from rotting, which would be a shame after this house had withstood the test of time as it had.

She sat down on the porch step and began to make a wish list of what she would do with this house, if it were hers. Just like Robby had said the owner wanted, if it had been her own, she would try to preserve the rustic ambiance while still making it nice and certainly utilitarian. She'd watched a lot of building shows on Saturday mornings and she'd toured any number of her uncle's finished homes back in Chicago, so she knew what she liked as far as that went, but she hadn't actually done much in the way of constructing the projects. Still, if some of those day laborers could handle this stuff, couldn't she?

After working until the sun set again, she went back into town and stopped into Home Depot there. She bought a book on bathroom remodeling and took it back to the hotel with her. On the way out the door, she noticed a Home Depot truck with a big "Rent Me" sign on it, and it only fueled the fire of wanting to start working on a project out there. If she could find a way to rent the truck to haul materials, she could have that bathroom usable in no time at all.

Back at the hotel she went across and brought back a sandwich from the restaurant. Then she showered and crashed on the bed with her dinner and the book. By the time she went to sleep at nearly midnight, she knew what she had to do, and in fact, had a materials list all written out for that bathroom. Now she only needed exact measurements, and permission, and to have someone pick out the new tile and fixtures.

First thing the next morning, she put a call in to Robby, but no one answered. She waited around a few minutes and then went across and ordered breakfast and brought it back again so she could listen in case he called the hotel back. When he never called by the time she was ready to go, she decided to leave and try again later.

Stopping once more at Home Depot, she took a spin through the tile and bath fixtures departments to see what was available before buying a tape measure and pruners. She also stopped at a department store and bought a radio. Sometimes it was so quiet out there that it made her crazy. She stuffed it down in her saddlebags and headed on out to the house.

Once there, her first priority was to cut that darned tripping vine clear out of the way. It had nearly flattened her a number of times. While she was at it, she went to the garage and searched for a shovel. She took it back to the vine spot, dug out a space, and then went down near the creek that ran along the edge of the yard and brought back a couple of large flat stones. Carefully, she crafted a solid stone step on the slight incline that had been tripping her for these last few days. When it was done, she was surprised at how good it looked there in the naturally landscaped yard. It fit in perfectly.

Inside the house, she measured up the bathroom floor and walls of the shower, and then stood gazing at it critically for several minutes, wondering what would look right there to make it easy to use, but still not seem like a modern remodel. That day as she continued to clean, she tried to picture in her mind what would look good.

She had the house about as clean as she was going to get it without a vacuum and real mop, so she moved on to the summer kitchen. She scrubbed the sink, swept the floors, and washed the windows, then took off some wood trim that had been added long after it was built and was, in her opinion, completely out of place with the beautiful hand-hewn logs. Next, she measured the windows.

That evening, on the way back to the hotel, she stopped at a linens shop and bought the bedspread and curtains she'd thought would be so perfect in there. She stuffed them and matching sheets down into her saddle bags and strapped pillows onto the back of her bike. She was way jumping the gun, but it would be incredibly nice to have a bed of her own to speak of soon.

Robby didn't return her calls that night, or the next morning, so she decided to just go ahead with her own judgment on the tile choice. If the new owner didn't like it, she'd rip it all back off. In the meantime, she was excited to get on with the program out there at the lovely, old farmhouse.

Knowing that she had no ID to rent the truck, she shamelessly smiled at the guy at the rental desk and sweet talked him into letting her take it, even without ID. Then she bought the tile and other materials and some curtain rods for the summer kitchen and then smiled again when he helped her load everything. On further thought, while she had the truck, she stopped at a furniture store on the way and bought mattresses and box springs for the two beds in the granary. She knew she was spending a lot of her own money, but from the way Robby had acted that morning with her, she didn't doubt that the owner would pay her back for any personal money she was dumping into this neat old house or her quarters.

When she arrived, she pulled the truck as close to the door of the summer kitchen as she could and struggled to unload one of the sets of mattresses, then pulled the truck over to the porch of the house and did the same. By the time she had the tile, underlayment, and materials unloaded, she was completely worn out, and had to take a break and catch her breath for several minutes before she could head back to town to return the truck and pick up her motorcycle.

Back at the house, she felt like a kid in a candy store as she contemplated beginning to tile the sides of the shower. It was going to take some work, but she couldn't wait to get started.

When she went to wrestle a sheet of the backer board in, it was simply overwhelming. It was too big and too heavy for her to maneuver through the doorways and then hold up on the wall, so she had to change tactics. She decided to cut it down to the size she needed right outside on the porch so it would be lighter to carry inside by herself. That was much easier, and before lunch, she had the backer in place and had the seams patched with the mortar.

While she let it set up, she went out to the granary and struggled again to lift the beds outside where she wiped them free of dust and then carefully washed them with the cleaner Robby had purchased for the wood floors. Even broken down into just head boards, foot boards and rails, they were heavy and she went and got an old wheel barrow out of the garage and, by carefully balancing, she was able to wheel them across the yard and to the porches.

She wrestled the one into the summer kitchen first and put it together, and then pushed and pulled and groaned, and managed to wrestle the box spring and mattress into place. When she finally succeeded, she had never been so pleased with herself in her life. She lay down on the bare mattress and rested from her struggles, then decided that just as soon as she had a way to cook she was going to check out of the hotel and move out here for good.

She dug her new linens out, made up her bed, and after hanging the curtains at the windows, wished she had the little table. At least she could go out to the garage and get one of the antique Mason jars and pick the wildflower bouquet to finish her beautiful new summer kitchen off as she'd envisioned.

With her room that much done, she went back out and wrestled the other bed into the front bedroom of the main house and then pushed and pulled its bedding into place as well, before going back to begin the actual tiling of the shower.

She'd chosen some six inch ceramic tile that looked like real mottled chocolate brown, tan, and gray stone she thought would go well with the weathered logs. At first she was able to apply the mastic and put them up whole, and she was absolutely smug at how well her wall was turning out on her first attempt at tiling, until she had to cut one to fit. She broke the very first tile she tried to cut, and broke the second one as well, and then got worried. She went back and reread the instructions on the tile cutter and figured out she wasn't doing it exactly right and tried again. The third time was a charm.

She broke two more tiles before she was finished, but she still had enough, and the shower was going to look marvelous when finished, if she did say so herself. Toward the end, she'd been too short to reach and, once again, dug through the garage and found an old wooden ladder that helped her reach the last couple of rows at the top.

As it got dark, she was so tired she wondered if she could drive the whole ten minutes back to the hotel without falling asleep right on her bike. It had been a long, strenuous, and completely satisfying day.

She stopped and got fast food on the way in, and after trying Robby one more time, sat on the bed in her room to eat before heading into the shower. She never made it. She woke up sometime after midnight still in her jeans and shoes with a half eaten sandwich in her hand, shivering on top of the covers.

Chapter 5

Robby pulled in to his building parking garage without worrying about anyone waiting for him. Hopefully, even the most money hungry women would be long at home in their beds by this hour. He got out of the Rover and yawned and stretched before heading upstairs to his condo. It had been another long three days out of town but this time it hadn't been all business. He'd gone home to see his family for a couple of days when his mom had called and told him his dad was sick again.

His dad had diabetes and his illnesses had gotten to be much more serious since he'd been diagnosed. They'd been such close friends his whole life. Seeing him like that was always a wake up call that his dad was a mere mortal like all the rest of us. Robby knew he probably wouldn't live to be an old man. It made him sadder than anything in his life ever had.

He got off the elevator, let himself in, locked the door behind him, and automatically went to check his machine. Dumping his messages as usual, he was surprised to find a message from Kelly and several times that she'd called and hadn't left messages. He wondered if something was wrong out at the house. Why else would she have called him several times when he'd left a message at the hotel that he was leaving and to call his cell if there was an emergency?

It hadn't been a terribly convenient time to be called away as far as just having hired her, but he hadn't worried. Maybe it was good that she know, right from the start, that there would be times he'd have to leave her in charge for awhile.

Short of burning the place down, she couldn't hurt it in the condition it was in, and somehow he knew he could trust her. He just wished he'd been able to go back out and see her under the ruse of checking on the house. It had been five days now since he'd given her the key.

When he finally dragged himself out of bed the next morning, he tried the hotel, but she wasn't there. He had some things he had to do today in his home office, and then he'd have to run out and check on the place. It was amazing how much that idea lifted his spirits. He'd known he was a little burnt out lately, but hadn't realized how much until he'd noticed how this little excitement over his new house and caretaker could perk him up.

He called to see if the new phone had been installed yet and was told it had, but when he tried it, he found that no one answered and he laughed thinking she hadn't known it was hooked up and probably hadn't even thought to plug in a phone. He stopped on the way there and bought a phone and a small microwave to use until they got the kitchen remodeled.

As he walked back to the Rover, he had another thought and went back inside to buy the most powerful push lawnmower he could find and the oil for it. He thought about a riding mower, but his yard was so diverse and uneven that he didn't think one would even be practical and had to settle for self-propelled. He still hadn't checked into finding a gardener or contractor, and the yard was probably going to have that house completely taken over soon if he didn't do something. On the way out of town, he stopped and bought another gas can and filled it, thinking back again to the last time he had done this, just a few days ago.

The last ten minutes from Tolke on, he drove faster than he probably should have but he couldn't help himself. He tried to tell himself it was the house he was looking forward to seeing, but knowing the shape it was in, that couldn't have been the only thing he was looking forward to.

When he pulled up to the front of the house and got out, he had to laugh. From somewhere inside the house he could hear the old Credence song about elephants in the backyard. Gazing around at the over grown lawn, it was somewhat plausible.

On the way into the house, he had to step over a mess on the porch that completely puzzled him. There were pieces of some kind of thin gray boards and he had no idea what it was.

The porch was a disaster, but when he went inside he was very pleasantly surprised. The house that had been dusty and dreary and somewhat stale smelling, was now clean and sun filled and smelled of the breezes that wafted in through the open windows. He followed the music and eventually found her in the bathroom, standing on an ancient ladder, doing something to the beautiful new tile that lined the walls of the shower.

The tile looked good, but not nearly as good as she did, standing there on that ladder with her back to him. He'd never seen her without her leather on and the figure those cut off jeans revealed was every bit as pretty as her hair and eyes.

He must have made a sound of some kind, because she gasped and whirled and the ladder she was standing on tipped and fell toward him. He caught her before she fell headlong, but she knocked him back against the bathroom wall and they both ended up in a heap on the floor near the doorway. The clip that had been holding her hair up in a loose knot popped off and it took a second to untangle the beautiful long red-brown strands, so she could even look up at him. "Robby! I'm so sorry! I didn't know you were here. You scared me! Are you okay?"

She carefully tried to stand up without stepping on him and then reached to pick up the funny shaped bottle she'd been using on the ladder.

He'd been tackled an awful lot in his days as a football player, but he didn't think he'd ever enjoyed it quite as much as he had this time when she'd just knocked him flat. She reached down to pick up the ladder and then glanced around for her hair clip, trying to comb out the tangles with her fingers before she twisted it all back up and secured it.

He sat up, then leaned against the wall, watching her and was still sitting there when she turned down the radio and asked, "Well, what do you think? Do you think the owner will be mad that I picked some tile out and started without checking with him first? I tried to call you several times, but could never get in touch with you."

He looked from her to the tile again. "No, I think he'll love the tile. The house looks wonderful! You've been busy. I thought it would take weeks to get this much done. It's amazing what clean windows will do. It looks great." He finally stood up and came closer to examine the tile. "You didn't tell me you were a contractor. Why didn't you say something the other day?

This is awesome. It's new and waterproof and nice, but fits with the logs beautifully."

"Honestly, I'm definitely not a contractor. I'm actually a registered nurse, but I've always wanted to try something like this. It wasn't that bad, really. I bought a book and read all about it. This is going to sound terrible, but I assumed that sometimes construction isn't the most technical of all occupations and decided to try my hand at it. I was hoping to have a functioning shower as soon as possible."

"That is the one thing that can't be lived without, isn't it? Are you okay? Did I hurt you?"

She shook her head. "No, I'm fine, but I think we toasted the nineteenth century ladder. I was almost done sealing the grout. Now I'll have to go find something else to stand on."

"Tell me what to do and I'll reach it for you." He took her bottle. "Registered nurse, huh? That's good to know in case of an emergency. Now, what am I doing here?"

She showed him how to seal the last few feet of grout and when that was done, she enthusiastically took him to see some of the other things she had accomplished. They went into the front bedroom and she showed him the bare bedding. "Do you think the owner will care that I pulled the antique furniture out? I just thought if he ever came he might want to be able to actually stay here once in a while. I mean it's still a little inhospitable. And the kitchen is still a mess, but it might be nice for him. There's a dresser and nightstand out there too, but it was all I could do to lift just the head and foot boards."

Robby smiled at her enthusiasm. "I think he'll totally appreciate it. How in the world did you lift the things you did?"

She sighed dramatically. "It was hard. Ridiculously hard. I was definitely wishing for some more muscle." She went toward the door. "Come see another idea I had. Do you think the owner would let me live in the summer kitchen? You should see this other bed. It seems like it's about two hundred years old. It's so cool! And there's a little table that matches it, but I couldn't move it by myself."

She almost skipped out the door and across the lawn, and he was surprised at the change from the wary, hesitant person who he'd thought was a kid who wouldn't accept a ride. Somehow she'd come to trust him, and her real personality was showing through, and she was a riot! As they went past the smokehouse, she laughed and said, "I considered living in here, but worried that I'd smell like a barbecue or something."

With a laugh, he said, "Wasn't there a commercial awhile back about how men liked women who smelled like bacon? Maybe living in a smokehouse is the key."

"Yeah, but what happens when the honeymoon's over and their sense of smell dies? The whole romance would end in the outhouse. Well, either the outhouse or the pig pen. Hey, I wonder what happened to the pig pen. If you have a smokehouse, don't you have to have a pig pen?" She stopped to show him her new step where the vine had tripped them and then continued on to the summer kitchen.

When he walked in, he couldn't believe the change. The only other time he'd been in here had been that first day with the realtor, but the impression then had been of a dusty, dingy, almost gloomy room with twisting pieces of trim hanging off the walls and logs that were almost devoid of color. Today, with the windows open and the curtains and bedspread that were such a clean, crisp contrast to the weathered woods, it seemed more like an advertisement for a fabric softener or something.

He gazed around in amazement. "Wow! This is great! How did you do all of this so quickly?"

"This was actually relatively straightforward. All I've done is cleaned it, took off that awful wood trim, and put up the curtains. This is just a great room. So, do you think the owner would mind if I lived here? There's already plumbing available, and room enough to section off a small bathroom there by the sink and cupboards."

He turned to her. "Kelly, I need to tell you something. I own this house. I just bought it. I'm not sure why I told you that a friend owned it at first. For some reason, I was a little worried because we were complete strangers. I know we still don't know each other well, but I hate feeling like I'm not being honest with you. It's been bothering me. It's mine, and I think you've done a wonderful job in just these last few days and, of course, you can live in here. Will it be warm enough when winter comes?"

Putting both hands on her hips she looked at him. "It's yours? Man, I wouldn't have worried quite so much about offending a stranger by going ahead with the tile if I'd known it was yours. Was the tile okay? 'Cause I can rip it all off and start over."

He chuckled. "The tile was beautiful. Tell me how much you've spent and I'll reimburse you. Include the bedding, and curtains, and everything. And I'll get an account at Home Depot so you can get what you need in the future. Where's your heavy table, and I'll help you carry it in while I'm here."

With her almost skipping back out the Dutch door again, he followed her to the granary and smiled one more time at her enthusiasm as she showed him the other furniture as well. Between the two of them, they moved her table and then the dresser and night stand into the front bedroom with the bed, where he sat on the bare mattress and asked, "How did you bring all this stuff on your motorcycle? Is there someone else who's been helping you?"

She explained about renting the Home Depot truck and he decided maybe he'd better think about getting a truck for his new caretaker. What she'd accomplished so far with what she had available was amazing.

It was almost noon, and they made peanut butter and jelly sandwiches in the kitchen, then took them and two paper cups and a jug of milk to the step of the porch. It was the only place to sit in the whole farmstead, other than a bed. They ate in silence for a couple of minutes, and then she said, "You know, I probably wouldn't have accepted coming to help here if I'd known you were the owner right off. You were right to not tell me up front. I needed to get to know you a little to trust you. Silly, huh? Because I didn't know the other mystery guy at all. But it's probably true.

"What are your thoughts on the bathroom floor in there? The wood is beautiful and has held up incredibly well considering, but it really isn't terribly practical. Do you want to leave it as it is? Or cover it up with something more water resistant?"

He turned to look at her as he finished chewing his bite. "I don't know for sure. These floors are so cool, but I wonder if leaving it in the bathroom will eventually lead to ruining it."

"We could try to finish it with something that's as waterproof as possible. A shower curtain seems more rustic, but a glass shower enclosure would help protect the floor better. Maybe you could put glass in, but use bronze hardware instead of chrome or brass or something. That would be less dissonant with the logs."

He was getting a kick out of watching her while he ate. "Why don't you put some ideas together that you think would be appropriate with the style of the house, and I'll try to get back out here in the next day or two and let you know. I'm sorry I had to go out of town the last few days. Next time call my cell if you have questions."

"You only gave me your home phone, remember?"

"Didn't you get my messages at the hotel? I left my cell phone for you when I left. Didn't they give it to you?"

She looked at him blankly. "They've never given me any message. Of course, lately I've been staying here late and leaving early. Let me go and find something to write with. Hang on." She got up to go back inside and he took another bite as he gazed around. He'd loved this place the first time he'd seen it, but today it felt so much more homelike with her working here and the house full of fresh air and sunshine.

Returning with the hotel notepad and a package of cookies, she took his cell number and he didn't think twice about giving it to her. The way she'd been today had been so far removed from the way other women treated him that it never even occurred to him not to give it to her.

With lunch over, she gathered up their paper cups and napkins and he went to his Land Rover and brought in the microwave and the new telephone. When he tried to plug it in, he found that the phone jacks in the house were the old kind and the plug wouldn't fit. He left the phone sitting next to the jack, and went back out and began to unload the lawn mower. Just when he was going to try to lift the heavy, unwieldy box out by himself, she showed up and without a word took the other side of it and helped him set it on the ground.

"Nice mower. I see you got the jungle taming model, which is good. Do you need a Phillips head or flathead screw driver?" She reached for the instruction bag that was taped to the top.

He looked up at her and laughed. He couldn't remember when someone had treated him this normally, male or female. She read for a minute and said, "Phillips. I'll find one for you. Just a sec." He watched her back as she disappeared inside the house again and smiled to himself. She was a kick.

Twenty minutes later, he had it put together and properly filled with gas and oil and was ready to attempt to mow his own lawn for the first time in his life. It was actually kind of fun. Ever since he'd left home for college, he'd lived where the grounds maintenance was done by someone else.

In another twenty minutes, some of the fun had worn off and he'd begun to sweat like he was in practice. He hadn't brought any clean clothes and decided to take off his shirts. He needed to put spare clothes and towels on his list to bring on another trip. If he attempted to mow the lawn again, he'd need to try out her new shower.

The next time he shut off the mower to dump the grass catcher, Kelly appeared from the house with a frosty can of pink lemonade. "That lovely avocado fridge isn't much to look at, but it works wonderfully. Are you feeling like Paul Bunyan or something yet? The lawn looks marvelous."

He accepted the drink gratefully. "Thanks. I haven't mowed a lawn in years. And I don't think I've ever mowed anything like this. I keep worrying that there are little deer or something hidden under all of this." He drank half of it down in a few gulps and said, "When I got here there was a song on your radio about tambourines and elephants in the grass. When it's this long there's actually that possibility."

She headed back into the house and turned to say over her shoulder. "If you find any elephants, I want to see them. I've never met an elephant." He laughed and choked on his lemonade. He'd met a few elephants in his day, but never anything like her. He went back to his mowing, still chuckling.

Back in his condo that night he was still chuckling at her as he got ready for bed. She was the most fun he'd had in years. Even just mowing the jungle lawn had been fun with her there.

Jason met him for lunch the next day and asked Robby as soon as he saw him what had happened. "What do you mean what's happened? What's happened what?"

Jason was peering at him like he was a bug under a microscope. "What's going on Rocker? Why do you look so... so pleased with yourself or something? Why are you so dang happy?"

Robby laughed. "So dang happy? Pleased with myself? What are you talking about Raime? There's nothing different about me. Have you ordered?"

"I ordered. The usual. There's definitely something different. How was your dad?"

Robby sighed. "He's not doing so well. It's awful to realize that your idol is human. Do you know that? How are Monique and Shania?"

"They're great. Look how cute Shania was this morning." Jason pulled out his phone and showed Robby a picture of her running through a fountain in the city park with her hair in corn rows with tiny ribbons attached to them.

"She is absolutely adorable. Must get that from Monique. What did coach have to say? Has Purcell found a promising tight end who he thinks we'll have a chance at yet? I'd love to lose Bocklin. I mean, I don't want to mess with a guy's life, but he's such a pain. There has to be someone out there."

"He'll find someone. So really. What's going on? Why the grin."

Robby smiled ear to ear and said, "What grin? What are you talking about, man? It's just me. 'Bout the only thing different in my life is I mowed my own lawn for the first time yesterday. It's good to have your own lawn."

"You're a terrible liar, Robideaux. You finally met a girl, didn't you?"

"Maybe. You got a problem with that?"

Jason laughed. "Bocklin is going to be crushed to find out that you really aren't gay. We've all told him about a thousand times, but he's convinced that since you don't use and abuse women the way he does, that you don't like them. So who is she?"

"I haven't really met a girl, but I did hire one to be a caretaker for out at that house and she's turned out to be pretty entertaining. I went out there yesterday, and she made me laugh. Really, it was mowing the lawn. It was therapeutic."

"Yeah, sure. I'll have to try that therapeutic yard work sometime. So what is she like?"

Robby waved a noncommittal hand. "She's just a girl, Jase. In fact, honestly, when I first saw her I thought she was a kid." He didn't have to tell him it was because she was covered head to toe in motorcycle gear.

Jason cracked up. "On second thought, Bocklin might have a heyday with a girl who can be mistaken for a kid."

Peter Holmes closed the thick file in his hand and absently tapped it with his finger. Maybe she really was dead. That night it had seemed too much of a coincidence that she disappeared the same day he had intended to get rid of her, but it had been more than four weeks, and his man had been able to come up with nothing. There hadn't been even a single call made from her cell phone number.

As far as they could tell, she hadn't called, written or even e-mailed her mother, or her uncle and his family. Her Facebook account had gone dead; there had been no charges on her debit cards or in her bank accounts. Her mother had even cleaned out her apartment finally and closed all of her utility accounts.

He tossed back the last of his drink and got up to go put the file into his home safe. Knowing she was dead was a huge relief, but in a way it was a shame. Even knowing that if she wasn't dead, he'd kill her himself, didn't make him forget that incredible hair. She'd had the most amazing hair. And eyes.

Back at the hotel for the last night, Kelly slipped out of

her clothes and got ready to shower. She thought back to that day at the house with Robby. He was very different than she'd thought he'd be when she first met him. He was so good looking that she expected him to be a jerk, but today he'd been adorable. She felt terrible for falling off the ladder and knocking him down like she had.

She studied a bruise on her upper arm that she knew she'd gotten in the fall and thought about the incredible vision she'd discovered when she'd come out to bring him a drink and found him mowing the lawn shirtless. *My, oh my, oh my, but he'd been built nicely! He did not have the physique of a business man.* That view of him had been the stuff of fantasies for sure.

She got in and out of the shower and realized she was completely out of clean clothes again and decided that, not only would she need to do some wash again tomorrow, but she had to go shopping and buy some things. In a little over two weeks she'd about worn the few clothes she'd brought to rags, not to mention what a pain it was to go to the laundromat with such a small amount.

Curling up on the hotel bed in her last clean undies, she started making a shopping list again and wished she'd been able to bring her car with her for this flight across the country. It would have been so much easier to carry things. Her car and her mom. That stupid news photo was practically haunting her and she wished there was a way to let her mom know she was safe and happy, at least for a while.

Then she had an idea. She'd always bought her mom flowers on tough days. Not just any flowers, but white daisies to make her mom remember to look forward with a perfect brightness of hope. It was their own secret, happy code.

She wondered if there was a way to have flowers delivered without anyone finding out where they were ordered from. If she had them sent to Uncle Roy with cash maybe they'd get there unnoticed by anyone scary. At least that way her mom would know she was okay. Tomorrow she'd check into it. She fell asleep, missing her mother and her Uncle Roy's family and wondering if any more patients had died because she hadn't been able to stop them yet. It was an incredibly troubling thought.

The next day after sending the flowers, she made three different trips from Tolke to the house to drop off clean clothes, new clothes, and a few groceries. She finally checked out of the hotel for good. On the last trip from town, she stopped at Home Depot again and bought the right kind of phone plug and the tool to install it, and a new lockset for the summer kitchen.

If she was going to be living in it, she wanted to be able to lock it up tight at night. It wasn't that she didn't trust Robby. Her trust for him was somewhat uncanny under the circumstances. He didn't frighten her one iota. It was the other human beings of this world and even just the fact that she was so far out in the country out there. She'd never lived out of a city and been that completely by herself at night, and she hoped with good locks that she wouldn't be afraid.

That first night by herself, she tossed and turned for awhile, and finally turned some music on low. After another long, restless wait, she eventually fell asleep. At least in the morning it was great to wake up there to the birds and the soft breezes, even if she was more tired than usual. She ate a bagel and some fruit, hung a shower curtain and took the maiden voyage in the new shower, then put on new, clean clothes to start her first full day here at the house.

Robby called late that morning on the new phone and asked what she needed. He said he'd be out that afternoon and she was ridiculously excited to see him again today. She had to keep telling herself it was just that she was lonely and going stir crazy from being so far removed from people, and not the incredibly masculine vision that kept playing in her mind of Robby shirtless. Whatever it was, it was wonderful to actually talk to a real, intelligent human being when he finally showed up that afternoon.

He brought the things on her list and a toaster, some lawn chairs, an outdoor barbecue grill, more groceries, some real dishes and a dish drainer, as well as linens for the other bed, some of his own clothes, and a set of towels and rugs for the bathroom.

She helped him unload it all, and then standing on the other side of the bed helping him make it up was the most natural thing in the world.

Later, he brought out a veritable stack of home improvement brochures and sat beside her on the porch step and asked her what her thoughts had been on the bathroom floor, and then they decided together on a glass shower door with bronze hardware.

Next, he brought out booklets of kitchen cabinetry options, and they studied them until they had an idea of what would bridge the gap from hand hewn logs to modern kitchen. They decided on knotty hickory cabinets that would be stained a weathered barn wood and then picked more bronze appliances and a bronze apron farm sink and bronze range hood. They decided to leave the bathroom floor wood and coat it with a couple layers of polyurethane, but in the kitchen Robby decided to use the same color tile as the shower wall, only larger. He picked out the faucet he wanted, but left the kitchen design entirely up to Kelly. At length he went back out and tore into the lawn again.

She came out on the porch and began putting the grill together while he worked at taming the yard monsters. By the time he was done for the day, she had the grill ready to go and was just working at attaching the new propane tank. She was pleasantly surprised when he came out with a rack of ribs and a mason jar of homemade barbecue sauce and fired it up to use it. She had assumed he would leave like he had all the other times. He put the ribs on to grill and went and showered and changed clothes, while Kelly tackled more of the strangling vines in the front yard.

His ribs were to die for. After they'd eaten them while sitting on chairs on the porch and cleaned up the mess, she went back out and sat on the step again, watching the sun go down in the west and listening to the crickets start up around her.

As the stars started to come out, he reappeared and sat beside her in the early evening quiet. Together, they enjoyed the peace without talking much. When she finally got up to go to her summer kitchen, all she said was, "Good night, Robby." But it was all that needed to be said. It had been an incredibly nice afternoon and evening.

It was amazing the difference that having him there in the house for the night made in how comfortable she was when she lay down. The tossing and turning of the night before was completely gone. She prayed and read her Book of Mormon, then turned out the light to listen to the crickets and the stream and drift off peacefully. This was a life she could get used to really fast.

The next morning, he was coming out of the bathroom with damp hair as she came into the house to shower. He looked so good she was actually a bit embarrassed at how he made her pulse rate jump. She had to remind herself that he was only her boss here, and that as soon as she had figured out how to stop Peter and the others and it was safe, she'd be going back home to Chicago. Telling herself that he wasn't a member anyway helped as well.

That morning they agreed that the kitchen design needed to be the next priority because the cabinets were going to take several weeks to arrive, so she spent the morning working on her little farm table with the brochures and a straight edge. When she came back in for lunch, she showed him what she'd come up with and the only suggestion that he had for her was to change the color of the granite countertops to one shade darker. He took the design and put it in his Land Rover with a promise to get the cabinets ordered on his way back home that afternoon.

She was on the porch stacking the pieces of backer board that were the remnants from the shower, when he came out and asked, "Should I get a construction dumpster ordered for out here, or can we try to put most of this kind of stuff into a trash dumpster for the garbage man?"

She thought about that for a minute. "The only really big things we'll need to get rid of will be the kitchen cabinets, and, honestly, I don't know which would be more environmentally friendly, to have a major bonfire project or haul them off to the landfill. At any rate it will be weeks before we're ready to take them out. Let's at least try to just use a smaller dumpster. But do we have one? And when is garbage day? How does that work this far out in the tulles?"

Her definition of where they were made him grin. "I take it you're not from somewhere this rural, huh?"

Shaking her head she admitted to him, "I'm from Wheaton, Illinois. All but downtown Chicago. There are no jungle lawns or gravel roads to be found there. I've never lived out like this. It's a bit quiet, and night before last, my first night here alone was a little sketchy, but all in all it beats the heck out of traffic and smog. How about you? Where are you from?"

"I'm from somewhere in the middle, both logistically and populationally. Is that a word? I grew up in a small suburb of Kansas City. The city center was a forty minute drive and the fields and farms were fifteen or twenty. It was perfect."

"So what brought you to North Carolina?"

He hesitated for a second and then said, "My work brought me here. At first I wasn't sure about it, but now I love it here. I'll probably stay here even when I retire."

She put the last of the larger pieces of backer on the stack and began to put the smaller scraps into a grocery bag. "I would think you're a long way from retirement at your age."

"Oh, I don't know. Sometimes people retire sooner than you'd think. In some industries the turn over rate is pretty high."

Putting the tied grocery bag on top of the stack, she turned toward the house. "Must be tough in acquisitions."

When she'd asked what brought him here, just for a second he'd considered telling her what he did professionally and then decided against it. Maybe she wouldn't really change if he told her, but he was enjoying being treated like a regular Joe too much to risk it. Plus she was doing a marvelous job here at his house and he didn't want to jeopardize that, either.

She had disappeared to somewhere up the stairs. He could hear her singing to the radio, and he could smell some kind of cleaner. He'd hardly even been up there and followed her up to the room she was cleaning and asked, "So, my little R.N. slash handy woman, can you build another bath up here or should I find a contractor to do it?"

She looked up and thought about that for a second and

then said, "I should probably say hire a contractor, but if you're willing to let me try, I'll give it a go. I may still have to hire someone, but can I check into it?"

"Absolutely. Your account is set up at the Home Depot by the way."

"Cool." She glanced up from where she was scrubbing a wall. "Do they carry vacuums?

He smiled at that. "I'll bring you a vacuum. I'll bring you another ladder too. Do you want me to wash this top part that you can't reach?"

"Yes, I would love it." She handed him her spray bottle and a sponge. "How come you don't work normal business hours?"

He shrugged as he began to scrub. "That's just the way my company works. Right now is their slow season. In another two months we'll be working like twelve, fourteen hour days, so it evens out."

He was working almost straight over the top of where she was scrubbing and she laughed when his stomach growled. Sheepishly, he asked, "Did you have anything in mind for dinner?"

"Does spaghetti sound okay?"

"It sounds great! Come on. I'll help you cook."

"You're apparently hungry." She began to pack up her cleaning supplies.

"Actually, I'm pretty much always hungry. Do you suppose I can eat spaghetti without wearing it? We have to get a table and chairs and somewhere to sit. The porch step and lawn chairs are fine, but we're just lucky it hasn't rained much the last while. We'd be eating standing up or sitting on a bed."

Waving her sponge at him, she laughed and said, "We're tough, Robby. We can handle whatever. And if it rains before you find a table, we'll take the lawn chairs to the little table in the summer kitchen. It could be a picnic of sorts."

She gave the wall one last wipe. "One of my professors at college was telling us that like half of the world's population still have dirt floors and no refrigerator. We Americans are spoiled rotten when you think in those kinds of terms. The weird part of that is sometimes the people with the most simple lives seem the happiest. Maybe we're missing the whole secret with our standard of living. Who knows?"

He looked down at her. "You're living relatively simply here. How's that going? Does it make for being happy?"

She was thoughtful for a minute. "I'm okay here. It's much quieter than I'm used to. And when you're not around, I usually have to have the radio going or it can get positively lonely. I miss my family here. Sometimes though, it's just peaceful instead of lonely. It certainly makes for being still and listening to know if God is there. Does that sound crazy?"

"No, it doesn't sound crazy. Maybe that's what makes the simple living civilizations happy is that they remember to be still and know God better than we do. It certainly can't hurt." He changed the subject. "You're family is welcome to come visit you here. Or you can go visit them if you need to. There's no reason to be lonely for them."

She glanced up at him and he had no idea what he saw in her eyes, but it wasn't good. Somehow talking about her family and going home to visit had brought back the fear or hesitation or whatever he had seen in her eyes those first couple of times in the Pancake House. It was thought provoking and he gazed down at her again wondering what those deep green eyes were keeping from him. And what the straight, pink scar on her forearm was from that she was absent-mindedly rubbing just now.

Chapter 6

Later that night, back home in Charlotte, he was still troubled by what he'd seen in her eyes that afternoon as they washed walls.   Something wasn't right there.   As far as a caretaker, she was perfect. He couldn't have asked for anyone to take better care of his house or work harder, but the more he thought about it, the more he decided she was hiding something. Or hiding from something.

He went to his computer and pulled up Dex Online and tried to find her under Kelly Shane in Wheaton, Illinois and wasn't surprised when he came up with nothing. He did another couple of searches and still struck out. He had been correct then. Something fishy was going on with her.

The strangest thing about that though, was after being around her, he didn't think she was necessarily being dishonest. In fact, he could just about swear she was as honorable as they come. She had been careful to leave receipts for him down to the penny, and she had spent her own money for him rather than seeming to be after his. That alone in his life was nearly earth shaking.

Still, he was trusting her with his house and a charge account. He probably ought to get to the bottom of this. He decided to go back out there the next morning and see about getting her social security number and W-4 signed.

They had only just talked about painting and what to do with the upstairs bedrooms the day before, so he was more than a little surprised to find her up there, standing on one of the lawn chairs barefoot, painting when he got there at a little before ten. He stood for just a minute admiring the view of her in her long shorts and T-shirt before saying anything to her. When he finally said her name, she gasped again, and her chair tipped as she whirled around to look at him.

He wasn't able to catch the plastic cottage cheese container she had been just about to dip her paint brush in, but he was able to catch her as she fell headlong. They both landed in a tangle on the floor again.

He took her gently by the shoulders and went to push her off, but she winced and he wondered if this time she'd gotten hurt in the fall. He pulled her hair back away from her face before trying to move her again. "Are you okay, Kelly? Did I hurt you?"

She groaned as she sat up. "No, I'm fine. I think I'm fine. I'm so sorry, again. I thought I was alone. You scared the lights out of me. Did I plaster you with paint?" She pulled her hair out of her face and wrapped it around her finger and tucked it into the back of her shirt. "Oh, good. It landed on the drop cloth. Are you all right? I landed on you hard that time. I'm sorry."

He grinned as he pushed her off with a wince of his own. "I'm just glad you're not a big girl who loves to dive. We are definitely buying you a new ladder today. One of those newfangled ones that are hyper stable."

She started to laugh as she carefully stood up, and he wondered what was going on for a second, until she leaned over and picked up a paint rag and started to wipe at his hair. He really began to worry when she laughed again and asked, "Did you ever want a milkshake? You know those bleach jobs the boys were getting a few years ago with light color on top of their darker hair underneath?"

Watching her with a fair amount of skepticism, he replied, "No. I never did. I'm really good with plain old dark brown, thanks. What are you trying to tell me?"

She tipped her head sideways and considered him for a minute, then gave him a heart-stopping smile. "You'd look good in a milkshake. If you ever did decide you wanted one, I mean. And if you don't want one right now, you'd probably better go wash your hair before that dries. It is kind of cute though."

"Cute? I'm twenty-eight years old, Kelly. I don't think cute is really the right word to describe a twenty-eight-year old man."

She scrunched her lips to the side while she considered and then nodded her head and said, "Yeah. It's the right word. With the milkshake you look about nineteen. Cute definitely works for nineteen-year-olds. Leave it in. No one will know you're an old guy!" She laughed as she rolled up the plastic sheet she'd been using as a drop cloth. "I'm just glad it was your hair I painted and not your beautiful old wood floor. It wouldn't be nearly so cute. You didn't by any chance remember a garbage can, did you?"

"Yes. And twenty-eight is not old, for your information."

"Whatever you say, Grandpa." She laughed again as she went past him to take the paint filled drop cloth down to the trash.

"Geez, Kelly, that was brutal. Grandpa? How old are you if twenty-eight is grandfatherly?"

"Twenty-three. Barely." She emphasized this last before she laughed again and skipped down the stairs.

When she met him coming back up with another cottage cheese container, he tried to dissuade her. "Don't go up and try that again today, Kelly. Wait until I bring you a decent ladder. I have a lot more renovation I need you around for. Plus, who would hassle me about being an old guy if you got killed painting?"

She smiled up at him. "Please tell me that's not your best argument for why not to die this morning." She continued up the stairs and he turned and was going to follow her until she continued, "Let me at least close up my paint and clean my brushes."

In the kitchen, while she cleaned brushes, he talked to her about what he'd found out about how much caretakers make. It wasn't very much, and she laughed again and said, "Whew! I'm rolling in the dough now, aren't I?"

Before he had a chance to continue and ask the real questions he'd come to ask her, she got more serious and said, "Robby, I need to ask you a favor. You can tell me no and to hit the road if you want me to, but I don't have any ID or social security card with me. It's only temporary. Sometime, I'll go get them. But in the meantime, is there any way you could either pay me cash or just hold my pay until I can get them to you?"

He was surprised, and then in a way he wasn't. He studied her intently for a minute, wondering what was going on and what he should do, and she met his gaze squarely while he did. Finally, he just asked, "Why?"

"Why don't I have them, or why should you still let me stay?"

"Both."

"I can't tell you why I don't have them, and you should let me stay because I'm honest even though I can't tell you, and I'm doing a good job for you, and you have nothing to lose if you don't pay me. It's not that I've scammed someone or am running from the law or anything. And I'm legal, I promise." She still met his gaze squarely, and he wondered what he should say to her about this.

He honestly didn't know what to do. He didn't want to do something foolish or that could get him in trouble. The press could have a heyday with stuff like this, but then he did trust her. He had from almost the very first and he'd truly felt like he was being prompted to ask her to come here to work for him.

Unsure of what to do about it, he said, "Let me think about it. I'm going to have a shower." He turned and went into his room and got his stuff and went into the bathroom. Now what the heck was he supposed to do? Just as he'd suspected, there was something wrong, but he certainly wasn't any closer to finding out what.

He didn't find his answer in the shower and on getting out he went in search of her. She was in the front yard with the pruners working on the vines that tangled all through the rocks and the trees on the hillside. When he walked up to her, she gazed at him with quiet, deep green eyes and just waited for whatever he was going to say to her. He decided to be honest with her. "I don't know what to do about you, Kelly. Let me think about it some more. In the interim just keep on here and whatever I decide, I'll make sure you get paid for all you've done and spent. I'll let you know as soon as I figure it out."

With that he turned and went back to the Land Rover, more than a little troubled. Not only would he miss her if she went, but he was somewhat crushed to know she wasn't being completely forthright with him. If she wasn't running from the law, why couldn't she tell him?

When he got back to his condo he got on-line and started digging for a reputable private investigation firm that wasn't in the North Carolina area. He was going to be in the Bay Area in a couple of days, maybe he'd hire somebody there to dig into what was going on with her.

It felt almost a bit sneaky to go behind her back, but what if she was the world's best actress and was after him for whatever she could get out of him. It seemed like a crazy way to go about it if that was the case, but he'd learned a long time ago to be cynical about things like this. He made his appointment, even though he wasn't happy about it, and he was still troubled about it late that night when he began to wonder if she wasn't in some kind of trouble that didn't include the law. That was the only thing that made sense now that he'd gotten to know her.

She had run. That was the only plausible reason, wasn't it? She was a nice girl. A beautiful, smart, competent, educated, nice girl. Something must have happened that made her leave her life behind without even ID or a social security card.

Or maybe she had them, but couldn't give them to him because they could be traced. Thinking back to that first day and the motorcycle helmet and leathers and her refusal to take his help, it all made sense in a strange way. Why else would she have left her family when she came right out and admitted she missed them? Why would a registered nurse be willing to "ride south and take whatever job she could get" when there was a need for licensed nurses in virtually every part of the country?

Unless she'd lied about being a nurse as well. Maybe she was one of those scammers who couldn't tell the truth if it was written for them to read. He didn't know what to think and dropped off to sleep troubled.

He didn't call her or go out there, and when he got to San Francisco two days later, he did indeed meet with and hire a private investigator to discreetly check into her without leaking the fact that Robby was inquiring after her. He would start in Wheaton, Illinois. Her bike did have Illinois plates. He could check on them. He had the guy sign a contract to keep his name and business confidential or not be paid a penny and face a law suit. It was hard nosed, but he'd had to become that way the last few years.

The private investigator actually got back with him on a preliminary basis that very afternoon simply to say that by working through all of the electronic options he had, there was no one from the greater Chicago area named Kelly Shane who was twenty-three years old that he'd been able to find out about. There were four Kelly Shane's, but three of them were older women and the fourth was an African American man in his thirties. Of course, he wasn't familiar with Chicago and what was happening there, so he was leaving to fly there the next morning to see what he could dig up.

By the time Robby flew home, he still hadn't gotten any more information and he was more discouraged than he'd been a couple of weeks ago before he'd met her. Things became more clear the next morning though when he signed for an express letter from the PI that contained enough information to make Robby sick at heart about whatever had made Kelly Shaye Campbell ditch her bloody car and all of her possessions and run away.

Thinking back, he was incredibly grateful that he'd listened when he'd felt like he should hire her. He still didn't know what she'd been so afraid of that she'd stage her own death, but knowing her, he knew whatever it had been; it wasn't that she was doing something questionable.

Now he knew there was a viable reason for her lack of ID, but he still didn't know what had caused her to run, and he certainly didn't know how to admit to her that he'd hired a private investigator to check into her background. Somehow that seemed so underhanded to him. At least now he knew enough to help keep her safe. It was funny because in a way they were both trying to lie low and had been trying to hide that from each other.

Robby called the PI back and asked him to stay in Chicago and see if he could find out why she had run in the first place. Then Robby loaded up an overnight bag, climbed into the Rover and hit the road for Kelly's house. Knowing what he knew now, he had no problem having her work for him indefinitely, and he'd find a way to pay her so neither one of them got in trouble.

He called the house from Tolke just in case she was somewhere in the house doing something that she could fall from when he walked in. He didn't want to scare her off of something again, no matter how nice it was to get tangled up with her those times. She picked up on the second ring and he could tell she was a little tentative about what he was going to tell her.

He tried to sound upbeat as he said, "Hey, Kelly. I'm in Tolke and I'm headed your way. I just don't want to scare you to death when I walk in this time. How are things going?"

"Fine. I'm just working on the wood in the upstairs bedrooms."

"You're not standing on anything to do it are you?"

She laughed. "No, Robby. You asked me not to, remember?"

"Good. See you in a sec."

Ten minutes later he walked into the bedroom she was working on and things went much more smoothly than when he hadn't called. He'd have to remember to call her every time. In fact, under the circumstances she needed a cell phone as well. He'd bring her one out next trip.

He stepped around her to examine the tongue and groove wainscoting she was nailing up on the lower half of the wall. It had been somehow stained to appear weathered and matched the logs on the exterior walls so well it was uncanny. "How in the world did you get new wood to look like this? Or is this reclaimed barn wood? It's perfect!"

"It does look great, doesn't it? I bought a book and it had this incredible recipe for wood weatherer. It's a scream. It actually calls for soaking a pound of galvanized nails in the solution. At first I wondered if it would work, but so far it looks good."

He could tell she was watching him and wondering what he had decided to do about her. He felt guilty for leaving her hanging this long, but he'd done the best he could. He came right out and reassured her first thing. "By the way, I decided to keep you no matter what I'll have to do about paying you. I decided I can't spare such a crack renovation expert, so we'll have to talk about how you want to be paid until we can make arrangements for your ID."

She came up to him and gazed at him and then finally said, "Thank you Robby. I'll make sure you don't regret that decision. I promise."

He put a casual hand on her shoulder. "You're welcome, Kelly, but I'm the one who should be thanking you. You've done more than I can believe in such a short time, and you've been able to stay with the character of the house better than I ever dreamed. You've done a beautiful job, and I'm grateful. Thank you."

She stood looking at him for a minute and then said simply, "You're welcome. Thank you for letting me do it." She turned and said over her shoulder. "Come see what I've done in the basement."

"Wait a minute. I have a basement? I didn't know I had a basement."

She laughed at him. "Come on, Rob." To herself, she mumbled and laughed again. "He doesn't know he has a basement. You're a corker, Robby Robideaux." As she led him to the stairs that were hidden behind the other stairs, she asked, "Isn't there an NBA player with a name just like yours? Rocky Robideaux or something like that?"

He glanced at her to see if she was teasing him, but she was focused on taking him down the stairs. "Yeah, I think there is."

"Is he related?"

How to answer this without her hating him if she ever found out. "Could be, yeah. How did you find this?"

"I just noticed there were a couple of basement windows in the back and searched until I figured out how you get to them. It's actually kind of cool down here. In fact, cool and cool. It's neat, but it's also about twenty degrees cooler than the upstairs. This would be the perfect place to store food to keep it fresh. Not to mention where to come to cool off in the summer."

"Wow!" He stood staring around. "A stone foundation.

This is wild. How in the world has this house not crumbled when it's only on a stone foundation?"

"I wondered that too, but look." She walked over to one of the basement walls. "It's not a stone wall, it's actually bedrock. The corners are sitting on bedrock and these stone walls are just filling in up to the logs. Whoever built this thing was a master. This house will still be around and strong in another hundred and something years if we keep taking care of it. What are you going to do down here?"

"Well, since I wasn't aware it was here until three minutes ago, I have no idea. The food storage idea was kind of intriguing. Maybe we could section off a storage room. But then we'll have to plant a garden to grow things to store in it as well." She didn't know it, but food storage and a garden had actually been one of the things he'd planned for here. He didn't have a garden at his condo because he couldn't, but he had his year's supply there, like the prophet had encouraged.

She looked at him. "I wouldn't have pegged you as a gardener. Is there still time to plant a garden? It's already nearly the end of May."

"I've never gardened here. I have no yard in town. It's a condo, but the growing season here is long. Probably until November. We should be fine. Do you garden?"

She nodded. "Some. My mother has killer tomatoes on the deck." She peered around the basement again. "A storage room would be cool, but don't make it an ugly cement storage room like most people have. This house has so much character. We should do something really cool. My uncle has done some neat wine cellars in some of those houses back home. I know it won't be a luxury home wine cellar, but we could do something awesome with these stone walls. You could light it like it was a mine or cave or something and maybe have a door with some glass that looked old like those jars we found, and you could back light it. It could be really cool."

He watched her talk, and her green eyes fairly glowed with her ideas. He'd have gone along with her even if they hadn't been great plans, just to watch her face and enjoy her spirit. She was the most refreshing girl he had met in forever.

"We could build a real, old wine cellar; we just won't put wine in it. I don't drink but cool and dark and dry is perfect for storing about anything. Come up with some ideas, and we'll work on it. In the meantime, I'll either find a local to help us get a garden started or find a tiller that is easier to use than the one my dad used to use."

He looked around the rest of the open space down there, broken only by the occasional humongous log post. "Maybe we could build a theater room down here with some of the rest of this. It would lend itself beautifully. We could stay with the mine idea and have neat old lantern light fixtures and leave these posts just like they are. If we put in a tasteful small kitchen area and some nice theater seating it would offset the primitive stuff and be great. What do you think?"

"I think it sounds perfect. And like a lot of work. There's enough here to keep us busy for several months already." Her face clouded up and he wondered if she was thinking about home and her family.

She didn't appear very happy and finally he asked quietly, "Will you still be around here in several months?"

Her eyes met his and then moved away. "I'm not sure. If I have to go, I'll try to let you know so you can replace me in plenty of time."

Putting a hand on her shoulder, he gave it a squeeze. "You'll be hard to replace, Kelly Shane. You've been amazing so far. You've done a great job."

She put a hand up to touch his and smiled. "Thanks."

By the time she went to her own house that night, Robby decided he had a ridiculously enjoyable school boy crush on his caretaker and wished he didn't have to go home the next day. He had meetings and another out-of-town trip to raise funds for his foundation that would keep him from helping her do exciting things like washing walls together.

The industrial strength lawn mower came in handy that day and the next. When he felt a touch too attracted to his little handy woman for his own good, he went out and mowed more lawn again. By the next afternoon, he'd finally mowed the whole thing one time. Of course, the part he'd mowed first was ready to be mowed again, but at least it wasn't threatening to engulf the entire place anymore.

That afternoon he also called a little restaurant that had the kind of tables he liked and ordered a dining table and chairs that would be shipped out in a few days. It was with a distinct sense of disappointment that he left. He really would have liked to stay there indefinitely and keep working on the house with her.

It was just as well. He had to teach a Sunday school class the next morning early, then fly out first thing Monday for a few days, and he was beginning to be rather too attached to his beautiful, auburn haired helper. He had to remind himself as he drove that he shouldn't get attached to someone who wasn't a member of the Church. But she was fun. She was really, really fun.

Peter was just getting ready to step into his Beamer to leave the hospital for the weekend when the man who had come to be his least favorite Chicago police officer nonchalantly stepped between his car and the next. Peter looked up at him, wondering what was up and hoping he wasn't here after more money.

The big officer leaned back against the next car and said casually, "You had me fooled, Holmes. I really thought you'd offed her. I guess you weren't lying. That time."

Instantly alert, Peter asked, "What are you talking about?"

"The girl. That redhead. Who disappeared so conveniently for you. There's been a private investigator nosing around about her. He's based out of the bay area. And her family didn't hire him. I'm still not sure who did, but that's your deal. Not mine."

Closing his eyes for just a moment, Peter had to fight the urge to swear bitterly, although this whole time he'd wondered. That had been too much of a coincidence.

Opening his eyes back up, Peter reached for the sheaf of papers Hartvigson had folded in his hands and asked tiredly, "How much this time?"

Chapter 7

When Robby finally loaded into his Land Rover and left after dinner on Saturday evening, the house felt positively lonely and Kelly had to turn her music on within minutes of his departure in order not to be almost gloomy there by herself. She got ready for bed and lay down and picked up her Book of Mormon, but kept catching herself daydreaming about Robby when she was supposed to be reading. Getting attached to him under the circumstances was foolish on several counts, and she gave herself a lecture and then made a mental note to find a local ward to go to, even if she wasn't able to have her records sent for. She hoped it would be safe enough to go to church here. She needed it so much in her life.

It had been almost four weeks since she had left Chicago on the run, and she'd never missed church for more than a week at a shot in her life. Even with reading her scriptures regularly, she was positively going through withdrawal. Plus she needed someone else in her life to talk to other than just Robby. He was great to talk to, but she was feeling far too attracted to him for comfort.

He was gorgeous and interesting, but he was also not a member and lived hundreds of miles from her home and family. She had no idea how long she'd be here or if someday she'd have to pick up and run, and she needed to keep her head better where he was concerned. While she was thinking about him and her life, she had a thought that hit her like a brick. What if he was married? She sat straight up in bed in shock just at the idea. She immediately got up and called him on his house phone.

When he picked up on the third ring, she didn't beat around the bush. "Robby, it's Kelly. I just had a thought and I need to ask you something. Is there a Mrs. Robideaux?"

He chuckled on the other end of the line. "No, why?"

She felt a bit embarrassed but she'd had to know. "I just needed to make sure. If there had been I'd have either had to quit or else you'd have had to bring her out with you when you come. I couldn't work for someone like this if you were. It had just never crossed my mind before tonight."

He laughed again. "That's good to know. If I get married anytime soon, I'll tell you. In the mean time you can go back to bed and rest assured that I'm single. Did you really think I'd be coming and working beside you like I have with a wife at home?"

"No, I didn't, but you never know. I've had some ugly wake up calls in the past. Some people have different values about things like that. Sorry I called so late. I just had to check."

"You can call whenever you need to. I'm glad to know you'd respect my wife if I had one. You're right. There are some with some extremely different perceptions of what's appropriate, but I'm single. There isn't a Mr. Shane somewhere is there?"

This time she laughed at him. "No, Robby. Good night."

"Night, Kelly."

She went back to bed and tried to read again, but still found her mind was pre-occupied. She put her book down, turned out the light and lay there, smelling the honeysuckle vine outside the window and listening to the stream. The nerves she had felt that first night here alone never even registered anymore.

She got up the next morning and made some calls and was, in fact, able to find a young single adult branch within about a half hour's drive from the house. She had to plan enough time ahead to be able to find it in a strange area and figure out how to get there on her motorcycle in a dress. She wore her leathers in and changed in the restroom and then settled in to almost bask in being back in church again.

When they asked her to introduce herself in Relief Society, she was somewhat worried at first, and she still introduced herself as Kelly Shane and as just visiting, but during the course of the meetings she came to decide that she couldn't live without church. She couldn't let fear rule her life and she prayed for comfort and the peace of mind that attending church would be safe. By the time one of the other young women invited her to come to a family home evening group activity the next day, she accepted the invitation without hesitation. She needed this in her life and was more grateful than ever before for the marvelous organization of the church.

Back home by herself, she fixed Sunday dinner and ate it alone. Then she read her scriptures for another little while and wrote in her journal. With that done, she lay down to nap and as she laid there, she tried to figure out what she was going to do when she got up. She didn't want to work on Sunday, but she had no friends or family, no TV or books or even church music. She'd been throwing herself into working on the house to fill her time and Robby had been here last Sunday afternoon, but the hours seemed to loom out there forever alone. She wished she knew someone who needed help or visiting because she was bored to tears here today.

After she woke up, she went for a walk up the stream and stopped near a deep, shady pool where she sat on a rock and listened to the music of the water playing over the stones. It was an idyllic place and she wished she had a hammock and a good novel to enjoy here.

After a while, she went back home and put on her leathers and helmet and went for a drive, exploring the area for over an hour.

On the outskirts of Tolke, she happened upon an extended care facility and without hesitation she went inside. She knew from experience that there were old folks in centers like this who desperately needed to be visited, and this evening she needed to visit just as much.

She checked in with the office and found out which couple of patrons were most in need of attention. She then had the good fortune of spending time with a handful of positively delightful, lonely old men and women who had compelling stories to tell, all in that comfortable southern drawl Kelly was learning to love. She climbed back on her bike an hour and a half later, knowing she need never feel as lonely and at a loss for something to do again, now that she had found this place. They needed her every bit as much as she needed them.

Back home, as dusk fell around Robby's house, she was

finally able to settle in and get ready for bed without feeling so at a loose end as she'd felt earlier that day. It would be good to work on the house again tomorrow to fill the time.

Monday morning she was up and working with a passion, and she was able to lose the unrest she'd struggled with so much the day before. She finished the wood wainscoting in the upstairs bedrooms and started on the tongue and groove ceiling. When she went out to the saw table she'd set up on the porch there was a big, old yellow tom cat that showed up and began to make a nuisance of himself.

At first he just sat and watched her work and at lunch she made the mistake of tossing him a sliver of ham from her sandwich. After that, every time she came out to make a cut, the darned cat would wind itself between her legs and practically trip her as she tried to walk. Twice she had to catch him when he came in the house behind her and throw him back out.

In a way he was company, and in a way he was a total pain and nearly tripped her with his attempts to snuggle.

That evening she went to meet with the kids from her branch for the family home evening activity she'd been invited to. They had a barbecue and a volleyball game at a park, and it was ridiculously nice to meet people and make new friends. She had had no idea how much she missed this kind of thing. She got back on her bike as it got dark, disappointed that it was over.

Tuesday morning the cat was still there and Wednesday when the new table and chairs arrived, he very nearly got run over by the huge panel van that came to deliver it. Kelly was so flustered at seeing the cat miss being squished on the gravel drive by less than a foot, that it took her a little while to be thrilled to actually have a place to sit and eat a meal.

Thursday, she strapped the canvas bag she'd bought for her laundry to the back of her bike and headed into town to the laundromat. She put her things in the washers and then headed across the way to the market and bought groceries while she waited. Once her laundry was in the dryers, she ran to buy the putty she needed to fill the nail holes in her woodwork.

When she returned to the laundromat, there was another guy there doing his wash. It only took about a minute for Kelly to wish that her things were done and she could leave rather than be the object of attention of this local, hot shot, macho type. He'd put his things in and was strutting around flexing his muscles and tossing a football into the air and catching it or pretending to make slow, exaggerated passes across the facility.

When he made a comment about how a hot little number like her would probably really know how to please a man and gave her a big, dumb grin, she didn't think he even had a clue how demeaning he was being. It was a sad example of how much of the world viewed women as simply objects. It brought back some ugly reminders of how she'd been treated sometimes in college by the football team there when she'd worked at their dining hall.

Several times he attempted to strike up a conversation with her, and although every time she tried to discourage him, he literally grabbed her arm as she went to leave to demand her phone number. Instantly furious to be man handled, she jerked her arm away and had to fight not to slap him as she turned to her bike. As she drove into Robby's yard, she was still completely disgusted with this stud muffin with a big ego and a small brain.

She unloaded her things and put them away, then started to make chicken primavera for lunch, still irritated at having had to put up with the guy's antics as long as she did. It had never even occurred to the brainless brute that she wouldn't be impressed by his ability to pretend to throw the ball. Let alone the fact that it had apparently never crossed his mind that women weren't placed on earth solely to please men.

She tried not to let it, but in a way it hurt that to some men women had no value beyond physical pleasure. She'd come to know her father had never seen the value in her mother beyond how beautiful she was, and it had become a tender spot over the years.

Realizing she was letting a guy she didn't even know make her uncharacteristically irritable, she made a conscious decision to try to forget him and had a pile of chicken, pasta, and vegetables bubbling in a pan when Robby showed up unexpectedly a few minutes later. He walked into the house and seemed to be following his nose into the kitchen. "Holy Toledo, your lunch smells awesome, Kelly! What are you making?"

She was so glad to see him it was almost a little bit embarrassing. "Chicken primavera. Have you eaten? I made a ton. I was just going to have leftovers for dinner sometime. You're welcome to have some."

"I will most definitely take you up on that! It looks amazing. Are you sure you don't mind? I'll wipe out your leftovers."

She laughed. "I'm so grateful just to have an intelligent human being to talk to that I would gladly hand over any leftovers. Did you see that the table arrived? They brought it yesterday."

He brought plates and glasses from the kitchen, and she brought the pan and a kitchen towel to set it on and went back in for milk and silverware and napkins. As they sat down across from each other, they both automatically bowed their heads and Robby asked a blessing. When he was done praying and they'd said amen, he asked, "Lonely week? Or just an unintelligent one?"

Feeling somewhat self conscious, she admitted, "Both. Sunday I went to a church in town, but I was still so lonely I went into the care center in Tolke and visited old folks. Monday I did go do something with some of the kids from here, but it's still been quiet.

"Then this morning I went to the laundromat and encountered the unintelligent portion of the deal. Some big, piece of meat, macho jock was strutting around the place trying to impress me with his ability to throw a football and demanded my phone number. Needless to say, I'm incredibly glad to be reminded that some men have brains and some respect. You're a breath of fresh air after the Tolke Neanderthal."

He chewed a bite of his lunch and gazed at her a little strangely, and she felt silly for being so offended by the laundromat guy as Robby asked, "I take it that you don't like football."

Trying to quell her earlier feelings of hurt, she replied, "Mmm. No, I don't exactly dislike it. In fact, I used to love it when I was younger. As gifted athletes, some of those guys are incredible. And in high school I'd pretty much decided they had the ultimate uniforms for showing off the guys uh, physiques. Terrible, huh?" She gave him a smile that was somewhat guilty because that sounded no better than the laundromat guy.

Continuing, she said, "But then I went to college and worked at the student cafeteria where the football team ate. It was a less than positive experience sometimes. Most times. On the one hand, they tended to be brainless and egotistical and had atrocious manners. And on the other, they spent a great deal of their time practically ordering me to go out with them as if it was this huge honor and actually asking a girl if she wanted to go was beneath them. Needless to say, I never went."

"So you don't mind football. It's just the players you dislike?"

She grimaced and felt even guiltier. "I'm sorry. I sound negative, don't I? I don't dislike either across the board. I just haven't had a terribly good experience with the players, and after becoming a nurse, I've had my share of trying to put a few of them back together. It's a sport that has way more than its fair share of injuries. To me that seems foolish. You only get one body in this life. Blown out knees and brain concussions in the name of a game are heartbreaking."

He was still watching her intently and she tried to back pedal. "At least to me it seems that way. I'm sorry if I'm offending you. Are you a huge fan or something?"

He hesitated. "Sometimes. I've always loved football, but you make good points." He changed the subject, nodding at the lunch. "This is marvelous. Where did you learn to cook like this?"

With a laugh, she said, "The student cafeteria. At least that's where I got a start. And of course my mom. I've always liked to cook. I worked in two or three restaurants in college. A couple had these great chefs that I tried to work beside as much as I could. Then I got too busy, and now I just have to get a book or watch them on TV. Do you really think it's that good?"

"It's great. Maybe I should pay you room and board so I can come out and eat with you and not feel guilty about canceling out all of your leftovers."

She shook her head. "You don't need to pay my board. I'll make you a deal. You make ribs occasionally and I'll cook for you anytime. Your ribs were phenomenal. They were to die for. Just call me and let me know when you're coming so I know when to plan for you."

"You don't know how much I eat, Kelly. I'd better pay your board. I'll leave some money in the kitchen. How have things been going while I've been gone?"

"Good, two of the upstairs bedrooms are almost done with wood. I'd be completely finished if I hadn't had to trip over the cat that has adopted me. I don't know where in the world he came from, but he's quite enamored. I made the mistake of giving him a bite of ham. Now he haunts me. I've had to throw him out of the house like six times."

Robby grinned. "Maybe he'll be good, intelligent company." He changed the subject and continued, "I have to go back to Charlotte tonight, but what can I help you with today? I brought a tiller by the way. It's small enough that even you should be able to use it if you want to. Or I'll do it. It will take longer to get finished, but it's great to handle."

"Oh, good. We should get started on a garden if we're going to plant one. You could work on that, or help me tape off and paint upstairs. That new ladder is great, by the way. Thank you."

"Good. Sometimes I worry about you working out here alone. I brought you a cell phone too this trip. You should have one with you when you're away from the house." He got up and began to clean up the lunch. "Thank you for feeding me. It was marvelous. Is there any thing you can't do well?"

She laughed as she went to pick up her own plate. "Oh, Robby. You have no idea. And I'm going to keep it that way. I have some world class failures that I have absolutely no intention of divulging. When I mess up, I really mess up. No half way for me. No, I go out in a ball of fire when I crash at something."

"That's better than being wishy-washy."

"Yes, even though I've failed with a passion at times. At least I try things whole heartedly. I'm afraid I made my mother crazy as a child. She used to call me 'Kelly the Intrepid'. There were times that I gave her gray hair. At least that's what she claims. She doesn't really have gray hair. I tried to tell her that at least she wasn't bored. She still grounded me when I pulled something too out of control. Mean huh?"

Robby laughed. "I would like to have known you as a child, Kelly. I'm sure you're right. I'll bet your mother was never bored."

That night Kelly thought about her mother when she went to bed. She really, really missed her. It had been five weeks since she'd run. The next morning she sent her mother daisies again. It was the fifth day of June.

Chapter 8

Robby and Kelly settled into a comfortable routine and between the two of them they got a lot done, in spite of the fact that the cat got more and more bossy as the days went on. For some reason, the first time Robby saw the cat he called him Ted, and the name stuck. The next time Robby showed up he had a cat litter box and a washer and dryer with him. "Now you won't have to put up with the local, stupid, piece of meat, macho, jock football player when you do your laundry." She looked so guilty about her assessment of football players that he laughed and added, "And if Ted gets stuck in the house at least he won't make a mess."

They tilled up the garden area and side by side they planted peas, beans, corn and tomatoes. Every once in a while they'd add something else that seemed interesting, and the tender green shoots came up almost miraculously within just a few days of being planted. Kelly got in the habit of weeding first thing in the morning before it got hot out, and their little garden looked amazingly good for two novice gardeners. Robby continued to mow when he came, and Kelly kept trying to tame the vines and added stone steps and small retaining walls, and the yard began to appear more and more loved and cared for.

The day that the living room furniture arrived, they celebrated with popcorn and Hot Tamales and a movie on the new, big screen TV.

There was no cable TV available here and since neither of them watched much, Robby had just gotten an account at the local video rental place in Tolke. They decided that when you walked in the front door, the house was finally really beginning to look like a home with real furnishings.

Soon after that, they took a day trip to the quaint little restaurant with the décor Robby liked and bought several more things to hang and decorate with. Then one day, Robby brought a painting with him that he'd bought for the big wall.

The crowning of the living room occurred when he showed up with a humongous ancient moose head and hung it over the fireplace. As they stood there peering at it, he looked at her with a completely straight face and said, "The old guy I bought it from says his name is Cuthbert."

Kelly laughed so hard that she leaned against him, and tears came to her eyes.

The headway in the house was slow, but it was steady and the day before the new cabinets were to arrive, they took the old ones down. That night they had a huge bonfire out in the gravel drive and roasted hotdogs and s'mores on it as it finally burned down. Robby laughed at her as she danced and sang around the huge flames.

Kelly asked Robby to hire the cabinet shop to install the new ones. They were so big and heavy that she just didn't feel she was up to it even with his help. The day the cabinet hangers were there, Robby headed to the nearby river to go fishing and Kelly tagged along. While he fished, she wandered along the bank or sat in the shade and read a book she'd bought the day before. Only a few pages into it she encountered a scene that was decidedly inappropriate, and she put the book down in disgust, lay her head back on the grassy bank and tried to take a nap.

She could have been drowsy, but his comment about snakes from all those days ago made her a little nervous. At length she got up and told him she was going for a walk up the river bottom for a while.

Her first assessment the morning she'd arrived in North Carolina had proven to be correct. Everywhere she'd been it was lovely. Sometimes wildly overgrown, sometimes rocky, but always it was a beautiful place and she wished she'd have been able to visit under more favorable circumstances.

Whenever she thought about home and her mom and the others, she felt guilty about not successfully putting a stop to the dangerous drug studies that had ended at least two lives that she knew of. She'd gotten safely away, at least for the time being, but something had to be done about Peter and Dr. Crowther, and

Peter was still dealing drugs as far as she knew too.

Several times, she wondered if she needed to try to contact the police again, or go back and check into things, but every time she had that thought, she would remember the way Peter had looked at her that day he'd caught her reading the patient file. She couldn't go back. At least not yet. Not until she found a way to do it without running the risk of being the next body. Peter would kill her if he could. She had seen that clearly in his eyes.

Thinking about Peter's look that day made her shiver in spite of the midday heat, and she wrapped her arms around herself as she continued up the river course. A subtle sound coupled with her prickly thoughts had her peering around the thick undergrowth wondering what she had heard. A second later, she detected it again. The hair on the back of her neck stood up, and she froze in place trying to identify the source of it.

It was weird; something she'd never encountered anything like before. Almost a chuckle, but not human in the least. Just when she decided it was time she turned around to head back toward Robby, she saw a shadow move under the bushes right at the very edge of the river just across from her.

Still frozen in place, the only thing she'd moved to see the shadow was her eyes. Mere seconds later she was completely astounded when the shadow deepened into the head and front half of a striking black cat that stood almost three feet tall at the shoulders.

If the cat hadn't been standing just twenty-five feet or so in front of her, she wouldn't have believed her eyes, but at that short distance with only the relatively flat water between them, there was no mistaking. She had heard of black panthers here in the Deep South, but for some reason she'd understood they were a tall tale of some sort. The wishful thinking of a group of people like the Big Foot enthusiasts or something.

The giant, sleek, coal black feline in front of her was absolutely no figment of her imagination, and she was frightened beyond being able to move, even before it somehow detected her and stared right at her with huge, golden yellow cat eyes. The eyes narrowed as they glared at her, and the animal's tail began to switch in the undergrowth, making the bushes behind it rustle as it moved. The cat took a single step toward her onto a rock out in the water of the river, and Kelly felt her lungs begin to heave with the shot of adrenaline that burst into her blood with that solitary move toward her.

She didn't know whether to scream, or turn and run, and she wasn't able to get her rigid muscles to even consider moving anyway. She felt like she was in one of those bad dreams where you had to get away, but you couldn't move, and she watched the panther in terrified fascination as it stared her down with one foot poised to come across the rushing water toward her.

When it had stepped out onto the rock, the rest of its body had emerged from the undergrowth and she could see that it was much bigger than she'd ever have dreamed a panther would be in true life. Just its body was between four and five feet long and its tail extended beyond that another few feet. She had expected a panther to be the size of a bobcat for some reason, but this cat was more the size of the female lions at the Chicago zoo. It was huge!

Still switching its tail and glaring at her, Kelly's breathing had gotten so labored that there was no question of trying to stay there calmly. Her lungs were going to burst, and still she was unable to move. When she thought she couldn't stand it a second longer and was going to hyperventilate, the cat at last turned and in one graceful lunge, disappeared back into the dense undergrowth it had appeared out of.

Finally, she was able to get her body to function and she turned as well to plunge headlong back down the path on the bank toward Robby. She'd only thought that she'd walked up the bank a few minutes, but it felt like miles before she burst through the bushes to see him there calmly fishing above a deep amber pool. With a huge sigh of relief that she'd made it to him, she literally ran into him before burying her face in his chest and struggling to control the tears that threatened. He wrapped his one empty arm around her and brought the other one as far around her as he could reach and not tangle her hair in the line that still extended into the river.

He leaned down to speak to her above the sound of the

current. "Kelly, what's wrong? Are you okay?"

Still breathing like her lungs would burst, all she could do was shake her head for a minute. At length, she simply got out one word, "Panther."

When Robby heard her finally say the one word with such a force of emotion, for just a second he thought she was mad at him for hiding the fact that he was a pro football player from her, but it didn't make any sense. How would she have just realized here on the river and if she was angry with him why would she rush to him and bury her face against him when just about the only other time they had even touched was when she'd fallen on him? She was obviously extremely upset about something. Her heart was racing nearly out of her chest, and she could hardly breathe.

Still trying to figure out what was going on, he gently raised her face to look at him and asked her again, "Are you okay? What's going on?"

All she did was bury her face against him one more time, and he wrapped his arms back around her still shaking shoulders. From right against his shirt he heard her say breathlessly, "There was a black panther. Just up the river. I thought it was coming across at me. I was so scared."

He pulled back from her in amazement. "What? You really saw a black panther?"

Tears overflowed her eyes and after one more glance at him, she buried her face again. "Oh, Robby, I was so scared."

He hugged her for a couple of minutes and then stepped back from her and leaned to set his fishing pole aside without taking his other arm from around her. "You really, truly saw a black panther?"

She gazed up at him with wide, tear filled eyes and nodded. "Yes, I really saw one and it was frightening. Sorry I'm being a baby. I usually love to see things like this." She wiped at the tears on her cheek. "I thought they were a myth or something. It was huge! It was like the size of a lioness at the zoo." She put a hand down to indicate how tall it had been. "It was this tall, Robby and I'm not kidding you! It stood and glared at me and switched its tail. It took a step right toward me when it saw me. I would have thought it would run from me not step toward me."

He put a reassuring hand on her shoulder and squeezed it, then said, "I'm sorry you were so frightened, Kelly, but actually, you were probably safe. A few people have seen them, but no one has ever been approached. The panthers have always run away. I almost wish they weren't so wary. I've wanted to see one for years and years."

After hesitating for a moment he asked, "Do you dare to go back and show me if I stay right with you? Maybe it's still around somewhere. I would love to see it."

Her face blanched, but she smiled anyway and said, "Robby, you're nuts. Haven't you been listening to me? It was a cat the size of a pony."

Gently, he asked again, "Would it be any less frightening with me beside you?" She hesitated while she considered that and he continued, "Do you have any idea how lucky you were to see it? Everyone here dreams of a glimpse of a black panther. They're incredibly elusive. Come show me where you saw it. It's probably long gone, but let's at least try."

She looked up and studied him with those deep, dark green eyes and finally she took his hand and turned to head back up the river. "I'll be fine with you beside me. It was through here."

She held his hand firmly, and he finally moved ahead of her as they walked. Only about an eighth of a mile up river she pulled back. When he glanced down at her she put a finger to her lips and pointed across the water to the other bank. "See the rock with the wet cat prints on it?" She pointed. "It came out of the bushes right there and just stood there looking at me and switching its tail. After a minute or two it began glaring at me and then stepped out onto the rock and acted like it was going to come right across the river at me. I was so afraid that I couldn't even move."

Robby checked out the rock that did indeed still have huge wet prints on it just across the way there, and glanced back at her. Holy Toledo! No wonder she was scared! The prints were nearly five inches across and the cat could have almost jumped across that space toward her. "Wait here." He squeezed her hand and whispered to her, "I just want to go across and see if I can still see anything. I won't go far, I promise."

Shaking her head, she took another step closer to him, gripped his hand tighter and barely mouthed, "No way. I'm coming with you. I don't want to stay here alone."

"You'll ruin your shoes."

"They're my gardening shoes anyway."

He shook his own head, trying not to smile. He wasn't going to complain about her being this close to him and holding his hand. He'd been wanting this for weeks now. "Okay. C'mon." He headed across in his waders and she stepped into the river right behind him.

At the rock, they paused and he put a hand down beside the prints to compare size and then looked up at her and raised his eye brows and was glad to see her smile. He pulled a camera and a tape measure out of his fishing vest and after stretching the little tape measure out beside the muddy print, he snapped a couple of pictures, put them away, and went to move on.

On the bank, he pushed back the bushes to reveal tracks in the mud where the cat had been standing when she'd first seen it appear. After looking at them, he pushed on into the underbrush with her right at his heels in the thick of it. Once a few feet away from the river, the growth thinned a bit and they were able to clearly see prints for several yards before the ground became too hard.

Walking as quietly as they could, they began to follow the path. After just a step or two, she took hold of his hand again and held it tightly and he could hear her begin to breathe heavily again. He didn't blame her. That cat must have been something else. His own heart was pounding.

In just a short walk, they came to a place where the growth thinned under some big, old trees and he was hesitant to step out of the cover of the bushes. They crouched down and he peered all around the little clearing and was just about to move forward when there was a strange sound up ahead. He felt Kelly grip his hand desperately hard. He looked at her, moving only his eyes, and she moved hers toward the unusual chuckling sound.

He could read the alertness in her gaze and stroked her hand with his fingers as he watched for the cat under the trees. They were rewarded for their stealth when the huge, coal black panther gracefully stepped slowly through the trees from left to right across the clearing not thirty yards in front of them. He felt her hand on the back of his vest and then silently he felt her hand him the camera. He wanted to take the picture, but he also figured that the cat would be able to hear the camera and would be gone the second he did.

He held off until the cat was almost back into the thick trees on the right side of the clearing and then aimed and shot without even raising the camera to his eye for fear the monstrous feline would bolt when he moved.

The click was almost imperceptible, but even so, the cat stopped and stared right at them. Robby felt like they were relatively well hidden with the brush around them and in the dim light under the trees, but the cat commenced to switch its tail and he came to understand just what Kelly had meant when she said it glared at her. It narrowed its eyes and he could see the distinctive yellow stare all the way across the clearing.

Kelly was breathing so hard that he felt terrible for bringing her back and scaring her a second time, and he could feel his own heart pounding like a jackhammer. Several times right in a row he shot photos, hoping he was, in fact, getting pictures of the cat. He hated to scare it off, but he wanted to record this once in a lifetime opportunity of seeing such an incredibly secretive cat of legend.

The fish and game had a reputation for refusing to acknowledge that these panthers even existed here in the southern United States. And he would probably never make these photos public, but he and Kelly would always have a record of what they'd seen this day.

At length, the cat finally turned and bolted into the darkest shadows under the brush and Kelly let out a huge breath that he matched with one of his own and she squeezed his hand again. He turned and put an arm around her and pulled her close and gave her an exuberant high five. She was almost too tense to return it at first. "Kelly, that was great!" He was still whispering for some reason. "That was so awesome! You were incredible! Thanks for helping me to see that. I've always wanted to see one! Even before I came here and before the whole Carolina Panther thing I've wanted to see one. Thanks."

She beamed at him and then shook her head and leaned it against his chest again as she laughed. "I think you're nuts, Robby. I think my heart is going to explode. Is it gone? It's not waiting out there to eat us, is it?"

He chuckled and hugged her to him, thoroughly enjoying being the one she turned to in her fear. "It's not waiting to eat us. We're fine. You're the best! Thanks." He hugged her again. "Come on. Let's go home and see how our new kitchen looks and get something to eat. You're heart will slow down as soon as we're back to the car, I promise."

On the way back, they followed a path to the river instead of struggling through the thickest of the undergrowth, and he held her hand all the way across the river and back to his pole. They were nearly back to the Rover before she finally let go and moved a step or two away from him, but he was still disappointed. It was terrible to be glad she'd been scared, but having her close had been great.

Unsure of whether the kitchen would be usable when they got home, he stopped at a drive in for fast food in Tolke on the way home. The kid who was working the drive through recognized him immediately, and Robby turned to talk to Kelly hoping to create a diversion so she wouldn't notice the reaction the employees were having toward him. She still seemed somewhat shell shocked from the panther, and he felt guilty again for making her go back, but she didn't even notice when the kid called him Rocker as he handed them their food. At least there was that.

The crews at the house were still working and rather than risk creating another stir with someone recognizing him, Robby turned to Kelly. "Can we go to your house for a while? We need to stay out of these guys' way for a little longer. Do you mind if we use your table to check out the photos on my laptop and see what we got?"

Yawning, she nodded. "Sure, whatever. Let's take another lawn chair with us."

He studied her face for a moment, and asked gently, "Are you okay? You still don't seem very happy. Are you going to be all right?"

She smiled and then nodded again. "I'm okay. With you there, I was fine. I'm so glad I could show you. I'm just tired from when you weren't there. Then I was terrified. I feel like I've worked a double shift today and I haven't done a thing. How bad is that?"

He got his laptop and picked up a lawn chair off the porch. "Adrenaline does amazing things. When you come off something like a scare like that, you really come down. But then you know that as a nurse. What made you want to become a nurse?"

"I wanted to do something that would help society. And there's always a need, anywhere you go. I figured if I had to work, I could and still fit in a family."

"What made you quit?"

She glanced at him and then looked away. "Oh, I just decided to take some time. It was kind of a spur of the moment thing, actually." He could tell she was hedging, but he let it go.

The private investigator hadn't turned up much more than he'd found originally when he continued to dig in Chicago about her. She'd been dating a doctor who practiced at the hospital she'd been working at, and he'd been considered a suspect in her disappearance even though he'd been the one to discover she was missing because she'd been planning to go out with him that night. Robby had read all the news clippings but nothing conclusive had ever been printed, and the police had pretty well put the investigation onto the back burner.

Robby kept hoping that one day she'd level with him and he could help her with whatever her problems were, but so far she hadn't trusted him with much. He thought back to when she'd run to him earlier that day when she'd been so frightened. He had to take that back. She trusted him; he was sure of it. It had been incredibly nice to be the one she ran to. He probably should've just taken her home instead of frightening her further, but it had been great to see it with her there beside him.

Once they got to the summer kitchen, he sat at the little table and began working on the laptop, and she pulled clean clothes from rubber totes under the bed and went back to the main house to change out of her wet jeans and shoes. While she was gone, he gazed around. Her room was neat and tidy and smelled like the vine that climbed outside the Dutch door and windows. He expected that she'd begun work on her own bathroom, but so far the room was just as he'd seen it that first time, except for a mirror that she'd hung and a couple of baskets that held shoes and some of her things.

There was a dress hanging from one of the window sills, and he made a mental note to encourage her to start working on her own bath and a closet. She needed that at least. And a comfortable chair and a dresser. He could bring them to her so she didn't have to struggle with the rental truck. Picking up the camera, he snapped a couple of photos of her bed and table to see if he could match them for her.

When she came back in, she picked up her hairbrush and ran it through her hair, then pulled it back into a pony tail and came to stand behind him with her hand on his shoulder as he finally got the photos to pull up on the screen. He was thrilled with how well they'd turned out after how they'd been taken. All she said was, "He was so much bigger than I'd ever have dreamed. Did you know panthers could be that big?"

He thought of some of the guys on the line and answered drily, "Yeah, I figured they could get pretty big." He clicked through a few more photos. "Do you think we should go to the fish and game people with these, or do you think they'll just brush them off like they do every other panther sighting down here?"

"Do they not take sightings seriously?"

He shrugged. "I believe their pat answer is supposed to be that people think they're seeing a panther but it's really just a misidentified coyote or house cat."

She put a slender finger on the image on the screen. "There's not much question about misidentifying what's here.

These pictures turned out remarkably well, especially for how they were taken."

"Which means the wildlife people will claim they've been Photoshopped."

She laughed. "You might be just a touch cynical. If you don't think the authorities will take you seriously, just put them on YouTube and let the masses enjoy them. You said yourself that everyone down here wants a chance to see a panther."

She went over and stretched out on top of her bedspread and stuffed a pillow under her chin. "Personally, I think I've had my fill of panthers. I'm almost embarrassed at how scared I was. I honestly thought he was coming across that river at me. It was awful."

He looked up and met her eyes. "But you were still willing to come show me. It meant a lot to me. That was a one chance in a lifetime for me. Thanks. Sorry we scared you again."

Sleepily, she blew off how it had bothered her. "It's okay. You'd already saved me, so I kind of owed you. Plus, it wasn't scary with you there beside me. You always have that effect." She closed her eyes, and he watched her for a minute before he went back to the pictures. He helped her not be afraid, but she helped him find the passion for life again. Before her, he'd lost it somewhere along the way.

It wasn't long before he could tell she had gone soundly to sleep, and, when he was finished with his photographs, he pulled up some other business paperwork and continued to work there at her little table. Late in the afternoon he saw the cabinet guys start to load up their trucks, and he headed back over to the main house to see how things had gone and do a walk through with their lead installer.

It was going to be a beautiful kitchen. She'd done a marvelous job designing it. He ran a hand over the stone countertop, thinking about the girl who slept out there in his summer kitchen. This house was far more home to him now than his condo, even though he'd had the condo for years and he'd only had this house for weeks. It had nothing to do with time, and honestly probably nothing to do with properties either. It was her. Her, and the fact that he was just him when he was around her. It was nice to be appreciated just for being himself.

Thinking about the fact that she still didn't know he was a pro football player made him somewhat uncomfortable. They had gotten to be very good friends over the course of these last weeks, and it was to the point that she was going to be offended when she finally did find out. But even knowing that didn't make him want to tell her. Theirs was an incredibly easy and comfortable friendship. He'd never had a female friend who was so straightforward since Ellen Durfey in the first grade, and that was only because in the first grade they hadn't even realized they were different.

He was still standing in his beautiful new kitchen when his phone rang. It was Jason and he hurriedly glanced at his watch as he answered, "Hey, Jase. What's going on?"

"I know this is stupid question, but where are you?"

Robby laughed. "At my house. Why? Where are you?"

"I'm at my house too, Rocker, but my house is only ten minutes from our meeting. You did remember that we have a meeting tonight didn't you?"

Rolling his eyes, Robby asked him. "Jason, in all the years that I've known you, have I ever missed a meeting? Even once?"

On the other end of the line Jason laughed. "Yes, once. You were in the hospital in traction at the time, but you missed one. You never miss meetings, but you've never had this dazed look you're wearing lately either. It's about time I come out and meet this girl who you thought was a kid who now works for you. Ever since you hired her, you've been missing in action."

"You stay away from my caretaker, Jase. She's doing a marvelous job and don't you ruin her. Hey, you'll never believe what I saw today. We were fishing and we saw a real black panther. It was awesome! I got pictures. I'll bring them."

"Cool. Who's we?"

"What?"

"Who's we? Who were you fishing with?"

"A friend. What do you care who I fish with?"

"It was her, wasn't it?"

"Her who? Raime, what is up with you? Why are you asking me who I was fishing with?"

"You're a mess, Robideaux." Jason laughed. "You never fish with anyone. And why are you out at that house every minute that you're in town? I have your women calling *me* to find out what's happened to you. You're smiling all the time. I can even hear it in your voice over the phone. What happened to the Rocker who was so burnt out and miserable a few weeks ago? And don't try to tell me it's therapeutic yard work. I know you too well."

Robby chuckled. "She's just a girl, Jase. I'll see you in a while. Tell Monique hello."

"Maybe you should bring her in with you. After the meeting we'll take her and Monique to dinner. Monique is a killer judge of character. We could check her out for you. Make sure she's safe."

"Safe for what? What could she possibly harm at that house? You saw it. Although it is getting much better with her around. I can't bring her, anyway. She doesn't know what I do for a living."

"What do you mean she doesn't know?"

"Uh, when she asked, I told her I work for a large corporation in acquisitions."

Jason totally busted up. "Acquisitions? What am I in? Distribution? You're gonna be in a lot of trouble when she finds out."

"Let's just keep her in the dark for a good long time, shall we. I'm just a guy to her and it's unbelievably refreshing. I'd like to keep it that way. I have to go or I'm going to miss a meeting. See ya in a sec."

"Hustle, man. See ya."

Robby closed his phone, still smiling. Yeah, he was going to be in a lot of trouble, but Jason's curiosity was a crack up. He'd be totally surprised when he finally did meet her. She was an extraordinary young woman in many ways.

Kelly still hadn't appeared from the summer kitchen, and he went back out to tell her goodbye. From her porch he could see her curled up in a ball still asleep on her bed, and he decided to just let her sleep. The panther had really shaken her up. Maybe it would be best if she just rested.

She appeared cold curled up there and he went back inside the house and pulled the quilt off of his bed and took it back outside with him. In her house, he gently draped it over her and then locked the door securely behind him. Leaving a note for her in the new kitchen, he locked that house up too and headed in for his meeting. If it wasn't so convenient to have a place close to the stadium, he'd sell the condo and just live out here. He was so much more comfortable here.

He shook his head when he realized what he was thinking. It wasn't here. It was with her, and he had to stop and take stock for a second. So he had a thing for her. She wasn't a member, and he'd better not get attached to her, although so far he couldn't find a thing about her that would keep her from the church.

She was a nice girl, and it was obvious. She was modest and clean living and had a wonderful spirit about her. She never said anything questionable like all the other women he knew, and prayer over meals had been a given with her from the very first. The one time they had spoken of anything spiritual, she had mentioned being still and listening for God. Maybe it was about time he told her about the church and offered her a Book of Mormon.

Chapter 9

Sometime late in the night, Kelly could smell him. That hint of aftershave she'd gotten when she'd run to him after seeing the panther. Still half asleep, she pushed the thoughts of the panther out of her head, breathed in his smell, snuggled deeper and went back to sleep, remembering how solid his chest had felt when she ran to him.

It was her stomach growling that woke her up. Man, she was starving! She rolled over and stretched and realized she was snuggled under the quilt off of Robby's bed. No wonder she thought she could smell him. She put her nose right into the soft flannel and breathed deeply. He smelled really, really good.

She laid her head back and sighed. There wasn't a doubt in her mind that her Father in Heaven had had something to do with her running out of gas that day. This situation was far too perfect to be a mere coincidence. The only problem was she was becoming seriously attached to Robby, and he wasn't a member of the church.

On the surface that didn't seem like that big of a deal because he was obviously a wonderful person, but deep down she knew falling for a non-member was a mistake, and she needed to not go there. When she finally found "him" and settled down and got married, she needed a husband who was strong enough spiritually to lean on, and held and honored the priesthood, and would do his share to help pull their family's spiritual handcart. She'd seen a lot of women who pulled them alone, her mother included, and she knew in her heart that pulling together was vitally important in the eternal big picture.

Not that she was getting ready to marry Robby, but how many times had she seen friends fall in love with someone who wasn't truly compatible with their value system just because they spent a great deal of time with each other?

That had happened to her own parents, and her mother had literally drummed it into Kelly's head over the years to make better decisions than she had made.

For that matter, whether she and Robby ever became an item romantically or not was one thing, but item or not, Kelly should have been making more of an effort to try to share the gospel with him. He was obviously a good man, with a wonderful spirit about him, and just because she was basically in hiding didn't mean she couldn't help him to find the true gospel of Jesus Christ. It was her greatest treasure, and, to someone without it, it would be the most tremendous gift. It was time; she'd known that for a while now.

As she got up to dress, she tried to figure out how to get him a Book of Mormon without giving her only copy away. She couldn't order one and have it shipped without a credit card and an address. Somewhere there would be a hotel or motel owned by an LDS person, or maybe she could just buy one from the missionaries here in this area or someone at the church. She made a mental note to take some money and ask someone on Sunday.

Walking into the pretty, new kitchen that morning fired her up! It was every bit as beautiful as she'd envisioned it. Even better. They'd set the cabinets and countertops and installed the sink. Now she just needed to install the faucets, lay the tile, and have the new appliances delivered. This was going to be awesome. She almost wished it truly was her own kitchen.

Not that that mattered. Robby had been amazingly good to let her make choices and have the run of the place. Money didn't seem to be a big issue to him. Maybe he'd let her get all the new dishes and furnish it how she'd like as well. Probably. He wasn't terribly picky about anything. Mostly he was just an incredibly nice, incredibly good looking guy.

Pulling out cold cereal, she went to the funny, old, avocado colored fridge they'd moved into the hall, got milk, and then took her bowl to sit on the front porch step like she'd gotten into the habit of before the table delivery. Ted kept draping himself around her as she ate, and she had to keep brushing his tail away from her face to take another bite. "Cat, I swear. You're making me crazy."

She gently shoved him across the step away from her

bowl. "Go away. Let me eat in peace, you little cuss." She smiled out at the beautiful morning. Ted was definitely in the way sometimes, but he was a great deal of company if she honestly admitted it to herself.

She and Ted were still eating breakfast when Robby's Land Rover pulled up the gravel lane. He got out and came to the porch and sat down next to them to gaze out over the yard. Instantly Ted started to lounge on him and Robby laughed. "How can you even eat with him here? He's like an amoeba or something. He almost rolls against you." He shoved the cat gently away. "Did you finally wake up?"

"Yes, but not until this morning. Thank you for lending me your quilt. Do you want something to eat? If you want, I can make you something."

"No, but thank you. I had breakfast meetings this morning. What are you going to be working on today?"

"The kitchen sink. What did you think? Did you like the kitchen?"

"I love it. I would never have been able to have pictured what you did in there. When I think back to what it looked like the first day when the realtor showed it to me, I can't even believe what you've done here. It's great. Your ability to envision is a gift. By the way, I already arranged to have the appliances delivered. They'll be here next week. Will that give you time to finish the tile floor?"

"It should. I'll try to hurry so we don't have to eat microwaved food any longer than necessary."

"We could grill stuff. The only thing I know how to do is ribs, but I know salmon is good on the grill. I kept a big catfish yesterday. Maybe we could try it."

"Fish is good grilled. I've never had catfish. What is it like? How do you cook it?"

"I've only ordered it, but it's okay. Down here they bread it with something and deep fry it. It's definitely greasy, but it's not too bad. Maybe we could try it for lunch."

At lunch time, she unceremoniously announced that cat fish tasted like mud, and Robby laughed so hard that he choked on his drink and she had to pound him on the back. At that she felt positively penitent and back pedaled. "Sorry, that was kind of rude." She took another bite and chewed thoughtfully. "Maybe it's just the way I cooked it or something. I'm just used to the marvelous seafood in Chicago."

"Actually, it was much better than the deep fried way. It must just taste like mud. So, how do you know what mud tastes like, anyway?"

She frowned thoughtfully. "Mmm. That's a good question. I must have eaten it when I was little or something, because the taste was familiar."

He cracked up again and then continued, "You always cook healthy. It's wonderful. I much prefer that to all the fried, heavy stuff. Are you an athlete? Why are you so health conscious?"

She shook her head. "No athlete. I played soccer in high school, and intramurals in college, but no. I'm a nurse. I just don't ever want to be one of the patients in the cardio wards or cancer floor. I have ancestors who had serious longevity. If I'm going to live to be a hundred, I want to feel good while I'm doing it."

"Good for you. But, still. Not every one can make healthy taste great. That's another gift."

Kelly laughed at him. "You just agreed with me that it tasted like mud. What are you talking about?"

"It was the catfish's fault. Maybe next time we should go to the coast to fish, or go clam digging or something instead."

"But you really like fishing on the rivers here, don't you?"

"Yes, but maybe they're called catfish because you're supposed to feed them to Ted."

She laughed again and whispered, "Ted didn't like it either."

At a little after four that afternoon, Kelly was lying half in, half out of the kitchen sink cabinet, hooking up the garbage disposal while Robby watched from the dining table where he was working on his laptop again. He had helped her hold the thing in place while she got it attached because it was heavy, but he was the first to admit she was far more adept at all of this than him.

In a way, it was highly entertaining to him. She'd never done a lot of it, but she'd buy a book and study how to do it and then give it a go. So far she'd done unbelievably well, other than having to go back and forth to Home Depot sometimes to get things she'd forgotten or gotten wrong the first time. Even if she hadn't been able to do that great of a job, he'd probably have let her have at it anyway, because he so admired her spunk and attitude.

He pulled his eyes away from her and back to his computer and was surprised to hear a knock on the front door. Kelly looked up at him and bonked her head on the disposal, and he laughed at her as he went to see who had wandered onto his private lane.

Upon opening the door, he busted up to see Jason standing there holding a grocery bag with Monique and Shania coming up the walk behind him. Shaking his head as he laughed again, Robby said, "You just couldn't stand it, could you? Your curiosity was killing you, wasn't it?"

Jason slapped him on the shoulder as he went past, and Robby bent down to scoop up Shania who was squealing, "Uncle Wobby! Uncle Wobby!"

Gazing all around as she came up the step, Monique smiled at him. "Robby, this is really nice. For some reason I expected all run down, but this is beautiful. And incredibly peaceful. No wonder you've gone underground."

He leaned and gave her a one armed hug. "Well, it still has a long way to go, but it's getting there." He ushered them inside and shut the door. "Come in and make yourselves at home as much as you can. There's not much furniture yet in some of the rooms. Come back and meet Kelly. She's just now under the kitchen sink, actually."

Jason gave him a look that was more than a little bit skeptical, and they followed him through the living room into the kitchen. Robby put Shania down and looked over at Jason as if to say, "I wasn't kidding", and Jason raised his eyebrows and shook his head. Shania walked right over to the sink cabinet and almost appeared like she wanted to climb in and see what was going on under there. Leaning down, Robby spoke to Kelly, "How close are you to being done there, Kel?"

She didn't raise her head, just said, "Another couple of minutes. Was that really someone at the door?"

"Just some locals who were lost. When you're through will you come talk to me in the living room?"

At that, she looked up and bumped her head again. When she noticed Shania's little face right there, she looked around and then glanced at Robby with big eyes, scooted out of the cupboard, and hurriedly stood up. She went to smooth her hair, then glanced at her hands and decided against it.

Robby handed her a paper towel off the counter, and she began wiping her hands as Robby introduced her, "Kelly, I'd like you to meet some very good friends of mine. Monique and Jason Raime. I work with Jason. And this little angel," He scooped up Shania and tossed her gently in
the air. "Is Shania." He turned to Shania. "Can you say hello to my friend Kelly Shane?"

With a shy smile that revealed a dimple, Shania held out her little hand and said, "Hello, Kelly Shane. It's vewy nice to meet you."

Kelly returned the smile and took the tiny hand in hers as she glanced at Robby. "Oh my, but you have nice manners. It's very nice to meet you, too, Shania."

Shania let go of her hand and turned back to Robby and wrapped her arms around his head. "Uncle Wobby, is Kelly Shane the weason you're nevo at you other house by us any mowa?"

Robby had to move her arms before he could start to answer, "Uh, well." Kelly started to laugh and Monique gave Jason a look and interrupted.

"Uncle Robby just wanted a break from the city and some of the people there, sweetheart. It's peaceful out here in the country, don't you think? Did you see that pretty kitty out there on the front porch?"

"Yes. Can I go look at the kitty, Mommy?"

Robby let her down and Monique took her hand and they

headed back the way they had just come in. As Monique went past Kelly, she said, "Excuse me for a moment."

As they went out, Jason reached across and offered Kelly his hand. "It's good to meet you Kelly. We didn't mean to interrupt what you're doing. I thought he was joking when he said you were under the kitchen sink."

She glanced down at her hand and wiped it on her jeans before she returned his handshake. "It's nice to meet you too. I'm sorry we didn't know you were coming, or I certainly wouldn't have been under the sink."

Jason gazed all around. "Wow, this place looks good. He said you were whipping it into shape, but I can't even believe how different it is. You've done a great job!"

"You've been here before?"

"Robby brought me out when the realtor showed it to him. Then I thought he was nuts to buy it, but now... This is truly cool."

"Well, I haven't done it all. Robby has helped and the cabinets we hired out. But it is coming along."

Robby shook his head and gave her the credit she'd earned. "She's done almost all of it. She has a knack for envisioning, and then she's worked about a gazillion hours. She's even willing to sacrifice life and limb." He walked up to her and scrubbed a black mark off of her forehead where she'd bonked her head. "That's why she has stuff on her head." He laughed, and she blushed, and Jason looked from one to the other of them.

Monique had come back in and ran a hand over the cabinets that were brand new, but appeared to have weathered for years. "I've never seen anything like these. They exactly match these marvelous old logs. I have to tell you, Robby. Jason said you'd bought this rundown old farmhouse cabin, and I expected a beater, but this house is great. Even the brand new part fits with the rustic old part. How did you do it?"

Robby nodded at Kelly. "It's all her fault. All I do here is try to tame the lawn and catch fish that she says taste like mud." He grinned at her. "She's the This Old House fairy."

He went to the grocery bag Jason had put on the counter

and peeked into it. "Hey, how did you know we needed to barbecue? Our appliances have to wait until the floor is redone." He turned to Kelly. "Check it out, they brought ribs, Kel. If you thought my ribs were good, wait until you taste Jason's! And potato salad and all kinds of goodies." He turned to Jason. "I caught a cat fish yesterday and we ate it for lunch. She told me it tasted like mud." He smiled over at Kelly. "In a really nice way."

"Hey, I cooked it. I'm sure it was my fault." She turned back to the Raimes and said in a stage whisper, "It really did taste like mud."

"Yeah, but the funny part about that was she knew what mud tasted like."

Monique smiled at her and asked Robby, "Didn't you ever make mud pies when you were little?"

"Made them. Not ate them. Who eats them? We gave them to the little neighbor kids to eat."

Kelly looked at him. "Robby! You truly let the little neighbor kids eat them?"

"Hey, we paid them. And we told them it'd make them as strong as us. They loved them. Said they tasted just like catfish."

Shania came in hauling Ted like a sack of potatoes, but he didn't seem to mind. Monique went to his rescue and Shania said, "You're kitty is so, so fat! You should call him Santa Clause." The adults laughed, and Shania peered up at Jason. "Daddy, do you weally work with Uncle Wobby? I thought all you did was play football with him."

All the adults laughed again, and Kelly asked Jason, "So, are you in acquisitions too, at your work?"

Jason glanced up at Robby and gave a lopsided smile. "No… No, I'm in distribution."

Looking from one to the other of them, Monique picked up Shania and said, "And I'm in motherhood. Can we see the rest of your house, Robby?"

"Sure. Come on. I'll give you a tour." He turned to Kelly. "Can I show them your house too?"

"Absolutely. While you guys are touring, I'll finish the disposal and get this mess cleaned up and out of the way." She reached to turn on the disposal and the other four headed toward the back of the house.

They were hardly out of the kitchen when Jason went close to Robby and whispered, "Mistook her for a guy? Yeah, right Rocker. You couldn't mistake her for a guy if you were blindfolded and unconscious."

"She had on a black leather jacket and pants and a tinted helmet and was sitting on a motorcycle. Okay?"

Jason shook his head. "It's still not possible. At first I thought Bocklin was going to hassle you. Now I think he's going to try to steal her. Why didn't you tell me she was like that?"

Robby laughed. "Like what? Is there something wrong with her?"

"You know what I mean. So what's up with you two?"

Shaking his head at his friend, Robby chuckled. "Jason, I've been telling you. She's just a girl. Okay, so she's raving beautiful. She's just a girl. A really nice, talented, intelligent girl who I personally am never going to expose to a scum dogger like Bocklin. Anyway, she hates football players."

"What do you mean?"

Monique came closer to hear his answer as well. "I think her exact description was big, brainless, piece of meat, macho jocks who are demeaning, egotistical and have atrocious manners. Oh, and I think Neanderthal was thrown in there somewhere as well." Both Raimes stopped dead still and stared at him, and he shrugged. "She worked at the cafeteria that fed the football team back in college. You can imagine what kind of a reaction she got. She said they never asked her out, they told her. It didn't go over well, apparently."

Jason's eyes had actually gotten big. "Apparently. She really said that?" Robby grinned a big grin and Jason added, "Geez. It sort of keeps it all in perspective doesn't it?"

"Yup." Robby shook his head with a laugh. "Any over inflated ideas I had about how tough and important I am are thoroughly flattened. But you know what? It's absolutely refreshing to be just a guy for once. I'm telling you. I'll never be the same."

Monique laughed. "I may have to try that with Jason. Do

you think he'll get that perpetual dazed look you have now?"

"Monique! You wound me. What's she trying to say, Jase?"

"Oh, just that you have that happy, doofus thing going on. You know she's going to be mad when she finally clues in, don't you? Now she's even going to be ticked at Monique and me, as well."

"Jason, right now, she likes me for me, and she's easy going and nice and undemanding. Don't you ruin her."

Monique looked at him. "After meeting her, I don't think she's going to change once she knows what you do for a living. She's just going to be mad."

"You know, she's red, but so far, I haven't seen a hint of a temper."

Shaking her head, Monique said, "Red temper or no, you wait. She's going to be hurt, but it's a lot easier to be mad than to be hurt. She's going to be mad."

Jason seconded the thought. "She's going to be mad."

"Well, maybe she won't find out." They both looked at him like he was being a doofus again. "Look, she doesn't leave here much. And we don't go places out in public often together. And there's no TV reception and not much radio."

"Summer camp starts in two weeks, Rocker. How are you going to hide what happens to your body when the season starts? She might be beautiful, but she's not brain dead."

They'd been hearing the disposal go on and off in the kitchen, but now it went off and stayed off, and they could hear her footsteps on the hardwood as she approached and asked, "Do you want me to light the grill, Jason? It might take a while to warm up."

"That'd be great. Thanks."

When she was gone again, they all stared at each other for a few seconds and then Robby sighed. "You guys are raining on my paradise. I was enjoying being blissfully anonymous. You're going to go and make me ruin everything."

Monique laughed and hugged him with one arm around his waist. "You underestimate her, Rocker. She's gonna be just fine. Trust her. You know in your heart she's no more of a money-hungry, notoriety seeker than I am. She seems like a rock. Come show us the rest of your house."

As they continued on through the house, Shania asked, "Mommy, what does bwain dead mean?"

Chapter 10

She'd been working on the kitchen floor tile for three full days when she finally put the last little piece in place. She packed up her mortar, picked up the tile cutter and trowels, and went to clean them before taking them to the basement to store until the next tile project. Wishing she could just go shower and fall into bed, she decided she'd better put signs by both kitchen doorways that the floor couldn't be walked on in case Robby came in before she was out of bed in the morning. He was big and if he stepped on anything, it would ruin it. She looked over the tile work with satisfaction.

It truly was beautiful. Once it was grouted, it was going to be incredible. She hoped he wouldn't mind that she had added a strip of wood in-laid into the tile work all around the perimeter.

She put out her signs and then opted for a bath instead of a shower. As the water ran she dumped in some bubbles, lit a candle, turned out the lights, and then slipped her tired body into the heavenly warmth and leaned her head back. Who would ever have thought that a project would make you so tired and stiff? It wasn't even all that big of a kitchen. It would have been great to have her Uncle Roy here to help her. As she let the warm bubbles relax her, she thought about her uncle and mother back home. She really missed her mom.

It was late when he finally landed in Charlotte in the pouring rain, but he wanted to go out to the house anyway. He was tired and the weather was abysmal, and, though the condo was closer, it didn't truly feel like home anymore.

He picked up his one bag and headed for the long term parking lot, grateful there weren't many people around at this time of night. Settling into the Rover, he turned his phone back on after his flight and then felt his gut tighten when he saw that the private investigator he'd hired to check into Kelly had called.

It was after ten Frisco time, but Robby called him back anyway and was appalled to hear that the man's office had been broken into. He assured Robby that nothing had been found to direct them to Robby, but he wanted Robby to know he thought they were trying to find out why he'd been digging into Kelly's past. Robby thanked him and then sat there thoughtfully for several minutes. Whatever Kelly had run from wasn't a thing of the past. That much was clear. And now they probably suspected that she wasn't dead after all.

He drove up the gravel lane and walked into the house and then pulled up short. There were no lights on anywhere, but the door was unlocked and the sound system in the living was still playing softly. He looked back out and double checked that her motorcycle was there. It was. He walked through the house and saw the sign she'd put out on the kitchen floor just a split second before he stepped down on it. Taking the long way around, he went to check on her in the summer kitchen. Maybe she'd just accidentally left the door unlocked and stereo on.

There were no lights on at her house either and he felt like a peeping Tom for just a second as he stood there in the rain, peering in to see if she was in her bed. It was nearly two AM, but the curtains were open and her bed was still neatly made up and empty. Back tracking, he called her name as he crossed the lawn again, this time truly starting to get worried. The PI had said they didn't find anything, but… He tried not to let thoughts of whoever she had run from in Chicago enter his head, but there was a chill he struggled to ignore.

Where would she have gone in the dark? The thought occurred to him that maybe she was out on a date with someone. Maybe that's why her bike was here and she wasn't. But would she have left without locking up? The thought of her on a date troubled him for some reason. He probably shouldn't have, but he'd come to feel like she was a little bit his. He pulled his phone out and hit her number as he walked back into his house and was even more troubled when he heard her phone ringing and saw it sitting beside a notepad on the kitchen counter. Where in the world was she?

Going through the house one more time, he saw the bathroom door shut, but didn't think anything about it. There was no light showing underneath it and he'd been calling her. If she had been in there she would have answered. He knocked just to be sure and then started in the basement and went all the way through every room checking for her. Finally, he opened the bathroom door and realized she was there in the tub in the dark. He'd knocked and called and now he almost panicked and went right over to her and grabbed her shoulder and shook her as he yelled, "Kelly!"

Slowly, she opened her eyes, and after a second when she realized he was standing there beside her bathtub, her eyes got wide, and she sunk further down in the water. "Robby! What are you doing?"

"Searching for you. Are you okay?"

"I'm fine. Go out."

Even though he left right then, he still worried that she was going to be disgusted with him when she got out. He heard the water start to drain out of the tub and then the shower start up. Man, she'd seemed so tired lying there. Tired and beautiful, but just thinking that made him feel guilty. Why had she been sleeping in the tub with no lights on at two in the morning?

He paced in the living room without turning on the light for a few minutes, and then stopped and looked out the window into the black and wet. He finally sat down and took his shoes off. Even if she was completely ticked at him for walking in on her, he was glad he'd come out here. Especially if there was something wrong with her. He hadn't been trying to be inappropriate.

It was just that ever since he'd learned from the private investigator that she'd staged her own death and run away, he'd known she had to have been in some kind of danger to have done something so drastic. She wasn't overly dramatic by nature. It had to have been something truly bad. And the phone call tonight had him completely keyed up. These last weeks since then, he'd been relatively complacent because he thought she was safe here. As safe as she could be anywhere, if she was being as cautious as he thought she was. Still, they needed to always be careful.

She was still in the shower, and he went into his room and changed out of his business clothes. He put on a pair of sweats and a hoody, then came back out and started a fire in the fire place. He turned off the stereo and stretched out on the couch, listening to the rain and the crackle of the flames on the wood. It was really nice here--so much nicer than his condo in the city. Kelly had looked like a tired angel in the bathtub in the dark.

When Kelly finally shut off the shower water and toweled off, she still hadn't truly warmed up after falling asleep in the tub. She had no idea what time it was, but the candle had burned all the way out and the water had been so cold that her teeth chattered before she got the shower water running hot.

She was glad he had come and woken her up. She would have probably awakened soon just from the cold anyway. But she knew it was late, and she would have been nervous showering and locking up and going to the summer kitchen by herself, in the dark and the rain. It had been weird to wake up and realize he was standing in the bathroom with her, but she could see the worry in his eyes. It *was* totally weird to be in a cold tub in the dark in the middle of the night.

She dressed and got out and went to search for him, wondering what he was doing here at this time of night in business clothes. She found him in the living room asleep on the couch with a fire going. He'd turned off her music and must have been listening to the rain. She leaned over the fire and stretched her hands to the warmth, letting the heat finally start to toast away the chill she was fighting, and wondered if she should wake him up or let him sleep.

When she was finally warm, she quietly pushed the logs way back and closed the screen doors tightly. She went into his room and brought back his quilt and gently tucked it around him and locked up and went up to her house. On second thought, she went back and left him a note on the bathroom mirror. "Robby, thank you for waking me. I was TIRED, but I was getting so cold and would have been a Popsicle if you hadn't come in. Thanks, Kelly". She did appreciate how he watched over her.

The pressure on her sinuses was painful even before she was all the way awake the next morning. She slowly sat up and then sneezed violently and grabbed for the box of tissues she kept on the floor beside her bed. *Great. A sinus infection.* Just when she'd been going to try to hurry to get the tile floor grouted and sealed so they could put the appliances back in. She gazed outside at the rain streaming down the windows and sighed. At least Robby was here. He'd cheer her up.

She dressed and went across to the house and was just about to open the lovely avocado fridge when she sneezed again. Somewhere behind her she heard Robby sneeze almost in unison, and she turned to regard him sympathetically. "You too, huh?"

He nodded and handed her a tissue from the box in his hand. "Let's not eat cold cereal this morning. Let's go back to the Pancake House and have something ridiculously high in calories or sugar. On the way home we can buy some cold pills and rent a movie." He sneezed again. "Or three."

"And some orange juice."

He gave her a half hearted grin. "You want to rent some orange juice?"

She laughed in spite of how she felt and followed him out to his Land Rover.

Pulling up outside of the Pancake House brought back memories. She'd first come here more than two and a half months ago, and remembering the fear and uncertainty she had been feeling then made her unbelievably grateful for this man walking in front of her. As he held the door for her, he smiled and said, "I met an incredibly beautiful girl in this restaurant one time. I've been fond of it ever since. Maybe she'll be here again today." She sneezed. "What? It could happen."

He pulled out her chair to seat her and she met his eyes. "You probably don't know this, but you rescued me that day, Robby. Thank you. I'd been praying for help and God sent you."

As he went to sit down across from her, he squeezed her shoulder and said, "You probably don't know this either, Kelly, but you rescued me that day, as well. I hadn't even known to be praying for you, but God in His wisdom sent you anyway. Thank you."

"How did I rescue you?"

"I was getting seriously burnt out with my life. That's why the new old house in the first place. Your coming has helped me not be so cynical and jaded. I'm a much happier guy. And I'm sure Jason would agree that I'm much nicer as well. He says he'd like to hire you to fix some of the other guys we work with." He paused and then asked, "How did I rescue you?"

Their eyes met and she had to look down. "I wish I could tell you everything, Robby, but it might get you in a lot of trouble. Just know that I had to leave and couldn't bring anything like my car or ID or debit cards with me, and I was alone and worried. You really were an answer to prayer."

"I might be able to help. Did you ever think about that?"

"Yeah. If I can ever figure out what to do, I'll ask you. In the mean time, just keep letting me work on your house in relative seclusion. Maybe by the time we get that wine cellar done, I'll have had an epiphany."

They ordered and small talked until their drinks came. Then, she turned back to him. "Speaking of God sending you. Can I ask you something?"

"Sure."

"Do you ever wonder if there is one church out there that is the right one? The true one? The one that God and Jesus Christ have organized and sit at the head of?"

"No. Do you?"

"Actually, no. Why don't you wonder?"

"Because I know there is."

"You do? How do you know?"

"I asked."

"Who did you ask?"

He looked at her and smiled. "God. Who do you think?"

"Oh." She had intended to try to get him to want to take the missionary discussions or at least read the Book of Mormon, but she had no idea what to say now and was almost relieved when their food came. She prayed before she ate for more than just to bless to the food. She truly wanted to share the gospel, but was feeling a bit stuck and needed inspiration.

Robby watched her face as she asked him the questions

about God. He could see her struggling to know what to say to him and in a way he was feeling the same things. For awhile now he had been wondering about how to share the gospel with her and had been surprised that after serving a mission and living and working this close to her he wasn't feeling this urgent need to convert her, and just this minute he was wondering if he didn't understand the reason why. With her pointed questions, it was starting to make sense now.

From the very first, he had been so surprised that she lived the principles of the gospel. At least as far as he could tell. He knew she obeyed the Word of Wisdom, and as far as he knew, she obeyed the law of chastity. She certainly dressed modestly and behaved appropriately around him. She was scrupulously honest and hard-working and had mentioned that she'd gone to church although he'd always been in Charlotte taking care of his own callings on Sunday mornings. Even some of the little comments she'd made, like becoming a nurse so she could still have a family even if she had to work, all fell into place.

He began to smile. All these weeks of the two of them hinting around about the church but never coming right out and saying it. She noticed his smile and asked, "What?"

"Do you ever wonder?"

"About what?"

"The one right church."

"No. I'm like you. I asked too. Why were you smiling?"

"Just happy I guess." He paused and then continued. "Have you ever been to Ireland? I'm assuming you have Irish ancestry with that hair."

"No, I've never been, and yes, I'm Irish. Why? Where did that come from?"

He shrugged. "Just wondered. I've been to Ireland. When I was nineteen I went for two years." He looked up at her and smiled. "It was a good experience for me."

He was watching her trying to figure out what he was saying, and it was all he could do not to laugh when her green eyes got huge and her fork stopped in mid air with a bite of food on it, just in front of her open mouth. Finally, she set the fork back down and asked, "What are you telling me, Robby?"

He laughed. "Nothing. Just that Ireland was nice. You should go sometime. You'd like it there." Her forehead wrinkled, and she looked at him hard, confused. "I went on a mission to Ireland, Kelly. We're both members of the Church. Only we didn't realize it until just this minute."

He could still see the wheels turning while she tried to assimilate this. Finally, she asked, "You only just realized?" He nodded. "How did we not figure this out sooner?"

"Uhm, we're both dorks? I don't know."

She sighed and picked up her fork. "It kind of makes me mad. I've worried for weeks about how to share the gospel with you. I've felt guilty as anything. For a while I rationalized that I just needed to be a good example. Then I didn't want to offend you. I hate that. I always waste so dang much energy worrying about stuff. If I'd just asked sooner I could have quit worrying."

She paused and then said almost to herself, "I wish I'd known you were an Elder right at first. I would have given about anything for a blessing." She gazed up at him again. "I was kind of a mess. But then I'm sure you knew that."

"I guess I owe you an apology. I didn't think you were a mess, but I did know you were troubled. I just thought you'd have thought I was crazy if I offered a blessing."

She shook her head. "You don't owe me an apology." She reached across and took his hand. "I'm just so, so grateful you came back and brought me that gas can. Who knows where I would have ended up?"

He squeezed her hand back. "You'd have been just fine, Kelly. If I hadn't been listening, God would have sent someone else who was. He's watching over you. Watching over all of us. As long as we're listening, He'll guide us. And you're a really good listener. You're going to be fine."

She pushed her hair back from her forehead. "I hope so, Robby. I hope and pray so. Sometimes I really miss my mom."

Tears glistened in her eyes and he tried to joke, "Don't cry. As lousy as I feel I'll cry with you and think what the waiter will think. He'll never let us rent any orange juice."

"Stop. I'm laughing and crying at the same time and I feel ridiculous. What kind of movies should we get?"

He pushed his plate back and put a tip on the table. "You choose. I'll probably just sleep through them anyway." He sighed and rubbed the back of his neck. "I gotta kick this thing quick. I have a huge week next week. Hey! You're a nurse! You'll know just what to do."

"Robby, if I honestly knew how to fix the common cold I'd be a peace prize winner. I'm afraid it's just those old standbys. You know. Rented orange juice. Sleeping through movies on rainy days in front of the fire. Just don't do stupid things like falling asleep in the bathtub. It took me until four o'clock this morning to get warm again."

He could actually feel himself blush. "Sorry I walked in on you. When I came in and the house was unlocked, the stereo was on, but no lights were, and you were no where to be found, it scared me. I thought maybe you'd gone on a date, but didn't think you'd leave the house unlocked. Then I saw the bathroom door was shut, but there wasn't a light on. Even when I called and knocked you didn't answer. You didn't even hear me when I was in there calling you."

"I was so tired. That tile floor wiped me out. Did you like it? Did you like the wood in-lay?"

"It's perfect. I can't believe you can do stuff like that when you've never done this before."

"Well, I'm sure I break more tiles than a professional would, but I'm also sure that you're still dollars ahead of what they would charge. I was hoping to get it grouted and sealed today, but I don't think I'm up to it. My nose would drip on it."

"No grouting today." He stood up and helped her to her feet. "We're calling in sick. Let's get some deep, melodramatic movie like Don Knotts and Tim Conway. Something with meaning, that will inspire us." They ended up with *Pillow Talk* and *Lady Hawke*.

When they got home, Robby went into his room to change back into his sweats, but he found more than he'd bargained for. He went in search of Kelly and found her in the living room. "Uhm, Kelly. Could you come here for a minute?"

She looked up at him and must have known something was up. "What's wrong?"

"There's a problem in my closet. Well, either a problem or a miracle. Ted had kittens."

"Seriously?" Her eyes got really big and he nodded. "Good heavens!"

They rushed back to the closet, and he showed her where Ted had indeed given birth on top of a bathrobe that had dropped off the hook above. They both knelt down to look, and Ted stopped licking her four new little felines to gaze up at them placidly. Kelly smiled up at him. "They're teeny. Look, she had four different flavors. How did she even get in here?"

"I have no idea. What do we do now?"

"I haven't a clue. I've never had kittens before. Have you?"

"No, but then I'm a human. It's impossible for humans to have kittens. I'm also male. That complicates things."

"You're forgetting that Ted was male, too. Should we leave them or move them out of your closet?"

"I think the damage is already done, and that robe will wash. She's probably pretty tired. Let her stay for now. We'd better put the cat box in here though. I'd hate to have to throw her new family out when it's raining."

She stood up and patted him on the shoulder. "You are far too much of a softy to throw kittens out in the rain. Don't even try to convince me otherwise. I'm getting to know you too well to even believe it."

Getting up to follow her, he admitted, "You're right." Absently, he added, "I hope they get cuter. They look like skinny little rats right now. I thought kittens were supposed to be cute little balls of fur that chase yarn."

"Give 'em a minute or two, would ya? They're like two hours old. Here's the cat box. I guess I should buy cat food too, next time. I kept thinking he would go home to wherever he came from."

"I think he's a she, Kelly. "

She swatted at him as she went by. "You know what I mean. Where did you put those cold pills?"

"In the fridge beside the rented orange juice." She laughed and shook her head and he asked, "What? Are you laughing at the rented orange juice or the cold cold pills?"

"Does it matter? Either way you're a lunatic. The lovely avocado fridge in the hallway is just the topper."

He gave her a tired smile. "It could be worse. I could be completely normal and totally boring."

"That's a great point, Robby. Will the food police come if we have popcorn with our rented orange juice and cold cold pills?"

"I'm not sure. Let's chance it and spend the day living on the edge." He smiled at her. "If the food police come, we'll put donuts into the mix and be sick."

"We're already sick."

He gave her a dramatic sigh. "Quit being so analytical. It makes my nose run."

"Your nose was already running, too."

"See what I mean? Should we watch *Pillow Talk* or *Lady Hawke* first?"

"If I answer that, are you going to accuse me of being analytical?"

"Of course not. I would never use a word like analytical when I'm this sick."

"*Pillow Talk.*"

He sighed dramatically again. "I was afraid you were going to say that."

She turned to look at him. "You were the one who chose it at the video store."

"I know, but I'm so tired, I'll probably sleep through it."

"If you fall asleep, I'll turn it off. Will that work?"

He sat on the couch and put his feet up on the coffee table. "That will work. Do we have any other blankets than the ones on our beds?"

"No. I'll bring yours in to you. Do you want pillows too?"

"Yes, please. And some socks. Would you mind? They're in the top drawer."

She brought them in to him and when he went to take them, she said, "Put a foot up here. Now the other one. Better?"

"Much. Thanks. You're a saint. Do you want me to help

you with your socks now?"

She laughed and admitted, "I haven't taken mine off since getting out of the shower last night. Fevers always make me cold, but thanks anyway."

He leaned sideways onto his pillow and pointed the remote at the TV. "Then I owe you one." He sighed and closed his eyes, and she smiled. It looked like she would be watching *Lady Hawke*.

That night when she went to tell him good night, she asked, "Robby, since we both know we're members of the church now, and since you're the only family I've got here in North Carolina, do you think we could have family prayer when you're out here? I've really missed it."

"Sure, Kelly. Anytime. My family is all back in Missouri, so it'll be nice for me, too. Do you want to pray right now before you go to your house?"

"Would you mind?"

"Not at all."

Chapter 11

They both survived their colds. The kitchen floor finally did get grouted and sealed, and the appliances were delivered and hooked up. The delivery truck drivers offered to remove the old ones, and Kelly was almost sad to see the lovely avocado fridge go after how many times they'd joked about it. When Kelly wondered what the next project should be, Robby encouraged her to start framing in her new bathroom and a closet in her summer kitchen. He even came in and started to help her frame them, but he smashed his thumb horribly the very first time, and she had to help him drill the blood blister out before sending him off to a meeeting.

The day before the huge week started that he'd been concerned about, he showed up with a dresser, a nightstand, and two rustic chairs that almost exactly matched her bed and table. That night when he went to leave, he told her goodbye, and then warned her that he didn't know exactly what his schedule would be like. "Things are going to be much busier for me for a while now, but try to call me if you need something. I may not be able to take your calls right that minute, but I'll check my phone when I can and get back to you. I'll come here when I can, but I'll be working long days sometimes."

She put an arm around his waist and squeezed. "I'll be fine, Robby. We'll be fine. Do what you need to do and don't worry. Good luck with your acquisitions."

"Thanks. Come pray with me, and I've got to go."

He didn't show up for four days and then, when he did, he came late at night and was gone again by six o'clock the next morning, and he seemed completely thrashed. Finally, on Sunday, when she got home from church at noon, he was there crashed on the couch in the sun, and she came in and gazed at him in concern. He appeared positively haggard. She went into the kitchen to see about dinner. She decided to make a meatloaf she could just keep warm until he was ready to eat.

When she was through cooking, she brought her Book of Mormon in and sat on the floor beside him and read. After awhile, when she became drowsy, she leaned her head back and closed her eyes. It was nice to just sit here beside him sleeping. She had missed him ridiculously this week. She almost wondered if he was okay. Whatever he was doing was really taking it out of him.

Tired as he was, he could smell her shampoo. He rolled over and opened his eyes to find her sitting there on the floor beside the couch with her Book of Mormon open next to her. She'd turned on her side and her arm was lying there on the couch beside him, and he wondered again about the cut that was now a pink scar on her forearm. There was something about that mark that really bothered him. He wondered if that was how she had left the blood in her car when she had run away. One of these days, he was just going to come right out and ask her what had happened.

He wished she would level with him about what had occurred back then to scare her so badly. He put one finger out and gently touched the scar and then pulled back and sat up. He was getting far too attached to her.

Before, he'd been telling himself he should stay away from her emotionally because she wasn't a member, and now that he knew she was, he almost wished he didn't know. That knowledge had cleared a path through his brain that made him feel like he could go ahead and fall for her if he wanted. The twenty-eight-year-old man in him who was so ready to settle down was stoked about that. He could see himself with her for the rest of forever in a heart beat. But the logical side of him kept repeating things in his head that encouraged him to be cautious and think this thing through.

In the first place, she'd come right out and told him just what she thought of football players. And granted the fact that he would only be able to play for a handful more years at the outside, football was his passion and he loved what he did, when it came right down to it. It was incredible to be one of the best in the world and know that you could dominate your competition at the highest levels.

Yeah, he got beat up sometimes. A lot. But he was gifted and he reveled in that. There was nothing better than the feeling when he caught a big pass. The rush was indescribable. But she was going to be thoroughly ticked when she realized he was an extremely famous football player. She'd be ticked and then, probably, want to get far away from him.

Not only was the football a problem, but she was from the Midwest and there was every likelihood that one day she would pick up and leave here just like she had picked up to come here. Especially, if whatever had caused her to run like she had in the first place was able to follow her here. And the final straw was that her trying to disappear didn't exactly dovetail with his fame.

The most troubling part of all was that the very thing that made him so comfortable around her was what ultimately would probably take her away from him. She was one of the few women around him who didn't make it clear she was offering, almost like some lovesick hound dog.

While it was absolutely refreshing, what it really meant was that she wasn't desperately attracted to him like the others were. She was friendly and neighborly, and even solicitous to him sometimes, but she had never truly flirted with him in the close to three months she had been here. Sometimes he wondered if she saw him as a big brother or something, and, frankly, it was a little deflating. Jason had been right. She definitely helped him to keep his perspective.

He ran a hand through his hair and had to admit it served him right. After years of not being interested in girls who were definitely interested in him, it was only fair to fall for one who wasn't. He sighed and touched a strand of her silky, red-brown hair.

No it wasn't fair. He'd been doing his best all these years to be wise and moral and honorable, sometimes in the face of big challenges. He'd stayed true to his values for long enough that there was a rather prevalent rumor that he was actually gay. He didn't much care about it, except for the fact that it reflected on the Church because he was a high profile member. He'd always kept the faith that eventually, when he finally found her, the obvious fallacy of the rumor would be dispelled. But the fact was, all these years, he'd been faithful.

That was good, but he was so ready to be done being single and settle down. Much as he adored Shania Raime, sometimes she made him sad too. He'd love to have one of her of his own. One with red-brown hair would be perfect.

He sighed again and dropped the lock of hair. He'd better get up and think about something else. He was a big part of the leadership of the team, and it was imperative that he be up-beat and passionate to get the season started off with some momentum. Showing the proper game face to the younger players was vital. He was great at this game and needed to teach the rookies coming up behind him. He needed a change of attitude right now.

He knew how to change his attitude. He started right in counting his blessings mentally and within just a minute or two he'd come full circle. Maybe Kelly wasn't madly in love with him, but she'd been a tremendous blessing to him and was a ton of fun. While she was here with him, he was going to enjoy every minute of her.

He picked up the lock of hair again and twirled it around his finger. Her hair was still amazing to him. She was fun and beautiful. Not to mention all the other characteristics he'd come to respect about her in the last three months. He was so glad he'd listened that day early last May. It would have been awful if God had had to send someone else and he'd missed her.

He rolled back over onto his back and closed his eyes again. And she was a great cook. Something smelled wonderful. Other than her shampoo.

Kelly woke up and went to move her head to ease the kink in her neck, but her hair was caught on something. She turned to see if she could untangle it and realized it was Robby's hand it was caught in. He'd wrapped a strand of it around a finger in his sleep. She reached back and tried to unwrap it with one hand without waking him up, but he opened his tired blue eyes and glanced over at her and she said, "Robby, my hair's caught on something. Could you help me? I can't reach it to untangle it. I'm sorry I woke you."

He was still half asleep as he unwound the tress and pushed it back over her shoulder, and she wondered how it had gotten wrapped around his finger in the first place. She leaned forward and stretched her neck as he rolled over and closed his eyes again. Her stomach was growling fiercely. Maybe she should go ahead and eat without him. Closing her Book of Mormon, she stood up and turned to gaze back down at him. Even thrashed, he looked good enough for dessert.

Just as she thought that, he opened those baby blues and gazed up at her. "What?" For a second she worried that he'd been able to read her mind.

She shook her head. "I didn't say anything. It was my stomach. How soon do you think you'd want to eat?"

"An hour ago. I just wanted to sleep even more than I wanted to eat. It smells like heaven. What did you make?" He sat up and ran a hand through his rumpled hair.

"Meat loaf, mashed potatoes and gravy, and asparagus with hollandaise. Chocolate mousse for dessert. Anything sound good?"

"All of it. I was late for meetings this morning and didn't eat. Then came straight here and had a bowl of cereal, but it's long gone. Head for the kitchen, I'm right behind you."

When they were seated and had prayed, she asked, "So how did your grueling week go? Are you as hammered as you look?"

He laughed. "That wasn't very nice, Kelly. No, I'm not hammered. Just tired. It takes a while to get back into the long day, high energy mode. How was your week? How is the new bathroom coming along?"

"Fine. Framing is heavier, more demanding work physically than the other stuff. I wish I was that big girl who loves to dive you were talking about that day. But the studs are in. Now I'm working on the electrical."

"Let me guess. You bought a book."

"Of course. It's a great book."

"You're not going to electrocute yourself while I'm thirty five minutes away are you?"

"No. At least I'm going to try not to."

"Good, because I would miss you."

Hartvigson. Again. Great. Peter Holmes motioned him inside his office and then closed the door behind him. "What?"

The big officer just chuckled at Peter's obvious distaste. "Why don't you ever act happy to see me, Doc? You'd think we weren't even friends, by the way you act."

Trying to hide his irritation, Peter said, "Look, I have a full schedule today. What did you need?"

"Just to tell you that the family of one of your patients who recently died has asked the department to check into it. I've already investigated and closed the case, but I wanted you to know. For our future business dealings. Information like that comes in handy." He smiled and turned to the door and said over his shoulder, "Have a good day, Doc. Pleasure doin' business with you." Peter could hear him chuckle again as he walked down the hall.

Chapter 12

She didn't electrocute herself, but she did slice the heck out of her hand the next evening when she was running the Romex into the boxes she'd attached to the studs for the outlets. The utility knife she'd been using slipped, and she cut deeply into the thick muscle at the base of her thumb on her left hand. She gasped and quickly closed her right hand over it to try to catch the blood that began to pour from it.

She grabbed a pair of socks from the top of the laundry basket sitting nearby to use to absorb the blood and apply pressure. *Oh, marvy, Kelly. You've really done it this time.* She went over to stand over the sink in the corner while she tried to stop the bleeding. This one was going to take stitches. A lot of stitches.

Staunching the flow of blood was a bit of a bigger job than she'd at first assumed, and she ended up standing over her sink for close to half an hour, soaking several pairs of white socks in the process. She didn't think the sight of blood bothered her, but for some reason, as she stood there, she began to feel woozy and light headed.

When the dripping finally stopped, she went in search of her leathers and helmet and motorcycle key. Putting the pants on over her long cut off jean shorts one-handed was hopeless and she gave up and struggled to get the jacket on and strap on the helmet, wishing the whole time that she'd had the foresight to stock up on first aid supplies in the new kitchen.

Sitting on the bike, she rolled her neck to try to wake up a little, grasped the right handle bar firmly and then rested the closed fist of her left hand on the other one, and pushed the ignition switch. She'd only gone a quarter of a mile, fighting to maintain control in the gravel when she gave that up as too foolish to keep up, parked the bike beside the road and walked home. She opted to leave it there rather than risk a cut hand *and* a wreck.

At home, she tried for a cab service in Tolke but there wasn't one. She debated about whether to call an ambulance or just take a cab from Charlotte. Deciding the latter would be less conspicuous, she went that route, but then realized when the office wanted to know her address that she had absolutely no idea what her address was. She tried to describe how to get there, but the dispatcher was having none of it. Finally, she asked them to hang on while she called Robby on the cell to find out the address.

Wondering if he'd even be where he could take the call, she was pleasantly surprised when he picked right up and she asked, "Robby, hey, what's my address?"

On the other end of the line he laughed. "4116 South Route 32, Tolke, North Carolina 47314, why?"

"I'm just calling a cab. I accidentally cut my hand and need some stitches. The bike is too hard to control. They're on the other line. Gotta go, thank you."

"Whoa, say that again. You're calling a cab to Tolke to go get stitches. What?"

"Robby, they're on the other line, I need to hurry. I cut my hand and can't handle my motorcycle. I'm just calling a cab. How are the acquisitions going today?"

"Acquisitions are great, Kelly. Tell the cab never mind. I'll be there as fast as I can to pick you up. Are you okay?"

"I'm fine, but don't come. You're too busy. Thanks anyway. The cab will be fine. I'll call you when I'm done. Gotta go."

"Kelly, I'm on dinner right now. I'm walking out the door as we speak. I'll be right there."

The line went dead and she took a deep breath, closed her eyes for just a moment and sighed, then went back to the other phone. "I'm so sorry to keep you waiting. You know, my friend is actually going to come and get me. Thank you so much anyway."

Hanging up, she flipped open the book and wondered where to have him take her when he got here. There was one small medical clinic in Tolke. She started to dial the number and then stopped and glanced down at her hand and groaned silently. This was going to take more than a local PA, and she knew it. Honestly it probably had to have a plastic surgeon. She sighed and opened the Charlotte book to search for a hospital.

She was waiting on the porch when he pulled up, with a dishtowel and a wash cloth wrapped around her hand. She climbed in and he looked at her hard, then pulled right back out. As they passed her motorcycle, he turned to her and asked, "How bad is it, Kelly? Are you okay?"

She opened her eyes and nodded tiredly. "I'm fine. A bit light-headed just now, but fine. But it's bad. My utility knife slipped when I was working on a wire. It's going to take some work."

At the stoplight in Tolke, he turned to her and when she showed him, he winced. "Good Crimonies! I'll say it's going to take some work. Did you take anything for pain?"

"A couple Tylenol. Every thing else thins the blood. I'll be fine. But I think I'd better go into the hospital in Charlotte instead of just a clinic here. Do you have that much time?"

"I have to go back to Charlotte anyway. I have a friend near my work, one of the team doctors for the Carolina Panthers. Let me take you to him and see if he has time to do this."

She leaned back against the seat and closed her eyes again against the pain that had begun to throb. "Thanks for coming to save me, Robby."

Robby glanced over at her as she sat with her eyes closed, almost sick at the horrible slice through her beautiful hand. He wished he wasn't so crushed for time right now. He did have an hour and a half dinner break, but they had evening meetings tonight broken out into teams, and he really needed to be there. Other than Jason, he was easily the leader of the whole offense. Even Jason looked to him for that fire in the belly when he needed it.

He pulled out his cell phone and dialed up medical support. "Hey, Jake. Can I talk to Doc Snyder? Thanks. Doc. It's Robideaux. I have a situation. Have you got a minute if I show up with a friend of mine who needs stitches? I need to hurry; I have critical meetings again in like twenty minutes."

"Sure, Rock. Whatever. You know where I am."

"Be right there." He looked back over at how pale she was and shook his head. This was one of the most vital meetings of the year, but he seriously considered blowing it off anyway.

Her hand was beginning to hurt enough that Kelly was a little out of it as he drove fast through the city, then pulled around to the back of the stadium. He drove right up almost under the edge of the building near the stands and hustled around to open her door and get her out.

With an arm around her waist and walking fast, he led her through a couple of short hallways and then into a clinic of sorts where a doctor in a white coat met them. It was an open area with several beds. On one of them there was a shirtless young man with a huge chest and shoulders in the bottom half of a football uniform. He was reclining with a cleat off and his foot iced and elevated. Another bed held a second player in a uniform. He was sitting up, but didn't look like he felt all that great.

Kelly knew just how he felt and was grateful to Robby for gently helping her up onto the high bed. A doctor came to them and, when Kelly pulled the towel away to reveal her hand, the doctor made a sound in his throat and looked up at Robby, shaking his head. "Robideaux, you need a plastic surgeon. This isn't something I can just stitch up. There are layers of muscle that have to be repaired here. I'm sorry. She's going to have to be taken in to St. Luke's Regional. I'll call over there and make sure they have a plastic waiting."

Appearing incredibly frustrated, Robby ran a hand through his hair and then dropped it to her shoulder and gazed at her. "Kelly, I know this is going to sound horribly cold-blooded, but I have to at least show up at this meeting. Can you wait here for awhile? Doctor Snyder will watch over you for me, and I'll hurry, but it might take some time. Could you stand to wait?"

She looked from Robby to the doctor and back and then shook her head. "Robby, I'll be fine by myself. I'm a nurse, remember. Just let me borrow a phone book so I can call a cab."

He considered that and then said, "No. If you can't wait, I'll just bail on the meeting." He glanced at his watch. "Come on, we'll go right now."

She put a hand to his chest, feeling horribly guilty. "NO! No, Robby. You don't blow things off. You would never miss a meeting you've committed to. I'm not going to be the one to change that. You're a man of your word. I'll wait. Go. Please."

He searched her eyes and then put an arm around her and pulled her to him in a careful hug and whispered, "I'll hurry." He turned back to the doctor. "Can you give her something for the pain? She's tough, but it's obviously hurting her. And take care of her for me, Snyd. I'll be back as soon as I can." He gave her shoulder another squeeze and turned and hustled out the door.

A second later, he reappeared and turned to the shirtless player and said brusquely, "Leave her alone." With that, he walked back out, and Kelly turned to look at the football player he'd spoken to. *What had that been about?* The player simply grinned at her, and she glanced away. He reminded her of those obnoxious players in college.

Kelly looked at the doorway Robby had just gone through and then glanced at the two football players again, before turning back to the doctor as he asked, "Do you want something for the pain?"

She sighed. "Something as in what? I've taken Tylenol."

"Do you need something stronger? Codeine?"

Shaking her head, she said tiredly, "No, no Codeine. I'll be fine. Will I be in the way here?"

The physician smiled. "No, young lady. As much clout as Robby has here, you could move in. Make yourself at home. Would you like something to drink?"

"No, thank you. Would it be okay if I just sat in a chair? And maybe got some ice. Ice might help."

"Take any chair you'd like and I'll bring ice." As he left the room he turned to the same player and repeated gruffly, "Leave her alone."

Without even a glance at the grinning player, she carefully slid off the high bed and walked to a nearby chair and sat down in it slowly. For some reason she was incredibly light headed.   She so wished she'd been more careful with that darned utility knife.

She leaned her head back and tried to pull her hair back out of the way, but it was difficult one handed. The cut was throbbing with a pound now, and she propped her elbow on the arm rest and lifted the hand straight up to elevate it. She hated to even think about how long this was going to take to heal.

Both players across the room were staring at her, and she would have been embarrassed if she hadn't felt so lousy right now. She was glad that at least her jean shorts were modest and clean, except for the blood that had dripped down her clothes. She closed her eyes and tried to concentrate on something other than how much her hand was hurting.

Seeing Robby in action here in the city had been interesting. He was much more dynamic and in control here than he was out at the house. There he'd been relatively laid back. And even though sometimes he arrived at the house in his business clothes, she'd almost forgotten how good he looked dressed for success.

The people here looked up to him. That was completely obvious. It was incredibly nice to know that people he worked around had a great deal of respect for him. She shouldn't be here making him have to choose between helping her and fulfilling his responsibilities.

She paused for a moment and searched her fuzzy brain to try and figure out why the doctor had said that Robby had clout here. He'd never mentioned anything about working around the Carolina Panther medical offices before. Maybe his company contracted out to the team or something. That must be it. At any rate, Dr. Snyder hadn't seemed unduly surprised that Robby had brought her here.

Dr. Snyder came back in with the ice and studied her for a moment. "You're sure you don't want anything for the pain?"

Kelly gave him a tremulous smile. "No, I'm not sure. Let me keep trying to stick it out. If it keeps getting worse, maybe I'll change my mind. The ice will help." Laying her arm up on the bed next to her, she discarded the bloody wash cloth, opened out the thin cotton dish towel so only one layer covered her skin, and then balanced the bag of ice gently on top. At first it was too heavy. She sucked in her breath and tried to flatten it out, so the weight rested away from the cut on her thumb.

She hadn't realized she had made a sound until she glanced up and saw both players watching her intently. Wiping the moisture off of her forehead and upper lip, she glanced away again. Codeine made her loopy and sick to her stomach, but maybe she should take some. She laid her forehead down on the bed beside her arm and decided she felt incredibly whiney just now. If her mother had been around, she'd have climbed right onto her lap in the big rocker and let her hold her even though she was twenty-three years old. This might turn out to be a long night.

Her knee began to tremble from the pain, and she hurried to lean up and cross her legs so she could force them to hold still. Glancing up at Dr. Snyder, he gave her a concerned look, then left the room for a second and came back with a small paper cup that held a white pill, and some juice and crackers. "Take at least one. There's no point in being stoic about it. If you're a nurse, then you know it's going to get worse at the hospital before it gets better."

She nodded. "Thank you." She tossed the pill back and washed it down and then munched two of the crackers before putting her forehead back down against the bed. The ice should be deadening it somewhat, shouldn't it? Her leg started to tremble again and she had to stand right up to get it to stop. She expelled her breath out through her lips and lifted the arm to elevate it and turned to walk back up the nearby hall for a minute. She hadn't eaten since lunch. Hopefully the medicine would kick in quickly and she could relax a little better.

Walking did help. She wasn't sure she was walking in a straight line, as dizzy as she was, but it helped. She slowly walked up and down the short hall for several minutes, waiting patiently for the relief she knew would come if she could manage not to throw the medicine back up. Codeine truly made her sick.

Finally, feeling greener and greener, she looked around for a restroom just in case she lost it in spite of her will not to, then sat back down in the chair. She'd die of embarrassment if she threw up all over the Carolina Panthers' medical office.

She tried to pull her long hair away from her face with her right hand, held it in place and put her forehead back down on the bed again. This time she pulled the ice bag over toward her so it was touching her brow. As she finally felt that first wave of airiness from the medicine hit her, she sighed with relief.

She was going to make it through this. Her hand would stop its incessant throbbing soon, and Robby would come back and save her. He always saved her. He'd become an absolute knight in shining armor to her. It wouldn't be long now. Modern medical chemicals were a wonderful thing.

She was still leaning on the bed like that when she felt a gentle hand on her back, and Robby spoke to her softly, "Kelly, are you okay?"

Turning toward him, she gave him a half hearted smile. "I'm fine, Rob. Are you through or do you have to go back?"

"I'm through. I'm so sorry that took so long." He crouched down close to her and tenderly brushed her hair back from her face. "You don't look so good, Kel. You're not gonna keel over on me when you stand up are you? You're really pale."

She shook her head and tried to pull her hair back one handed. "No, I'm just a little woozy. I finally gave in and took some codeine." She tried to smile. "I should warn you that I get stupid on codeine. It makes me feel ridiculously blonde."

He lifted her gently to her feet and pulled her hair back for her. "Sixty percent of the women in the country would be offended at that comment." He slipped an arm around her shoulders and pulled her to lean against him. "Come on. Let's go get you put back together."

She sighed as they left the building. "This might not be all that much fun."

"No. Probably not, but I'll hold your other hand and we'll make it through. You're the strongest lady I've ever known."

"I should have just hired an electrician."

He shook his head as they walked. "No, Kelly. You can't set aside your passions to live safely. It's worth going through the stuff, even big stuff like this, to live large. The ones who play it safe miss out on all the most vital parts of this life."

She let him help her into the car. "You're truly wise. Either that or me taking codeine makes you extra not blonde."

"Extra not blonde?" He laughed as he pulled out with a squeal. "How many pain pills did you take?"

"Just one, but I should also warn you that they make me really sick to my stomach."

He slowed down. "Sorry, I'm feeling guilty for making you wait for me."

"Don't feel guilty. I love that you're a man of your word. I'm just grateful that you came and saved me, Robby. When we get there, could I get a blessing? And then you need to drop me and go back to your house so you can rest. Don't you have another big day tomorrow?"

"I'll give you a blessing, but I'm not going to just leave you. Don't be a dork."

She gazed over at him and smiled slowly. "I can't even believe you just called me a dork." She shook her head. "That is so not a you word."

"It's not a you word either, so don't be one. I couldn't just dump you off at the hospital."

"Robby, I'm a nurse. I've spent a million hours in a hospital. I'll be fine."

He shook his head. "I'm not going to argue about this, Kelly. You're not up to it."

They drove the rest of the way to the hospital in silence. When they got there, Robby leaned across the SUV, placed his hands on her head, and gave her a short, softly spoken blessing. Then, he helped her out so gently that she looked up at him, confused. She'd thought he was mad at her, but he wasn't acting mad at all. He returned her look and then when she tripped over nothing in the parking lot, he put a strong arm around her again to help her inside.

Kelly was amazed when as soon as they got inside the door they were taken to a cubicle immediately, even though there was a waiting room full. She glanced up at him in surprise and he shrugged and said, "Doc Snyder probably made the arrangements. Hopefully the plastic surgeon is waiting here somewhere."

She was indeed even more grateful that she'd accepted the Codeine when the surgeon began to inject her hand with anesthetic. In spite of the narcotic, the pain was excruciating and when she gasped, Robby stood closer to her and gripped her good hand in his large one. He pulled her against his chest with the other arm. "Try not watching. Sometimes, that works for me. If I don't look and try to think of something else, it's not so bad."

Through gritted teeth, she asked, "Do you do this often?"

He shrugged. "Uh, occasionally."

Within just seconds her hand began to numb. She tried to relax and took a deep breath and said, "Remind me to donate to the research of anesthetics when I become independently wealthy, would you? They are definitely divinely inspired." She leaned into his chest and sighed in relief. Now that the hand wasn't screaming in pain, the Codeine made her so comfortably mellow. She closed her eyes and breathed his smell in and enjoyed being hugged close to him after just having felt so miserable. "Thanks for rescuing me again, Robby."

She could hear the smile in his voice even without opening her eyes. "Anytime, Kelly. I'm sorry you got hurt. This may call for more rented orange juice and cold cold pills. Or cold pain pills. It's too bad we don't have the lovely fridge in the hall still. But we could rent more no brainer movies."

Still leaning against his chest, she laughed softly. "You're a dork."

When the surgeon was finally done with her, and her hand was bandaged to the point it would be hopelessly useless for days, Robby led her back out and helped her into the Rover. She hadn't even considered he would take her anywhere but home, and she was surprised when he pulled into the parking garage of a several story building just a few minutes later. There was actually a live security guard at the gate, and Kelly looked over at Robby, but was too thrashed to even ask what was going on. She supposed he needed to run an errand before dropping her back home. She closed her eyes and was almost asleep by the time he opened her door and gently helped her out of the Rover.

He took her arm and she went with him mutely, wishing

she could have stayed in the car sleeping while he did this. When he unlocked a door and stepped into a dark and silent home, she finally understood that this was his condo here in Charlotte. He tossed his keys on a table and led her through into a hallway. At the door to a bedroom, she paused as he went in and stepped into a walk-in closet, and came back out with a humongous T-shirt.

When she looked at him, wondering what was going on, he said, "I hate to do this to you, Kelly, but under the circumstances I don't have a lot of options. It's almost two o'clock in the morning and I have to be back in meetings at six thirty again. I don't want you to be out there alone hurt, anyway. Can you stay here in my guest room tonight until I can make arrangements for someone to go stay with you in the morning?"

She had no idea what to say and just nodded her head. "Sure, Robby. Whatever. I don't need someone to go stay with me. I'll be fine. It's just a cut."

"You heard the doctor say you'd cut the nerves and they were going to be horribly painful for a few days. He thinks you're going to have to take more pain medicine than you took tonight, and you were already a bit blonde, remember? Someone should be with you." He changed the subject, before she could object. "I'm going to have something to eat right fast. Do you want something?"

She shook her head. "No, thank you. Which door is mine?"

He walked further up the hall and reached in and turned on the light. "Right here. Wake me if you need something." He turned and gave her a sad smile. "I'm sorry about your hand. Good night."

"G'night, Robby."

She stepped inside the room, too tired to even worry about staying at his house with him for the night. She just hoped that none of his neighbors assumed they were sleeping together. She struggled to get out of her things one handed and then put on the T-shirt and prayed and gratefully slipped into the bed.

She thought again about the early pioneers of this country. What would they have given for the blessings she had enjoyed tonight? The clean, innovative hospital with the mercifully pain killing drugs. The talented surgeon, and now a clean, heavenly soft bed where she was safe and watched over. One more time she thanked her Heavenly Father for sending Robby to rescue her again.

In the middle of the night she woke up in unbelievable pain and went in search of the bottle of pain pills they'd given her last night. She found them on the table in his entry and glubbed two down with a glass of milk, then paced the hallway, silently, until they took effect enough for her to be able to go back to bed at four-fifty in the morning. The doctor had warned them about how painful this would be, but she hadn't truly thought it would be like this.

The next time she woke up, the house was dark and silent. She glanced at her watch, wondering why it wasn't morning when it felt like such a long time since she'd gotten up in the night. She reached up and turned on the light beside the bed and was surprised to see it was almost noon. Unless she'd slept through the entire day and it was almost midnight. She struggled to a sitting position and went to the window and pushed back a corner of the blind. Outside it was bright daylight, and she sighed in relief that she wasn't completely turned around in her head.

She went to put her clothes back on, but then paused when she remembered how bloody they were. She gazed down at herself in the huge T-shirt, wondering if she would be modest enough in it if Robby showed up here, while she was laundering her things in his washer and dryer. It came almost to her knees and she decided it was fine. She carefully bent to pick up her clothes and go in search of his laundry room. Putting her clothes in to wash, she headed once more for the pain medicine, and helped herself to more milk and some toast, before going back to bed while her things washed.

When she'd laid down, she hadn't meant to go back to sleep, but she was pretty much out of it when a knock woke her, and Robby poked his head in the door. She turned over and tried to peer up at him, but her head was fuzzy from the pain medication, and it took her a minute before she could focus. "Hey, Robby. Sorry, I'm still here. How is your day going?"

"Good. How are you feeling?"

"Mmm." She groaned. "A little zoned. The pain medicine is toasting me."

"I put your things in the dryer. Do you want some lunch with me?"

"Yes, what time is it?"

"Twelve thirty."

"Have you got a robe I can borrow?"

"Sure. " He disappeared, and came back and tossed the robe onto the bed. "I'll be in the kitchen."

She dragged herself up, put on the robe and rolled up the one sleeve several inches, then gazed in the mirror at her hair and wondered what she would brush it with, even if she felt up to trying. She shook her head and went to find him. In the kitchen, she felt stupid because he looked like he'd just showered and dressed and she was a complete wreck, but there was nothing for it. She walked up to him and extended her right arm. "Do you think you could help me roll this thing up some?"

"Sure." He stepped back and looked her up and down with a huge grin. "If I didn't know what you'd been through last night, I'd swear that you partied too hard. That is some wild hair you've got going!"

She tried to push her hair back and then gave him a tired smile. "It could be worse. I could be covered in blood still. What are you eating? It smells divine."

"Chinese take-out." He reached into a cupboard and handed her a plate. "I figured you could eat it whenever you came out from under the codeine. You were seriously gone when I left at six."

"I'd taken two pills at four-thirty. The doctor was right. The pain is over the top. I'm being a complete noodle."

"Oh, good. You'll go perfect with the Chinese food then. How's the pain right now?"

"Fine. I took more medicine not quite an hour ago. Just don't ask me any tricky questions or make me sign anything. It would never hold up in court."

He raised both hands defensively and then reached to help serve her out of the little cartons. "Which ones do you want?"

"Is any of it the really spicy stuff?"

"Nope."

"Then a little of everything. What's the least conspicuous way to leave your building?"

"In my Land Rover tonight, when I come get you."

They took their plates to the table and she prayed and then said, "No. You missed your dinner last night because of me. We're not doing that again."

"What are you going to do? Walk?"

"Even North Carolina has a cab, Robby. Or maybe one of the guys in my ward would come get me."

He finished a bite, and then offered, "I'll make you a deal. I'll get fast food and eat it as I drive."

"Is this week as grueling as last week was?"

He considered that for a minute. "Yes."

"Then, no."

"What do you mean?"

She twirled a lo mein noodle around her fork and looked at him. "You were hammered last week even without skipping meals and running injured employees around. You don't have time to take me home. Relax instead. I'll call one of the guys."

"How about if I have one of my guys take you? After all, it was my place you were working on when you were hurt."

"Let me think about it. You have a very nice place here, by the way. It's exactly opposite of the house. Why did you do that?"

"I told you I wanted a change."

She gazed all around. "You definitely got a change. How is your company affiliated with the Carolina Panthers? Are you contracted with them?"

He stared at her hard for a minute. "Yes, why?"

"Was that a bad question? Why did you look at me like that?"

He hesitated. "It wasn't a bad question. I'm just wondering what you're thinking. Were you uncomfortable there last night with those players?"

She shook her head. "Honestly, I hurt too bad to even care about them. Why did you tell the one to leave me alone?

The doctor did the same thing when he left the room."

Robby made a sound of disgust. "Bocklin. He can be an idiot around women. He's the classic stupid, piece of meat, macho Neanderthal you knew in college. I just didn't want him to hassle you."

"He didn't hassle me. I was just in pain. In pain, and tired, and hungry. I was being such a whiner. Sorry. I hope I didn't embarrass you in front of anyone."

"You didn't embarrass me. Quite the contrary. There's a rumor raging around the place about my mysterious, auburn haired beauty. I think I've earned a whole new level of respect around there."

She laughed softly and shook her head in disbelief. "You are so full of bologna, but I'll let you butter me up anyway, to counteract the fact that I have no hairbrush or toothbrush."

He finished his plate and stood up and took it to the sink. "I'll have whoever I ask to take you home, bring one of each when they come. What time do you think you want to go?"

"I don't care. I don't want to be any more inconvenience, so whenever someone can come. I'm just going to rest and try to sleep off the pain and medicine whether I'm here or there. It's not like I can do much for right now, anyway."

He squeezed her shoulder and headed for the door. "Until they get here, make yourself at home. See ya."

As the lock clicked behind him, she finished the last of her Chinese and took her plate to the sink in the kitchen, rinsed it, and straightened up. She got her things out of the dryer and for a few minutes she wandered around the condo looking at it, then yawned and decided to go lie down again. The medicine wiped her out. She was so sleepy.

Once that afternoon, she woke up needing more medicine and ate more take-out with it. Then she read the Book of Mormon for a few minutes until she drifted off again, hoping she'd hear the door when her ride came.

She actually slept straight through until she heard a key in the lock of the door and pulled herself out of sleep to get ready to go. As she moved, she realized she'd gone too long without a pill. The pain was out of control again. She got up and struggled into his robe to go greet her ride and tell them she'd be right there, but she was surprised when it was Robby she met in the hallway.

Glancing at her watch, she realized it was almost nine o'clock at night. She ran an embarrassed hand through her wild hair and groaned. He must think she was a complete slob. When she looked up at him, she decided he seemed nearly as hammered as she did, and she asked, "What happened to you? Are you okay?"

He chuckled half-heartedly. "Aren't I supposed to be asking you that? Not the other way around? How did you do today?"

"Fine. I've just been sleeping. Are you sick?"

He shook his head tiredly and rubbed the back of his neck. "No. It was just a long day. Do you want to get dressed to go home or just wear my robe?" He smiled at her and handed her a hair brush and a tooth brush.

Something was wrong, and Kelly stared at him hard, wondering what was going on. He was not the crisp, neat, well-dressed business man she had said goodbye to after lunch. She walked up to him and put a hand to his forehead. "What's going on Robby? What happened to you? I saw you less than eight hours ago."

He met her gaze steadily, as if trying to decide how to answer that, and then finally gave her a guilty grin and said, "You're gonna be disgusted at me. I played football with some of the guys at work today and got creamed. But I'm fine, so just lay off, okay? I'm too tired to hear about Neanderthal prejudices. Can we just go home?"

"Sure, whatever. I'll hurry and get dressed. What exactly is the technical definition of got creamed?" *Holy moly! Creamed was a good word. He was all but limping.*

He shrugged as he turned back toward the kitchen. "I got bumped around a little is all. I went into it thinking those guys liked me. Now I'm beginning to wonder. Do you want something to eat here or should we just go?"

"Just enough to take some more medicine. Or should I drive? How creamed are you?"

He laughed and stretched his back and rubbed his thigh. "Pretty creamed, but I'll drive. Get dressed and I'll find you something to eat. Or how about if we stop at this little Greek place just down the block and get souvlakis to eat on the way? Do you like Greek?"

"I like it all unless it's terribly greasy or too spicy. Greek sounds wonderful. I'll be right out." His house line rang as she went back to dress. It had rung probably twenty times today, and she'd ignored it while she was in and out of sleep, but there had been a number of different women's voices leaving messages on his machine. She'd almost wanted to go push the button and see what all these ladies were saying to him.

Three minutes later, when she was dressed and her hair was combed and her teeth brushed, she came back in and heard him grumbling as he was dumping the messages that had been left. He'd play each one for about two and a half seconds before hitting the delete button. Finally, she asked if something was wrong, and he said, "No, I just hate doing this everyday. Are you ready to go?"

She came over and gazed at him and asked, "Then why do you do it?"

"Do what?"

"The message thing?"

"What do you mean? Do you want me to just let them stack up forever?"

She gave him the look and went over and pushed the power button on the machine. "Robby, if you don't want to dump a bunch of messages, turn it off. Is there anyone hyper critical that you need to hear from who doesn't have your cell number?"

"No, but if I don't let the machine pick up, I'll just have to listen to the phone ring a thousand times when I'm here."

She reached down and unplugged the phone out of the wall. "Robby, this is your home. You don't have to let anyone intrude on the phone anymore than you're obligated to let someone in your front door who isn't welcome."

He appeared almost amazed, and she had to laugh. "I think sometimes we forget that they are modern *conveniences*.

My mother was great about that. When Sister Beck gave that conference talk about letting less negative influences into our homes, my mom cheered and threw a pillow at the TV.

"We started just turning the phone off when we didn't want to be bothered. It was an epiphany for me. It had never even occurred to me that I wasn't obligated to take a call if I didn't want to. You'll love it! You'll feel incredibly powerful when you pull that plug! Shall we go?"

He shook his head and laughed. "We shall go. What's wrong with your stomach?"

She glanced down to where he was looking at something poking out of her shirt over her belly button. She covered it with her hand. "Don't see." She waved the all encompassing bandage on her left hand. "I could manage the zipper, but there was no way I could get the button done up and there was also no way I was going to ask you for help. I'll have to find some pants I can manage until this thing is off. We're not going anywhere but home, are we? Will anyone other than you be seeing me?"

"Nope. Just plain, old me. Let's go home."

Chapter 13

The next morning he called her cell phone at just before six when he was getting ready to leave. "Sorry to wake you, Kelly, but I'm just thinking. I brought your motorcycle back, but you can't drive it and you can't do much with your hand. I know you don't like TV all that much and there are only a couple of books and movies. Are you going to go crazy here without something to do?

"Do you want to come into Charlotte with me and you can have my car for the day? You could drive an automatic one handed, couldn't you? You could sight see or shop. I just don't want you to feel stranded and at a loose end."

She was so asleep she hoped she understood what he was asking. "You must know me well. I'm going to be climbing the walls. But today I think I'm still going to be a zombie on pain pills. I wouldn't dare drive. Could I take you up on that when I'm not so sore? Are you going to be coming here any of these next few days?"

"I can come any night. I'll call you tonight and see how you feel. In the mean time, don't do anything too dangerous, okay?"

"I won't. I promise. Thank you for asking. Have a good day."

"You too. See ya." She hung up and laid there thinking about him. *He was such a sweetie.* She wished they could be more than just friends sometimes.

The kitties' eyes had opened while she'd been in at his condo, and they were getting more and more alert and wiggly. They were not only adorable, they were also a lifesaver as far as keeping her entertained while she was indisposed. She felt guilty about hanging out in Robby's room with the kittens, so she moved them into the living room beside the fireplace and then held one of them for hours when she was so sleepy and lethargic.

When Robby called, she opted for one more day there at the house with the pain medicine. As she taped a bag around her hand so she could shower without getting the bandage wet, she was hoping by the next night she could be off the strong stuff completely.

When he showed up late that night, he looked like heck again, and she looked at him hard, but didn't ask. He'd been so ready for her to say something about him playing football that day that she felt guilty. Instead of mentioning that he seemed hammered, she took him in to see the kitties. He was so enamored with them that she watched him instead of them while he played with them. He laid on the floor next to where she'd put them and let them crawl all over his hands and arms.

Within minutes he had fallen asleep there on the hardwood floor with them, and she went and gently woke him. "Come on, Robby. They are adorable, but you have another huge day tomorrow. You need to sleep where you can rest. Go in and go to bed."

He yawned, and sighed, and got up to go. "Thanks, Kelly. I would have been stiff and cold. They are really, really cute now, aren't they? See you in the morning. I need to leave at ten to six."

Waking up the next morning, her hand was still ridiculously tender, but she wanted to go into Charlotte with him anyway. She was still somewhat mopey, but being here alone with nothing to do was making her nuts, even with the kitties. He must have known she still wasn't up to much because he took her to his condo again and left her to relax for the morning and said he'd bring her the Rover on his lunch break.

As she took a pain pill, she mentally committed that it would be the last one and from then on she would use only ibuprofen or Tylenol, whether the hand was bad or not. She was so tired of feeling drowsy and out of it. And she definitely wanted to be completely with it when she drove his car. She went back to bed in his guest room for a couple of hours and then got up, washed the bed linens, and helped herself to his desktop computer to research the must-see sights of Charlotte.

By the time he picked her back up at a few minutes after

eleven, she was awake and excited to go out on the town for the first time in literally months. When Robby had first asked her the other morning, she'd been hesitant because she had only gone to a couple of places in Tolke without her helmet and leathers to hide behind. But she'd gained so much confidence with him here. It had been three months since she'd disappeared from the Chicago area, and North Carolina felt like a world away to her.

She'd prayed about it and felt good about going, and she decided she needed to repair any damage she may have done with Robby's associates. Those few men who had seen her the other day had certainly not seen her at her best, and she planned today to make Robby proud if by chance anyone else happened to get a glimpse of her.

Wearing a nice, dressy pant suit and heels, with her hair long and shiny, and just a touch of make up on, she knew when she saw Robby's face as she walked out into his living room that she looked good. He just stood there and looked at her for a minute and then made her crack up with an exaggerated cat call and whistle. She laughed and put her arm around his waist. "Knock it off. Apparently I look okay? I didn't know if anyone from your work would see me, but if they do, I wanted to undo the damage I did the other day coming in haggard and bloody."

"You look hot. If I wasn't paranoid that someone at my work would offend the tar out of you, I'd go show you off. Where are you off to this afternoon? Have you got plans or are you just going to fly by the seat of those extremely flattering pants?"

"Stop. I have no idea how to take you like this." She pulled a note out of her pocket as they left his condo and headed down to get in his car. "I'm going to go to the Mint Museum of Art, then to Levine Museum of the New South, and then the botanical garden at the university. And if I have time after that, I'm going to go to the farmers market. What time do you need me to pick you up?"

He held the door for her to get in and went around to the driver's side. "I guess that depends on how good you're feeling. If you're up to a long day, come back at nine tonight. If you're still going a little slow, come back at five-thirty, and I'll take you to my condo to relax until my evening meetings are over. Do you want to just call me? Or text. I won't be able to answer a call in the middle of things."

"I'll text you. Now help me make sure I know exactly how to get back to wherever you'll be."

"It's easy, just find the football stadium, and go to the east side. I'll meet you at the front door of the big building right there almost in the parking lot. The route to the stadium is marked on all the freeways. In downtown look for Mint, Graham or Morehead streets. It's big. You can't miss it."

She turned and gazed at him across the car. "Robby, I'm not a guy."

He glanced over at her, and looked her up and down for a second, and smiled. "You can say that again."

"So you can't say find the stadium and go east. Which way is east here? Let me watch where we're going and before you get out sketch me a map. Guys know east. Women follow the map and turn at the second light."

"Are you trying to help me understand how the female mind works, Kelly? Because I've been trying to figure that out for decades now and have finally given it up as hopeless. Can it really be explained as follow the map and turn at the second light?"

She laughed. "Well, no. But east? No. You have to at least give me the stadium is round and concrete and there's a blimp flying over it. Mostly just draw me a simple map."

"Okay, Kelly. Watch this. See this big brick colored building. Turn here. I don't know what number of light it is, but turn at this light. It's either red or green or yellow. Go straight and just when you're going to crash into this round cement colored building, that incidentally has no blimp flying over it, turn like this." He swerved left and she had to grab the arm rest. "And drive up to this big, squarish building with all the windows." He turned to look at her with a grin. "How was that?"

"You want me to turn like that?" She shook her head and laughed. "Brick colored and squarish? Robby, what percentage of the buildings in the United States do you suppose are squarish?"

"Okay, squarish was nebulous, but brick colored was viable."

"Brick colored? No way. There are fifty colors of brick."

They'd pulled up to the building and Jason stepped away from a group of about fifteen men, half in football uniforms and half in street clothes, to walk toward Robby's Rover. Robby rolled down the driver's side window and asked Jason, "Raime, what color is brick colored?"

"Red. Brick red. Why?"

Robby laughed and opened his door to come around and open hers. "I just needed you to clarify that for Kelly."

She stepped out, smiling. "It's a guy thing. It's like east. Hi, Jason. Could you please explain to Robby about how women think and remind him that I'm not a guy?"

They walked back around and she stood beside the driver's side door that Robby held for her. "He wants me to go east to the squarish, brick colored building without the blimp." She laughed as she slid behind the wheel and moved the seat forward. "Have a good afternoon. Try not to get creamed, Robby. I'll be sure and turn just like you said. See you later." She laughed again as she drove off and did indeed squeal his tires as she turned out of the parking lot.

Jason looked at Robby and then at all the others who had been watching her get out and come around the car. When she squealed off, he shook his head. "You can't be still having issues with mistaking her for a guy."

Robby laughed. "Are you kidding me? Did you just see her?"

"I did and so did everyone else." He nodded at the other men. "They're all already curious about the mysterious red head from the other night. I think you've just achieved mythical status just by her walking around the car. I hope she doesn't honestly think I can explain how women think. Is that even possible?"

"Heck no! Come on. We've gotta dress. We should hustle."

"Does she know about you being a football player? What was that crack about you getting creamed?"

Robby shook his head. "The other day after I was so banged up, she wanted to know what was wrong with me, and I told her I'd played football with some of the guys from work and got creamed. She thinks it was a pick-up game."

"Geez, man. You are gonna get so busted! You think the guys creamed you. Why don't you just tell her and get it over with?"

Robby stopped walking and turned to him. "I'm just a guy to her, Jase. Someone she's comfortable with. She's never tried to get me to sleep with her, or buy her things, or be seen with her. I can promise you, if she saw a reporter coming with a camera she would run. She doesn't want my money, or fame, or me to even hold her hand. Which I should change. But my point is, she likes me for me.

"Do you know the other day when I took her home after having her hand stitched up, she couldn't do up the button on her jeans. Do you know what she did? First off, she said that there was no way she'd ask me for help with it. That's what a nice, moral girl she is. And in the second place, she said it was okay because I was the only one who would see the funny bump under her shirt, and I didn't matter.

"I mean she said it more tactfully than that, but... It was the most incredible feeling. She likes me because she thinks I don't play football." He shook his head and kept walking.

"Yup. You're gonna get creamed. You need to get that doofus look off. It's going to be hard enough to get these guys to focus on something other than what just drove off in your Rover without you looking so dang happy. Snap out of it."

Robby gave him a huge smile. "I'm just happy to be enjoying these two-a-days. What are you talking about?"

"You just remember that when she comes back and everything you own hurts. Don't limp in front of her."

Kelly came into Charlotte with him for two days in row, and then on Sunday, when he came back in to go to his home ward, he dropped her off at the ward she'd been attending in Midland. Before he pulled away from the church, he asked again, "You're sure you can find a ride home? Because, I can come back and get you."

She waved a hand at him. "I'm sure one of the guys here will take me. Have a great day off." He headed out of the parking lot, wanting to cuss under his breath. She sure didn't question "one of the guys".

He wanted to go right back to that church and make a formal announcement from the pulpit that she was his deal and all the other guys could keep their helpfulness to themselves. He shook his head as he drove. He needed to get a handle on his life with her. All this time, he'd just been enjoying her, but today he felt positively possessive. He had to step back and analyze that.

For months, she had been one hundred percent dependant upon him, and it had been kind of nice. In getting honest with himself today, he realized that while he'd been thinking he was protecting her, he'd also been basically keeping her a prisoner. If she chose that, that was one thing, but right now she couldn't even drive her motorcycle to go buy milk if she wanted.

Not only that, but he had to be honest and admit that he didn't want other guys driving her home. But if that was true, then what did he want from her? He probably ought to figure that out before it was too late. The status quo couldn't just go on forever. He wasn't sure what he wanted and what to do about her, but he did know that he adored her and would stay with her forever if he could. As he pulled into his ward house, he made a mental note to call and get her a truck she could drive one handed. Then, she could carry whatever building materials her heart desired, whenever she pleased.

On Monday morning, when he was gone again, Kelly was relatively pain free but one handed. She was wondering what in the world she was going to do with herself. Robby had invited her back into Charlotte with him, but she didn't want to spend the whole long day alone among strangers again, and she knew that bringing her clear out here meant an almost two hour longer day for Robby, on top of his killer schedule right now. She didn't understand the drastic change in his working hours, but the fact that his days were grueling was impossible to miss.

She dug around and did actually find a few things she could do well with just one hand. Their little garden had begun to produce like a machine, and she found that with a small paring knife she could harvest the produce quite nicely.

And she could certainly write fine and spent most of Monday afternoon designing the new wine cellar and theater room they'd talked about.

She also decided to ask him about making one of the ground floor bedrooms in the main house a master suite for him and turning another one into an exercise room. He'd had a beautiful exercise room in his condo, and she'd love to be able to use it as well. Ever since the panther sighting, she'd been somewhat hesitant to jog or take walks out here by herself, and the exercise room would be great when Robby wasn't here to do stuff with.

She'd been in the garden for more than an hour Tuesday morning, when she got a call on her cell phone. It was Robby asking her to go open the gate for a delivery he was having made there this morning. He didn't say much and got right off the line and she wondered what he was having delivered that he was being so close mouthed about. She went and opened the gate and was back in the garden in her cutoffs when two vehicles pulled down the lane.

One was a brand new black Chevy truck and the other was a car with dealer plates. The driver of the truck got out and came over to her with a clipboard, and asked her to sign a form that simply stated a truck had been delivered. She was so caught off guard by the whole thing, that she'd signed Kelly S. Campbell before she realized what she was doing.

After she signed, the truck driver took his clip board and got into the car and it drove back up the lane, leaving Kelly to wonder what was going on. Why was Robby having a brand new truck delivered? She couldn't help herself and brushed off her hands and feet and knees and went and got into it and checked it out. The only time she'd ever even been in a brand new vehicle was when Ryley made her go with him to the car shows back home. She and her mother had always bought used vehicles to save money.

The truck was incredibly nice. It had all the bells and whistles, and power everything. It even had a sunroof, and she was more confused than ever. This had to be the delivery Robby wanted her to open the gate for. She went into the house to find herself some lunch, hoping just a little bit that he'd bought the truck for her to use, and wondering just how well off he was. So far, in more than three months, money had been a non-issue. A non-issue to the point where she almost wondered if money was not an issue to him at all.

She made herself a chef salad and took it to the porch step. She'd put all the kitties out on the porch for the day, and they thought they were in kitten heaven out there with the vines and the steps and the occasional bug to predate. Ted came and tried to commandeer her salad. Kelly had to push her away several times before she finally got the hint and went and sprawled on the walk where the kittens immediately pounced on her.

That afternoon, Kelly wrestled the ladder into the kitchen and after carefully rigging a paint bucket, she began to stain the kitchen ceiling. Her right arm and her neck soon got tired, but she could do it well one handed and was pleased with the results. It was tedious work because of the heavy floor joists from the floor above that comprised the ceiling.

She had to literally stand with her head up between the four by twelve timbers to get into the cracks and crevices. Then every so often she would have to get down and move her ladder over a foot or two and climb back up and go at it again. At least it was something she could accomplish while she waited for her hand to heal. She turned her music up loud and sang along as she stained, pausing from time to time to roll her neck and shoulders.

When dinner time rolled around, she settled for two fresh, home-grown tomatoes, sitting on the step and then put the kitties to bed in the living room. She went back to the kitchen, locking the front door behind her, to get back to her staining. If she worked late, she could have it finished tonight and could start a coat of urethane on it in the morning.

Chapter 14

The vicious throb in Robby's head had burgeoned to a full grown pound and he wondered if this film was ever going to end. He'd taken a hard hit in the afternoon practice and the pounding in his head had only gotten worse during this evening's meetings. Theoretically, training camp was to make their team better in preparation for the upcoming season, but for the unsigned free agents who had only this three and a half week window to prove themselves, it was a do or die situation. They had to prove what they had to offer the team now or they'd lose their chance at playing pro football, unless another team somehow happened to pick them up.

One of the free agents was a promising left tackle named Kendricks that Robby sincerely hoped made the cut. He had the stuff to be great, but Robby didn't necessarily want to be the one to be tackled any more. The guy was killing him. After the first few hits that initial week, Robby had thought the defensive line coaches would tell the guy to take it easier, but apparently not. It was hard to make a winner who was fighting for a career back off, but the last thing they needed was for one of their own team to be seriously injured.

And even though it seemed egotistical, Robby knew he was one of this team's greatest assets. Both in playing football and in leading the team's attitude and work ethic. He rolled his neck there in the dark hoping no one noticed it and then surreptitiously rubbed his temples. Man, this one was a kicker. The film finally ended, the coaches called it a night, and Robby headed for his vehicle.

Jason caught him in the parking lot. "What did Doc say about your head, Rocker?"

"I didn't go see him."

"I saw that hit, Rock. You acted dinged after. You should have had it checked."

Robby went to shake his head and decided against it. "These young guys are watching us like hawks right now, and you know it, Jase. We're the work ethic of this team, and they're going to do exactly what we show them to do. Playing injured is just part of the game. I can't slack off now."

"Slacking is one thing, Rocker. Brains aren't really optional."

"I'll be fine. Just let me get home to Kelly."

"You're going all the way out to your house tonight? Or is she at the condo?"

Robby looked at him. "Jason, she stayed at the condo in the guest room one night because we got out of the Emergency Room in the middle of the night, and I had to be back here. That's the only time she stayed."

Jason put up a hand defensively. "I'm not accusing you of anything dastardly, Rock. I know you don't do that. Okay, we'll go to your house."

"What's this we'll?"

"I'm taking you. Get in the car and shut up."

"I'm fine, Raime. Just leave me alone and let me get going. I'm tired."

"'You're making a big deal of this and the guys are watching. Just get in."

Robby sighed and got in the car. "The only reason I'm going along with this is because I had a truck delivered out there this morning. She can bring me back."

As they pulled out of the lot, Jason turned to him. "Lean the seat back." He reached behind them and handed Robby a pillow. "There might be Cheerios stuck to it, but it's soft. Shania will share."

He drove for a while and then said matter-of-factly, "I've considered this and decided you should marry Kelly."

Robby opened one eye and looked up at him. "Oh, you have. Why is that?"

"I don't know, but you need her."

This time Robby didn't open his eyes. "I'd marry her in a heart beat, but we've never so much as gone on a date. There are some things you don't know about her Jason. She staged her own death and ran from her home in Chicago last April sometime. I knew something was wrong, but didn't know what and decided that since she was living in my house I should get to the bottom of it. I hired a PI and he found out she was missing and presumed dead, but he didn't know why she did it.

"I've asked her about it in a roundabout way, and she admitted she'd had to run, but she said she couldn't tell me why. My theory is she thinks if I know I'll get in trouble. Anyway, she could never be in my spotlight. And I sometimes wonder if whoever she ran from will find her, and she'll be gone again."

"You probably ought to demand an explanation. You have more clout than she'd ever dream of as far as fixing her troubles, whatever they are."

"I can't. Not until I level with her about who I am."

"So then level."

"She'll hate me."

"She adores you, Robideaux. She's never going to hate you. She's a rock and you know it. She'll be mad, but she'll get over it."

Robby sighed. "I hope so."

He had Jason just let him out, and as he drove away Robby was unbelievably glad to be home. The mellow, yellow porch light on the logs, the glow from the windows, and the faint sound of her music felt incredibly welcoming. The door was locked, so he dug out his key and let himself in. The kitties raced across the living room floor to their corner as he came through, and he smiled to himself as he followed the music to the kitchen.

He should have been surprised to see her standing on the ladder at ten o'clock at night with her hurt hand, but he wasn't. That was his Kelly. He didn't want to scare her by either yelling over her music or touching her, when she didn't know he was here, so he went to her radio and turned it off, instead. His intentions had been good, but she still whirled so fast toward him that she fell, even though the ladder stayed upright.

The brush flew from her hand as she saw him and tried to catch herself, but it was too late. She let out a small scream as she fell backwards against him and they both landed in a heap on the floor again. This time he didn't even try to move. He just laid his head back and groaned. "We are hiring the roof out. There is no way I'm letting you climb that high."

She carefully sat up, without leaning on her hand. "Robby. I'm so sorry. I didn't expect you tonight. Are you okay?"

Still lying there, he said, "I'm fine. I'm sorry I scared you."

At his tired tone of voice, she crawled over and gazed down at him. "What's going on?" She put her hand to his head. "Did you play football again?"

Her hand felt wonderful and he decided he wasn't going to answer her question. "I just have a headache. Your hand feels incredibly good. Do you think you could rub my head?"

Her own forehead grimaced with worry. "Sure. Do you want me to do it here? Or would the couch be more comfortable?"

"The couch. Just give me a minute. Are you through with whatever you were doing?"

"I was staining. It'll wait." She stood up. "Give me your hand." She leaned back and pulled for all she was worth and helped him up. "Go put something else on, and I'll be in the living room."

"Thanks." He changed into a pair of warm-up pants and a T-shirt, and went back into the living room, where she was waiting on the end of the couch in the dark, holding a kitten. "How's the hand?"

"Hand's good. How's the head?"

"Head's bad." He sat on the couch and leaned over onto her lap as she put the kitten back on the floor with the others. "I'll be fine. Rub it for a minute, and I'll go to bed and sleep it off."

She put her hand into his hair and began to massage his scalp, rubbing in small, gentle circles. "Have you taken anything?"

"Aspirin and Tylenol." He wasn't going to mention that they hadn't touched the throbbing pain. "I'll be fine." She started to run her fingernails through his hair in long, slow strokes, and he sighed. He had known he would feel better here.

He relaxed against her and let her hand ease the tension and smooth out all of his wrinkles. She'd turned the music back on low, and he tried to place the quiet, acoustic guitar he was hearing. It was some old balladeer from the seventies, but it was too hard to think, and he gave it up and just felt the soothing pressure of her fingers.

She left his hair and rubbed the knots in his neck, gently up and down the length of the muscles. Her fingers felt like heaven. He turned his head and she worked on the other side. She moved up the back of his neck into his hair line and hit a bruise, and he tried not to groan.

She must have known it was tender because her touch got softer in that spot, and she went back up to the top of his head again and then around to his temples and forehead. This time she came down the side of his face and worked on the muscles of his jaw. He wished he'd discovered this kind of therapy a long time ago.

He was almost asleep when she said, "Put your legs up on the couch and stretch out Robby. If I let you go to sleep here, is your alarm set on your phone?"

"Yeah."

"You need to leave at a little before six, right?"

"Yeah. Do you think you could drive me in? Did your truck come?"

"Sure, I'll drive you in. Yes, the truck came."

"Did you like it? I was worried about having you be stranded while you can't ride your bike."

"I loved it."

"You'll look pretty in a black truck." He sighed again. Maybe he would just sleep right here.

He didn't remember her getting up and covering him with the quilt and shutting off the music, but he woke up there alone, sometime in the middle of the night feeling miraculously better. He went into his bedroom for the rest of the night and laid back down, remembering how her hands had helped him so much the night before. He really owed her one.

He owed her another one when she gently woke him the next morning and then fed him a wonderful breakfast before loading him into the new truck and heading out as the sun was coming up. He was still sick and tired, but nothing like he'd been the night before. She had been a miracle treatment.

They drove in silence until, at length, she asked, "I don't suppose you'd consider calling in sick, huh?"

He shook his head gingerly and laid it back and closed his eyes again. "Can't call in sick."

Then when they got close to the stadium, she gently touched him. "Robby, you'd better start waking up. We've passed the brick colored building, and I'm just about to swerve around the corner to the round cement building without the blimp."

He gave her the smile that she was hoping for and sat up. "I guess I'm on then. Thanks for rescuing me last night and bringing me in. I think I'm going to live."

She was gazing at him with big, dark green eyes. "I'm so glad to hear that. If you need me to come back and get you, just call me."

He met her eyes and then glanced away. "I'll be fine, but thanks. I'll see you sometime. I'm not sure when. Take care." She didn't say anything as he got out and shut the door. He looked back at her before he walked away. He'd better be honest with her soon about what he did, or she was going to be incredibly hurt.

Jason met him coming across the parking lot and peered at him about as closely as she had when he'd left. "How's the head?"

Robby gave him a grin. "Never felt better. How's yours?"

"You're actually a pretty good liar. You do seem a whale of a lot better than you looked last night though. What did Kelly say?"

"Not a thing. Just filleted me with those big, green eyes. I'm hoping she just thinks I had a headache."

"And not a brain concussion, like I do."

Robby opened the door of the building. "We walked into this with our eyes open. And you know what? I still love to play football. After you, my distributing friend."

Just several minutes after practice started that morning, one of the assistant coaches approached Robby and said, "Coach Bracken wants to see you, Rocker. He's in the offensive film room."

Robby took off his helmet and began walking across the field. He knew what was coming; he just didn't know whether Coach was going to be grateful that he was trying to be a strong leader or ticked that he was sacrificing his own body to do it. At any rate, he was glad not to be the recipient of any more hard hits just now. Even after Kelly's hands last night, his head still pounded.

Stepping into the film room, he set his helmet on a table at the back and clunked up the aisle in his cleats to where the head coach was sitting in the dark watching a film of yesterday's afternoon practice. "Hey coach. Flynn said you wanted to see me."

"Have a seat, Rocker. I'd like your opinion on something."

Robby sat down next to this man who he'd gained a huge amount of respect for over the last six years. "What do you want to know?"

After fast forwarding through the film for a second, Bracken stopped it and started it again in real time. "Watch this play and tell me what you think."

Robby turned his attention to the screen and watched the play that culminated with Robby catching a long pass just as Kendricks completely annihilated him. It took several seconds for Robby to get back up and when he did he leaned over with his hands on his knees for a moment or two. He was still moving slow and weaved slightly when he went back to the huddle. The coach clicked pause and turned to Robby.

Without hesitating, Robby gave his opinion. "Hendricks is good, Coach. I think if it were up to me, I'd sign him. He's tough. He's taken me down consistently these couple of weeks."

"Between you and me, he's going to be a Panther, but you and I both know that's not why I called you in here. How many million dollars do you suppose the franchise has got invested in you, Rocker?"

Robby smiled big at him. "A gob."

"And how many more million would we stand to lose if you were out of commission?"

"A couple of gobs."

"I know why you're doing what you're doing, and I want you to know that I appreciate it, but don't make me swear at you, Robideaux. You know I hate to swear at you Mormons. Just to prove that I'm aware I need your example out there with the young guys, I'm going to give you the opportunity to get knocked around a little by Seiverts today, but he knows about your head and will act accordingly.

"And Jason is going to forget you exist as a receiver and you're going to be okay with that for awhile. And just to show that I value your brain, I'm going to keep Kendricks away from you for a few days. Is there anything else I should be doing with you right now?"

"Not a thing, Coach."

"Good." He clicked off the projector. "For the rest of the morning, I want you either obviously answering questions for me out there, or with one of the other team coordinators. I don't want your helmet even on your head. Is that clear?"

"Yes sir. Thank you, sir. You may not believe this, but I appreciate it. I've felt like swearing myself."

"Well, don't do it, Rock. You're the last bastion of hope that there truly are saints for some of us old warriors. Don't burst our bubble. Now tell me something. Is there any truth to the rumor I'm hearing?"

Robby smiled again. "I can't answer that Coach until I know what the rumor is."

"That you have a strikingly beautiful red headed friend hidden away somewhere?"

"I do have a very pretty friend, Coach."

"And are you finally going to settle down and tie the knot?"

Robby laughed right out loud. "No, sir. I'm not. We're just friends in the first place and just between you and me, she hates football players. In fact, she doesn't even know I play football. She's not from here and obviously isn't a huge fan. She thinks I'm a business man."

At this, the coach finally softened his gnarly demeanor. "Really? You're kidding me. Is that possible?"

Robby smiled. "I told her I was in acquisitions. Then Jason told her he's in distribution. We're both dead meat when she finds out."

"Man, I'll say! Don't you dare let an angry chick jeopardize my team. If something happened to both you and Jason, I'd have to kill myself. That's completely off the record of course."

"Of course, Coach. Maybe we could have her kill Bocklin if she becomes murderous."

"Now, there's an idea I hadn't thought of with Bocklin." Bracken smiled. "I may just run that by the legal department. And that's off the record, too."

"Of course, Coach. We were both kidding."

Bracken put back on his stern head coach face. "Head coaches never kid, kid. Now get back out there and keep that team whipped into shape. And you protect your head. Protect your everything."

"Yes sir, Coach."

Chapter 15

Kelly watched Robby walk away from the new black truck with mixed feelings. In a way, she was glad she had been able to help him last night to feel better and to rest, but in a way the feelings she was starting to have for him worried her to death. That long look he had given her as he stepped out was so thought provoking. There were these incredibly strong feelings that transmitted between them, but there were some communication gaps that short circuited things to the point of frustration.

What had he been thinking when he'd looked at her? She had no way of knowing what went on behind those striking blue eyes. Sometimes she thought he thought of her as a cute neighbor kid he'd hired to work on his house, and sometimes she thought he truly cared about her. That was hard to figure out because he was always such a nice guy. From that first day, when he'd gone out of his way to bring a gas can to an unknown motorcyclist, she'd known he was a server.

And what if he did care about her? If he did, she couldn't act on his feelings for her anymore than she could act on her feelings for him with her life the way it was now. Her life was in such limbo here. So many times, she'd thought she needed to go home and find a way to deal with the situation at the hospital and get on with her life, but every time, she'd been so uncomfortable with the idea that she'd put it out of her mind. The look she'd seen in Peter's eyes that afternoon would come back to her, and she'd realize again that she was far too out of her league there to take it on without someone powerful who could help her.

Over the months, she'd come to have no doubts that Lt. Hartvigson was involved with the mess at the hospital. He had been too smug, and simply the fact that he wouldn't even begin to check into things there had to indicate that, didn't it? She knew that people sometimes didn't take her seriously because of her appearance, but he hadn't even begun to consider checking into the hospital. She was still worried that somehow she'd gotten Robby in trouble with the law for letting her stay here, even if it was because of a crooked cop.

Still, as she drove the half hour or so home to Robby's house, she knew in her heart it was time to get serious about getting back to Chicago. The patients at the hospital were still at risk of becoming the next statistic, and she was in way over her head here with Robby. Something had to give or she was going to end up with the smashed heart of the century.

With no idea even where to begin, she finally decided to stop at the library and start by checking into who was involved with Peter at the hospital. Then she decided that not only did she need more privacy than a public library but she remembered that because she'd never been able to produce ID and proof of residency, they wouldn't issue her a card or even let her use one of their computers.

She drove on home and got more cash, then headed back into town to purchase a computer. There was nowhere in Tolke to buy one, and she was just about to head on toward Charlotte when she thought of the pawn shop at the other end of town. Maybe they'd have something used she could work with. It didn't need to be fancy or powerful.

Finding a good, used laptop that was wireless enabled, she went home, wondering if she'd have to do something extra to the service at the house to be able to use it. She'd seen Robby use a laptop there, but had no way of knowing if he was just working on documents or if he'd been online at the time.

She unlocked the door and even the adorable little kitties didn't make her smile as she went in and set the laptop on the kitchen table. This was the beginning of the end, and she was smart enough to know it. The headlong flight from home had been so heartbreaking and scary at first, but it had turned out to be a wonderful experience for her here in North Carolina. The thought of ending it all and returning home was even more heartbreaking.

But she couldn't do this forever. She had to face reality at some point and today was where she needed to start. Somehow that look on Robby's face as he'd walked away had made her know that. She plugged in the laptop and opened it with a sigh.

That afternoon, she drove back into Charlotte to the plastic surgeon's office to have her hand checked. He took the huge bulky bandage off and checked it over good and declared it healing nicely, then took out about half of the exposed stitches. He rebandaged it with a much smaller wrap and sent her home. Her thumb was still immobilized, but it was unbelievably nice to have her fingers back.

Dr. Peter Holmes had given it some thought and had come to the conclusion that there were no other options. The nurse who had been buying Oxycodon from him had to be dealt with. For months now she'd been the source of a neat little profit, but yesterday she had tried to turn the tables and had threatened to turn him in for dealing if he didn't agree to supply to her at no charge from now on. There was no way he was going to be on the chain of a half witted, overweight nurse. Having a cop own him was bad enough.

He'd give her a free supply all right, but it was the kind that was going to be her last hit.

It was Wednesday night and although it added more than an hour onto his day in drive time, Robby wanted to go out to the house instead of to his condo. He got into his Land Rover and started it up, thinking about how Kelly's hand had felt on his head last night. Her touch had been incredible. As he went to pull out of the lot, he remembered how she had looked at him that morning as he got out of the truck, and he pulled the car over to the side of the lot and paused.

Maybe going out to the house tonight wasn't that great of an idea. He needed to get his head on straight about her and decide what he truly wanted where she was concerned. He needed to quit just letting things evolve, however they did. He wasn't seventeen anymore. And he wasn't just a business man.

They both had some issues. Granted, his were the kind

that most people dreamed of having. Money and fame and attention. But under the circumstances, for her those things were at the least going to hurt her and at the worst, could put her in a lot of danger. He wished he knew what she was up against there in Chicago.

More than a little disappointed, he turned for his condo instead of the house. It was probably for the best anyhow. That extra hour was foolish as long as the days were during camp. At least the worst of it was almost over. There were only three more days of the two a days and then the evening meetings would be over. They had the Fan Fest at the stadium and then several season opener fundraisers for the various players' foundations, one of which was his, but at least some of the pressure would be coming off, as far as setting the pace for the younger men.

Thinking of the fundraisers, he reminded himself that he needed to find a date for a couple of the parties. Everyone else would be with someone and going solo just fed the flames of both the eligible status and the whispered innuendos about his being unsure of which sex he was attracted to. At least Kelly had settled some of those rumors lately, when she'd cut her hand.

He thought about her hand touching him last night again. He was supposed to be this rough, tough football player, but last night he'd just wanted to be taken care of, and she'd stepped in beautifully. Beautifully and temptingly. He had wanted to kiss her in the kitchen, even when she'd just flattened him and he felt awful.

He wondered if she'd agree to be his date for the parties. And if she agreed, would she be safe there with any possible press that would show up? He'd have to check into both the security and what kind of news coverage they would have before he approached her. It would be fun to take her to a dressy party. Much as he usually hated those things, she would liven things up a bit. She probably looked totally hot in a party dress.

She was still on his mind as he pulled into his complex and went upstairs. The phone began to ring almost before he had the door unlocked and he walked in and glared at it. The maid must have plugged it back in again. He glanced at the machine and saw a flashing twenty-seven. Holy smokes! He was *not* dealing with them tonight.

The machine kicked on and he heard Jenna's voice say, "Rocker, I know you're in there. I just saw you drive in and I know you're too polite to ignore me when you're standing right there next to the machine. Let me come u..." He reached down and unplugged the phone from the wall. Kelly was right. That did make you feel incredibly powerful. He unplugged the machine as well and headed for a bowl of cold cereal. Kelly had been good for him. What was he going to do about her?

Wednesday and Thursday nights, he stayed at the condo telling himself he was being responsible, and it had probably been a good idea, as far as resting. But on Friday afternoon, when Coach Bracken announced that evening meetings had been canceled and things wouldn't be starting up the next morning until ten, Robby knew, without a doubt, that he was going home to Kelly.

He didn't care if they didn't do a thing but wash walls again. He wanted to see her. He had missed her ridiculously these last couple of busy weeks. He wasn't even going to stay long enough to have dinner with the team.

Just past Tolke, he called her to make sure he didn't surprise her, but she didn't answer the house or her cell. That made him worry and disappointed him at the same time. He hoped she was okay and that she wasn't out on a date. He couldn't think of any other reason for her not to answer her phone.

Pulling up to the house to find her mowing the lawn in shorts eased his mind immensely. He felt somewhat guilty for not having gotten to the lawn this week, but dang, she looked good out there mowing. He just sat in the Rover and watched her for a minute.

One good thing about being away from her these last couple of days, he'd made a decision about her. He wanted to be with her, and it was time she knew he wasn't a business man in acquisitions. Maybe once they got that out in the open, they could get to the bottom of what she was so desperately afraid of back home. Then they could explore being more to each other than a homeowner and caretaker. It was a rather involved sequence, but they had to start somewhere.

Now all he had to do was figure out how to tell her. He'd been grappling with that one for two days solid. He really didn't want to wreck their friendship over this.

He got out of the Rover and went to sit on the porch step and watch her. She was almost done with the last section, and he certainly wasn't going to act all macho and try to steal the last forty feet from her. Not when she had legs like that to watch. She shut off the mower and took the grass catcher to dump it, and he got up and went inside to get her water bottle out of the fridge.

As he came back out, she had started the mower back up and was pushing it toward the garage. Once it was inside, she shut the big doors and came back out and threw herself out, spread-eagled in the middle of the front lawn, in a dramatic swoon. He came over to her and dribbled the cold water from her bottle on her flushed face as she tried to catch it in her mouth. Some went up her nose and she coughed and turned over and then sneezed and gave a small scream while he laughed at her.

She now had grass clippings in her ponytail and all over her clothes and grass stains on her tennies. He started to pick the grass out of her hair and laughed again when she said, "Whew! I've been mowing for weeks, I think." She glanced at her watch. "Okay, maybe only three hours, but there have been a couple of Tuesdays in that time." She gazed up at him and put her hand to his head. "You look better. How are you feeling?"

He took her bandaged hand and turned it over and then back again to examine it. "Much better. Ravenous. Do you have dinner planned or should we go on a quest for interesting food?"

"Is chicken cacciatore interesting enough? Do you like Italian?"

He broke into a deep, exaggerated Italian accent. "Do I lika da Italian? Of course, I lika da Italian. I am da Italian. Whatta you thinkin'?"

She laughed at him. "Really? You're Italian?"

"Heavens no. I'm like twelve generations of French, but I sound good, don't I?"

"I wouldn't know. The only Italians I know in Illinois sound like a bad gangster movie. But that could be the Chicaga accent. You sound more like a happy version of the spaghetti and meatball guy on *Lady and the Tramp*."

"Oh, man. That cannot be a good way to sound. I thought I had that Old World thing down."

They walked toward the house and then she started to detour to the side. "Where are you going?"

"I need to go get the grass off and change. I don't want to leave a trail through your house."

"Kelly, it's just a house. Can't you do the water dog thing and shake it all off or something?"

She shook her head and laughed. "Could you demonstrate the water dog thing for me? I don't believe I'm familiar with that." She pulled her ponytail around and began to try to run her fingers through it.

"I'm not coordinated enough to do the water dog thing. Sorry. You change; I'll make a da pasta and finda da violin and old wine bottle candle."

"The pasta's made, but good luck with that violin and candle. I'll be right back."

He watched her walk toward her house for a minute and then went back to his Rover. He didn't have *Are You Lonesome Tonight*, but he had some Italian tenor music that would make her laugh if it was belting over the stereo when she came back in.

He was right. She walked through the back door laughing. She came and wrapped an arm around his waist, and he laughed with her as she asked, "Where in the world did you find that music? It's perfect."

"It was in my car. I have a bit of everything. What can I help you do?"

"I think all that's left to do is toast the bread. How are you with a broiler?"

He took the loaf of French bread she handed him. "Good, as long as I have four or five timers set."

"Then you'd better do the bread. I have to have seven timers, and it still comes out a little dark. How was work?"

"Good. I was actually scheduled to be there late again, but there was a change of plans. Speaking of work, I have some parties I'm kind of obligated to attend next week. They're actually fundraiser deals for some of the Carolina Panther players' foundations. For cancer kids or at risk youth or whatever. Would you be willing to put on a party dress and come with me to them? We wouldn't have to stay very long. Just show up for a while. Do you like parties?"

He was watching her face, and he saw the concern. "I love parties. Especially after becoming a recluse here, but if there are pro football players, won't there be a lot of cameras? I'm terribly allergic to cameras."

"I knew you'd say that. I checked on what kind of press will be allowed. I actually have three to go to, but one will have a ton of coverage. The two I was talking about you coming with me to should be okay."

She gazed at him seriously for a couple of seconds and said, "If you think it's safe, I would love to. I am going to tell you what happened someday, Robby. Just not until I'm sure that I won't get you into the mess."

"How would just telling me get me involved?"

"I don't know, Robby. I wish I did. Because I'd love some help. But not yet."

"Did it ever occur to you that I might be able to help you?"

"Of course. But what if it backfired?"

He shrugged. "I've got people who deal with backfires."

She met his eyes sadly for a couple of seconds and then said, "Soon. I'm working on it. I'm just so not sure what to do. Give me some time. In the mean time, just let me lie low in North Carolina."

He put a hand on her arm. "I'm a patient guy, Kelly. Just know that if you ever up and disappear one day, it will kill me. I'd lots rather take a chance and be involved than be left behind wondering if you were safe." They stood gazing at each other like that until both the buzzer on the stove and on the microwave went off, and Robby went to take the garlic bread out of the broiler.

They went to the table, and Robby prayed and part of the prayer was for Kelly to be safe and watched over. Afterward, she reached over and squeezed his hand. "Thanks, Robby. I appreciate that. When are your parties and what do I need to wear?"

"Next Friday and Saturday. And Monique would probably be the better one to ask about what to wear. I'll pay for whatever she thinks you need. I never know about things like that. I always just wear a suit and cuff links and call it good."

"I'm sure a suit and cufflinks on you are more than good. How long are you going to be working this nasty schedule?"

"It was going to be through tomorrow, but even my morning meetings are pushed back. It's still going to be much busier than I was this summer, but the grueling part is over. In the next few weeks I'll be going out of town a lot more. Which reminds me. No ladders when I'm out of town. Do something safely on the ground when I'm gone. Okay?"

"You know Robby, it's not the ladders. It's you. I never have a problem unless you walk in the room unannounced."

"Yeah, well, just to be safe, how about if you just read a good book while I'm gone, and I'll help you make up for lost time when I'm home."

She smiled. "I would just hate that if you forced me to read a good book. Honestly, right now, the garden is producing so fast that I could spend weeks just doing something with all of it. What would you think of getting a freezer?"

"Get whatever you want. Maybe you should let them deliver it so I don't have to try to be out here at a certain time. What are your plans for tonight and tomorrow morning?"

She nodded at the boxes of canning jars on the counter next to the new canning kettle. "I'm bottling your tomatoes. What are you doing?"

"I'm thinking about going fishing. Want to come with? If you'll come with me, I'll come home and help you with the tomatoes."

She smiled. "Can we stop on the way home and buy some salmon?"

"Absolutely. And I'm not even going to tell the little catfishes you said that."

"Cool. 'Cause I hate it when the catfish are offended. Are you going the same place we saw the panther?"

"I didn't think you'd be very enthused about going back there, but we can if you want."

Shaking her head, she said, "I don't care, just out is good as long as I'm not alone."

"Are you too lonely here, Kelly?"

"No. Just this last week some. The kitties are company. And the truck has helped. But I'm typically relatively outgoing. I'm not usually a loner by nature. I'm getting used to being without my mom and my uncle's family. But sometimes I catch myself talking to the radio. I was okay when you were here more."

"I'll be here more again. Just give me a few more days. Grab your jacket and I'll get the gear."

Chapter 16

Checking with Monique had been good advice. It seemed she was a pro at these fancy parties, and she knew exactly where to take Kelly to get her dresses and then right where to find shoes and jewelry to go with them. Monique even recommended a hairstylist, and by the time Kelly met Robby at his condo on Friday evening, she was comfortable that she wouldn't embarrass him when she went with him that night. He must have agreed, because he smiled appreciatively when he opened the door to her and walked all the way around her to check her out.

"I was right. You do look hot in a party dress." He smiled and whistled and then gave her an exaggerated frown. "Now I'm going to have to fight all the other guys off, though. I hate that. Fist fighting in cuff links is so tacky."

She laughed. "You're such a smart aleck sometimes. Do I look okay? Honestly?"

"You look perfect. And I wasn't being a smart aleck."

"Well, you should know that I'm out of there at the first thrown punch."

He chuckled. "I'll try to remember that. All set? Should we go?"

"It's your party. I'm just here for the ride. I hope they have food. I should have gotten a snack."

That made him laugh right out loud. "Kelly, anything even remotely affiliated with a football player has food. Tons of food. What have you been doing today?"

"This morning I plumbed in a Jacuzzi tub in the summer kitchen and canned green beans, and this afternoon, I got a manicure and had my hair done. I'm not sure what that says about me, but you asked. How were things in acquisitions?"

He held the door of his Land Rover for her. "It means that you're incredible. A one in a million." He shut the door and came around and got in. "If I tried to tell someone who saw you as you are now that you'd just plumbed a tub and canned, they'd think I was lying. You're the only girl in the world who could pull that off."

"Thanks. I didn't think I was digging for compliments, but maybe I was. I'm just worried that I look like a plumber or a pioneer woman. I don't want to embarrass you."

He smiled across the car at her. "Lighten up. They're just stupid, piece of meat jocks, remember? This is not a big deal. Relax. We're okay."

"You may have to remind me a time or two. I don't think I've ever even met a pro athlete before. Do you have to do these kinds of things often?"

He nodded and pulled at his collar to loosen it a little. "From time to time."

"Do you enjoy it?"

"Usually. I don't often stay very long. There's a lot of drinking and that gets old fast. But they can be fun. The food is usually good. And it's typically for a good cause." He grinned across at her. "The girls are beautiful. At least the auburn-haired ones."

She gazed at him wondering what to think. "Are you sure you're French. That sounds to me like blarney. Maybe you're part Irish."

"Ah, the Irish do have the blarney, but the French. The French men are supposed to be second only to the Italian men in being able to talk to women. And the Italian men lie. The French don't, so to me that means that really the French men are the winners."

"Is that a good thing or a bad, Robby?"

"I guess that would depend on what the French men are talking to the women about."

"So do you speak French?"

"*Oui oui*, Madame. I speak some French. *Vous fait*? Do you?"

"Enough to say, *Zhe no compre pas.* But I think it's easily the most beautiful language of all."

"That's why the men can talk to women. The women don't even care what they're saying. It's just the way they say it."

"Are you sure the French men never lie? 'Cause this is sounding a little suspect to me right now. You must have a lot of experience in speaking French to women."

"Some may lie, but I never do. You're just a bit confused because of my interesting Italian the other day. Here we are. Are you ready?"

"I hope so. Coach me through this, okay?"

"Miss Shane, someone who looks like you do tonight needs no coaching. Just smile." He helped her out and grinned. "And eat."

The food was good, just as he'd said. And the girls were beautiful. That was true too. Kelly was frankly somewhat stunned at how many women tried to come on to Robby. He had started out with his hand gently on the small of her back, but within just a few minutes she wanted to put a sign on him that declared he was with someone. After a while, she whispered, "Is it always this way for you?"

He gave her a lopsided smile that was more than a touch sad. "I told you I wanted peace and seclusion. I wasn't lying."

"Why?" He looked at her and smiled an honestly amused smile. "I mean. That was rude, sorry. You know what I mean. I mean you're very nice and handsome and everything, but am I missing something?"

"You know me better than all the rest of these women. You tell me."

"I've buried myself already. I'll start doing that just smile and eat thing now."

"Come on, we'll at least find one of those stupid little hors d'oeuvres plates that are so hard to carry around." Another woman was approaching, and Robby took Kelly's hand and led her in the opposite direction.

Kelly glanced up at him, and he apologized, "Sorry, but she is the most predatory woman I've ever met in my life. In fact, you're probably at risk of physical injury from her just because you're with me."

That made Kelly laugh. "I could take her, Robby, but fist fighting in heels is just so tacky."

"But, I'm not like you. If you two started punching, I'd watch. Just for a second, of course."

"I was just kidding, Robby. You'd watch? That's terrible."

"Hey, I just said I didn't lie. Not that I was all well behaved." They needed to dodge another female and finally, Robby asked, "I know you're hungry, but would you be terribly offended if we just went out on the dance floor and danced for a few minutes. Maybe that will give us some breathing room."

"No, I wouldn't be offended. But do you think that will stop them?"

"I can only hope. Let's at least try. Although, I hate to dance. Except slow ones."

"So, just ask the band to play slow ones for a while. They won't mind. They'll probably be glad to."

"That's a great idea." On the way to the floor, Robby did indeed stop and whisper to one of the band members who nodded, and they spent a heavenly half hour simply dancing close and talking occasionally. Kelly enjoyed it enough that she began to try to mentally back off. That's all she needed was to be one of a herd of hundreds of women who had a thing for him. This night had been good for her that way. Now that she knew what he was up against with women, she would be much more careful to watch herself.

When the band finally played another fast song, they went in search of food and then had to deal with the mingling women again. Kelly was surprised when even a couple of the men came up and started talking to them, and then one said, "So, Robideaux. Are you ever going to introduce me to your friend?"

With a smile that didn't quite reach his eyes, Robby answered, "Nope. I'm not. But nice try, Birch. See you around, huh." Robby put his arm back around Kelly's waist and said close to her ear, "Should we dance again, Kelly?" They headed that way, and she turned to glance at him as he said, "It would seem I'm not the only one who needs space from predators."

She waved a hand noncommittally. "Ah, they're just those big muscle, small brain types, Robby. We are not going to waste energy bothering with them."

He didn't say anything, just gazed at her, and he almost seemed sad. She wondered if she had offended him and thought back over what she'd said. It hadn't been kind, and she shouldn't have said it. She touched him on the arm. "I'm sorry, Robby. I shouldn't have said that. We can bother with those men. They are children of God even though they have outsize egos."

Shaking his head, he continued walking. "Kelly, I don't want you to have to put up with men who have big muscles and small brains. Are you still hungry?"

"No. I'm fine. I've had enough."

"Shall we just go then?"

She looked over at him wondering where his smile had suddenly gone. "Sure, Robby. Whatever. Have we stayed as long as you want? Or have I offended you?"

"No. You haven't offended me. I'm just tired. It's been a long week. I don't usually stay a whole lot longer than this anyway. Let's go home."

As they wended their way slowly to the entrance, mingling occasionally as they went, there were still women coming up and talking to Robby as if Kelly was invisible, and she wasn't sure how to react to it. It helped when he took her hand and just hung on to it. When the one most predatory woman came up to them, Robby was almost rude he walked away so obviously.

Near the door, they met Jason and Monique coming in, and they stopped and talked for several minutes. Robby seemed to become more animated again, and Kelly breathed a little easier. Still, when they reached the Land Rover, they drove in silence for the first several minutes. Finally, Robby broke the silence. "I'm sorry about that Kelly. I should have warned you better and probably asked your permission to hold your hand. I promise I wasn't just using you in there for crowd control."

She wasn't sure how to answer that at first and had to think about it. Finally, she decided that she needed him to just come right out and talk to her if she could manage it. She wasn't sure why the party had tended to depress them both, but she wanted to understand and fix it. "Robby, can I ask you a favor?"

"Sure." He glanced across the car at her.

"Could you pull over and talk to me for just a second so I can see your eyes and try to understand what's bothering you?"

"Yes, but while we're at it, can you help me understand why you subtly pulled away from me after we'd been in there awhile?"

He pulled into the drive through of a fast food restaurant in the town before Tolke and as he rolled down his window, he asked, "Are you still hungry? Would you like something else?"

She decided she was going to be happy and positive and see if she could find his smile again before they got home. "Yes. Dessert! How about a hot fudge sundae? With anything they have as far as nuts and bananas and cherries and whipped cream and stuff."

"Man. That sounds incredibly good. I think I'll have one, too. And a sandwich." He ordered and when their food came, he pulled the car over to the middle of the parking lot under a street light and shut off the engine. Then he turned to her and began to unwrap the sandwich. "What did you want me to talk to you about?"

She wasn't honestly sure how to say it and decided to simply ask him right out, "Well, what happened in there? Where did your happy attitude go? Was it just all the women? Or did I somehow offend you?"

He silently chewed his sandwich for a moment or two while he thought and then shook his head and said, "No. You didn't offend me. And I'm sorry I lost my happy attitude. And yes, all the women steal the energy from my life. But do you realize that they stole your energy from my life too?"

She felt her forehead wrinkle as she tried to figure out what he was saying. "What do you mean?"

"I mean... Remember when I got home last Friday night and you were mowing the lawn? Do you remember how you let me pour water on your face and you laughed until it got up your nose? Remember tonight when you first saw me and we were joking about plumbing and having your nails done? And French men and fighting with cufflinks?

"Or, think back to when you cut your hand and I was at the hospital that night with you. Or even the other day when I had such a bad headache. Do you remember how comfortable you were with me? I hugged you at the hospital when you were having your hand injected, and you weren't afraid of me. You rubbed my head for nearly an hour and you weren't afraid of me. So why were you uncomfortable with me in there?"

She looked at him wondering what he was getting at. "Was I truly that much different in there?"

"Not at first."

"And then?"

"And then you began to pull away from me."

"I'm sorry, Robby. I didn't mean to. It was just hard to comprehend how many women really wanted to be with you. I felt like one of your herd in there."

"Isn't that silly, Kelly, when the only one I had asked to be with me in there was you? I could have taken any one of them."

"But honestly Robby, isn't that why you asked me? So you didn't have to deal with the stampede?"

"Yes and no. I could have gone alone, or even stayed home you know. Yes, I don't like how those women swarm. I hate it. I know it has nothing to do with my wonderful talents and personality. None of them even know me. But if it was just that, then why do I like to come out here with you and the cats?"

"Because I don't swarm?"

"No, Kelly. I can go home to my condo and lock the door and unplug the phone, which is heavenly, by the way, thank you. But I can go be alone and no one is swarming. I still want to come out here instead. It's not just that you don't act like a herd animal.

"It's more than the fact that we aren't predatory. Aren't we honestly friends? Don't we enjoy being with each other? I like to be with you, Kelly. I trust you. It's safe to be with you. But tonight, after you saw how those others were, you got afraid of me."

She thought about that and nodded. He was right. Those women had compounded the worries she'd been having about how much she did indeed like him. He gazed at her sadly as she nodded, and then asked one little word. "Why?"

What to tell him? It was hard to bare her soul even a little. "Because we are friends, Robby. Because I do like you. I love you dearly. So then when I saw how those women reacted to you, it intimidated the heck out of me. What in the world would I have to like compared to all those beautiful women who are throwing themselves at you? And honestly Robby, I couldn't live with myself if I acted like some of those women."

"Sheesh. Thank goodness for that. Do you want the cherry off my Sunday?" He offered it to her and she took it and tipped her head up and bit the cherry off the stem. He wiped some whipped cream off of her chin and asked, "Do you truly not know the answer to what you have compared to them?" She just looked at him, unwilling to get any more gut honest than she already had.

He changed gears and asked her, "Kelly, what if I told you I was wealthy? Because I am. Not as well off as some, but more so than others. And the stupid thing is that I worked hard to get here and it's nice. Except for the money grubbers. But what if I told you I was? Would that change how you felt about me?"

She considered that. "I guess I can't say for sure, Robby, but I'd like to say I don't think so. I've known from almost the first that you were well enough off that you could afford two homes and aren't too concerned about money. Why would I care if you were well off?"

"I hope you wouldn't. I hope you wouldn't care if there were a lot of things about me I haven't told you. But there are some things about me I'm relatively sure you're not going to like. And it makes me tired."

At this point she was totally lost and didn't have a clue what to say, so it took awhile to even know what to answer. "That's where your smile went." He gave her a sad nod. "So are you going to tell me what's going to bother me?"

"Nope. I'm putting it off for as long as I can get away with it. I've had more fun with you these last three months than I've had in the last three years. Maybe you'll always like me and be my friend."

"Now you're scaring me, Robby. What's going on? Why would I not be your friend?"

"Do you trust me, Kelly?"

"Oh, Robby, of course I trust you. You know that as well as I do."

"Then you're just going to have to keep trusting me. Because I'm not telling you any more."

She met his blue eyes and only had to consider that for a second or two. "All right. I'm okay with that, Robby. I do trust you. Implicitly. Whatever your issues are, we'll figure it out. Not only have you trusted me when you had no good reason to, but we have far too nice of a friendship to mess it up. I'm sorry you have reasons to doubt me. I'll try to do better."

"It's not a doing better thing. You've been great. I guess it's a how durable or malleable are you, thing. And when it comes right down to it, we are what we are, I guess. What can we do differently tomorrow night so you won't feel like you're one of my herd? Tomorrow is going to be a sit down dinner, by the way."

She leaned her head back against the seat and took a deep breath. "Let me think about that one. I guess very first, I need to just choose not to feel like one of your herd."

"Would it help to remind you that I asked you?"

That would depend on why he asked her, but she didn't tell him that. "That will help." She gave him a smile. "Maybe, if I picture you washing walls with me. Or playing with the kitties. Maybe, then I'll remember that you're just Robby, and I'm just Kelly, the woman who washes the walls and feeds the cats."

He was looking at her like he wanted to say something to that, but then he simply nodded and went to turn the key. "It's a start. Let's go home and play with those kitties. Have we got any no-brainer movies? What have you got?"

"*Sahara, The Princess Bride,* and *Transformers.* Oh, and *McClintock.*"

"You have awesome taste in movies." He pulled out onto the highway. "Do we have popcorn?"

"Yes, and you ask for it every time, but do you ever actually eat any of it?"

"Not much, but it smells like a movie. It's important."

She laughed at him and he gave her a wan smile across the car. "My dad and I used to watch movies together. You would like my dad. What's your dad like?"

She took another bite of her sundae before she admitted, "He, uh, he left when I was two. I don't even know what he looks like."

The car was quiet for several seconds before he said, "I'm sorry." After a few more seconds, he thought out loud. "That's bizarre, isn't it? I'll bet you were marvelous when you were two. Why would a father do that?"

"My mother has spent the last twenty one years trying to reassure me it wasn't my fault, but sometimes I wonder if it wasn't because of me. She says he was just weak charactered and hadn't ever learned to settle down and be responsible."

"Kelly, when a man walks away from his family, there's no question that it's anyone's fault but his own. Especially not a two year old child's fault. How sad for him that he's missed out on everything in your life."

"I had an uncle who was close, and he kind of filled in. What is your father like?"

"I'm exactly the opposite of you. My dad was my best friend. He helped me deal with my bossy sisters. Except for just a short time when I was a teenager and totally obnoxious, he's been my number one fan, always." He reached up and loosened his tie. "He's been sick lately. He has diabetes and it's making him seem so much older than he should. He's only fifty-nine, but he's aged about ten years this last little while."

"Diabetes can do that. A lot of people don't worry about it as much as things like heart disease, but it can be awful. It's because it's hard to regulate, I think. Do you get to go home and see him often?"

"Quite a bit. And they come here sometimes. The whole family will be coming in a couple of weeks. You'll get to meet them. It's really fun when they all come, although I'm always relieved when they leave too. I have three married sisters and eight nieces and nephews. It always takes me a second to recover. I have a couple of little nieces who are mini dynamos. They remind me of you, actually."

"Is that a good thing? Are they good dynamos, or do they fall off ladders on you?"

He chuckled across the car. "It's a good thing."

Chapter 17

They drove back into Charlotte together the next evening because she had left the truck at his condo overnight, and he dropped her to have her hair done, then went to run some errands. He picked her up, then took her back to his house to dress. As they were unlocking the door, the phone began to ring, and Robbie grumbled, "The maid keeps plugging things back in. I even left her a note this time."

As they were coming in and shutting the door, the machine kicked on and a voice said, "Hey Robby, its Jenna. I know you're there because I just saw you pull into your parking garage. Can I come up and see you for a while? I know that you're lis…"

He picked up the phone with the bright yellow Post-It taped to the top and without preamble said, "Jenna, if you just saw me, then you know I have a friend with me. Isn't that just a little weird to want to come up? Look, I don't mean to be rude, but we're just heading in to a fundraiser. And you know I'm in the middle of training camp. I'll call you if I want to do something, okay? Just leave me alone for awhile, all right?"

He hung up without even waiting for her reply and turned to Kelly. "Sorry about that. I'll find someone to write the maid a note in Spanish. Maybe that will work. Do you have everything you need to dress?"

"I hope so. What did you mean, training camp?"

"That's just what my company calls the meetings and work we're doing right now with all the long hours." He went off toward his room. "How long do you need? Can we leave in twenty minutes?"

"Sure. I'll be ready." She gazed at him, hoping that phone call wasn't the beginning of another long night of being at least among his herd, if not one of them.

He must have known exactly how she was feeling

because he came back over to her and lifted her chin and gazed right into her eyes. "We're going to have a good night, Kelly. No matter what happens there or who is around to bother us. We're friends no matter what, remember? I'm just the guy who washes walls with you, and we're not going to let anyone else decide how we feel. I'm going to stay happy, and you're not going to pull away. If we have to, we'll go hide on a dance floor again."

He grinned at her. "As a last resort, we'll break into fisticuffs."

"Fisticuffs? Is that a real word?"

He gave her another smile as he headed for his room. "I'll have you know I got As in English in college. Fisticuffs is a word. Just like dork."

Fifteen minutes later when she came out of her room after dressing, dork was the absolutely last word that came to mind when she saw him in his suit. He'd looked good last night in navy blue, but tonight in black he was incredible. His hair that was so dark brown it was almost black, just touched the collar of his white shirt, and he looked nothing short of magnificent. She felt ridiculously out of her league. How was she ever going to keep from falling seriously in love with this man? And she knew more than ever that would be a huge mistake.

Her heart almost sank when she saw how he looked, but she decided to do her best to keep it light. "Oh, my, Robby, keeping the herd at bay was a great theory before you were dressed. Now it's out of the question. The only choice we have is for you to wear a paper bag over your head. No, no that wouldn't work either. The physique looks too good in the suit too. Do you have any of those big robes we wore to graduation? That's our only hope." She turned her back to him and asked, "Could you help me with this necklace? I can't work the clasp with this splint."

Taking the necklace from her hand, he bent to put it on her, and fiddled with it for a minute. "I don't know that I can work the clasp either with my big, clumsy hands. There, I got it." He glanced up and caught her eyes in the mirror across from them on the living room wall. "It's gonna take more than a graduation gown to disguise you tonight, Kelly. You look like a princess."

He put both hands on her shoulders and gazed at the two of them in the mirror. He stood another several inches over her, even in her heels and his dark good looks set off her lighter skin and shining auburn hair piled into curls and tendrils around her face and down her back. She knew the slim fitting black dress she wore showed off her figure to perfection. Even Monique had insisted that she buy it the moment she saw it. They were a striking couple and there was no denying it.

Now she just hoped they could pull off this worldly beauty and style without ruining the friendship they had enjoyed so much these last months together. She looked up and met his glittering eyes again, wondering if what she needed wasn't a suit of armor instead of evening wear.

That train of thought made her remember that even if they couldn't put on a real suit of armor, they could put on the whole armor of God. It was silly, but the fact that he looked so incredibly good seemed like a negative. But that was backward wasn't it? Between how good he looked and knowing they were going to be dealing with the other women, she truly felt in need of spiritual reinforcement. She needed to know how to cope with the way she felt about him. Turning to him, she asked, "Could we pray before we go, Robby? For some reason tonight, I really feel like I need that. Would you mind?"

She could feel him searching her eyes, but she didn't volunteer anything else and at length he said, "Sure. That's a good idea." They turned to kneel at the couch together and when he reached and took her hand as they bowed their heads it felt natural and right. She bowed her head next to his and was grateful when he volunteered. "I'll say it."

As he began to speak, she felt a literal rush of reassurance. This is how she would picture him in her mind when she started to feel like one of the herd. When the overwhelming feelings of being lost in the sea of beautiful women who wanted to be with him hit her, she'd remember this moment and realize that in spite of his appearance and the money he had warned her about, he was just Robby. The man who prayed beside her.

Their shared faith could bridge the gap and help her to not be intimidated. The only problem was that knowing he was a man of faith only made her feelings for him stronger. And that was a problem that could leave her trampled in the wake of the emotion. She knew that, and it scared her.

Listening to his soothing, low amen, she added her own prayer that she would know how to deal with all of this. Robby stood up, and still holding her hand, helped her to her feet. She let go of his hand and put hers to his cheek. "Thank you, Robby. I needed that. You always help me. Thank you. I'm going to be just fine now. Shall we go?"

He went and held the door for her. "I just wish we had a fairytale carriage waiting."

An hour and a half later, Kelly felt the evening was going reasonably well, all things considered. They'd made it inside and had survived the onslaught during the time everyone mingled before being seated for dinner, and even the fact that there had been a photographer inside hadn't been too threatening. Robby seemed to understand that she didn't want her photo taken and had gone to trouble to keep the photographer at the other end of the room from them.

Now, seated at a round banquet table, with Jason and Monique on one side of them and another two couples as well, she began to relax. The man she remembered Robby referring to as Bocklin who she'd met at the hospital was on her immediate left, but he had a date with him, and she assumed he would behave himself accordingly. She ignored him and wondered what was for dinner. She was starving.

The food was good, and she ate quietly and listened to the conversation going on around her while watching the people at the other tables as well. She'd been trying to pick out who the football players were as she ate. Other than Bocklin, she had picked out a couple who she thought might have been, but it was hard when everyone was in evening dress. She probably wouldn't have even known Bocklin was if she hadn't seen him that night at the stadium medical offices.

They were into their fourth course and Bocklin had

slowly migrated from asking her a casual question or two to be polite, to giving her pointed looks. Then he made a couple of low comments, almost whispered in her ear that left her in absolutely no doubt that he would continue to flirt with her in spite of the date that was sitting just on the other side of him, and Robby at her side.

As the dessert was served, Kelly had begun to wonder what was on the agenda for tonight, once the meal had been concluded when Bocklin's date excused herself and went to the powder room. Almost immediately, he turned toward Kelly and began to talk to her with thinly veiled inferences. Kelly reached under the table for Robby's hand to get his attention and put an end to Bocklin's outrageous flirting.

With Robby's eyes on him, Bocklin laughingly began to joke. "That night with Doc Snyder I almost didn't believe my eyes, Robideaux. I'd had you pegged for at least a switch hitter and was surprised to see you with a pretty girl. And the way she looks tonight, I'd almost like to arm wrestle you for her and take her off your hands."

Kelly rolled her eyes and Robby smiled at her reaction and said, "I'll bet she'd just love that, Bocklin. Big, macho guys like you are her specialty. But wouldn't your date be just a hint offended?"

Bocklin turned to Kelly and gave her a long, slow, come-on glance. "She'd get over it. She'd understand. She's seen Kelly here and can tell that she does something to a man's blood."

The smile died right out of Robby's face and he dropped the charade and said coldly, "Knock it off, Bocklin. We're having a nice dinner here. Don't ruin it. Save the barbarianism for the field."

Bocklin came right back with, "What's the matter, Rocker? Not afraid of a little competition are you?"

Kelly's water goblet stopped dead still on the way to her mouth. Her mind began to race as she turned to look at Robby and the others around the table.

She met Robby's eyes for just a split second and wasn't sure what she saw there, and then Bocklin went on. "It's too bad we both play offense. I've never had a chance to prove to you just how much better I am on the field, but I've proven it a hundred times over off. Not willing to engage in a contest for a girl? Or do you just know that I'm by far more masculine and that she fires me up?"

At this, Robby's eyes began to glitter, and Kelly could see the anger in their depths. She squeezed his hand under the table as she turned to Bocklin and asked sweetly, "Is that really true? Do I fire you up, Bocklin?"

He eyed her sickeningly, gave her a suggestive grin, and assured her, "You know you do, baby."

Furious to the core, Kelly hid it well as she sweetly replied, "Well, this should help then." With that she simply tipped her full water goblet and let the ice cold liquid land strategically in Bocklin's heated lap.

Immediately she began to pretend it had been an accident. "Oh, dear. I am so sorry." She handed him the napkin out of her own lap and went on in the same sweet voice, "That was so clumsy of me. Please. Accept my full apologies. I can't imagine how that happened. It somehow just tipped so quickly."

Bocklin swore, stood up and glared at her and then around the table. Just then his date came back and looked at him and the others in surprise. He wiped at his pants with the napkins and then growled at the innocent woman who had had the misfortune of accompanying him, "Let's get out of here, Candice." He turned to Robby. "She's all yours, Rocker. With my blessing."

Robby answered him sarcastically, "Why, thanks, Bocklin. That's so generous of you."

After Bocklin was gone, there was a moment of silence. Kelly looked around the table, first at the other couple and said, "Sorry about that. I shouldn't have done it, but..." Then she turned to Jason and Monique who appeared almost panicked. She continued on and met Robby's eyes. For just a moment she felt herself wanting to cry and ask him why. Then she just wanted to get away.

He put a hand on her arm. "I'm sorry that we got seated with him..."

She shook her head and interrupted him. "He wasn't a

problem. And his behavior isn't your fault, *Rocker*. Excuse me please." With as much dignity as she could find in her shriveled up heart, she stood up and walked toward the exit and the restroom.

Out in the hall, when she was almost to the door of the ladies room, she saw the side exit to the street and just kept on walking. She wished she could have just kept on walking right out of the belly deep, heart-breaking embarrassment that felt as if it were going to choke her.

Outside, she hailed a waiting cab without a backward glance and got into the car and let it pull away before she let the tears that had been threatening for the last few minutes fall and drip onto her exquisite party dress. *Geez, she had been an idiot.*

At Robby's condo, she struggled to control the tears as she got out. She paid the cabby, waved as she walked past the security guard, got into Robby's truck and headed for home, still wondering how she had been so stupid as to not have realized that not only was he a football player, he was a world class one.

She had probably led Peter and the others straight to her by being seen with such a super star. And she'd probably gotten him into trouble for hiring her as well. The press would have a ball with this. It brought a whole new meaning to the word fool.

She cried all the way to the house, and tears still dripped down her cheeks as she pulled up the Internet to look up Rocker Robideaux, Carolina Panther, and eligible bachelor extraordinaire. What she found there made her completely heart sick. So much for thinking about washing walls, or playing with the kitties, or even him praying with her.

Standing up, she kicked her beautiful shoes off into a corner and began to take the pins out of her hair, then took her toiletries bag and a pair of pajamas, and headed for the shower. Gazing in that mirror tonight, just for a minute, she'd actually thought about forever.

At the door to the summer kitchen, she turned and looked back at her little home. What was she going to do now? She'd have to leave before Peter found her here. Which didn't matter anyway. Robby wasn't about to think about forever with her when he could literally have his pick of any girl on the planet.

It was no wonder he had a herd. Those girls would have been a mere tip of the iceberg. She began to cry again as she went over to the main house and got into the shower. *How had she been this incredibly foolish and naïve?*

She showered until the water ran cold and then went to her house, turned out the lights, and climbed into bed. She didn't even pray. She had no idea what to pray for and didn't want to admit even to God how stupid she'd been.

Forty minutes later, when she heard his Land Rover pull up, she buried her head under the pillow and tried to stop crying. When she heard Robby talk to her through the open window beside her bed, she pulled the pillow off and spoke through her tears. "Go away."

Her head rang with a jumble of thoughts. How did this happen, and what was she going to do now? How in the world could she live without his help and protection? And what did she do with this hopelessly broken heart? The one thought that resonated clearly and strongly was that a future with Robby was completely and totally out of her reach in every way imaginable.

She had no idea what time it was when she finally cried herself to sleep.

Crimonies, what a night! He had had some days that had ended in a ball of fire, but this one had to be his all time topper. He should have known it. He should have known that things were going to go into a nosedive from the second they'd walked into the condo to the sound of the phone. He sat on the leather couch in the firelight and picked up a kitten and put it into his lap.

He tried to look back on his life to figure out how in the world he had gotten to this place. And where was he? This was insane. They couldn't even make a movie of this, the screen play would have been too implausible. He gazed up at the ceiling and spoke out loud, "Okay, Lord. What did I do so wrong in my life to deserve this mess?"

Ten years ago he had dreamed of making it big, and all the things that would mean. Then, a few more dollars and being able to play more football solved every issue he had. He never dreamed he'd be twenty-eight years old, single, and with a thousand new issues, and less clue than an eighteen-year-old about how to deal with them.

Leaning his head back against the sofa, he closed his eyes. *Man, she had been beautiful tonight.* She'd looked so good it had almost scared him, and it had taken every bit of his self-control not to lean down and kiss her neck as he'd put her jewelry on for her. But, he'd wanted to. Man, he'd wanted to. Only knowing she'd have completely run away from him emotionally made him resist.

Poor Kelly. Poor, beautiful, sweet Kelly. It had been more than two hours since Bocklin's idiotic revelation, and she was still out there crying.

After another few minutes of thinking and worrying, he smiled as he thought about how she had dumped that whole glass of water on Bocklin to help cool him off. That had been the most classic thing he'd ever seen. Coach would have loved it!

The fire began to burn down, and he watched as a log burned through and fell. At least she was still here. He'd never been so relieved in his life as when he'd driven up to find her bike still parked outside. In the morning he'd have to find a way to start making it up to her.

But how did you fix something like this? He hadn't done anything except be exceptionally talented and lucky and successful. How could you fix that and why would you want to? It had taken years and years and an incredible amount of work to get here. This should be a good thing. Why did it feel so insurmountable?

He put the kitten down, got up, and shut the fireplace screen. Maybe things would seem better in the morning.

Chapter 18

The sound of a spoon hitting a bowl in the kitchen alerted him to the fact that she was up and getting herself breakfast. He put down the Book of Mormon he was reading while he'd been waiting, and went to go start patching things up. In the kitchen he found a box of cold cereal on the counter, poured himself a bowl, and followed her out to the front step of the porch. She was sitting there in a pair of sunglasses, barefooted, and in shorts and a T-shirt, munching. He dropped down beside her with his own bowl and leaned his arm against her shoulder.

For a minute or two all they did was eat beside each other, and then finally, without looking up, she said, "You're a jerk."

"I know. And I'm sorry."

Again, they ate in silence until she asked, "Aren't you missing church?"

"It's stake conference today. I was sort of hoping I could come out and go to your ward with you this morning."

"I'm sick."

"Where are you sick?"

"You're not my mother."

She took another bite and chewed it. "My eyes are too puffy to go to church today." He went to take her sunglasses, and she shrugged him off. "Don't. I look awful."

He turned to her and very gently took her sunglasses off and gazed into her eyes. "You don't look awful."

She put the glasses back on. "Don't lie to me Robby. Don't lie to me anymore anyway."

"I'm not lying. And I've never lied to you. I don't lie. I told you that."

"I'm in acquisitions? Come off it."

"I'm a wide receiver. And you weren't all that honest with me either Ms. Campbell."

"Shaye is my middle name. I don't lie either. Really.

Were you just trying to make a complete fool of me in front of your friends? Because if you were, it worked out quite nicely."

"Oh, stop it. You know I wasn't trying to make you look bad. At first, I just didn't know you. You've seen what I'm up against. I knew I was being prompted to hire you, but I didn't dare tell a stranger all about me, and then hand her my phone numbers and a key to my house."

"Well, you could have told me once you knew you could trust me."

"You'd made it perfectly clear just exactly what you thought of football players, Kelly."

She made a sound of disgust. "The local stud muffin and a bunch of college Neanderthals who can't pronounce their own names. You're not exactly what I was talking about, Mr. NFL MVP."

"In all honesty, there was probably a time that I was a college Neanderthal."

"You? Playing stupid isn't going to get you out of this one, Robby. *Rocker.*"

He turned to her and took her glasses off again. "Look, Kelly, I am what I am. I'd apologize for what I do if I thought it would help. But, I am what I am. I'm sorry you hate it. I wish you didn't."

She gazed at him with big, sad eyes and then turned away. "Why didn't you tell me?"

"You're the only woman who doesn't like me because of my football. You're the only woman who doesn't like me *because* of my football. It's totally frustrating and totally refreshing at the same time. For all these months I've known we were friends because we liked and respected each other. It honestly was my own personality, me that you were friends with. Not because I'm Rocker Robideaux. It's been priceless to me."

Without looking up, she asked, "Are you firing me?"

"Of course not. Why would I fire you? I'm not the one who doesn't like you. I've known about you for months and have still wanted you around. Are you firing me?" She looked up at him. "You know what I mean."

"I don't know what I'm going to do." She sighed and set

her bowl beside her on the step and admitted sadly, "I'm completely lost this morning."

He put his bowl down too and reached for her hand. "Kelly, why do you think I didn't tell you I was a pro football player?"

She put the glasses back on. "Because you didn't want another harem girl. I've seen the girls, Robby. I do understand what you're up against."

"Kelly, I just didn't want our friendship to change. I wanted to be able to come out here and mow the lawn without it being a big deal. I'm just the guy who washes the walls, remember?"

"No, Robby, you're not. Maybe you were right to keep me in the dark. It was fun while it lasted. It was. But, reality is reality."

"You make it sound like me being wealthy or well-known is the end of the world, Kelly. I can't be all that bad, can I? There must be *something* good about me still."

She put her head down on her knees, wrapped her arms around them, and her shoulders began to shake. Sliding an arm around her, he pulled her over against his chest. "Don't cry Kelly. Please don't cry. If I'd known it was going to make you this upset, I would have told you. I promise I would have. I just wanted to keep enjoying you for longer. Can't we go back and pretend I'm just a business man?"

She shook her head without raising it and sniffled. "I have to go home."

Her voice was muffled, and he pulled her hair aside. "I'm sorry. I can't hear what you're saying very well."

Raising her tear-streaked face to him, she repeated it, "I have to go home, Robby. I didn't realize the kind of publicity I was potentially exposing myself to. They probably already know where I am.

"They'll kill me. And I have to stop them. I still don't know how, but those poor patients are dying, and there's no one to stop them. They're getting away with it. And Peter is dealing drugs." She wiped her eyes and put her head back down. "And I can't stay here with you like this. Knowing who you are now, it would be insane."

He stroked her head and continued to hug her against him. "We've done okay, Kelly. We can keep on doing okay. Why can't you stay? If you left, I'd die without you. And what about Ted and the kittens?"

She finally did relax against him, but then shook her head and said, "You don't understand, Robby. They'll kill me and drag you into this whole mess. The press would have a field day with me. I can't do that to you. I have to go."

"Go where? Who would kill you?" He pulled back and lifted her chin. "Out with it Kelly. You need to tell me what's going on. The nice thing is that along with the horrible money and the fame comes power. You'd be amazed at what I can do because of who I am. Let me help you."

She looked up at him quietly, then sighed and began. For several minutes she told him the tale of what had happened at her work back in Chicago, and he finally understood why she'd run away nearly four months earlier. He rubbed the pink scar on her fore arm, knowing now that he'd been right about the blood in her car.

Shaken and unsure of how to go about taking care of this, he decided to try to lighten things up. "You dated a psychiatrist? I don't know, but that sounds crazy to me. Talk about insane."

She shook her head, and he finally got the merest hint of a smile out of her. "This isn't really a laughing matter, Robby."

He nudged her. "Well, you didn't really laugh. I'll have to research some good psychiatrist jokes. I'll bet there are tons of them."

"You're probably right." She nodded at his empty cereal bowl. "I know you're still starving. Go get you another bowl. Or do you want some real breakfast? I can make you something."

"Real food does sound good, but I can make it. Come finish talking to me while I cook. What time is your church? I can't remember."

"Eleven o'clock. We're in the same stake. But I honestly don't feel like going. My head is pounding."

He stood up and reached a hand to pull her up too. "Well,

if you'd quit bawling." He smiled and put an arm around her shoulders. "That can't be good on a headache. And I know headaches. Let me finish eating, and I'll rub it for you."

As they went into the front door, she looked up at him. "You had a brain concussion, didn't you?"

"I don't know for sure. Jason thought so. That's why he brought me out that night. I know from your perspective I'm stupid, but the younger guys on the team look to Jason and me as role models. I couldn't call in sick that day. And it was worth it to be a strong example. Coach knew what had happened and pulled me out the next day to consult with some of the secondary coaches, so at least I wasn't still getting knocked around."

Still watching him with big eyes, she asked, "Does that happen often?"

"No. I've had a couple over the years. I know this is going to sound suspect to you, Kelly, but I honestly do try to take care of my body. It's the only one I'm going to get, and it's also how I earn my living. I'm an athlete. My body is a big deal to me." She glanced at him up and down, and then continued on to the kitchen with him following. *Now what had that look meant?*

She sat at the bar, and he dug through the fridge and surfaced with bacon, eggs, and hash browns. "Are you still hungry? Do you want some too?"

"I didn't think so, but bacon and hash browns do sound good. Mostly, I just want to go back to bed. I think I'm going to wear my sunglasses even indoors today. Just these kitchen lights are too bright."

"Go lie on the couch and I'll bring your food to you when it's done. Do you want ketchup?"

"Yes, please."

"Hold one of the kitties, and I'll be right in."

When he got to the living room, she was sound asleep, so he went into his room and brought her the quilt off of his bed and covered her with it and sat on the chair across from her, watching her sleep as he ate. She didn't look like a princess anymore this morning. More like a tired, auburn haired angel.

Monique had known that Kelly would be sad, but Monique hadn't understood just what Kelly's situation was, and had vastly underestimated just how sad. Kelly must have cried a good portion of the night from the looks of things. He gave himself a wry smile. This was the first time in his life that a female had been devastated that he was rich and famous.

At least she wasn't gone. That was a good thing. Although he knew she still had every intention of leaving him sometime in the near future. He finished his breakfast and took their dishes back to the kitchen, loaded the dishwasher, and cleaned up. Then he took his cell phone and went out to the front step again to make phone calls.

He wasn't exactly sure how to go about getting the mess in Chicago cleaned up, especially if there was a rogue cop involved, but he'd figure it out. That was the very least he could do for her in exchange for all she had done for him. After all, she had helped him find his passion for life again. It was an incredible gift.

He'd call a friend from college who was now an All-American Hall of Famer who played for the Chicago Bears. Maybe he could point him in the right direction. Then he'd see if he could sneak into the back of the stake conference.

Kelly woke up there on the couch in the dim light of early afternoon. He'd put his own quilt over her as she slept and his smell made her cry all over again. What was she going to do about Robby? She sighed, knowing she needed to be gearing up to tell him goodbye. Whether the mess with Peter was resolved or not, she couldn't continue to stay here falling in love with Robby Robideaux now that she knew he was, in fact, Rocker Robideaux. It would be foolish and pointless.

She snuggled deeper into the sweet smelling flannel and went back to sleep. Her head still ached, and she couldn't face this day yet anyway.

When he came in from church, he found the tears still on her cheeks. He'd known she'd be upset at him, but he'd had no idea she'd be this deeply sad over things.

He walked on into the kitchen to start making lunch, wishing he wasn't right in the middle of such a demanding time of the season right now. It would have been good to be able to take some time and baby her, but then the busy time of the season was probably why this whole thing had flared up anyway.

It was just as well. They'd needed to get things out in the open, if only so they could get to the bottom of her troubles back home. It wasn't like they could go on living like they had been forever, but, oh, it sure would have been nice.

No, on thinking about it, he didn't want just the status quo. It was time he moved on in his life. He'd wanted to settle down for so long, but just hadn't found her. Now he'd found her, but he had to work through all of their issues before he could even try to talk her into marrying him.

As he got steaks ready to go on the grill, he tried to make a game plan in his head for how to go about fixing his relationship with her. Their first pre-season game was this next Saturday, and then the next one was the following Thursday and was against the Bears in Chicago. That felt like another one of those things that couldn't be coincidence.

In the meantime, they had the Fan Fest celebration at the stadium Wednesday night, and practices every day this week and next until they flew out for Illinois. Kelly was going to get the last of her stitches out tomorrow, and he was going to take her during his lunch hour, if she'd still let him.

Somehow, he knew she was going to be back to that fearful girl he'd first met until she got over worrying about who had seen them together. Even in that she had a viable concern. If what was going on back home was truly the way she had described it, then even the smallest press coverage truly could be putting her life in danger. Maybe he shouldn't try to go with her to get the stitches out.

Picking up a platter of steaks and corn on the cob, he carried them to the grill on the front porch, glancing at the couch as he walked past. Seeing her eyes open and watching him, he slowed. "Feeling any better?"

She hesitated for just a moment and then nodded her head. "Yeah, I'm fine."

He studied the lines on her forehead and then continued on to the grill to put the meat on, and came back inside as she sat up on the couch. "I thought you said you didn't lie."

"I don't. I am feeling better, and I'm fine."

He sat next to her and pulled her back down to lean onto his lap and began to rub her head. "Are you feeling better physically or emotionally?"

"Both."

"You don't sound positive about that."

She sighed. "I'm going to be fine, Robby. Just give me some time to adjust and figure this out. I'm tougher than I seem." She closed her eyes.

"I know that. I actually know you pretty well, considering. I was going to ask you. How much contact have you had with your family? Do you want me to take something to them when I go to Chicago next week for a game? Or we could even try to smuggle you in to see them."

Without opening her eyes, she said, "I don't have any ID, and I couldn't risk being seen, but thank you anyway. It was a heavenly thought. Maybe you could just mail a letter from there when you go."

"You don't have to have ID or be seen. I'll charter a jet. You could stay right in the plane. I could go get them and bring them to you. Or have Jason do it while I stay with you."

She opened her eyes. "No, Robby. You're not going to start spending forty-leven dozen million dollars on me just because now I know that you can. A letter will be enough until I can get things settled and get home. It'll just be nice for them to know I'm okay. I'm sure my mom has been worried."

"I've sent her flowers a couple of times. Daisies. I always used to send her daisies when she was having a bad day. We had this thing where daisies symbolized pressing forward with a perfect brightness of hope. I didn't feel like I could send a card with them, but I'm sure she understood I was trying to tell her I was okay."

He pulled her long hair out and straightened it with his fingers. "I can't even imagine having your child just up and disappear the way you did. It would kill a parent. What you were able to do in such a short time was amazing. You're so smart. I would never have thought to do everything you did."

She raised her head and gazed at him. "You don't honestly think I thought that day through alone, do you?" He met her eyes and then she laid her head back down. "The Holy Ghost helped me every step of the way that day, Robby. I could never have made it safely away without Him."

He brushed the hair back from her brow. "I'm so glad you recognize that and know how to listen." He gently lifted her head. "Let me up, Kel. I need to go turn the steaks." A minute later, he came back in and pulled her back down. "Let me rub the other side." As she turned her head, he asked, "Did you decide you don't hate me, Kelly?"

"Of course, I don't hate you, Robby. I could never hate you."

"Then why were you so upset?"

She sighed and turned her face into his belly. "I'm just sad, Robby. Sad and worried. I knew we couldn't live like this forever, but I didn't really want to face it quite this soon. I'm just going to miss you."

Robby wanted to lift her up in his arms so he could look her in the face and tell her she wasn't going anywhere, but he couldn't. In the first place, he would help her move himself if he felt like she was in danger, and secondly, he knew he was going to have to win her over on this one fair and square. To do that, he had to fix the issues back home first so he could even start trying to help her learn to deal with his life.

He ran his fingers through her hair again, feeling like he wanted to almost tug on it and let her know that he needed her, but he couldn't. Not this fast. "Don't bail on me yet, Kelly. I've got a very powerful friend in Chicago who's going to subtly start checking into things from the top down so they can roust out the crooked cop and shut your crazy boyfriend down. Please don't leave me just yet, okay? I'd be so lonely without you."

Chapter 19

Peter Holmes was half asleep with a drink in his hand in front of the TV. He was idly flipping through the channels when he stopped stock still and flipped back a channel. Just for a second he thought he had seen Kelly. The hair had been different, but that color and figure were unusually striking. The last channel back was one of those what's-going-on-with-the-rich-and-famous type shows and he clicked on, knowing she wouldn't have been in the society news.

He flipped back through and couldn't find her again, and went back to the channel he'd originally thought. Would she have been on the celebrity show? She had been beautiful, but she had also been smart. She wasn't dumb enough to stage her own death and then become involved with someone the press would follow.

Leaving that channel on, he watched for a second. It was a story about an NFL player's charitable foundation. The story was about one of the fundraisers being held by members of the Carolina Panthers football team.

Peter watched disinterestedly until he caught another glimpse of the woman who he thought could be Kelly. It hadn't been a close shot, but it definitely looked just like her. Her and some tall, dark man in a black suit. He couldn't tell if it was really her, but he was going to check it out anyway. The likeness had been uncanny.

When the news clip was over, he clicked off the remote and dragged himself out of the chair, half-embarrassed that he still found himself attracted to a woman he had every intention of permanently silencing. He swore under his breath. She had so gotten under his skin.

Kelly took her motorcycle into town the next day to go to the doctor. She hadn't ridden it in weeks because of her hand and the new truck, and it was still somewhat awkward, but this morning she chose to take it. Strapping on the helmet, she was pleasantly surprised again to remember just how unrecognizable she could become within seconds in her leather garb and gear. She should still use this whenever she didn't need to carry something. It truly would be harder for Peter and the others to find her if she was this covered.

Before she pulled out, she decided to keep her stash of money, the gold wristband, and the title in the bottom of one of the saddlebags just in case she ever did have to run again at a moment's notice. She'd have to get a lock for the saddle bags, but being prepared was a good idea, considering.

Robby had made a point of making sure she had plenty of money in the jar in the kitchen cupboard. Some of it was her pay, but mostly he was just being incredibly generous. She had never counted it, but there had to be thousands of dollars in there. This time, when she put money in the saddlebags, she put in a hairbrush and toothbrush as well, just in case.

She drove in to the stadium to meet Robby because he wouldn't let her back out of their prior arrangements, but when she saw a handful of players and the small crowd that had gathered out front, she pulled over to the other side of Robby's Land Rover and parked where he'd just be able to see her when he came out. She saw him exit the door, and she acknowledged the stir he created in the crowd with both a sense of pride and almost a feeling of doom.

Rolling her neck under the heavy helmet, she tried to dispel the disappointment that flooded her again. Before realizing who he was, she had begun to wonder about forever with him. Knowing now, the resulting let down was bitter. Forever with Rocker Robideaux was so far out of the question it was ridiculous.

She focused on watching him approach to keep her mind off of her disappointment, but soon realized that was a mistake and had to focus on her leather riding gloves in order to get how good he looked striding toward her out of her head as well. As he got close, she pulled out, telling herself little errands like this with him needed to stop. He was too high profile, and she was too vulnerable to heartbreak. Doing this was simply asking for trouble.

The Land Rover arrived at the clinic before she did, and Robby stood waiting for her in the parking lot. She parked the bike and walked over to him, glad he couldn't see how happy she was to see him. She needed to get a handle on her feelings. Until Saturday night, she hadn't realized just how attached to him she truly was. It was already going to kill her to say goodbye as it was, not to mention how embarrassing it was to know in her heart that she was definitely another one of his herd.

As he put a casual hand around her waist when they walked through the doors, she mentally shook herself. She had to get a lot more serious about finding a solution to Peter Holmes and associates, because she was way past the point of when she should be going home.

Peter's man followed Rocker Robideaux for four days and never saw a glimpse of the girl in the photo he had been given. He'd followed him from the stadium to his condo in the city and all around the town of Charlotte. He'd been at the celebration with the fans and had even sneaked in to view a couple of the practices with a handful of other fans.

He was certain he had the right Carolina Panther. He'd gotten a copy of the show Peter had seen and viewed it three times to be able to identify the man for sure. Rocker was definitely the man in the clip, but he wasn't seen with the red head again.

Finally, the man resorted to asking around about the girls Rocker was known to hang out with and learned that most people hadn't ever seen Rocker with a red-headed girl at all. One man even gave a disgusting grin and said, "That Rocker. I don't he think he really likes women. I think you want to be checking for a boyfriend where he's concerned."

Armed with that last bit of news and a packet full of photographs of Rocker sans the red head, the man boarded a plane and went home to report to Peter Holmes.

When Robby came home that night to find Kelly finishing installing a jacuzzi tub she'd had delivered in the summer kitchen, he breathed a sigh of relief. Maybe things were going to be able to get back to normal around here.

And if she was still installing a tub in her new bathroom, she wasn't planning to leave immediately. He was so glad that he wanted to have a hallelujah breakdown, but he acted completely nonchalant instead. He walked into the new bathroom and gazed all around. "This is going to be great, Kelly! I love the old fashioned copper tub design. And the jets will be awesome."

"It is going to be nice isn't it? Now if I can just get this connection to stop leaking. Maybe it's just that my hands aren't strong enough. Can you get this to turn?"

He knelt beside her and leaned in to see what she was talking about, and then easily turned the wrench she'd been struggling with. She reached over and opened a valve and they watched the connection intently for several seconds to see if it showed tell tale signs of leaking. When it didn't leak even a drop, she said, "Cool. Thanks. I've been hassling with that thing for an hour. It almost makes me mad that you did it that easily. Have you eaten?"

"No, I was hoping for home cooked food here. Have you got anything planned for dinner?"

"Grilled salmon and a salad. But I haven't started it yet. Are you starving?"

"Of course. What else can I help you do here before we cook dinner?"

"Would you mind helping lift the toilet onto the drain pipe. It's too big for me to lift, but it should just take a minute."

Robby smiled his biggest smile at her. "Toilets *are* my specialty. Hence the name, Robby's Plumbing, Home of the Porcelain Throne. Didn't you see my ad in the yellow pages?"

She glanced up and said drily, "Must have missed that one, sorry."

"You missed out! It has a lovely cartoon of me with a plunger for a scepter."

She rolled her eyes. "You should have been a used car salesman instead of a wide receiver." As he stood up, she offered him her hand to pull her up. "How was practice?"

"Good. Bocklin is still ticked. It's probably a good thing that he plays on the offensive with me on days like today when we scrimmage. How is the hand?" He reached for it and examined the long, purple scar that ran along the bottom of her thumb and palm. "Gosh, other than the scar, it's perfect. How does it feel?"

"Tender and weak and positively liberated without the splint."

"I thought he said it still needed to be splinted."

She looked guilty as she admitted, "He did. I just took it off for a second to see if I could turn that wrench." She leaned down and picked up the splint and slipped it back on. She blew a tendril of red brown hair out of her eyes and led him to the toilet she'd assembled. "Can you lift this to there?" She indicated the drain pipe and bolts she'd installed in the floor.

He leaned down and took both of her hands and then gazed into her face. "Kelly Shaye Campbell, if I help you with your potty, will you forgive me for being an NFL player once and for all?" She looked up at him and then down at their hands and then back up with big eyes, and he smiled at her in encouragement.

With a completely serious face, she replied, "I don't need to forgive you for being an NFL player, Robby. That issue was all mine. I was being terribly prejudiced, and I realize that now. I'm working on leaving that all behind. You didn't do anything wrong. What you are in trouble for was not being up front with me, but I understand that and you're forgiven. Now I just have to figure out how to deal with working for a superstar."

"Wow, I didn't know you worked for a superstar! I just thought he was a regular, normal Joe." He picked up the toilet and gently put it down on the drain pipe and bolts. "Is that where?"

"That's where. I'm so glad that you're a regular Joe with big muscles."

"I thought you hated muscles."

She looked up at him seriously again. "Oh, Robby, you're so confused. There's not a woman on earth who doesn't adore muscles, as long as there's a brain that's bigger than they are. Did you not understand that?"

"No, I guess I missed that part. Do I have a big enough brain to be one of the good guys?"

She laughed. "You're definitely one of the good guys."

While they were eating, he reported on what was going on in Chicago, hoping to put the brakes on her determination to leave soon. "My friend went to the Chief of Police for Chicago and told him what you thought was going on. He wants to know if he could meet with you if he flew down here sometime. I told him I would bring you with me to the game. Is that okay with you? We should try to get things resolved quickly so you don't feel like you have to leave."

What he had said obviously spooked her, and she asked, "There's not a chance that the Chief of Police would be involved with something crooked, is there?"

He shook his head. "I guess there's always the chance, but Mark thinks he's honest. And he and I and Jason will all three be with you. I would think you'll be okay. There's not a whole lot higher you can go, unless we go to the feds. And we'll do that next if this doesn't work.

"Plan to fly up with me on Wednesday afternoon next week, and we'll come home late Thursday night. You can stay right on the plane and we'll try to get your mom and uncle, and whoever else and bring them to see you. I'll take some private security men to watch over us."

"Isn't that going to cost a fortune?" She didn't appear terribly happy about it.

He shrugged and finished his bite. "I told coach I was going to charter a plane, and he mentioned it to the owner who is flying up for the game anyway. We'll fly up on his private plane with him, and it's not going to cost anything. Monique and Shania will be coming as well."

"And you don't think we'll have to have my ID?"

"Not unless we were going out of the country. You should be fine. And maybe you'll get to see your mom." Her eyes lit up and then tears spilled over, and he got up and came around and leaned down next to her chair. "Don't cry, Kelly. I didn't mean to upset you."

He put a hand on her shoulder and rubbed it slowly. "We're going to get to the bottom of this and then you'll be able to come and go as you please. You'll be safe and won't have to keep worrying or ever run away again. And you'll be able to know you protected those people at your hospital. It's all going to work out in the end."

She turned and buried her face against him and cried softly. Finally, she said, "I hope so, Robby. It would be so nice to see my mom."

He held her as she cried for a few minutes and then she wiped her eyes on her sleeve and looked embarrassed, as she said, "Sorry. Go back and eat your dinner before it gets cold."

Still watching her closely, he asked, "Are you going to be okay?" She nodded and sniffed. On the way back to his chair, he said, "Good. Have you ever flown in a private plane before?"

"Heavens no!"

He chuckled, "Then you're in for a treat. The owner will love you. He's the perfect southern, rich guy. He has this unreal accent and wonderful manners with just a touch of redneck. You'll have a ball."

"I'm sure I will. He has a touch of redneck, and he owns a pro football team?"

"Just enough redneck to make you completely comfortable around him. You'll see. It'll be fun. Everyone should ride in a private jet at least once in their life."

There were times, like that night as they knelt and prayed together in the living room before she went to her house to go to bed, that she felt like things were back to normal, and they were going to keep on as they were and be fine. And there were times, like when he came in for breakfast the next morning in a Panther warm up suit, looking like a movie star, that she knew their worlds would never truly mesh.

She took one look at him as she put a breakfast quiche on the table and mentally backed herself right into her shell. She couldn't just keep living like this. She was going to get her heart broken into a million small pieces.

He left for practice and she headed for the garden while it was still cool out. After harvesting baskets of produce, she took them into the kitchen and began to bottle what she knew they couldn't use before it spoiled. Then, with the canner processing, she went out to finish hooking up the last of the plumbing in the summer kitchen bathroom.

With that done, she gazed around at the luxurious new room. It was a perfect mix of the clean, simple, rustic building and era, and yet the latest in modern convenience. It was going to be wonderful to have her own private bathroom. Then she reminded herself that she was going to be leaving soon. She tried to be objective about it as she reasoned that it would be a great residence for whoever he hired to take her place as a caretaker here.

The thought of someone else getting him breakfast and sending him off to practice made her heartsick. She struggled not to let the tears that weighed on her heart fall out of her eyes, as she took stock of what her next project was going to be.

Everything she and Robby had discussed in the main part of the house was finished except for the master suite. And after that, there was the wine cellar and theatre room in the basement still to do. Without knowing for sure what her plans were going to be about going home to Chicago, she decided just to move forward as much as she could, and if she had to leave before she was finished, he'd simply have to find someone else to tie up the loose ends.

She was such an emotional basket case that she was driving herself nuts. Robby was probably sick to death of it. She wasn't usually a whiny, weepy kind of a girl, and, frankly, it was awful. She had to get a handle on all of this.

Thinking too much upset her, and she tried not to, but her mind would flit from sadness about leaving to worry about Peter. She'd catch herself thinking about how Robby looked, or how he made her feel when he was around, and she'd daydream until she realized what she was doing, then she'd mentally berate herself for letting her mind set her up for even more heartbreak.

She had been honest with him about trying to leave her prejudices about stupid athletes behind and had been focusing on the positive about Robby and his career. Since that momentous night, she'd gotten cable hooked up and begun to watch the news religiously. Not a night went by that Robby wasn't one of the stars of the sports portion and often was mentioned in the main part of the local news as well, for one reason or another. He and Jason were involved with all kinds of local events and charities, and the people of North Carolina obviously loved their star athletes.

And he *was* a star athlete. It hadn't been terribly hard to see that not only was Robby the same gorgeous, articulate, intelligent man she'd become friends with, but he truly did have the marvelous physique of a world class athlete. He was almost graceful, he was so effortlessly agile. He moved like a big, powerful cat and the team name of panther fit him like a glove, now that she realized it. He had that same innate, coiled strength she had feared when she'd wondered if the panther they'd seen was going to spring across the river at her. It was no wonder he could play at a world class level. It was also no wonder she was hopelessly attracted to him.

The only way she found to combat the tug of war for her sanity was to throw herself into her working agenda with the same passion that she had when she'd first come here. Then she'd been trying to overcome the loneliness and fear, now she was trying to overcome her feelings for Robby and more of the same fear.

Toiling like a maniac did work though. She was able to handle the emotional struggles, and she got a lot done. At nights she was able to fall into bed tired enough that she didn't lie there awake in an emotional stew. Sometimes, when Robby was there, she knew he watched her with an unfathomable expression, but she was doing the best she could to handle her feelings for him and his station in life. She knew he wasn't happy with the distance she worked so hard to keep between him and her emotions, but it was the only way she was going to survive this. She had no choice.

Chapter 20

By the time his first game arrived, she had the master bedroom stripped and stained, and had installed a new set of French doors out to a private deck she'd framed in. It didn't have the decking installed yet, but it was still a lot of headway for those short few days.

Saturday morning, the tension between them was almost palpable. She wanted more than anything in her life to be able to go in to his game, but she couldn't even ask about coming, not to mention the fact that it would have been incredibly foolish to put herself in that kind of limelight with him.

At breakfast, she tried to act like it was a normal, happy day, but the fact of his station in life had never loomed bigger in her psyche. She was struggling like never before.

He must have known what a mess she was because he was watching her like a hawk. At least he seemed to be okay, and she was immensely grateful for his mental toughness and emotional stability. It would have killed her if her chaotic mindset had rubbed off on him and thrown off his game.

She spent the first part of the morning installing decking and he disappeared, which was a good thing. It was hard enough to keep up her mask of nonchalance that she was grateful he hadn't volunteered to help for once. Toward late morning, he showed up and after quietly watching her work for a few minutes, he said, "I need to leave. Do you want to come and pray with me?"

Wordlessly, she took off her knee pads and accepted his hand to stand up and follow him back into the living room. They knelt side by side, and he took her hand again. "Would you pray this time, Kelly?"

She bowed her head and began to pray. She thanked their Father in Heaven for their blessings, and then asked for His help in blessing Robby to play well, and be protected, and to enjoy playing the game that he loved. She asked that the men who played around him would be able to feed off of his spirit and his passion, and to play to the best of their abilities as well, and that they would continue to be lifted by him and his character strength. She prayed for the coaches and support staff that they would be open to the Spirit to know best how to make the decisions they would be called upon to make to have a successful game.

As she wound down, she asked that Robby would be blessed for being the shining example to the world that he was and that he would be able to continue to be a force for good with the fame and exposure he had earned. Lastly, she asked that she would be able to be strong enough to handle the tasks she needed to deal with. Thanking for their blessings one more time, she closed the prayer.

Robby gazed up at her with an expression she wasn't sure she could understand, and then helped her to her feet without letting go of her hand. They stood staring at each other for a moment without saying anything, and, finally, she said, "Good luck, Robby. I hope you have a wonderful day. I'll be praying for you."

He put his other hand to her cheek. "There's no way I couldn't have a wonderful day after a prayer like that, Kelly. Thank you. Take care here. I'll be praying for you too." He let go of her hand and wrapped both arms around her and gave her a long, sweet, close hug, then gently kissed her on the temple before he let her go. He looked down into her eyes. "Will you be careful when I'm gone?" She nodded.

"Are you planning to be on any ladders today?" This time she shook her head. "Good. I'm not sure that would be a good idea today. I'll see you tonight."

With one last long glance, he turned and walked out the door, and she let out the breath she'd been holding and let her shoulders slump. She went over and sat on the floor beside the couch, picked up the kitty that crawled into her lap, held it to her face, and let the tears come. After a minute, when the kitten became bored with her and crawled away, she pulled both knees up and put her head down on them and sobbed out her heartache and sadness into the faded knees of her jeans. His tender kiss almost made things worse.

Sitting like that she prayed one more time. She asked God just one question. Why had He let her get into a position like this? It didn't feel fair. She'd been trying. She had never been perfect, but she had always truly tried to be obedient and an example to those around her. She had always been one to strive to be the best and help those less fortunate. She was morally clean and obeyed the Word of Wisdom and paid her tithing. She honestly tried to do it all. So then why had God let her get into a mess like this, where she would end up so unhappy for the rest of forever?

She had only been trying to do what she felt like she needed to when she started checking into the deaths at the hospital. Any good, honorable citizen would have been compelled to do the same thing. She had heard that no good deed went unpunished. She was sure Satan tried to make certain that was true, but today she felt like she needed more strength than she had to get through this.

It was all so backward. This should be a happy day. She remembered how energetic and up beat everyone at the university would be on game days. That's how she should be feeling. After all, it wasn't everyone who got to live and work this closely with such a celebrity player before he went in to be the star on the field.

She sighed, then got up and went back into the master bedroom, telling herself to count her blessings and think more positively on the way. Maybe she was just being hormonal. That would explain why her heart was breaking as he went to play his first game of the season. That must be it. It couldn't be that this day was drumming into her head over and over again that she'd been the worst kind of fool, and would regret falling in love with him for the rest of eternity.

Trying to ignore the tears that blurred her vision, she strapped back on her knee pads, picked up the drill, and went back to fastening down the decking. She just needed to work harder and faster and long enough to get her mind off of things. That was all.

She worked straight through until just before two when the game was going to start, then went and made herself a Shrimp Louie salad and took it to the living room to eat while she watched. It may have been a subtle form of masochism, but there was no way she was going to miss getting to watch him play, at least on TV.

It had been years since she'd watched a game and she'd forgotten how much she used to love this sort of thing in high school. She and Ryley had watched together, laughing and shouting at the TV and each other, as one team or another got ahead. Ryley had teased her when she mentioned just how good those guys had looked in their tight uniform pants, and she had hassled him about his enthusiasm for the cheerleaders. She had accused him of liking the cheerleaders better than he liked the sport, and he'd thrown pretzels at her. It wasn't really true. Ryley had loved the sport, but her taunt had gotten a good reaction, anyway.

Kelly settled onto the couch and then decided to go back out to her house and get a pillow and a blanket to cuddle up in. She didn't want to be tempted to steal the one off of Robby's bed when she got tired later. As hard as she'd been going lately, she got sleepy as soon as she sat down for very long, and today probably wouldn't be much different, in spite of the fact that she'd be watching Robby this time.

The game started with a bang and the Panthers hit the ground running, literally, and then threw two long passes and had, indeed, made the first touchdown within just minutes of the opening play. It was Robby who caught the second pass and made the score. Kelly finally understood that Jason was the quarterback. That must have been where his comment about distribution came from. Kelly would have smiled, except that her stupidity still hurt so much.

At half time, the Panthers were ahead fourteen to six and as the cheerleaders came onto the field, Kelly started to get up to go get herself a drink. As she stood up, she recognized the woman who Robby had repeatedly and overtly tried to avoid that first night at the fundraiser. Kelly was glad the players were already off the field so at least she didn't have to watch this woman hound Robby on national TV. Poor guy. Knowing him as well as she did now, she knew that women like this truly did make him flat out miserable.

He ought to settle down and get married. He'd be so much happier that way it seemed. Although on further thought, that probably wouldn't stop women like this cheerleader, who were so ridiculously tenacious.

Kelly sighed inwardly as she walked to the kitchen. She knew Robby truly would be happier married. She knew him well enough to know he'd love a married lifestyle. And she truly would try to be happy for him when he finally did settle down and tie the knot.

It was just that the thought of him settled with someone other than her was more painful than she wanted to face, and yet she had to face the fact that, of course, it would be someone else. Someone who could match Robby in all of the ways he was so extraordinary. Someone without her baggage. Someone who wouldn't get him in trouble with the law and the press and who was smart enough to at least realize who he was without having to be fairly hit over the head before figuring it out like she had.

The whole time she'd been working on his master suite, she'd had to constantly watch her thoughts so she didn't bludgeon herself to death emotionally, knowing she was fixing up a bedroom for him to share with another woman. It had been a constant battle, and she'd be glad when the bathroom and closet were complete, and she could move on to the basement and forget about Robby and a faceless wife.

The second half of the game, Kelly was getting tired and more mellow. When Robby caught several passes and made two more touchdowns, she was too happy for him to keep her emotional guard up and not be thrilled. She was as proud as if he were her own personal NFL star. As the game ended, the crowd came unglued and the network sportscasters began to do their thing. Kelly sat still for a second trying to understand what she had just been watching and what she had seen Robby do as an NFL player.

He was an extraordinary talent and would have been fun to watch, even if she hadn't had a clue who he really was, but knowing him and knowing what an honorable, hardworking man he was as well became almost mind boggling. Once again, she wondered how in the world she had lived this near him for more than three months without realizing he was Rocker Robideaux.

The team was leaving the field and the network was trying to corner a couple of the key players as they left to get quick interviews with them. Kelly watched as Robby and Jason were approached when they headed for the locker room together. A pushy, blonde woman with a microphone forced herself between them and began to ask them questions in rapid-fire style. Both of them were still breathing heavily from just having won the game, and Kelly wanted to reach into the screen and tell the brain dead woman to leave them alone. Couldn't she see they had left it all on the field?

Robby gazed directly into the camera and Kelly felt like time stood still for a moment. It was as if he was looking right at her. Finally, he drew his attention back to the woman newscaster, as he paused at the door of the locker room and said, "We had a lot of help out there. It was a team effort. We didn't do it alone." He looked up into the camera again and then ducked into the locker room door.

The chattering woman went off again, but Kelly just reached over and clicked the remote to turn off the TV. Robby had been speaking to her, thanking her for praying for him. She knew it without a doubt. She got up and took her bedding back to the summer kitchen, wishing she knew what to think and feel about him. After that look that had made her feel like it was just her and him, in spite of the millions of others who had been watching that game, she was more mixed up than ever.

She put the quilt and pillows back on the bed and then dropped to her knees beside it and asked for a greater insight into just what she should be doing in her life. Getting up again, she lay across the bed for a minute to listen. She desperately needed more inspiration here.

Most of the crowds were gone and only a handful of people still waited outside the doors to the locker rooms and sports medicine area. Knowing Kelly was clear at home and Monique was long gone as well, Robby and Jason had lingered in the clinic part of the facility, having their bodies iced and worked over. Both tired, they had been content to let the younger guys blow off steam and strut around, then go face the team groupies, while Robby and Jason wound down in relative seclusion.

When the technician wandered away for a minute, Jason turned to Robby and asked, "How is Kelly handling all of this?"

Robby shook his head and gave him a sad smile. "I don't know. She's kind of a mess."

"Still hates football?"

"No. I don't know that she ever hated football, honestly. I think she just didn't like the way the players tried to demand that she be with them. I think she really likes football, and I know she respects the work and the effort we go to. It's not the football that bothers her. It's the level of the football. For some reason, the fact that I'm relatively good, and pretty well known is what gets to her."

"Is it that she's afraid of being discovered by all the publicity?"

"Oh, there is that. But that's not the problem. I mean, I'm sure that's why she didn't come in today, but no. She somehow can't seem to process the fact that I'm just me, and we're still the same two people we were two weeks ago. She has this brick wall she drags around with her to keep between us. Every once in a while, she forgets she's afraid of me and then we're friends just like before, but most of the time she can't face me emotionally."

Jason shook his head. "Just give her time, Rock. It can't be easy to learn to deal with all of this in a few days. We were in the middle of it, and it took us years."

Robby gave him a grin. "Yeah, and we were both those mindless, macho guys like she made fun of."

Jason waved a lazy hand at him. "I was. You were never a macho jerk. You were probably even decent in high school. I was an idiot. Monique would have murdered me in those days."

Robby thought about that for a minute. "You know, I think you're right. She wouldn't have even gone out with you."

He laughed. "It's just a darn good thing you'd had some of the rough edges knocked off before you met her. You'd be useless without her."

"Don't I know it." He adjusted the ice pack on his shoulder. "D'ya spose it's safe to venture out there yet?"

Glancing at the clock, Robby nodded. "It should be. Most of them should have migrated off with the prima donnas. An old salt like you should be fine. I'm going to hang out for a little while longer. Get a massage before I go. Give Shania a hug from Uncle Wobby."

Jason grinned as he got up and stretched and began to undo the ice packs around his hips. "It's too bad we can't all find women like Shania. This whole fame thing hasn't even registered with her yet. As far as she's concerned, I'm just a fun guy. She likes me clean or stinky or tired or sore or however. She just likes me."

"Oh, stop your whining. Monique does too, and you know it. I've seen her hug you when you were disgusting, and she didn't even blink."

Heading out the door, Jason threw over his shoulder. "Kelly's the same way about you. She just doesn't dare believe it right now. Give it time. See you Monday."

Robby leaned back on the table and moved the ice pack on his thigh. He hoped Jason was right. If Kelly really did pick up and haul back to Chicago, it was going to kill him.

The massage therapist came in, and he turned over and lay on his stomach to let her work on his back. He knew Kelly loved him, but somehow he still wondered if she'd leave him anyway. He needed to find a way to help her understand that he was just a regular guy.

It was almost seven when he pulled up in front of the house. The main house was silent and there was nothing cooking when he walked in and he hurriedly glanced back outside to see if her motorcycle was still there. It was, and he ran a hand through his hair.

Geez, it was bad when he wondered if she'd leave him the first game of the season. He went up to her house and saw her crashed on top of the blankets on her bed. Heading back to the main house, he had to smile at her. Maybe his playing had put her right to sleep.

He got back in the Land Rover and returned to Tolke, picked up a pizza, and brought it back to her. She'd probably feel stupid that she'd fallen asleep instead of fixing dinner, but he was ravenous. At least she had been able to rest. Peace for her was in short supply these last days. He knew it; he just hadn't been able to find a way to help her with that, yet. He was going to keep trying.

He started a fire in the fireplace and, leaving the pizza on the table, went back to her house to wake her up. Letting himself in, he went to her and rubbed her back for a minute until she finally opened her eyes. She stared up at him in surprise. "Robby! Are you home already?" She looked at her watch and groaned. "Oh, I'm so sorry. I didn't mean to fall asleep. I'll hurry and make dinner."

She went to scoot off the bed, and he laughed at her. "Kelly. It's okay. I brought pizza. I hope you don't mind."

She ran her hand through her hair. "I don't mind. I'm just sorry I didn't have dinner ready for you after your first game. You were marvelous! Congratulations."

"Thanks. Apparently you watched. Was it torture to make yourself watch football?"

She turned to look at him, and then said, "I deserved that. I'm sorry about my bad attitude before, Robby. And no, I loved watching you play. I told you I used to love it. And I certainly haven't ever been able to watch someone I know be the star. I thought it was great! Are you okay? You didn't get hurt did you?"

"I'm fine, thanks."

"Oh, good. I was praying for you, you know."

He smiled at her. "I know, Kelly. I could feel it, honestly." He picked up her hair brush from the dressing table and brushed the tangles out of the back of her hair. "Come on. The kittens will have figured out how to get into the pizza box. We'd better hurry."

In the living room, she tossed all four kittens out on to the front porch, then sat on the floor between the couch and the coffee table, crossed her legs, and opened the pizza box. "Oh, my gosh, this smells good! We should order pizza more often. Holy cannoli, you brought a big pizza! How are we ever going to eat this much?"

He laughed, "I always skip lunch before an early afternoon game. We're not going to have any problem finishing this pizza. I'll say the prayer."

He prayed and they dug in. He watched her face as they ate. She went through this roller coaster where she would be comfortable with him and then he could practically watch her remember that he wasn't just Robby and she'd pull away emotionally. Then, as he talked to her, she would relax again and then later, it would start all over.

He could almost see the tension. When the meal was over, he wasn't surprised that she got up, went back to the deck she was building and started screwing down the decking again. He wasn't sure whether to help her or leave her alone, but now with his belly full of pizza, he was tired to the bone and stretched out on the couch in front of the fire.

It was after eleven when he woke up and lay there, listening to her still doing something in the other room. What to do about Kelly? She was going to work herself to death in a single week if she couldn't find a way to channel the stress more easily.

At midnight, when she was still going strong, he wandered in. She was marking out the walls and fixtures for the new bathroom and closet on the wooden floor of the bedroom she was converting. She glanced up at him and smiled when he came in, but the smile didn't reach her eyes

He came over to her and took the hand that held the tape. When she looked up at him, questioning, he asked, "Having a hard time sleeping tonight, Kel?"

Looking guilty, she admitted, "I'm sorry. I should never have let myself fall asleep this afternoon. Am I keeping you up?"

He shook his head and took the other tools from her hands. "No, I was just thinking. Let's go for a walk, what do you say?"

"Sure. Whatever." He put down her tools and took her hand. They crossed the room to the new French doors and headed out onto the new, partially finished deck. They crossed the bare joists carefully and then he helped her down the couple of foot drop, and took her hand again as they set off up the gravel road. He walked with her for more than twenty minutes before he heard her take a big, deep breath and let it out. Finally, she was going to start winding down.

After another ten minutes, he felt her shiver and let go of her hand to put his arm around her and pull her close. "I guess we should have brought jackets. Shall we turn back? Do you think you'll be able to sleep now?"

She let out another breath. "I hope so. I'm sorry I'm a basket case, Robby. I'm trying to get a handle on it, I promise."

"I have no doubt you'll figure it all out and be fine, Kelly. You don't need to apologize. Just tell me what I can do to help you."

"Oh, Robby, if I knew I'd tell you. I swear I would. Walking has helped. Thank you."

He stopped and turned to her. "Is there any way you could tell me what's bothering you?"

She gazed up at him with wide eyes there in the dark. Finally, she gave a miniscule nod of her head and turned and started walking again. "I'm just having a hard time trying to process my situation and living here with the whole Robby as an NFL Hall of Famer national icon. I'm sorry. I was surprised, but I had no idea how hard a time I would have."

"You don't need to be sorry, Kelly. I'm the one who's sorry. If I'd known it was going to make you this unhappy, I'd have told you sooner. I promise."

She smiled up at him. "You think rocking my world sooner would have been better? Robby, you need to understand something. It's not that I dislike football, I realize that now. Today I loved football. It was great. I've always loved football. My bad attitude came from how some men who happened to be college football players treated me. The problem with you isn't football, and it's not even a problem with you. I'm just... It's just that..."

She sighed. "I don't know what I'm trying to tell you, Robby, but please don't think this is all because you didn't tell me you played football. I'm sorry that it's hard for me to be a mere mortal beside you. I'm sure I'll be fine when I can stop worrying about Peter finding me."

She folded her arms across her chest and rubbed her bare arms to get warm. He put his arm around her again and headed for home, walking quietly for a time. He had no idea what to say to that. Finally, he said, "Kelly, you're no more a *mere* mortal than I am. Think about it. You're not listening to the Holy Ghost when you say things like that. Aren't you forgetting that you're a daughter of God?"

They had reached the house and he headed across the lawn toward her house, but she stopped him. "I've got to go back and clean up my mess."

He shook his head. "Just leave everything right where it is, and you can come back to it on Monday. I'll lock the new doors up." He paused, wondering if he should say something and then went ahead and asked, "Kelly, would you like a blessing?"

She looked up at him almost in wonder. "I would love one, thank you."

He took her hand and continued on to her porch where he handed her into a lawn chair. "What would you like help with, Kelly?"

That took her a minute. "Strength, Robby. I just need the strength to do what I need to do without falling short. Strength and more insight. Sometimes, I don't even understand why God let all of this happen to me. It makes me want to whine."

That made him smile at her. "You are the least whiney person I know. I wish I could be half as good about that as you."

He placed his hands on her head and paused for a moment to listen and compose himself, then began. He wasn't surprised when he felt inspired to bless her to know that she was strong enough to handle everything she would encounter and that she would be given the insight she needed.

He was surprised that he felt he should tell her not to hesitate to continue listening to the promptings of the Holy Ghost in order to stay safe. He blessed her with several other things, then ended with the counsel to not forget exactly who she was, and that she was a worthy companion for the greatest of God's children. He closed the blessing and paused again to assimilate what he had just told her. The part about staying safe scared him, even though he would never admit that to her out loud.

She stood up and looked up at him and wrapped her arms around his waist. "Thank you, Robby." That's all she said, but she didn't let go for a while. He just stood there with his arms around her, wondering when he was ever going to get the guts up to kiss her the way he wanted to. He thought about the staying safe part again and held her even tighter and kissed the top of her head.

When she looked up at him a moment later, he said, "Kelly, I didn't really mean to caution you about following the Spirit to stay safe. That definitely came from somewhere up above. It makes me want to keep you with me every second of the day. You will be careful, won't you?" She nodded. "Good, because I'd be lost without you. I love you, Kelly. I'm sorry I upset you so much by not being completely forthright." He brushed a thumb across her cheek. "Good night. I hope you can sleep now."

He turned and walked back across the lawn to his house, let himself in the new French doors, and locked them behind him. He looked across the new bedroom she was creating, and there was no way he could stop himself from picturing her as the wife who would someday share it.

Walking through the house, turning off lights and locking doors, he heard the little kitties scratching at the front door and opened it to let them in. They all raced inside and immediately began to tackle and wrestle each other. He smiled at them as he went to the bathroom and brushed his teeth. He was glad Kelly had her own convenient bathroom now, but he kind of missed seeing her just before she went to bed with tousled hair and a sleepy smile.

He prayed and went to bed, more at peace than he'd been for a couple of weeks now. That blessing had probably helped him more than it had helped her. He knew what was wrong now. She was afraid of getting close to him because of who he was.

He just hadn't realized it before tonight. He turned over and gathered his pillow into his arm. Somehow, it was all going to work out. He knew it in his bones. His tired bones. It had been a long day.

Chapter 21

Peter Holmes had been sitting in the dentist's waiting room for more than forty minutes, and to say his patience had worn thin would be a serious understatement. He picked up yet another People Magazine and began to page through its mindless drivel and suddenly froze. The photo he was staring at of Kelly and this Rocker Robideaux was sharp and clear and there was no mistaking it this time.

He folded the magazine and stuck it under his arm just as the hygienist stuck her head in the door to call him back to take his appointment. He reached over and picked up his suit jacket. "I'm sorry, something has just come up. I'm going to have to reschedule. I've been waiting too long to stay. I'll send my bill. I typically make a hundred and eighty dollars an hour, and I've been waiting for..." He checked his watch. "Fifty-two minutes." He got up and went out the door, leaving a rather flustered hygienist in his wake.

Kelly placed another two by four against the base plate on the floor and held it against her knee as she toe nailed it into place. The nail was more than half way in when she hit it off center and bent it. What the heck was going on here this afternoon? She couldn't even pound a nail, for heaven's sake! This was the fourth one she'd bent. That was more than she'd bent on all the other walls put together, and she was only getting started on this one.

She stood up in disgust and let the half nailed stud lean against the wall. Not only was she making a mess, but she was a nervous wreck as well. All afternoon, she'd been anxious.

She gazed around the bedroom she was in the process of turning into a master bathroom and walk-in closet and rolled her shoulders to loosen them up. Pounding and holding the studs for so long made her insanely stiff. She was going to need another roll of Romex soon. Maybe she'd take a break and run into Tolke. Perhaps that would settle her nerves, and she could get back to her hammer with more accuracy.

She picked up her purse, locked the door, and went to get into the truck, then for some reason, went back inside and got into her leathers and picked up her helmet. The Romex would fit into her saddlebags, if she worked at it.

At the first light in Tolke, she pulled up and stopped behind the car in front of her, and then decided she was going to go get a sandwich before she picked up the wire. There was a small sub shop just next door that had a marvelous cheese steak.

Stepping into the first set of doors of the little deli, she started to reach up to take her helmet off and literally froze. Peter Holmes was standing not two feet away from her, in the small foyer between sets of doors, talking to what had to be a local. The overall clad, elderly man was pointing down the road she had just come in on, and gesturing broadly at a map Peter held as Peter listened.

The blood raced from her head so fast that she had to resist the need to lean against the wall. Forcing herself to move, she stepped around the two of them and her arm literally brushed Peter's in the close quarters. But he was so intent on what the other man was saying, that he didn't notice. She turned and went into the women's restroom that opened off the foyer, hoping the sudden dizziness she felt didn't make her stumble before the door closed behind her.

Standing just inside the bathroom door, she leaned against the wall to regain her equilibrium while she listened to their muffled conversation just outside. How had he found her? Robby. Someone had seen her with Robby.

It felt like hours that she leaned there, but it must have been only minutes before they moved off. Taking a huge breath and praying for all she was worth, she went back out the door and deliberately walked back to the motorcycle she had inadvertently parked directly next to the car that now held Peter. As she started up the bike, Dr. Crowther emerged from the sub shop and climbed into the passenger seat and once again, she prayed that the head rush wouldn't make her faint.

Her breathing was coming in gasps and she literally forced herself to back out and pull back around the parking lot to head for Charlotte. So, they'd come together to silence her for good.

She eased the bike into the street, thanking God for her leathers and helmet, and that she'd been too anxious to work at home anymore this afternoon. She shuddered to think just what would have happened if they'd caught her out there alone.

As she drove, she remembered what Robby had said about her up and disappearing. She needed to find a way to let him know she was okay and that they hadn't taken her, but how? If they had found her, they had found him first. She had no doubt that there was someone watching him to find her. She didn't dare go anywhere near him.

On a whim, she stopped at a flower shop near the stadium, and without taking off her helmet, sent Robby a bunch of daisies to be delivered immediately. That way he'd know that at least she was okay when she left. Glancing at her watch, she realized practice would be over in fifteen minutes. Maybe there would be a way she could at least try to say goodbye.

Thinking about where he would try to meet her, she drove around downtown for a few minutes until finally, as she passed the brick colored building, she wondered if maybe he wouldn't look for her here. It was the only place other than the obvious that they had talked about much. Kelly knew that he knew she wouldn't come near the stadium or go home. She pulled the bike into a parking lot near the brick colored building and sat on it waiting. Hoping.

Robby had been having the most uncomfortable feeling all afternoon, and when he got into the locker room, he just about panicked when one of the trainers came up to him and handed him a bunch of daisies. "I know this is kind of weird, but these came for you. The delivery guy asked that you get them right away."

He knew exactly what they meant the second he saw

them, and his blood pressure went through the roof, but he tried to act calm as he glanced around the locker room. He didn't see anyone unusual, but he knew if they had found her, it had been through him. At least she'd gotten away, but away to where?

Dressing in record time, he grabbed the daisies and headed for his Land Rover, scanning the fans and the people gathered around outside, racking his brain to think of where she would go. He felt like swearing and breaking something. Even if he could think of where she would go, he couldn't go anywhere near there for fear of leading them right to her.

Still, he had to try to help her. He had to know if she truly was okay. He drove out of the parking lot and automatically turned for home, although he knew full well she wouldn't have been able to send the daisies if she had been there, and she would never go back there once she knew she'd been found.

He pulled up to the light at the brick colored building, still trying to think like she would. He glanced left and saw her on her bike, there in the lot next door. For a full thirty seconds he stared at her from behind his sunglasses, with her looking back at him from behind her tinted helmet. As the light changed, she tipped her head ever so slightly and then pulled away and gunned the bike out of the lot.

He didn't even dare follow her with his eyes for fear someone was watching, and as the bike left his peripheral vision, he thought his heart was going to rip out of his chest. Slowly, he drove the rest of the way to his condominium and once in the lot, he called the security company he used sometimes.

When he'd successfully arranged for a couple of guys to hang with him for a few days, he put his head back against the head rest and tried to quell the urge to throw up that came to him. Here he sat with extra security while she ran alone. And to where? They had thought they were so close to getting to the bottom of this with the Chief of Police on Thursday that they hadn't made any contingency plans. He had no idea even where she would head, except maybe away from Chicago.

He was still sitting in his car when Jason pulled into the parking garage and parked beside him. He got out of the car, and they headed into his condo because he didn't want to take a chance at talking where they might be overheard. As they walked in the door, the phone rang. Robby grabbed it and literally threw it against the wall, then leaned down and jerked the cord out of the jack. Jason just looked at him quietly as Robby sat down on the couch and put his head in his hands.

Jason sat in the chair across from him and waited. Finally, Robby raised his head, ran a hand raggedly through his hair and said, "She's gone, Jason. They found her here somehow, and she ran. She's gone. We were so close!" He got up and paced to the window. "How did they find her?"

"Where did she go?"

He gazed out into the North Carolina sunshine. "I don't know, Jase. I don't know. I should have hired her some security. I should have made a plan. I just thought we'd have the whole thing handled before anyone knew where to look for her. How did they find her?"

Kelly left Charlotte on I-85 going south and made it clear into Alabama before she stopped for the night. As she climbed off of her motorcycle, she gazed up at the moon and it was comforting to know that the same moon shone down on North Carolina. At least they occupied the same planet still, even if it felt like he was unbelievably far away.

She made arrangements for her room without taking her helmet off and then hefted the saddle bags inside with her before locking the deadbolt behind her. It was eleven o'clock at night, and she took off the leathers, showered, prayed, and then climbed into the big, lonely bed, tired beyond belief.

Her spirit was more tired than her body. She had plenty of money with her and made a decision to stay here for a couple of days so she could rest and give herself time to get used to the idea that her life as she had known it was over again, at least until she found a way to get the mess at the hospital shut down. She knew that Robby would continue to look into it from his end; and, maybe with the information she had given Robby, as well as what her uncle had, and what she had given to the first police investigator, if it hadn't been destroyed, they could shut things down and put Peter away so she could go home.

She turned over onto her stomach and tried to figure out just where home was. She'd lived in Chicago for twenty-three years, and she'd lived in North Carolina for not quite four months, but there was truly no question. Her heart was so decidedly in North Carolina that it was scary. Even knowing that it was foolish beyond belief, she had to admit that Robby was her life now.

Holy cannoli she had set herself up for heartbreak! She turned back over and looked at the textured hotel ceiling in the dark as she thought about how stupid it was to have her life revolve around him, and then got side-tracked thinking about how much she missed him already.

When she realized where her thoughts had gone, she mentally berated herself. She couldn't do that. She needed to be realistic about being in love with an NFL superstar. Maybe this turn of events would actually be good for her, regardless of how painful it was right this minute. She was gone from Robby. She'd had no choice, but the break was made. It was something she'd never have been able to just do otherwise, and she knew she needed to walk away sometime. She curled up into a little ball and hoped Heavenly Father would help her be able to do this. Being done being friends with him may have been wise, but it made her cry herself to sleep anyway.

Robby made it through practice on Tuesday by shear force of will, and then drove on home to the house in a daze. He'd known she wouldn't be there, and he wouldn't have even come, except he was worried about Ted and the kittens. He found the house locked, but he knew someone had been inside, and he went up to her house with fear in his heart.

Her door was ajar and her things had been rummaged through, although he doubted they had found anything of value to them. He knew she had always been careful, and it wasn't like they could find her ID or social security number. About the closest they were going to come to her by going through her stuff was to find the occasional long auburn hair stuck to a blouse.

Robby picked up the sweat shirt she had left draped over the back of her chair and took it with him back into the house. He wandered into her new master bedroom and noticed the dangling stud with the bent nail. He was so glad she had sent the daisies and then waited to let him see her. He'd have died if he'd just come home and found her gone. For the thousandth time that day, he wondered where she was and if she was safe.

He thought about staying at the house, but couldn't face it here without her. Putting Ted and the kittens outside, he left them enough food to last them for a few days and then went back inside again and gathered up the videos that she had rented to return. Everything about the place made him think of her, and he wasn't sure if this was exactly what he needed, or if he was just torturing himself, but he couldn't help it. It even smelled like her, and when he finally got back into the Land Rover to leave, he was more lonely than he ever remembered being.

Peter put his carry-on onto the conveyor that would send it through security and then stepped forward to the metal detectors with Crowther right behind him. He was still seething over the fact that they'd apparently been so close to getting Kelly, and yet she'd gotten away.

When the guard put the hand held metal detector closer than Peter felt was necessary while scanning him, Peter had the urge to slug the man. At least he wasn't patting him down. They'd been so close!

He picked up his bag and cursed viciously under his breath. She had obviously left that old house where she was staying in a hurry. How had they missed her? He hated to admit it, but he was going to have to tell his man at the drug company what was going on. He was going to be furious. Peter cursed again at the thought.

Robby still caught the flight to Chicago with the team owner. His spirit was too tired to keep up the charade of being fired up with the team any longer than he had to, and he opted to essentially hide on the private jet. During the flight, he was thinking about her again, and he realized she would be watching him from wherever she was. He didn't doubt that, and it helped him to get his game face on after all. In fact, her being gone may help him to play even better because he was so deeply angry about all of this that he was incredibly cool. He almost felt like being violent.

Thursday morning he met with the Chief of Police Darryl Benoit, explained what had happened, and gave him all the information he had. Robby told Benoit that Kelly had an uncle who knew what was going on, and that she had given her carefully compiled notes to an investigator Hartvigson before she had run the first time. When he left after talking to the man, he decided Mark had been right. He did think he was on the up and up and that the matter would be checked into.

As they stood up to go, Chief Benoit shook his hand. "Thank you for your help, Rocker. I'm sorry for what you're going through and that she had to run away again like this. On the off chance that she contacts you, I'm going to get on this information this very afternoon and if I have questions, I'll get them to you. We may be able to just ask some questions of the right people, but I doubt it. We're probably going to be putting someone into this hospital undercover, which may take some time. And I'll check with her uncle and dig here to see if there is still any evidence she left before.

"I hate to think that one of my officers could be involved, but the simple truth of the matter is that it may be. It wouldn't be the first time. Especially not in this town. And be more careful than you ever dreamed of being, because the powers that be in the pharmaceutical industry are dangerous. If her friend is working with the big dogs to short cut the system, they'll use every bit of technology and muscle they have to put Kelly out of the picture. I may have the law on my side, but until she's no longer a threat to them, she's in danger.

"At any rate, we'll be doing our best to get a handle on this so you can get her home and safe as soon as possible."

Robby looked at him and asked bitterly, "That's great,

Benoit. But how in the world do you get her home and safe when no one knows where she is or how to get hold of her?"

"I don't know the answer to that, Robideaux, but if anyone can do it, you can. Good luck out there today." He smiled sadly as he got up to go. "Don't you dare tell anyone I said that."

Chapter 22

After leaving the police chief in downtown Chicago, Robby found a phone book and looked up her Uncle Roy Delaney and took a cab to his house. He didn't know if he'd be home, but he figured he had a better chance at getting to talk with her mom without scaring her to death if he spoke with the uncle first. At least, if her mom knew as little about football as Kelly had.

He got out of the cab and asked the driver to wait while he went up to the porch and knocked on the door. It was answered by a middle aged woman who didn't recognize him, and he asked, "Is Roy Delaney by any chance here?"

The woman looked at him somewhat warily and said, "Yes, just one moment please."

When Roy came to the door, Robby saw that he recognized him right away, and he was glad. It would probably be easier to make him believe him if he knew who he was. Roy said, "I'm Roy Delaney. And you're Rocker Robideaux. Come in. Come in. What can I help you with?"

Robby came in gladly, hoping no one was watching her uncle's home just now, and glanced around. "Is there somewhere we could talk in private, Mr. Delaney?"

"Certainly. Please, call me Roy." He took him into a den and shut the door. "Now, what is it that you needed?"

Robby dove right in. "I know this is going to be a surprise to you, Roy, but your niece Kelly has been working for me for the last three or four months. I was actually bringing her here with me and was going to let you come and see her, but Monday someone from the hospital she was working at when she left here, found out where she was, and she took off again. I know that is incredibly discouraging, but I at least wanted to let you and her mother know that she's been fine. When I last saw her Monday, she was okay. They don't have her that we know of."

Roy did, indeed, appear stunned and he backed up and sat down on the sofa behind him. "Kelly's been safe with you, but she's gone again?"

"Yes, I'm sorry we didn't contact you sooner. For a long time, I didn't know what was going on. Kelly finally told me about a week ago, and we've been working with the Chief of Police here to try to get to the bottom of what sent her running in the first place. He will probably be contacting you, by the way. Anyway, she's been afraid to contact you. But I wanted to let you know that she's safe. Or at least she was. She's still on her motorcycle, and I think she has money. I just don't know where she went."

"How did she come to work for you?"

"That's a long story, Roy, and I have a game I have to be getting to. She actually ran out of gas one day near my home, but that will wait. I was worried that if I just showed up to talk to her mom that she wouldn't believe me and that I'd scare her. I was hoping you'd know who I was. Do you think you could help me tell her mom?"

"Sure, sure. She just lives down a block or two. We can go right now." He leaned out the door and yelled, "Mother, is Ryley still here?" Coming back inside, he motioned Robby to follow him as a younger man who somehow resembled Kelly, but with brown hair came toward them. His eyes widened as he recognized Robby, and Roy said, "Ryley, we're going to take Mr. Robideaux here to see Aunt Sharon about Kelly. Come with us, would you?"

Without asking questions, Riley joined them as Roy led them through to a garage, and as the door opened, he noticed Robby's cab and said, "If you want, we can take you to see Sharon and then back to your hotel or to the stadium. You can let your cab go."

"Yes, if you have time, I'd appreciate that." Robby went to pay the cabbie while Roy and Ryley pulled out of the garage, and then he got in the truck with them, and they headed down the block. At a modest rambler about two minutes away, the three of them got out and went to the door and went inside without waiting for it to be answered.

When Robby saw her mother, he knew where Kelly had gotten her beauty. Her mother looked just like her, only older.

Sharon gazed from one to the other of them, and Ryley took her by the arm and led the whole group of them down a short hallway to a living room where they sat down. Roy sat next to Sharon and took her hand. "Sharon, I don't want to upset you, but this man here, who, by the way, is an extremely famous football star. LDS football star. This man is Rocker Robideaux and he came to tell us that... You know, I think I'll let you tell her, Rocker. You told me so well."

Robby looked at her and gently said, "I've been watching over Kelly for a few months now, Mrs. Campbell. She's been doing well, right up until Monday afternoon. We think she's still fine. We know she got away okay, but she has run away again. The people she was so afraid of somehow found her. We're not sure how."

At first the blood drained from Sharon Campbell's face and then it flushed. She put a hand to her chest. "You say she's okay?"

"She was perfect Monday afternoon. And I know she got away okay. I just couldn't go after her because I'm sure I'm the reason they found her in the first place. She's probably safe. She has money and she's on her motorcycle again with her helmet on and I'm sure she'll keep it on. You can't even tell she's a girl with it on. She's probably okay; we just don't know where she went."

"Who's we?"

"Well, me and some of my friends. She's been working for me, in a manner of speaking. And when she finally told me about a week or so ago what was going on, we've been working with the police chief here in Chicago to get to the bottom of the mess at her hospital. She was actually going to fly here with me today, so she could meet with the Chief and hopefully get to see you. I'm sorry we didn't make it that far."

Sharon was so shocked that Robby was a little worried about her, and he reached across and touched her hand. "I'm sorry we didn't contact you sooner. Kelly hasn't dared to contact you for fear they would find her. She was hoping you'd know she was okay when she sent you daisies."

Sharon started to cry, and Roy put an arm around her and patted her shoulder. "Don't cry, Sharie. He's been the answer to our prayers. And she's been okay these months. I don't think he's lying to us. He has a reputation for being the most well behaved player in the whole pro league."

Robby touched her on the arm. "I'm not lying to you, Mrs. Campbell. I have taken good care of Kelly. Actually, she's taken good care of me." She looked up and met his eyes and he said, "I love your daughter, Mrs. Campbell. I want to marry her and be with her forever. We just have to find her first."

Kelly began to wake and stretch, then groaned. It had been too long since she'd ridden for eight hours straight, and she was stiff and tired, on top of being lonely and discouraged. She got up and ordered breakfast and got into the shower. At least this time, she'd put a set of scriptures in her stash in the saddle bags.

When her breakfast came, she ate and got out her Book of Mormon and read for a while, then went back to sleep. She wished there was a magical way to make time pass so the Chief of Police back in Chicago could look into things, and she could get back home, to one home or another.

The next time she woke up, she went down to the lobby and checked out the flyers for the local attractions in the racks to see if there was anything that seemed appealing to her here, or if she should get on the bike and keep on rolling for awhile. One thing was different about running this time. Her time spent with Robby, and knowing she had been okay the first time she took off, made her so much more confident that she could survive this. This time, she knew she'd be okay; she just also knew how lonely it was going to be. There were tons of things looked interesting, just not alone, and she decided to leave again in the morning.

Robby would be going to Chicago the next day. She thought about almost getting to see her mom and uncle and Ryley and struggled not to be completely depressed as she went into the gift shop to see if she could find a bathing suit. She found a suit and bought a T-shirt to cover it up with. Who knows? Maybe she'd end up with a whole collection of souvenirs to show for her stint of being a runaway.

The next morning, she put her leathers on, got back on the bike, and headed west into Mississippi. In the early afternoon, she got a room and watched Robby's game. He looked long into the camera again, and she turned her face into the pillow and sobbed. Not only was she lonely, but even though she knew it was wise to be done being friends with him, the thought of being without him killed her. She'd never known anyone who was so strong and so gentle. She'd leaned on him until he'd become not only her best friend, but also her foundation. Her ballast. He was the one who kept her steady in the water, and life without him sounded long and lonely.

On waking the next morning, she left with an old Bob Seger song about rolling away playing in her headphones and went on into Louisiana. She rode until she got too tired, and the next day she got up and left again. Somehow, the road didn't seem as lonely as the empty hotel rooms, and she was able to let some of the heartache go and start to try to talk herself into facing essentially starting over again.

She was about a million miles into Texas when it started to spit rain, and she pulled into the town of Abilene and got a room. She was tired to the core and unspeakably lonely, but she knew she was better off than the others. At least, she knew she was safe and okay. Robby and her family could only wonder and worry.

She hung out and rested for a day or two again, while she waited out the rain. She went shopping and bought a few clothes, and on Sunday she went to church in the booming metropolis of Chalk, Texas. Population six hundred seventy nine. She didn't even have any idea what kind of church she was going to, she just saw everyone filing in and decided she wanted the peace desperately. She ought to be safe out here in the middle of nowhere.

There were women there in slacks, but she went into the

restroom and changed anyway, then slipped into the pew. She literally soaked up the spirit like a sponge. Parts of the service were somewhat hard to swallow, and she certainly left with a sweet testimony of the truthfulness of the gospel of Jesus Christ of Latter Day Saints. But the Spirit had been there just the same, and she sang along with those around her gratefully.

After the service was over, she went back into the restroom, changed back into her black leather, donned the helmet and climbed back on the bike. This time, she sang hymns for a while as she rode north out of Texas and into the panhandle of Oklahoma.

She went up into Colorado and spent more than a week riding higher and higher into the mountains there, until she woke up one morning, and it was full blown autumn in the Colorado Rockies. She'd never seen anything quite like it and decided to stay right where she was for a couple of days, in spite of the fact that the mornings were downright cold. She got a room at a mountain resort and swam and sat in the hot tub as the steam rose from the outdoor pool into the cold, clear mountain air.

Robby knew there was a problem within moments of stepping out of his Rover in the parking lot of the stadium. He was typically the first one here to practice, and the three cars parked near where he usually parked should have tipped him off to not even get out, but he wasn't expecting trouble at six-thirty on a Thursday morning.

Two big men got out of each car and started to walk toward him, and he automatically began to pray, as he hit the alarm button on his car key. Two of them grabbed him as a third one slugged him, and then demanded, "Where is she?"

Only knowing he had a game the next day and that she would be watching, kept him from tearing into them, in spite of the fact that there were six of them. He shook his head and fought his instant fury. "You tell me! She's gone and you know it!"

One of the men who had an arm, jerked it up behind his

back as the leader hit him again and then ground out, "Where? Where'd she go?"

The sadness of the reality that he didn't know calmed some of the anger, and he was able to simply say, "I don't know."

They either believed him, or the two other cars pulling in, and the security guards who came out at the same time got to them, because they slammed Robby back against the Rover hard enough to leave a dent, then got into their cars and squealed away.

Jason climbed out of his car and strode up to him, as Robby got out his cell phone. He first called the cops and the security company again, then turned to Jason and rolled his eyes as they headed for the building. He hated it when he had to have body guards around all the time. Hopefully, Chief Benoit was getting somewhere up in Chicago.

One night in her room, she was flipping through the channels and realized Robby had a game the next day against the Denver Broncos in Denver, only sixty miles away from where she was. Thinking about Robby being so near made the loneliness feel overwhelming, and she got back out of bed and went down to the exercise room to work out some of her emotional frustration.

She had passed the front desk on her way in, and on the way out she asked the young male clerk if there was a computer anywhere she could borrow for just a few minutes. He let her borrow the one right there on the front desk, and she quickly pulled up the Chicago newspapers and scanned them for any kind of a story about Peter or the hospital. She found nothing, and more depressed than ever, she looked up when the game was going to be the next day, then went back upstairs and went to bed. She missed Robby so much more than she'd missed her family the first time she'd run away.

Even knowing she was a fool, didn't make her stop wanting to see him again. Watching him play the next day would be like picking at a scab instead of letting it heal, but she was going to do it anyway.

She dreamed of him that night. Of his hands on her head when he'd given her that last blessing and of how he had hugged her when she'd been so hurt after cutting her hand. Waking up to come back to the reality that she would probably never even see him again left her feeling unbelievably bleak. She was too emotionally bereft to just stay there by herself, even in the beautiful mountains, and got up, packed up the saddle bags, and rolled down the highway alone one more time.

Pulling out of the parking lot, she had to decide whether to turn left or right. It tore at her lonely heart to know that it didn't really even matter. No one would know where she was when she got there, and it didn't matter what time she arrived. About the only thing that registered right now was the fact that it was uncomfortably cold riding here in the mountains in the morning. She turned east and faced into the rising sun, hoping to warm herself some as she drove.

After awhile traveling the smaller, winding mountain road, she turned onto the interstate and shortly saw a highway sign stating the distance to Denver. Even the air felt warmer just knowing he was somewhere not too far away. It would be so nice to see him play today, even if that wasn't the smartest thing to do as far as learning to live without him.

She followed the signs into the city center, hoping to keep this feeling that he was close. It wasn't wise, but it was so comforting. He'd always been that way for her. The stability and security he had brought to her life at a critical time had been like being rescued at sea. It was no wonder North Carolina was home to her after that.

The freeways became more congested the closer to the city center she got, and she decided to get off onto the surface streets and find a place to stay. It was funny, even after living in a huge city for most of her life, after being at Robby's house, this much civilization felt almost overwhelming today. Maybe it was just the motorcycle in the crush of traffic.

She stopped at a traffic signal and looked around for a moment and realized the stadium was just through the block. Maybe she would forget watching the game on TV for once and go watch him in person. Certainly, it would be safe to do so here.

Maybe she could even get a seat near where the team came into the stadium, and she would actually be able to see him up close.

At the ticket booth, she took the heavy helmet off and bought a ticket. The clerk at the window smiled smugly when she explained that she wanted to be near where the away team came through. "Don't we all, honey. There are a couple of guys on that team who are absolute dreamboats!"

She stopped and fanned herself dramatically. "Have you seen that Rocker Robideaux? Now, if he ain't a doll! Half the women in these stands today will be daydreaming of actually meeting one of these guys and living happily ever after. Ain't never gonna happen, but it's a nice thought. Here you go, sweetie. And aren't you lucky? There's one seat right down on the tunnel." She handed Kelly her ticket, and Kelly walked away a little dazed. Nothing like a wake-up call.

It was almost two hours until game time, and Kelly put her helmet back on and returned to her bike, wondering what she should do to pass the time. She was hungry, but didn't want to take her helmet off until she absolutely had to. She decided to leave the stadium and drove around until she found fast food and then just went to the drive-through. She put the paper bag with the sandwich into her saddle bag, and then went to a nearby park, sat on the grass, and took off her helmet again to eat.

Forty-five minutes before kick-off, she went back to the stadium, and because of her small bike, she was able to find parking right near the entrance. Even this far from either Chicago or North Carolina, she was hesitant to take her helmet off, but she finally did and went in and took her seat that was indeed, just above the tunnel. Upon sitting down, she looked around and watched the people coming in. She had never been to a pro football game before, and it was interesting to see the fans as they poured into the stadium. Most were men, and she attracted her fair share of attention as a lone woman in head to toe black leather. She was glad when the seats filled, and she didn't feel so obvious.

By the time the game was ready to start, she had calmed enough to begin to feel a quiet focus, in spite of the crazed behavior of some of the fans around her. It was strange. Just knowing he was somewhere near had such a grounding impact on her. The stress of the last days dissipated into the enveloping sound and heady energy, and she was able to relax and just wait. She had no idea if she'd even be able to recognize him in all the gear the same as every other player, and she knew he wouldn't have a clue she was here, but regardless, being this close helped her. She was glad she'd decided to come.

The crowd, the music, and even the PA system were deafening as the game finally got underway. As she realized the away team was starting to appear, her heart contracted almost painfully. She glanced down the tunnel alleyway and watched the men approach, some acting loud and pumped up, and some unbelievably quiet and focused. He was still carrying his helmet, and she recognized him instantly and was surprised at how he affected her. He put his helmet on and was fastening it.

By the time he went past where she was sitting, the tears were streaming down her face. Maybe this wasn't such a great idea after all. Seeing him brought back every little memory and feeling, full force.

Embarrassed, she dug in her jacket pocket for anything to mop her tears and was even more self-conscious when a man sitting next to her silently handed her a napkin from the hotdog he was holding. She took it with a brief nod and tried to stem the flow, but it was impossible. Being without Robby felt like trying to live without air.

She thought back to what the ticket clerk had said about him and felt like an absolute idiot, but she still couldn't help her tears. She struggled to control them the whole first half and was down to just the odd tear that would escape to trail down her cheek every few minutes by the time the team reappeared for the second half.

Robby was on an incredible roll. She'd never seen him quite like this. He made catch after catch and two touch downs, and it had begun to sound like the Raime and Robideaux show. It was hard to tell from this distance, but he almost seemed angry, and she didn't know what to make of it. Maybe he was always like this, and she just hadn't ever been able to tell because she was watching on TV, but his barely leashed aggression was unfamiliar to her.

The napkin she had been using to soak up her heartache was a limp, soggy rag when the man next to her quietly offered her another one. She met his kind eyes when he asked, "Are you okay?" She started to nod yes, and then stopped, and gave him one brief shake. Who was she trying to kid? She was a complete mess. He reached over and rubbed the back of her shoulder. "Anything I can do?"

She tried to smile through her tears and failed miserably. "No. I'll be fine. But thank you." He rubbed her shoulder one more time.

At least his solicitation helped her to get some control. The second half was better, and she had finally dried her eyes by the time Robby caught his fourth touchdown pass of the game. The crowd of Denver fans in the stands became disgusted. Almost singlehandedly, Robby had humbled them immensely.

A few minutes later, when Denver got a touchdown, the furor was right back to its earlier pitch and Kelly just let the insanity go on around her. She almost felt like she could hide in it and nurse her fragile control and try to get a handle on her incredible loneliness here in the middle of thousands of screaming people.

At length, the game ended. The Panthers had won soundly, and the fans around her taunted and screamed obscenities at the Carolina players as they headed back up the tunnel. Another obnoxious woman sports caster with a microphone was poised at the mouth of it waiting to pounce on the star victors as they came back to the locker room.

Kelly stayed sitting as the people around her grumbled and started to stand up and begin making their way outside. Below her, she could see Robby and Jason approaching, and she wished she could just reach down across the tunnel and touch him one last time so she could tell him goodbye. It was hard enough to know she had to walk away, but it seemed so wrong without speaking to him when they'd become such good friends over the months.

As they entered the tunnel, the sportscaster approached them. Robby and Jason exchanged a glance that seemed to communicate some silent signal, because Robby turned away from the mike and Jason smoothly fell into step with the reporter. Robby took off his helmet and wiped his head with his taped forearm, and Kelly could see the fatigue that emanated from him. Once more, she wished she could reach him, this time to offer some gentle support so he could safely wind down with her like he'd been able to back home.

He was right there, just twenty or thirty feet away. But there was no way she could even let him know she was there, and she knew it. Being seen speaking to him on a news camera would be like advertising where she was. Not only that, but just like the ticket agent had said, there were any number of women just like herself sitting here in these stands wishing for just a word or two with Rocker Robideaux.

Knowing all of this, she just sat and watched him go by and felt her heart shrivel as he did.

Just before he disappeared out of the tunnel, someone to her left threw a plastic cup and it landed in the tunnel near him. As the security guards that accompanied the team went into action, Robby glanced up as well. He looked over to where the offending spectator was about to get escorted out of the stadium, then he glanced up to where she still sat so quietly, and their eyes met.

He stopped dead still just for an instant, and Jason, who was right behind him, followed his gaze up into the stands and saw her as well. Jason nudged him and Robby broke his gaze and looked all around them for a split second. Then, he looked back at her again. She didn't know what to say, and she could tell that he didn't either. Then, seeming to almost drag his eyes away from her, he ducked out of the tunnel with Jason and the reporter and was gone.

She still sat there, woodenly, wishing she hadn't come after all. It was going to be harder than ever to go climb on that bike. She waited for a few minutes for the crowds to thin, then picked herself up and dragged her tired body and spirit up the steps to the concourse and made her way outside. Every ounce of her energy had been sucked out, and it was all she could do to reach the parking lot and strap on her helmet.

With one last, long look up at the stadium, she straddled the bike and started it up. As the tears began to fall down inside of her tinted shield, she pointed the bike south. If there was life after Rocker Robideaux, she sure couldn't see her way to it.

Robby showered and dressed and then as the others headed for the entrance and the buses, he backtracked and went back out to the tunnel that led to the field. When he got there, the stands were empty, just as he'd suspected they would be. He leaned against the side of the concrete tunnel and wondered if it would be okay for a man who had just had the most record-breaking game of his pro football career to break down and cry.

Jason found him there and just stood there with him until Robby turned to him and said, "Tell coach I'm flying home private. Tell him I saw an old friend and missed the plane. Tell him whatever. I can't face them all right now. I'll fly home tonight."

"I'll tell him." Jason put a hand on his shoulder. "It's all going to work out, Rock. Someday. Take it easy." Robby nodded, and Jason went back inside.

Robby stood there like that for most of an hour, thinking. The security guards had cleared the building, and the custodial staff had nearly finished cleaning before he went back through the empty locker room, picked up his bag, nodded to the two off-duty policemen who were waiting for him, and wandered out into the sunshine on the outside. He had them take him to one of the hotels near the airport where he made arrangements for a private flight back to Charlotte.

Settled on the airplane, he leaned his head back against the seat and let his thoughts go to her. Man, she had looked like Christmas morning there today. She'd seemed sad, but even sad, she was beautiful. He could hardly believe it when he'd looked up there. If that idiot hadn't thrown the cup, he'd have never even known.

She'd lost weight, and her smile had seemed lost, but she was still the other half of his soul. As painful as it was to get just a glimpse, at least he knew she was safe and okay. That had been the hardest thing he'd ever had to do in his life, to see her and not talk to her or even acknowledge her. How long until this would be over?

He'd checked with Chief Benoit four times in the last two and a half weeks since she'd been gone. The notes Kelly had taken and left with the investigator were said to be nonexistent, and when the police had begun an internal investigation, they had indeed found that their investigator had been involved with taking money from the hospital scheme for more than a year. They'd had to put someone undercover at the hospital, so this could take weeks. And when this Peter was put away, he'd still have to find Kelly and bring her home. Even that was an issue, because she was intimidated by his career.

He sighed and closed his eyes. The passion she'd brought to his life had drained out like a sieve these last couple of weeks. The only thing that was saving his game was the anger that came to the surface when he played. Never one to be bad natured, there was a slow burn down in his gut that he channeled to keep him focused on the playing field. He'd lost some of his gregarious attitude in the locker room, but Jason had picked up the slack for him. He owed him big time.

At least he was playing better than he ever had in his life. It was like the only time he knew in his heart she was with him was when he was playing. He knew she was watching. Much as the bad attitude about football had been a problem at first, now football was the only connection they had.

This was all so stupid. There had to be a way, with all the modern technology, to be able to communicate safely, or even to keep her where she would be safe. The only problem was that to do that they needed to find her and bring her home first. And she was watching out for him and his reputation now too, as well as trying to stay away from Peter.

He opened his eyes and looked out the window. This was twice now that she'd been right there almost within his reach, and he'd had to let her disappear again for her own safety. It was the most sickening feeling he'd ever known, but there wasn't a thing he could do about it.

He thought back to Chief Benoit's caution about how

powerful the people who were after her were, and then caught himself. If he dwelt on how much danger she was in, he'd go crazy. He focused on the fact that he'd seen her today with his own eyes, and she was okay. Not happy, but alive and well and beautiful. He had that at least.

Closing his eyes again, he prayed for her once more. He needed to remember to give all this over to God better. He knew God could handle this and had to let Him; otherwise, it was going to eat him alive. He prayed for her safety and to lose this spirit of fear, and realized as he did so, that he wasn't just afraid for her physical safety. He was afraid she was going to leave him because of who he was.

He added a plea to his prayer to soften her heart and help her know that he loved her and only her, forever. It wouldn't be much easier to take if she finally found safety and then wouldn't stay with him.

He prayed silently as they flew until he finally felt that sweet peace fill his heart and then thankfully leaned his head back one more time to sleep for the remainder of the several hour flight back to Charlotte.

Chapter 23

Kelly woke up and turned over. The sun was starting to come in through the window of the little hotel that had been her home for more than three weeks now, and it shaded the textured ceiling a pastel pink. She stretched and glanced at her watch. Nearly seven thirty. What was she going to do with herself today? It had begun to be the project of the year to fill the hours, but she seemed to have found a niche here in this sandy little town in southeastern Arizona.

She'd come here because it was warm and had stayed because the sweet old couple who ran the motel had been so kind to her when she was sad and lonely. They had also been the ones who had helped her to find a way to fill the long hours of her day when she didn't have ID to find work.

Opal and Harv Rueben had seemed to sense that she was at a loose end and on the second day Kelly had stayed here Opal had asked her if she would like to go and visit her parents at the old folk's home with her. Kelly had accepted eagerly, and that trip had neatly salvaged her sanity in one two hour span. Every day since then, she had gone to spend hours visiting the elderly at the modest extended care facility. They were as lonely as she was, or even worse, and she had quickly learned to love these sweet, sometimes emotionally neglected, elderly people.

Every morning she would stop into the hotel office and ask to borrow the computer. She scanned the Chicago area's newspapers for any sign of a breakthrough there, and then would go see the old folks. Sometimes, she would go horseback riding with Opal and Harv's son. Tim Rueben had helped his parents buy and set up the little motel, and Kelly was sure he did most of the running of it as well. She got the impression he'd done it so that his parents felt like they were earning their keep while he took care of them as they began to age. He saw to it that the only thing they had to do was man the front desk for a few hours in the morning.

Tim was soft-spoken and gentle, and had helped the huge, bloody hole in her heart to start to scab over. She was still so lonely and discouraged that she wasn't sure she would ever truly find her smile, but these good people had given her hope.

Kelly had fallen right in love with Harv and Opal the first day. They had helped her so much by just taking her in that she felt like she should pay them for her keep and for their companionship. Tim had also quickly become a good friend, and she was incredibly grateful she had been able to stop and perch, if only for these few weeks.

Rolling out of bed, she put on her swimsuit and a cover up and went down to eat in the little café that never had more than three people in it. She wasn't surprised when Tim showed up as she was finishing and pulled up a chair at her table. "Hey, Kelly. What's for breakfast this morning?"

She smiled up at him. "Don't even pretend not to know. You may act like your parents own this place, but I've figured out that it's all a ploy to make them feel needed and that you've hired real managers and just don't tell them. You were probably the one who picked out the menu for breakfast."

"You've done a lot of figuring out, haven't you?" She nodded with a smile and he went on placidly, "I've been figuring some myself. You ever going to tell me why you're traveling around the country alone and check out the Chicago newspapers every morning?"

She felt the smile fade from her face and glanced up to meet his hazel eyes. They were warm and friendly and caring, and she wondered if she dared to level with him. She wished she could level with someone. Emotionally, she was barely staying afloat here. She'd never been troubled like this, even after she'd run the first time, but then she'd never felt anywhere near as strongly about anyone as she felt about Robby, either.

Still, Tim was too nice of a guy to burden with her troubles. She knew he was beginning to have feelings for her and would be hurt because she couldn't return them. She looked back up at him, then finally tried to smile again as she said, "It's a boring tale, Tim. I'd hate to make you yawn. What are you up to today?"

"Puttering until I decide to go into my office and tend to business. I was wondering if this beautiful redhead who's staying with my parents was going to go swimming this morning. If she is, I'm going to go too because she looks so good in a suit that it would be a shame to miss it." He gave her a lazy smile. "I'm a good listener of boring tales."

She looked at him again and was thoroughly embarrassed when tears welled in her eyes and started to run down her cheeks. She put her napkin to her face and tried to staunch the flow, then stuck out her bottom lip to blow her hair out of her eyes as she tried to smile. He watched her in concern for a second, then reached across and took her hand. "I'm sorry, I didn't mean to upset you."

Shaking her head, she said, "It's not you, Tim. I'm just in a mess. If you're willing to listen, I need to talk. Eat, and maybe we could go for a walk or a ride."

"I actually ate at six." He got up and helped her out of her chair. "Do you want to walk or ride?"

"Let's just walk. Do you mind?"

"Of course not. Can I hold your hand?"

She glanced up at him and gave him a watery grin. "You're being incredibly subtle this morning, aren't you? You can hold my hand, but I have to be honest and tell you that my heart isn't interested in a new romance right now. And after the story, you might not want to be anywhere near me."

He took her hand and led off down a path near the deck of the café. "What, are you some kind of criminal or something?"

"No, just unlucky and stupid."

He laughed softly. "Talk about your subtle. Let's hear it."

As they walked, she told him about Peter and the hospital and even about going to North Carolina and working, without going into detail about who she was working for, and how she felt about him. When she finished, he asked, "How were you able to work without ID?"

"Uh, well, at first I just said I didn't have it with me, but I eventually told him just what I've told you. He mostly just made sure I had the money I needed, and he paid for everything. I didn't actually make all that much, but he kept me safe and fed and hidden."

He turned to gaze at her for a minute, and then asked, "What are you not telling me about this guy, Kelly? And what's the stupid part? So far you just seem unlucky."

She teared up again. "Oh, Tim. You're going to think I'm so completely brain dead. But I honestly didn't know. I'm sure you've figured out that we became very good friends. I didn't think it was a problem. I mean, I thought he was just a business man. You know?"

He wiped at her cheek with his hand. "And he wasn't a business man? Are we talking drug dealer? Married? What?"

"No, no. Not that bad. Well, I don't know. He turned out to be an NFL superstar."

He turned and started walking again. "Let's see, North Carolina. Is he black or white?"

She gave him a pointed look. "White. Jason's married. I'm stupid, but I'm not a home wrecker."

"Rocker Robideaux. Hosanna, you weren't kidding NFL superstar!" They walked for a few more minutes, and then he quietly asked, "Are you pregnant?"

"Tim!" She turned to look at him, aghast. "Of course not! We weren't sleeping together. He would never do that! I would never do that!"

He pulled her hand again and returned to walking. "So, then I don't get it. What's the problem? What are you so stupid about?"

She looked at him like he was mindless. "I fell in love with Rocker Robideaux, Tim. Can it get any more stupid than that?"

For a few minutes they walked in silence, until he mused, "He has a great reputation for being the straight arrow of the league. Maybe it's not as stupid as it sounds. It's not like he's a womanizer. How close were you?"

Kelly glanced at him, wondering why he was asking her this. "Why do you want to know?"

He chuckled. "Yes, I'm interested in you, Kelly. I

haven't tried to hide the fact, but I also care about you. I'm just wondering if this romance was all one sided. Were you both involved or was he just being kind and you truly were being stupid?"

"What do you mean? How do I describe being involved?"

"Kelly, did he hug you and kiss you and tell you he couldn't live without you? Or did he treat you like a caretaker?"

His question made her sigh. "I was the caretaker, although he did tell me that he loved me once. But it wasn't romantic love. We were just very good friends. Buddies. I knew that he wanted to come home because I was there, but it was because I didn't chase him like the others. He was always saying how nice it was that he and I were true friends. He certainly didn't kiss me. Well, the top of my head once when I was sad, but no, I was just stupid."

Again, they walked in silence for a time, until he asked, "So, is there any point in my being interested, or are you terminally in love with Robideaux?"

His forthrightness made her laugh. "Being subtle again, Tim?" He smiled and shrugged, and she admitted, "I don't know how to answer that. I would certainly hope this isn't terminal, but then I've never felt even remotely like this about anyone before either. Why would you be interested in someone possibly terminally stupid anyway?"

"No one says love has to be logical." He rubbed her hand with his thumb. "So what's the plan now? What are you just hanging out waiting for?"

"Honestly, I'm hoping that someday soon, it'll be safe to go home."

He glanced at her. "Home to Chicago? Or home to North Carolina?"

His question made the tears start again, and she shook her head sadly. "I'm not going back to North Carolina. That would just be compounding the stupidity. I need to get on with my life. I just don't want to die in the process."

"How long has it been?"

"I left the last week in April the first time, but the Chief of

Police has only been involved the last seven weeks or so since I left North Carolina."

"Have you talked to anyone back home?"

"Not since I left."

"You haven't talked with Robideaux?" She shook her head. "So you're just watching the papers. Can you stay here until things break loose back home?"

"That depends on how long it all takes. I haven't been able to work without ID, so it depends on how long my money holds out. I definitely need to stay somewhere where it's warm, because I can't buy a car, and the bike doesn't do snow."

"You can stay here as long as you need to, Kelly. Don't worry about the money. How long do you think the investigation is going to take?"

"I keep hoping it's going to be any day now, but who knows?"

"And you think something will show up in the papers?"

"I assumed so. Do you think it could already have come to a head?"

"I don't know, Kel, but it's possible. Someone should check into it in depth. It'd be a shame for you to be a man without a country for no reason. I travel occasionally on business. If I checked into things away from here, I wouldn't give you away."

She searched his eyes. "Would you mind doing that for me?"

"Of course not." They stopped and gazed out over the desert before them. After another minute, he turned back to her. "You have to at least tell him goodbye, you know." She knew he was right, but it felt like it was just making a foolish situation worse. "You, yourself, said he took good care of you. Even if he didn't love you back, he must have been concerned."

She thought about that. She didn't doubt that Robby loved her. She knew he did. He just wasn't in love with her the way she was with him. Tim interrupted her thoughts with a revelation. "I'm going out of town tomorrow."

She turned and looked at him. "Where are you going?"

"Does it matter?"

"No, I just wondered."

"Iowa. Should I talk to your family, the Chicago police, or your superstar?"

"Can I give you my family's numbers and Robby's and you could just see what you can find out?"

"Absolutely."

"Thanks. And thanks for listening to me. Your family has saved me. It can get lonely on the road alone."

"I understand. Sometimes it even gets lonely when you're home."

Robby unlocked the door of his condo and stepped inside and instantly there were kittens everywhere around him. He finally had the phone under control, but the cats had him corralled. The house was so lonely without Kelly that he'd brought Ted and the kittens in to the condo, but five cats in one house were too much. He hated to give them away before Kelly got home, but he couldn't live like this.

With a grin, he called his attorney. "Howard, I know you do legal stuff, but I need some help. Who could I get to help me find legitimate homes for four kittens?"

The attorney on the other end of the line laughed. "You're calling me about kittens? Honestly, Rocker. Aren't there about ten thousand girls who could handle this for you?"

"I want the cats to have real homes, Howard. Not just get taken because I asked."

"How much are you willing to fork out to find real homes, man? Because I'll take them for you, but I'm pricey."

"You're worth every penny. Come get the cats."

"You so owe me."

"No, you're still in my debt over that woman you set me up with from your ward. You'll never get out of debt for that one."

"You've got a point. Call me anytime you have cat troubles. See you, man."

Robby had hardly hung up his cell phone, when it rang again. It was a number he didn't recognize and he answered it wondering who it could be. "Hello."

"Is Robby Robideaux available please?"

The man's voice wasn't familiar either and most people called him Rocker. "Who wants to know?"

"I can't tell you who I am, but I was told you might be able to tell me if the issues in Chicago had ever been resolved."

Robby stood stock still, wondering how to answer this. He almost whispered, "Is she okay?"

"No. She's heartbroken. And lonely beyond belief. She's been watching the papers, but hasn't seen anything. Is it safe for her to go there yet?"

"Not yet. Is she going there instead of coming back here?"

"I believe that's her plan. When it's safe."

Robby's heart jammed against his Adam's apple. "I'm sorry to hear that. Why?"

"Your situation isn't exactly compatible with being invisible."

"But she won't always be running."

"No, but you'll always be Rocker Robideaux."

That made Robby want to swear and ask what was wrong with being Rocker Robideaux, but he already knew the answer to that. Instead, he quietly said, "Tell her that I love her, please. And that I miss her."

"I'll do that. Much as I hate to. I don't think she'll believe it. She's pretty aware of your popularity."

"My situation makes me appreciate her more, not less. Tell her to watch the rockerrobideaux.com site. If anything breaks loose in Chicago, I'll post it."

"I'll tell her. I don't think appreciation is what she's in need of."

Totally frustrated, Robby ground out, "Look, not that it's any of your business, but I do appreciate her. I'm also in love with her. I'm not going to give up, and you can tell her that. I've searched for her for twenty-eight years. And I'm sorry that my being famous hurts her, but I can't live without her. Just tell her I love her."

"I'll tell her. She's a great girl. Take care, Robideaux."

"You too." The call ended with a click, and Robby stood there staring in shock at the phone in his hand. She was okay then. It had been more than a month since that game in Denver, but he still wondered about her a thousand times a day. Why would she not believe he loved her and missed her?

He pulled back up the number on his phone and called the phone company, but all he found was that it was a public pay phone in a hotel in Des Moines. That was reassuring and disappointing all at the same time. Just in case, he phoned Chief Benoit and gave him the number. Man, he missed her.

He went in and began to fix dinner, and she owned his thoughts, as usual. Why would she not believe him? She had to know he adored her, didn't she? He thought back to their friendship and their conversations and how they had treated each other. She had to know he loved her. How could she not have known? Maybe he hadn't been all pushy about it, but only because he worried she would run from him emotionally, just like she'd ended up running physically.

He'd told her once. And she'd told him the same thing a couple of times. He knew she loved him. Had she not understood that he'd meant he was in love with her and wanted to be with her forever?

This was so frustrating. At least she'd apparently found another friend who was looking out for her. Robby tried not to think negative things about that male voice on the phone. Kelly desperately needed a friend right now, and he knew it. He wouldn't begrudge her that. He was just insanely jealous that someone else could be with her when he so desperately wanted to be.

When dinner was done, he took it to the table, prayed over it, and started to eat as Ted decided to haunt him. He pushed her away with his foot. "Go away, Ted. Not now. Go away and let me think of her in peace, would you?"

Back in Arizona, Tim took her for another walk. Holding her hand again in the cool desert dusk made it incredibly tempting to not pass along what he'd said that he would, but he also knew that he had to. He knew her heart was in North Carolina.

After they'd been walking for a few minutes, he nonchalantly said, "I thought you said you were just being stupid and that he wasn't in love with you."

She stopped and turned to stare at him with big eyes. "What are you talking about? Who?"

"I talked with Rocker Robideaux yesterday. He has a tad different take on just what your relationship is than you do." He paused, but she didn't say anything, and he went on, "He thinks you're Mrs. Robideaux. The one who he's been searching for for twenty-eight years."

After staring at him with a questioning expression, she turned and started walking again. "You must have misunderstood, Tim. He never said anything like that to me."

"Well, maybe you'd better clear the air with him then, because he didn't really beat around the bush. His exact words were, 'I'm in love with her, and I'm not going to give up. I'm sorry that my being famous hurts her, but I can't live without her. Please tell her I love her and miss her.' Does that sound the slightest bit wishy washy to you?"

This time she stopped and stared at him with a shocked expression on her face. "He said what?"

Tim gave her a sad smile. "You heard me, Kelly. I think the man is smitten."

She still just stared, and then tears welled in her eyes, and she turned to continue walking, shaking her head. He put a gentle arm around her shoulders. "Don't cry, Kelly. This is what you wanted wasn't it?"

Wiping at her eyes with her sleeve, she said, "I do love Robby, Tim, but this can't be right. We've lost something in the telling or along the way. You wouldn't believe what his life is like as far as women. I went to a couple of fundraisers with him and was appalled. I'd never seen anything like it. They just throw themselves at him." She kept walking, and then went on, "It doesn't matter anyway. It's not like I can even talk to him, let alone see him."

"He said to check his website, rockerrobideaux.com, and

he'd let you know what's happening in Chicago."

She sighed, and wiped at her cheeks again. "Thanks for checking for me. I appreciate it. How was your trip?"

"Lonely." She glanced over at him as he admitted, "I understood perfectly what he meant when he said he's been searching for you for twenty-eight years. I'm only twenty six, but still." He rubbed a thumb over the back of her hand as they walked along. "If things don't work out with him, would you consider coming back to the end of the universe and living?"

She gave him a damp smile. "I think I am terminally hopeless, but sure, I could consider that."

"With all due respect, sir, we need to move on this or both doctors are going to disappear instead of just one. Let's bust what we've got, and then find this Holmes, if he doesn't turn himself in. If he's smart, he'll walk into the department and hand over his files. He'll figure out that his little empire is gone soon enough when we shut it down, and Miss Campbell will be the least of his worries. For that matter, he's probably already left the country, and we'll never see or hear from him again. We know he's been transferring money out all along."

Chief Benoit folded his arms across his chest and considered that, then shook his head. "You're forgetting that he's a psychiatrist. A crooked psychiatrist. Psychs tend to be a little twisted anyway. Who knows what he'll do? And he won't have much to live on in Mexico, if he's already run. We froze everything we found. He may still go after Kelly just on a vendetta."

His investigator didn't reply, just stood looking at him as he continued to think. At length, the chief turned back to his desk and said, "Shut 'em down and haul the rest in. I'll send someone to keep an eye on Kelly just in case. If we traced the phone call back to her in Arizona, they might have too. Or when Robideaux goes after her, Holmes might just follow him. If Holmes shows up, we'll grab him then."

Peter Holmes sat in front of his computer and pushed the "Make Transfer" icon one more time, then erupted into a hailstorm of cursing when the same red disclaimer saying, "Transaction denied!" popped up yet again. He'd been trying to move funds for hours and every single account but one had been blocked.

Years! Literally years of his life had just been somehow electronically ripped away, and his operation seemed to be crumbling in his hands. This couldn't be happening!

And just when he'd found Kelly again. At least he could eliminate her. Finally. He hadn't even known where Tombstone, Arizona was until he'd gotten here late last night.

He took a deep breath and forced himself to calm down. He'd get rid of her and then get to the bottom of why nearly all of his accounts weren't working. He'd tie up this last loose end here and then smooth things back home. Everything would be fine. Their operation couldn't be over. They'd made a lot of money over the last couple of years at Altium and had barely begun to tap the well.

He should have never become involved with Kelly in the first place, but hadn't been able to help himself. Even knowing that she'd caused so many problems and had to disappear didn't change the attraction he felt. He'd never seen hair like that.

Chapter 24

Ted was like Velcro Cat as Robby worked around his house, and she about tripped him as he answered his phone. He glanced at the little screen and hope filled his heart as he answered, "Hey, Chief."

"We've got them, Rocker. We got the evidence to make things hold up in court for both the doctors and a couple of others who were involved."

Robby closed his eyes in relief as the chief went on, "You wouldn't believe what these guys have been up to. They were short cutting clinical trials and so far we think they've lost seven patients. And they were going to push the patents through on these drugs and let them be prescribed. Who knows how many people would have eventually died if Kelly hadn't started digging? Who knows how many drugs they've already licensed like this? What a mess. And her boyfriend did have a neat little narcotics racket going as well."

Robby took a deep breath and let it out as he ran a hand through his hair. "So can she come home? Is it safe?"

"She can come home. And she should be safe. Everything is shut down, and we don't even need her testimony now. We'll probably ask for it just to be sure, but she should be fine. However, I have to be honest and tell you that we don't know for sure where the boyfriend psychiatrist is. He's disappeared. He's all but broke, and my guys think he's gone to Mexico, but the fact is, we just don't know. She should still be safe. Holmes knows that if he tried to come after her now, he'd only get in deeper. If he's as smart as we think he is, he'll come in and try to plea. Kelly should be completely off of his radar."

Robby sighed. "Thank you, Chief. If you ever need anything, I owe you big."

"No, you don't. Especially after we lost this guy. I hate

to even admit it, but you should be aware. Take care of your girl. She's had a rough go, but she has saved lives. Tell her that. I wish more people were like her. I'll be in touch the minute Holmes turns up."

Closing his phone, Robby leaned down and picked up Ted, who had been practically tripping him as she wound in and out of his legs. "She can come home, Ted. She can finally come home." He went in to his computer to update his website with the information he'd just received. "She can come home if she will." He put the cat down and patted her. "You'd better pray too. And pray that she's definitely not on Peter's radar."

As he booted up and waited for the screen to come up, this all seemed surreal. How could something that had loomed over her life and even his for so long, all be resolved so quickly? Of course it wasn't so quickly, the weeks and months had dragged on, and until Peter was arrested, it definitely wasn't all resolved, but according to the Chief, she should be fine. In the space of just a few minutes, Kelly's exile was over. Just like that. It didn't even seem possible.

Tim was watching Kelly check the computer just as she did every morning, and he saw her face blanch and tears come to her eyes. He came over and stood behind her with a hand on her shoulder as he read what she just had.

All it said was, "Kelly, Chicago is a wrap. Please hurry home. Can I pick you up? Call me. I love you, Robby". It was unbelievably succinct for something that had troubled her life to the extent it had. It seemed too simple of a resolution even to him who had only known of her struggles for a short time.

She looked up at him and asked almost hesitantly, "Now, what do I do?"

"What do you want to do?"

She shook her head. "I'm too mixed up to even know. What do you think?"

He crouched down beside her chair and asked her gently, "Isn't Robby Robideaux who you should be discussing this with?"

Closing her eyes, she began to cry quietly and finally admitted, "I have no idea. I'm so confused."

He stood up and pulled her into his arms. "Kelly, I can't tell you what you need to do except that you and I both know that you need to talk to Rocker. You owe him that. You owe yourself that."

He held her like that while she cried until his chest began to get damp. His mom came past and looked at him with raised eyebrows, and he just shook his head at her. Finally, Kelly pulled back and he looked into her face. "Better?" She nodded. "Good. What can I do to help you?"

"Oh, Tim." She hugged him with one arm around the waist again. "You've been so good to me. I'm sorry I've been such lousy company. You deserve so much more."

"Ah, if you throw me over for a wildly famous and wealthy pretty boy, I'll get over it. She's out there somewhere. I just need to keep looking." He smiled at her. "What are you going to do?"

She dropped her head. "I don't know. I'm sure he just means he cares for me as a friend. It's not like he's in love with me." Tears started down her face again and he handed her a tissue from a box on the desk as she continued, "I need to go home to Chicago. I can finally go see my mom."

"You're going to ride a motorcycle across the country to Chicago in late October? Don't you think that sounds uncomfortably brisk? There are snowstorms all through the upper Midwest right now. Can I offer to take you or let you borrow my truck?"

She shook her head. "That's kind of you, Tim, but no. That would be too much to ask you to take me, and how would I ever return your truck? I'll be fine. I'll buy some heated leathers somewhere, and I'll just have to hang out if I hit bad weather."

Tipping her chin up so he could look into her eyes he asked, "Are you sure you don't want to go home to North Carolina? You know he could afford to send a private plane for you, and you wouldn't have to cross the country alone and cold."

Sadly, she shook her head. "Of course I want to go home to him, Tim. But it would be foolish. I just need to get on with my life and start trying to forget about how I feel about him. And there's no reason for him to spend a bucket of money on me with a private plane. He is kind. He'd do it, but I can't. I'm afraid to see him. I'm afraid to even talk to him. I know I'll just have a harder time walking away if I do. Then it would only be worse."

For several seconds he searched her eyes until she squeezed his hand, took a deep, resigned sounding breath, and went to leave. He caught her sleeve, wondering what he should do here. "Make me a deal, Kelly. At least wait until in the morning. Can you do that? Give us one more day and then you'll be fresh to start."

After considering that, she said, "Let me think about it. I really should just head out, but you guys have been the best to me. Give me some time to figure out a game plan, and I'll get back to you."

She walked to the front door of the hotel and let herself out, and he picked up his cell phone. She wasn't considering staying until the morning, and he knew it. He still hesitated for a second and then pushed the number she had given him before for Rocker Robideaux.

Robby was dressed and headed out of the locker room to his car when his phone vibrated. He continued on out the door and into the parking lot before he picked up the call. In his hurry to answer it before they hung up, he didn't check the number, just said, "Robideaux."

When he heard the voice on the other end, he stopped dead in his tracks. "Rocker, you don't know me. It's Tim Reuben from Arizona. I called you a while back for Kelly. She's here. Although, she's just about to climb onto her motorcycle and head for Chicago. She checked the website this morning and after crying like her heart was broken, decided to go there instead of to North Carolina. But she loves you. If you're serious about her, come get her. I've asked her to stay until in the morning and she said she'd think about it, but I don't think she truly will. I offered to take her or let her take my truck, but she refused."

Robby hesitated for an instant, wondering what he should

do. He didn't want to demand she come to be with him, but at the very least he was going to make sure she got home safely to Chicago until he could try to talk her into marrying him. "Tell me where to come. I'll leave as soon as I can find a plane."

"Fly into Sierra Vista. It's small, but it's closer. We're twenty minutes east. I'll have a car waiting. Call me from there and I'll tell you how to find us. We're in Tombstone. Where the shoot out at the OK Corral was. But you'd better hurry. I'll flatten her bike tire just in case."

"Slash it if you have to. I'm on my way."

"Good. She's going to be mad at me, but she really does love you."

"I love her too, Rueben. And be aware that the old boyfriend psychiatrist who has been after her hasn't been picked up. The Chicago cops think he's left the country, but keep your eyes open."

"I have been, trust me. Watch your own back. See ya."

Robby closed the phone and stood there for just a second thinking about her. She was in Arizona. Getting through these last weeks had been just going through the motions, without her. He felt like he'd lost a limb or something even more vital. Just knowing where she was and that she was safe, and he'd be seeing her gave him more energy than he'd felt in weeks.

Jason came out the door and walked up to him and then did a double take and looked at him hard. He didn't even have to ask, but he did. "You found her?" Robby nodded, almost hesitant to speak it out loud and Jason became all business. "Where are you headed?"

"Arizona. But she isn't sure she wants to come back here. She's still worried about me being Rocker Robideaux."

"Hang with her, Rocker. She'll figure it out eventually. At least get her home safe to her family while you work on her. Are you going to be back for practice in the morning?"

They started walking to their cars. "I'm going to try. I haven't even found a plane yet. If I haven't figured it out by morning, I'll call."

Jason stuck out a hand at the Land Rover. "Good luck, bro. Tell her hi from Monique and me. We'll be praying for you."

"Thanks, man. I'm going to need it."

Mirages created by the mid afternoon sun danced in the desert out in front of the rental car Robby had picked up on landing. The closer he got to Tombstone, the more nervous he became, and he hoped it was simply that he was excited to see her, and not that she was in danger. He glanced in his rearview mirror and then repeated the prayer for her safety that had become almost a mantra. The Chief had seemed to think she'd be fine. He hoped he was right.

Robby worried about her safety, and about her reaction to him showing up here unannounced. He'd have to make it perfectly clear that he wasn't just assuming she would want to be with him. He was more nervous than he ever was before a game. Man, he'd missed her.

He pulled up in front of the little motel this Tim Rueben had directed him to, and looked around for just a minute. It was pretty much the end of the earth, and Robby wondered how she had come to find this place. He got out of the car and went into the motel office where a tall man with powerful shoulders and quiet hazel eyes looked up to greet him.

The man stood and extended a hand. "Rocker, Tim Rueben." He nodded at the motorcycle out in the parking lot with the flat tire. "She isn't very happy with me at the moment over her tire. She's not very happy with anyone or anything. I think her heart is bleeding to death. She actually called a tow truck to come and pump the tire up for her. I believe he's on his way here now. You owe me. She's in room 106."

"I do owe you. Anything you want, it's yours."

The man met his eyes and gave him a sad smile. "What I wanted, Robideaux, is a beautiful red head with big, sad, green eyes, but her heart is in North Carolina. How about if you just let me in on the secret to the strength she has, in spite of the mess she's in, and we'll call it even."

Robby nodded. "I'm good with that, but the source of that strength is her Father in Heaven. She's incredible that way."

He glanced out toward the bike. "Does she have any idea I'm here?"

Tim grinned. "Not a clue. You're on your own."

Robby returned the smile. "If I wasn't so incredibly stoked to see her, I'd be scared to death. Thank you for calling me."

"You're welcome. One more thing, Robideaux. Something isn't right here. I can't even tell you what it is. Just a feeling."

The same nerves Robby had been fighting as he drove from the airport ratcheted up a notch, and he met Tim's serious look. "Keep your eyes open."

Tim nodded. "They're open. And my handgun is close. I'll watch. You just see to it that you don't break her heart."

On the way out the door, Robby said, "I think it's my heart that's in danger here."

He walked down the small sidewalk and headed for the room with the number 106 on the door, noticing the tow truck that pulled up near her motorcycle as he did. A man climbed out in a pair of gray striped coveralls, pulled an air compressor tank out of the back, and approached her bike.

Just as Robby raised his hand to knock on the motel room door, it opened. Kelly stood there, dressed in her leathers and helmet, with her saddlebags hung over her shoulder.

Robby couldn't see her face to know what she was thinking or feeling, but she stood stock still. He froze as well, for a long moment, and then she reached up and pulled the helmet from her head. That incredible hair cascaded out again the way it had all those months ago in that Tolke hotel parking lot. Her huge, green eyes were wide with surprise, and he just stood there, wondering what to say and wanting to hold her and never let her go.

Finally, he simply said, "I think I fell in love with you the very first time I ever saw you take that helmet off. My heart has never been the same since. Hey, Kelly."

The green eyes got even wider, and he could see the different emotions of shock and then happiness and then uncertainty flit across her face and she said, "Robby. What are you doing here? How did you find me?" She slowly lowered the helmet.

His eyes searched hers to know what she was feeling as he said, "I came for you. You knew I'd come for you as soon as it was safe, didn't you? I brought a plane so you don't have to ride your motorcycle."

She hesitated, then said haltingly, "Thank you. I had no idea."

She looked down and then back up, and her eyes told him that Tim had been right. She was headed to Chicago and not back to him.

Unsure of what to do, he paused, and then decided to lay it all on the line. "I was hoping to take you home to North Carolina with me, Kelly. Please tell me you're not leaving me. I can't live without you."

Her forehead creased as she looked at him in open confusion, and then tears slowly seeped into her eyes as she sadly shook her head. "I can't come back and work for you, Robby. It would be a mistake. I should just go back to Chicago and try to get on with my life."

"Please no. You are my life, Kelly. Why would it be a mistake? We have a great life at home. We can get it back, I know we can."

The tow truck driver looked up from her bike, and Robby noticed that Tim had come out of the office and paused on the walk a short distance away as well. Frustrated at the audience, Robby went to reach for Kelly, but she backed off and wiped at a tear that ran down her cheek and said, "Don't Robby. We did have a great life, but it wasn't based on reality. We both know that. It would be foolish to go home with you. I'd only end up getting hurt. I appreciate you coming, but I'm not tough enough. I can't go back and work for you."

"Then don't work for me, Kelly. I'm sorry, I had no idea you were worried about getting hurt. I would have hired someone else to do all of that if I'd realized. But I need you. I honestly can't live without you. These last weeks have been miserable."

She sighed and then admitted, "Robby, I'm not talking

about a work accident. It's just that... I mean... We're not..."
She paused and then said, "I just can't. That's all. It would be
too hard." She hesitated, and the tears started in earnest, and he
took a handkerchief out and handed it to her. Then he took her
helmet and saddlebags and set them on the hood of his car and
pulled her gently into a hug.

"Kelly, I know what I do bothers you. I know it does, and
I'm sorry. I'm so sorry. Please forgive me for being a
professional football player and being famous. It won't always
be that way, I promise. In time, everyone will forget I ever
played football, and I'll just be the guy who mows your lawn and
washes walls with you."

She sniffled and shook her head against his chest.
"Robby, you're Rocker Robideaux. I'm just Kelly, mere mortal.
I can't do it."

In an infinitely gentle tone, he said, "Kelly, I can be
patient forever. I'll take you home to Chicago for now, and live
with that as well as I can through this season that I've already
given my word on. But, you have to know, I'm not going to give
up on you. I'm going to keep trying to talk you into marrying me
until I'm ninety and no one in the world remembers me, or that I
ever played football. I'm never going to give up. I've waited
twenty-eight years to find you; I'll wait another twenty-eight if I
have to until you can cope with me."

She pulled away and looked up at him in utter surprise.
"Marrying you! Robby, what are you talking about?" The tears
were still wet on her face, but there was confusion in her eyes.
Lots of confusion.

"Of course marrying me, Kelly. What did you think I was
talking about?" The sad green eyes were shocked, and he began
to realize that she didn't understand at all.

Her eyes narrowed as she looked at him, questioning.
"You were talking about getting married? Why in the world
would you marry *me*?"

He ran a hand through his hair with a sigh and then turned
back to her, took both of her hands in his and said gently,
"Maybe because I love you and can't live without you and want
to be with you forever and ever and ever. Maybe because you're

the best thing that has ever happened to me and life without you beside me is miserably lonely. Maybe because from the second I realized you were a girl under that helmet, I've never been the same. Maybe because I want to wake up next to you for the next eighty-six-million millenniums and have nine children who look just like you."

Her eyes widened even further as he went on. "Maybe because you're the most fun, as well as the most peace I've ever known. Maybe because we haven't finished the wine cellar, and I need you to sit on the master deck with me and watch for elephants in the grass. Maybe because I can't even begin to imagine how lost I would be without you in my life."

She was watching him with those incredible eyes, and he began to wind down and reached up to gently touch her face. "I can't explain it very well, Kelly, but it feels like you are the other half of my soul. There could never be anyone other than you to share that beautiful master bedroom with. I honestly do love you. I'm desperately in love with you. Is there any way you would consider marrying me?"

Where before she had looked confused, now she looked stunned. She was speechless for several moments and then finally, hesitantly reached up and put a hand to his forehead in concern. "You got creamed again, didn't you? Did you get hit in the head again?"

He groaned in total frustration. "Kelly! Of course I didn't get creamed! Are you listening to me? I'm trying to ask you to marry me here! Don't ask me if I'm brain dead! Just say yes!"

The tears were gone and she was looking at him almost warily. "Robby, you've never so much as even intimated anything like this. How can I not question you? Are you being serious?"

"Yeah." He gave a short, humorless laugh. "I'm pretty dead serious. You know me, Kelly. I wouldn't joke about getting married."

She softened, but was still obviously confused. "I didn't think you would, but why haven't you said anything like this before? I had no idea you felt this way. Why didn't you tell me?"

He put a hand up into her hair and gently closed his fist. "You've been a little afraid of me, Kelly, since you found out I played football. And before you found out, I was walking on eggshells just hoping you weren't going to kill me when you did find out." He pulled her close again. "I wanted to tell you, Kelly, but I felt like you would panic and leave me. Then when you did leave, I realized what a mistake I'd made in not telling you."

He let out a deep breath against her hair. "These last weeks have been hell, Kelly. I missed the most important catch of my life. Now that I've found you again, I'm not going to make the same mistake twice." He pulled back and searched her eyes. "Think about it. Think about me. You know me, Kelly. You know I adore you. Don't you?"

Deep in her eyes he could see understanding. She knew how much he cared, but doubt and fear warred with the hope he saw there. He sighed again and pulled her back close. "For a long time, I thought it would be best just to be friends with you and have you work for me until you could learn to care for me, in spite of me being Rocker Robideaux. But all that changed the day I had to watch you ride away alone in order to keep you safe. That was the worst day of my life, Kelly. And that day in Denver was even harder."

He paused for a moment and admitted, "I realized then what a huge mistake I'd made. I should have told you exactly how I feel. Maybe if I had, these last weeks wouldn't have been so miserable." He looked down at her and gently brushed a thumb across her cheek and said huskily, "I can't even tell you how many times I've prayed for you to be safe and happy. I'm so sorry for not making a contingency plan to keep you secure and guarded. My only excuse is that I didn't think they could find you. I didn't really understand what you were up against until Chief Benoit explained how powerful those people were. Please forgive me for not taking better care of you."

She kept looking from his hand to his eyes as she said, "There's nothing to forgive you for. You weren't responsible for me or the mess I was in. Even I wasn't the one who caused that.

I was just in the wrong place at the wrong time and then knew I had to do something about it. Sometimes, I even wonder if that wasn't the Lord's plan all along. I certainly don't blame you because they found me."

When she ended, he just looked at her, trying to read her and finally, sadly, he said, "I'll take you to Chicago and then I'll fly up a couple of times a week to be with you. I'm sorry, but I have to finish out the season because I gave them my word. Then, I'll break my contract and retire and move to Chicago. If you can't agree to marry me, are you at least okay with that?"

She started to cry again and leaned into his chest and said, "Robby, you can't break your contract and retire at the height of your career for me. You love football, and you're incredibly gifted. Everyone looks up to you. You're a huge example to the world. You can't walk away from all of that for me."

He spoke against her hair, "I've lost you twice, Kelly. I can't do it a third time. It would kill me. I'd a thousand times rather give up football than be without you."

Through her tears, she whispered so quietly he almost didn't catch her words, "I don't want to be without you either, Robby. Chicago sounds so lonely, honestly. I do love you, and I would love to marry you, but I don't know how to be enough for you. I'm just me. How could I ever do it?"

He wrapped his arms around her tightly. "Just exactly the way that you did it before you had to go. I'm not sure what you think I need in a wife, Kelly, but you're it. Trust me on this one, please." He leaned back and tipped her face up to look at him. "Please." He looked into her eyes again. "I've been searching long enough to know without a doubt. What more could I ever want? You're sweet, and smart, and fun, and perfect, and I love you. You're the only woman I've ever wanted. You're the only one I ever will."

She looked up at him, and he could see the love, but there was still doubt and he tried to reassure her, "I know the publicity is a pain, Kelly. I'm so sorry. I'll do my best to protect you from it, but you're the one. The only one. I'll do whatever it takes to prove that to you in time."

Finally, the hope in her eyes gave him hope as well, and

he asked, "Kelly, do you really think everything that brought us together and that we've been through was just coincidence?" She shook her head and then dropped her gaze and he said, "I don't either. If you can't trust me, or even yourself, can you trust God?"

At that, she looked up at him, and he could see the understanding fill her heart as she nodded and asked, "Yes. I really can trust God, can't I?"

"Yes, you really can trust God. So can I. He knows everything. Even how much I love you."

He lifted her chin again and then watched her eyes as he leaned down and slowly, gently kissed her for a long, long moment and then said, "I love you, Kelly Shaye Campbell. If I ask you one more time to marry me are you going to turn me down again?"

She dropped her eyes and shook her head, and he sighed as he hugged her tightly. "Oh, good. I'm not sure my ego could take that again in front of your mechanic."

He glanced up at the approaching tow truck driver, wishing he would get lost. Couldn't the man see this was an important moment? At least Tim had disappeared somewhere. Shaking his head in disgust at the lack of privacy, Robby turned back to Kelly and pulled up short. He saw pure panic in her face, and then he heard the driver say almost silkily, "Hello, Kelly."

Wondering what was going on, Robby glanced at the man to see utter evil in his eyes and an ugly black gun under a shop rag pointed at Kelly. Understanding dawned. This had to be Peter Holmes. He felt the same panic grip his own heart and a primal need to protect her flood his veins.

As Robby watched, the dull metal gun barrel shifted almost lazily to point at him. He heard Kelly suck in her breath as the look on her face changed from panic to sickening resolve, and she asked almost pleadingly, "What do you want, Peter? This has nothing to do with him. Leave him out of it."

In that same smooth voice, Peter calmly said, "I'd love to, doll, only I think he should come along with us. Keep us company. Why don't all three of us take a little drive, shall we? He can drive, in fact. Get in the truck." He motioned with the gun.

Kelly gave Robby the most heart wrenching look of sadness and fear, but then she turned to Peter, shook her head, and said firmly, "No, Peter, leave him alone. I'll go with you. Just leave him out of it."

The evil in Peter's face seemed to compound. Robby could read the fury and knew what was coming as Peter went to strike Kelly with the gun. Without even thinking about it, Robby stepped in front of her and struck at the gun in Peter's hand, knocking it away from Kelly.

It went off twice as Robby instinctively followed the first hit with a vicious blow to Peter's jaw. Something under Robby's arm burned white hot, and her motorcycle, two parking spots over, exploded into flames, showering them with pieces of metal and shattered plastic.

Peter's head snapped back from Robby's blow and as Peter fell, he lost his grip on the gun and time slowed to an eerie crawl as he scrambled to grip it. Just as he was able to right the gun and move to point it again, two more shots rang out from somewhere else.

Robby instinctively shoved Kelly away from Peter and tackled her to the ground beside his rental car. He rolled almost on top of her as there was another shot, and then for a moment that felt like eternity, there was silence except for their labored breathing and the sounds of the burning motorcycle.

Two men left the motel on the run. Seconds later, someone said, "He's down. We're clear."

After a moment's hesitation, Robby lifted his head to see Tim and another man standing over where Peter lay still. Robby took a huge breath and looked down at Kelly lying almost underneath him.

She gave him a shaky attempt at a smile and said, "Just like old times. Us in a pile."

He rolled off of her and tried to smile back. "Yeah, but this is the first time I took you down. Are you okay?"

Shuddering, she said hesitantly, "I'm … I'm fine. I'm glad I'm wearing leather. Is he…? Is he…?"

Wrapping an arm around her, he said gently, "I don't

know. Don't look. Tim's taking care of things, and I think there's an officer with him. Are you sure you're okay?"

"Robby!"

The alarm in her voice had him rolling back over onto her and looking around frantically until she added, "You're bleeding! A lot!" He sat up and she scrambled to her knees and grabbed the tail of his white dress shirt, yanked it up and almost screamed his name, "Robby! You were shot! Why didn't you say something? Are you having trouble breathing?"

He looked one more time to where Tim and the officer were and then sighed and stood up. Reaching behind his neck, he pulled his shirts off and then raised his arm to look at the ugly two-inch gash in the muscle under it that was dripping blood. He wadded the shirt and pushed it against the wound, and then offered her a hand to help her to her feet. "It's fine, Kelly. It's a scratch. It didn't actually go into me. It just sort of cut. Some surgical tape and I'll be good as new."

She put both hands on her hips and shook her head adamantly. "Oh, no! Oh, no you don't! This time, the only one who is watching is me, and there's no reason to be all tough about this. You are going to the hospital for stitches!"

"No, Kel. Honey." He put up a hand as if to defend himself. "Honestly. Tape works better. Stitches tend to rip right back out. Tape is a little more forgiving in my, uh, line of work."

She looked at him like a veritable mother hen for several seconds, her face ashen, and finally blew out a breath and said, "Well, get in here then. Opal has a big medical kit behind the front desk."

Purposefully not looking to where the others were, they walked past the smoking motorcycle and she said, "Ryley's gonna kill me when I tell him I blew up his motorcycle."

Wrapping an arm around her shoulders, he said, "Thank heavens it was only the bike. I'll buy you a new one."

"No." She shook her head. "No new motorcycle. I hate motorcycles. Your rental car is a little the worse for the wear as well. It now has a bullet hole."

"Make that two." He opened the motel door for her and then hurriedly replaced his shirt compress when he dripped blood on the entry tile. Trying to keep her talking, he asked, "You hate motorcycles? Really?"

She nodded as they walked behind the front desk. Picking up the kit, she took it into another office to the side, and shut the door behind them. As she dug through it, he lifted his arm again to examine his injury. It didn't hurt all that much, and he was actually grateful for it. It seemed to be keeping her mind off the fact that someone had just tried to kill her. The only hint that she was thoroughly shaken up was the color of her face and that her hands were shaking as she searched.

He wasn't that strong. Every time he thought about her almost being killed, he wanted to completely envelope her in a hug and hold her safely to him almost desperately.

Setting out an assortment of scissors, tubes, tape, and a bottle of some kind, she began to inspect the wound, and he couldn't help himself. He put his other arm around her, pulled her tight, leaned his face into her neck and wanted to almost breathe her in to know she was okay. She pushed him back and blushed. "Robby. What are you doing? I'm trying to work here."

Feeling both disappointed and then guilty for actually wanting to kiss her neck just now, he gave her a lopsided sad grin and said, "Sorry." She gave him the look and went back to fixing him, and he watched in utter fascination. He hadn't forgotten that he adored her, but she was even more adorable than he remembered. He still felt the need to pull her to him.

Whatever she was putting on him stung and to lighten the moment, he teased, "Ouch, Kelly. What are you doing to me?"

When she looked up, tears glistened in her eyes. He put both arms around her. He'd known this was coming. There was no way she could handle this shooting without it finally hitting her. Still, he was surprised as she crumbled into his chest and sobbed, "You saved my life. But... Just another couple of inches and ... Robby... You would have been killed."

He held her tightly for a few moments and then said, "Shhh. Shhh. I'm fine. We're fine, Kelly. We're both fine. A mere bullet couldn't have really gotten me." He pulled back and tried to smile down at her. "No crazy psychiatrist mechanic is going to get past me to you."

She looked up at him and rolled her teary eyes. "Be serious, Robby. You're hurt. Stop acting like it's nothing."

Shaking his head, he said, "You're all backward, Kelly. It's the last nine weeks that have hurt. And we are okay." He pulled her close again and wrapped both arms back around her and whispered, "Someone wanted to kill you, Kelly. But it's over. He's never going to bother you again. It's over and you're still here. And alive and well."

He grinned as well as he could. "And beautiful. It's finally over. I really wasn't joking. Try not to think about it. It will only frighten us and I don't want to think of anything but how nice it is to finally be back with you. Now, hurry and finish taping me. I'm bleeding on your jacket."

She nodded silently, and he reluctantly let her go and went back to watching her as she worked to pull the edges of his skin together. When she was finally done, she looked up at him and he couldn't help himself. He looked into her sweet green eyes and leaned back down and gently kissed her for another long moment, then sighed and hugged her to him gently and admitted, "I've wanted to do that for... For a really long time, Kelly."

He held her like she was glass and then, finally, pulled slightly away and said softly, "You know. Just before someone started trashing our vehicles, I was about to ask you if you would marry me."

Her big eyes came back and so did the bright tears and he asked, "Would you be disgusted with me forever if I proposed to you this morning?"

She just looked at him steadily for the longest time and then shook her head.

"Should I go back over all the reasons why I love you and want to have nine children with you?"

That made the color finally come back to her face, and she looked down and shook her head.

Glancing at his bare chest, he asked, "Should I go find a clean shirt?"

She looked at his chest as well, shook her head again, and gave a shy smile. "Definitely, no."

He chuckled and kissed her one more time and then got down on one knee right there in the motel office. "Kelly Shaye Campbell, would you do me the honor of becoming my wife for time and all eternity?"

She nodded through tears, pulled him to his feet, and slipped back into his arms and said softly, "Yes, Robby Robideaux. Rocker Robideaux, I would be honored. If you think I can do it, then I would love to. You're stuck with me forever and ever."

"And ever." He leaned down and kissed her again. Tentatively at first and then with all the emotion that had threatened to consume him these last weeks. Sweet, incredibly warm kisses that he'd dreamed of for months; that he'd been praying they would eventually finally discover. They had been such a long time coming and were definitely worth the wait. After a moment of tender hesitation, Kelly returned them kiss for heavenly kiss.

When he eventually lifted his head, he smiled and knew it was all going to be okay when he heard her take a deep breath, lean against him and whisper, "Nine children, good heavens."

The End

About the author

Jaclyn M. Hawkes grew up in Utah with 6 sisters, 4 brothers and any number of pets. (It was never boring!) She got a bachelor's degree, had a career and traveled extensively before settling down to her life's work of being the mother of four magnificent and sometimes challenging children. She loves shellfish, the out of doors, the youth and hearing her children laugh. She and her incredibly attractive husband, their family, and their sometimes very large pets, now live in a mountain valley in northern Utah, where it smells like heaven and kids still move sprinkler pipe.

To learn more about Jaclyn, visit www.jaclynmhawkes.com.

Journey of Honor (excerpt)

He pulled up and got off his horse and was just about to speak when he heard the sound of a cocking gun. The wagon flap moved and the barrel of a pistol appeared, followed by Giselle's head. When she realized who it was, she dropped the muzzle of the gun and took a deep breath and then whispered with her accent, "Oh, Mr. Grayson, you frightened me. I thought you were Henry Filson. What are you doing?"

That's exactly what he was asking himself just about now. "Uhm, you're not going to believe this, but I've come to see if you would consent to marrying me." He put up a hand. "It's just to be able to get you away in the morning, and we'll have it annulled when we get to your valley. It's either that, or stay here and deal with Filson and a trial, and waste more time getting started west."

She looked totally confused for a minute, and then said, "Just a moment." Her head disappeared back inside the wagon cover and he could hear her whispering quietly to someone and then a bare foot and lower leg appeared through the flaps. He realized she was getting out.

He went forward to help her down and she turned to look at him with big eyes in the darkness. She was wearing a nightgown covered with a long robe and her hair was loose and hanging around her shoulders. She was even prettier than when she'd been all dolled up and he questioned again to himself what in the world he was doing, while he waited there to see if she was going to laugh or cuss him.

He was completely amazed when she looked up at him in wonder and asked in a soft, sweetly Dutch voice, "You'd do that for me? Really?"

He didn't know what to say to that. He'd never experienced anything in his life that would help him figure out what to do in this situation. Finally, he just said, "Uh, yes. I would. But honestly, it's not being totally unselfish. Without you and your grandparents, we can't leave either until we find someone else to take your place. The army won't let trains of less than twenty wagons start out."

He paused for a minute and then decided that being absolutely forthright was in both of their best interests. "I give you my word to be a gentleman. I wouldn't expect anything other than your help in getting underway. You needn't worry."

She laughed a sweet laugh at him in the dark and said with her intriguing accent, "Worry? You have just taken a huge load of worry off of me! I don't doubt that I can trust you. I knew that the moment I saw you on the hotel boardwalk. And I fully intend to help all the way across this great journey. I will be glad to. I am more grateful to you than I can say right now. I would love to marry you to get started in the morning. I would be thrilled!"

For a second, he thought she was going to come right up and hug him. Just when he felt relieved that she didn't, she actually did. Just as quickly, she pulled back and looked up at him with a sober face. "Tell me what you need me to do."

Still a bit shaken, he simply said, "Be ready to go into town a little before sun up. We'll meet with the sheriff, get married and be back and ready to leave at first light."

All she did was look up at him with those wide eyes and say, "Okay." With that, she turned around and climbed back into her wagon without a backward glance at him. He walked away in the moonlight in a stupor. He got clear back to his own wagon before he remembered that he'd ridden his horse to hers and he had to go back and get it. Gathering his reins, he was turning to go when she poked her head out again.

Feeling a little sheepish, he said, "Sorry. Forgot my horse."

The Outer Edge of Heaven (excerpt)

Luken Langston pulled his pickup truck into the parking spot in front of the bunkhouse and shut off the engine in the lavender gray light of dusk. Opening the door and stepping out, he stretched his tired back and reached back in for his leather work gloves and the rope that lay coiled on the seat. He slapped the rope against his dusty pant legs and boots and breathed deeply of the evening smell of river bottom and beef cows. To some that may have been a questionable smell, but to him it was home in its purest essence and he loved it.

His stomach growled and he wondered if there was any real food in the bunkhouse fridge, or if he'd have to either settle for junk, or head back up to the main house before crashing tonight. He'd been up since four thirty that morning and was too tired to go for food, even though he'd skipped dinner. Maybe there was some fruit left, or some milk. Fo lived on milk, so there should be some. Or maybe that was backward. His boots sounded loud on the wooden porch boards as he mounted the two steps.

He tossed the rope onto one of the hooks inside the door of the bunkhouse, threw the gloves onto the shelf above it and reached to unbuckle his chaps. Hanging them beside the rope on the hooks, he pulled his shirt off over his head in one single motion. He dumped it into the laundry hamper next to his bunk as he kicked out of his boots and spurs, grabbed clean clothes from a drawer and headed for the shower.

Thirty seconds later, he decided a hot shower was the greatest invention known to man and resolved to sleep right there under the pounding, steamy spray. This had to be the purest form of heaven.

The need to sleep there cooled with the last of the hot water and he got out, dried off, and wrapped the towel around his hips as he stood at the sink to shave. The aftershave he slapped on helped to wake him up enough that he decided he would go in search of real food, even if he had to go up to the house. It had been a grueling evening.

He usually let the hands have Sundays off except for the barest minimum of feeding chores, but this afternoon he'd had a whole herd of heifers go through a break in the fence and get into a grain field. It had been a pain rounding them all back up, moving them alone, and then repairing the fence. The field would never been the same, at least not this year.

Slipping on a clean pair of jeans, he walked out of the bathroom, shirtless and bare footed. He was half way to the fridge when there came a light knock and then the bunkhouse door opened. A beautiful stranger with blonde curls and long legs stepped inside and called out for Fo. She didn't see Luke there in the half-light and came in several more steps, calling as she came and then abruptly pulled up when she finally saw him. Both of them were speechless for a second and then she stammered, "Oh, I'm so sorry. I didn't know there was anyone else in here. Please forgive me."

To buy these or any of Jaclyn's other books, please visit spiritdancebooks.com or call 1-855-648-5559

www.ingramcontent.com/pod-product-compliance
Lightning Source LLC
Chambersburg PA
CBHW070220260626
47160CB00002B/622